Soul on Fire
Cast Iron Farm Series Book Three

Ali Spooner

Also by Ali Spooner

Single Books
The Ghost of East Texas
The Trophy Wives Club
The Bee Charmer
Ruined
Back in the Saddle
Open Your Heart
South of Heaven
Shotgun Rider
The Settlement
Love's Playlist
Cowgirl Up
Twisted Lives
The Epitaph
Terminal Event
Bailey's Run
Series
The Island Series
Neptune's Ring
Venus Rising
The Hunter Series
The Devil's Tree
Bound
Sasha Thibodaux Series
Sugarland
Bayou Justice
Line of Sight
Strong Southern Women Series
Diamond Dreams
Gator Girlz
True North
Cast Iron Farm Series
The Mountain Whispers
The Star Child
Soul on Fire
Co-authored with Annette Mori
Heart Strings Attached
Free to Love

SOUL ON FIRE

ALI SPOONER

Affinity
Rainbow Publications

2021

Soul on Fire
© 2021 by Ali Spooner

Affinity E-Book Press NZ LTD
Canterbury, New Zealand

1st Edition

ISBN: 978 1 99 004905 7

Editor: CK King
Proof Editor: Alexis Smith
Cover Design: Irish Dragon Design
Production Design: Affinity Publication Services

ACKNOWLEDGMENTS

I would like to thank my fans for following my stories, providing great feedback, and encouragement. Writing wouldn't be so much fun without you. Thanks to Affinity, Irish Dragon for the cover art and the team of editors, readers, and publishers who continue to help me grow as a writer.

DEDICATION

I'd like to dedicate this story to all the dreamers out there, who relentlessly follow their hearts. Your bravery in stepping into a new chapter of your life inspires me to continue dreaming. As I follow each of you in your pursuits, successes, and failures it gives me confidence to expand my goals for the future. For that, I thank you.

TABLE OF CONTENTS

CHAPTER ONE

As the summer rolled along, Whit helped Mitch and Brad plan their first overnight adventure on the Appalachian Trail. She had purchased them each a set of waterproof trail maps for their packs, which would allow them to study the southbound trek they would begin in a few weeks.

Eli scowled, as she watched the weather forecast for Thursday when the boys were scheduled to head south. "It looks like some rain will be moving in tomorrow." She paced the living room floor.

"That will be an excellent experience for them. Mitch and Brad have rain gear, and we will have the potential of trekking through lousy weather when we hike for two weeks." Whit smiled at her lover. "They will be just fine. Besides, I put a GPS tracker on both of their phones. The boys are just going three miles."

Eli still frowned. "I know, but I will worry the entire time they're gone."

Whit smiled and ran her fingers down Eli's face. "I'd be worried about you if you weren't."

Carol giggled from across the room. "You two are so adorable."

Eli whipped her head around to look at Carol. "What?"

"You, my dear, are worse than an expectant father. Relax with the knowledge that you and Whit have trained them well to handle any situation."

"We could give them an hour's head start, then I could follow them," Eli suggested.

"No," both Whit and Carol responded.

Whit shook her head. "If you did that, the boys would lose the confidence you have instilled in them. Let them live."

Eli snickered. "I guess I am a tad overprotective."

"More than just a tad," Carol replied. "They need to show you how well they can do on their own. Their hero can't always guide them, so trust them to do the right things. If they don't make a good decision, they will choose another avenue until it is the right one."

Eli grumbled. "I know."

Carol smiled. "Your dad didn't keep your training wheels on your bicycle until you were ten. He was always there to dust you off and kiss your booboos, but he allowed you to fail and learn."

Eli flopped down on the couch beside Whit with a heavy sigh. "I know y'all are right, but it's so hard to let them grow."

"Everything will be fine," Whit told her. She covered Eli's hand with her own.

Eli could feel the crystal necklace pulsing against her skin.

Mitch and Brad came in from feeding the animals. Mitch must have noticed the worried expression on Eli's face.

"Is there something wrong, Aunt Eli? You look like you've lost your best friend, but I see them both sitting with you," he teased.

"No, I'm fine. It just hit me that you two are going out on the trail tomorrow, alone."

"Everything is going to be fine. If it rains, we get wet. We'll both probably need a good shower anyhow," Mitch said.

Eli smiled at his comment. "Probably so. I'll worry until I see you two come back safely."

Brad looked at Whit. "Should we get her a valium or something?"

Eli tossed a sofa pillow at him. "No, silly, it just means I love your two goofy asses."

"We know that. Trust me. Whit has drilled us on every possible thing we need to know to hike three miles down and three miles back." Mitch looked at Brad.

"At least three times over," Brad added. "We'll be gone after breakfast tomorrow and back before supper on Friday."

"I guess we need to plan a big meal for Friday then." Carol's comment lightened their spirits.

"How about bacon cheeseburgers and tater tots? Lots of them too." Brad grinned.

"That's easy enough. I'll make some ice cream, too." Eli finally smiled.

"We can make a huge breakfast in the morning and send you boys off with some biscuits to snack on tomorrow," Whit added.

"Are your packs all set?" Eli asked.

"Yes, ma'am. We want Whit to double-check us tonight, though," Mitch replied.

"That's a good plan. Carol and I are going to start on dinner. Why don't y'all check the packs now?"

"Yes, ma'am." Mitch offered a hand to Whit to get her off the couch.

†

"What are we cooking?" Carol asked.

"I thought we could grill chicken on the flat top to go with leftover veggies, and I want to try Hasselback potatoes. I saw a recipe for them on the Internet, and they look awesome."

"Okay, just tell me what you need me to do." Carol waited for instruction.

"Wash eight of those baking potatoes for me and dry them for starters." Eli grinned at her friend. "I'm so glad you've decided to stay up here longer. It's been fun having you here."

Carol moved next to Eli at the sink. "Do you think Whit would consider renting her cabin to me?"

Eli stopped washing the chicken. "Are you thinking of moving here?"

Carol nodded. "I've been giving it some thought. I'm fully vested in my retirement and thought I might check into openings at the local schools."

"That's fantastic news. What about you and Julia?" Eli grinned.

"Maybe we could move in together, if we can find someplace suitable. Julia only has a tiny apartment. I don't think it would work, and we both love it out here."

Eli shrugged. "Why don't you ask her about it after the boys leave tomorrow? She hasn't talked about the cabin much. It's been in her family for a long time."

†

Eli guided Carol through the first phase of prepping the potatoes. "You know me; I've got to put my spin on the recipe. We're going to use butter and dry ranch dressing for the basting sauce instead of the herbs. Baste them good and bake them for another forty-five minutes, basting every fifteen."

"That even sounds delicious," Carol said. "When do you want me to fan the slices open?"

Eli smiled at her friend. "You can go ahead and do it now to get the sauce deep inside."

"Wow, something smells wonderful in here," Mitch said, as they entered the cabin.

"Your aunt is trying out a new recipe for baked potatoes," Carol informed him.

Eli grinned at Mitch. "Hey, Mitch, can you whip up some of the white BBQ sauce for this chicken?"

"I'd love to, Aunt Eli."

"Are your packs all set?" Eli asked Brad.

Brad nodded. "Yes, ma'am. All we need to add is our water bottles and last-minute items."

"What do you need help with?" Whit asked.

"Brad can set the table. It's too early to heat leftovers just yet, but you can get them ready. Thanks for double-checking the packs."

"My pleasure." Whit started pulling dishes from the fridge.

†

"Damn, that's some good sauce." Carol spread the white sauce over the chicken breast and poured some on her plate to use as a dip. "The potatoes turned out pretty good, too."

"I could eat them every day," Mitch said, before putting another bite in his mouth. "I like the ranch and sea salt on them. Crunchy on the outside and soft on the inside."

"What are you guys taking for food?" Carol asked.

"We've got jerky and trail mix and some MREs, as well as a small stove."

Carol cocked her head at Mitch. "What the heck is an MRE?"

"Meals ready to eat," Brad piped in. "It's the same type of meal our soldiers eat while on deployment if they are away from camp. High in protein and calories, but easy to prepare with minimal effort."

"Easy to pack, too," Mitch added.

"Are you using the hammock tents?" Eli asked.

"Only if the shelter isn't in good shape. Otherwise, we'll use our sleeping bags in the shelter," Mitch replied.

"First-aid kit?" Eli asked.

Whit grinned. "In both packs. Even a snake bite kit."

Mitch shot a wink to Whit. "I'm beginning to think you don't want us to go, Aunt Eli."

Eli raised her head and stopped cutting her food. "I want you to go, but I damn sure want you to have everything you might need."

"The Xbox and TV are too big for our packs," Brad nonchalantly answered.

Eli broke out laughing. "I get it. You haven't even turned on an Xbox since you've been here."

"Do we even have one?" Mitch asked.

"I thought you brought yours up here?" Brad said.

"Nope, no time to waste on games." Mitch grinned. "Seriously, Aunt Eli, if we pack anything else, we might need to take a Gator."

"That kind of defeats the purpose of hiking." Eli smiled.

"My point exactly." Mitch reached over and put his hand on her arm. "Will it help if we call every hour?"

Eli made a motion to answer, but Whit interrupted her. "Absolutely not, you two are on an adventure, so you need to enjoy it. Your Aunt Eli will just have to get her panties out of a wad until you get back. Call if you need anything, or if you can send pictures."

"Get my panties out of a wad. Really Whit?" Eli grumbled.

"Yes. Now, let's finish this great meal in peace."

Carol laughed and took another bite of chicken. "Damn, this is good."

†

Eli pulled the bed linens over their bodies. She took Whit's hand and placed it between her bare legs. "See, my panties aren't in a wad," she laughed.

"Well, no, ma'am, they aren't." Whit took Eli's invitation and stroked her lover into a glorious orgasm.

"Remind me to have you check my panties again tomorrow," Eli chuckled.

"With pleasure." Whit kissed Eli deeply. "Let's get some sleep, so we'll be fresh in the morning to see the hikers off."

†

When Eli woke the next morning, she found Whit was already downstairs. She listened and heard the soft humming noises Whit made when she was making biscuits. Eli grinned and, after relieving her bladder, dressed and went downstairs.

"Good morning, sunshine," she said and kissed Whit's cheek. "You need a refill?" Eli walked to the coffee pot.

"Not yet, sweetie."

Eli started her coffee. "Are we the only ones awake?"

"Nope, Mitch is in the barn feeding the animals, and Brad is in the shower."

"They must be excited. Is Mitch checking for eggs?" Eli asked.

Whit pointed to a basket at the end of the counter. "Brad collected eight and fed the ladies before hitting the shower."

"I guess I need to pull out some meat to go with those eggs and your biscuits." Eli opened the refrigerator. "Ham, bacon, or sausage?"

"Do the ham and sausage. We can keep the bacon for the burgers tomorrow night."

Eli removed the packages from the fridge. "Did the boys pack toilet paper?"

Whit started laughing. "I got them some nature friendly, it can be covered up, and they won't have to pack it out."

"Eww, just the thought." Eli groaned.

"I can see why you've never considered hiking as a pastime," Whit teased.

"I'll admit, I enjoy my creature comforts too much, but pooping in the woods is not my idea of a good time."

"Gross," Carol said, as she walked in on the conversation. She wiped the hair from her face. "I'd have to agree with you on that one, Eli. Sorry, Whit."

"No need to be sorry. Hiking is not an easy lifestyle. I hope it will teach the boys how much they have to appreciate and what they take for granted when we start the AT." Whit continued cutting biscuits. "I think every teen should go for a few weeks of hiking for that reason."

"That is a good idea," Eli agreed. "I'll be much more comfortable when you join them for their trip, though."

"I do not doubt that Mitch and Brad would be okay, but I'm looking forward to it. I'll be missing you, but I'll have a trip to remember with the boys."

"You're starting to make me jealous," Eli teased.

"You can always choose to come with us," Whit reminded her.

Eli grinned. "I'd bitch and moan the whole way. I'd rather support your adventure from a comfortable bed."

"I understand that. I don't think these old bones could do it either," Carol said. "What can I help with?"

Eli pointed to the basket of eggs. "You can whip those up and add some of the shredded cheddar cheese. I'll scramble them once I get the meat cooking. Have a cup first, though."

"I think I'll climb the stairs and use your potty. The singing coming from the bathroom says Brad is taking a long shower, and I need to seriously pee."

"Yeah, he can be a bit of a diva in the shower," Eli said. "I'll start your coffee."

"Thanks." Carol headed for the stairs.

Eli started brewing a cup and returned to cooking the meat on the flat top. "I know you won't make it far on this trip, but maybe when you get closer to home, I could join you for a section of the hike. I know it may be a summer or two from now."

"I think that would be fun. Maybe, after Mitch graduates next year, we can hike longer than two weeks. It may be more difficult once he starts technical school or whatever he decides on doing."

Eli turned to Whit. "That's true. Maybe even on spring break, if the weather is good."

Whit picked up a large pan of biscuits. "Will you open the oven for me?"

Eli opened the oven door and closed it once the pan of biscuits was safely inside. "That's enough for the boys, so what are we going to eat?"

"Oh, you were hungry?" Whit teased. "That's a double batch. Even Mitch can't eat all those."

"What can't I eat?" Mitch asked, as he stepped inside.

"The three dozen biscuits Whit just put in the oven," Eli explained.

"Nope, but I'll be sure to fill a Ziploc full of them," Mitch replied.

"I've no doubt any of them will go to waste." Eli looked at Mitch. "Scrambled eggs with cheese good for you?"

"Sounds wonderful, Aunt Eli."

"Thanks for feeding the animals this morning," Eli said as she flipped some sausage patties.

"No problem. Is there anything you need me to do before we leave?"

Eli turned to look at Whit. "I can't think of anything. Can you?"

"No, I think we're in good shape, but thanks for asking." Whit looked at Mitch. "I know you have a small camp stove, so have you considered breaking down a fly rod to take with you? A little bit of oil and some meal, and you could fry fresh fish. I know there's a small creek along your trail south."

"That wouldn't be a problem. It's a great idea. We can save the MREs for another trip."

Whit held up her hand. "I'd still take them, just in case, but if you can catch fresh fish, that would be so much better."

Carol returned and began getting the eggs ready to scramble.

"What can I do?" Mitch asked.

"Go ahead and set the table and pull glasses down for juice."

Brad wandered into the kitchen.

"Hey, beautiful," Mitch teased. "I don't think you need to pack your hair product for this trip. Grab a hat to cover that head."

"Nothing like brotherly love first thing in the morning." Brad chuckled. "We may meet girls on the trail."

"Should I text Hayden what you just said?" Eli warned.

"No, ma'am. I just don't want to scare anyone. Looking at Mitch first thing in the morning will be scary enough. Are there Bigfoots in North Carolina?"

"There have been many reports of sightings on the AT," Whit told them.

"Just be careful they don't confuse you two for juvenile Sasquatches," Eli teased. "I can't imagine how I'd explain that to your mom."

"They'd bring us back quickly when they see how much we eat." Mitch laughed and set plates on the table. "Speaking of which, we're taking our fly rods, to see if we can have fresh fish tonight."

"Cool idea," Brad said.

Mitch pointed at Whit. "It was all her idea."

"I should have known," Brad stated.

Eli just shook and finished the meats. She poured the eggs on the grill. "You two can go ahead and pour drinks." She handed Carol the platters of cooked meat. "Eggs and biscuits will be up shortly.

"Mind if I grab some apple cinnamon jelly?" Brad asked.

"That's what we made it for, silly." Whit ruffled his hair.

Carol rubbed her hands together. "Yummy. I loved that stuff when your mom made it at Christmas."

"Brad and Whit made a nice batch and hopefully will make more as the jars empty," Eli said. "It is a tasty treat."

Whit pulled out the biscuits and stacked them on a platter. She took the bowl of scrambled eggs from Eli, put a spoon in them, and carried them to the table. "Here we are," she said.

Eli carried their coffee to the table. "Dig in."

Mitch filled three biscuits with ham and sausage and wrapped them in a napkin. When he looked up to see her watching, she smiled. "Making sure you have a stash to take with you?"

"Yes, ma'am. Is that okay?"

"Perfect, Mitch. If we don't have enough, we can cook some more," Eli told him. "I'm pretty sure no one will leave the table hungry."

Eli passed the jelly to Brad. "You've got your maps, and you know where to pick up the trail, right?"

Brad nodded. "Yes, ma'am, we just need to fill up our water bottles and grab our fly rods, and we'll be good to go."

Mitch's phone rang, and he laughed. "It's Dad." He answered the phone and put the call on speaker.

"Today is the big day. Are you two all set?" Mark asked.

"Yes, sir. Aunt Eli and Whit have quadruple checked our packs."

"Great. I just wanted to tell you both to have fun. Have you left yet?"

"No, sir, we're finishing up a monster breakfast, so say hi to everybody."

"Hey, everyone," Mark said with a giggle. "I'm very excited for you, boys. I wish I were there to go with you."

"We'll call and tell you all about it when we get home tomorrow night."

"Alright, son. You two have fun and take pics if you can. Love y'all."

"Most," Mitch answered. "Talk to you soon."

"Bye, son."

Mitch looked at Brad. "Do you want to bet on Mom calling as soon as we hit the trail?"

Brad grinned and looked at his watch. "That would be about right."

"Keep those phones handy," Whit teased. "I promise to hide Eli's today, so you'll have some peace."

"Hey now, I'm sitting right here and hear every word you're saying. I promise I won't bug the boys...too bad."

Mitch walked to the pantry and pulled out two Ziploc bags, handing one to Brad. "No time like the present."

"I've already filled your water bottles. They're in the freezer," Whit said. "They didn't have time to freeze, so you can drink off the bat if needed." She pulled out a small bottle of oil and a bag of corn meal and handed them to Mitch.

They packed the biscuits, water, and cooking supplies in their backpacks. Mitch looked at Brad. "Let's grab our rods, and we can get going." The boys shouldered their packs.

Eli felt her eyes fill with tears. She pushed the tears back with her hand and followed the boys out to the porch. "Be careful, have fun, and we'll see you sometime tomorrow. Call if you need anything."

"Will do. Love you, Aunt Eli." Mitch hugged her. "Don't let your eyes leak," he whispered into her ear.

She nodded and hugged Brad. "See you soon."

Carol and Whit joined her on the porch. They waved and watched, as the boys disappeared up the trail to the top of the mountain.

"Damn, I should have gotten a picture," Whit said.

"Next time, I won't let you forget," Eli promised.

"It's a damn good thing I've got your backs." Carol smiled, and her phone pinged when she sent them a picture.

"Thanks," Eli said.

They walked inside and cleaned up the kitchen. Whit looked at Eli. "Why don't we drive around a bit and show Carol more of the area since she's interested in making this home?"

Eli knew it was Whit's way of keeping her busy, so she didn't worry about the boys. She smiled at her lover. "Sounds good. Maybe we can hijack Julia for dinner at the steakhouse tonight?"

"Sounding better by the minute," Whit responded.

"I'd never pass up a good dinner with great friends," Carol added. "I'll give her a call."

CHAPTER TWO

"I'm going to shower and get dressed. Why don't you ask Whit about renting?" Eli suggested to Carol.

"Alright. No time like the present." Carol grinned.

"I'll be down shortly," Eli said and climbed the stairs.

"So, what was that all about?" Whit smiled.

"I was talking to Eli earlier about maybe looking for a teaching job up here. I'm fully vested in my retirement in Florida, and I'd like to see where a relationship with Julia may lead. She only has a tiny apartment in town, so I wondered if you would consider renting your cabin to me or maybe us in the future?"

"Now that's an interesting thought," Whit replied. "Let me think about it for a bit." She grinned at Carol. "I think it would be a total possibility. It would have to come furnished though. I've got no place to store the furnishings."

Carol smiled. "I don't have much in my apartment. I could sell that and move here with my basics. I may be jumping the gun on a relationship, but at least give some thought to the idea and what you would want for rent. Even if Julia's not ready for the next level, I want to be here."

Whit nodded. "I understand that completely. Let me talk it over with Eli while you keep romancing Julia. I think you make a cute couple."

"Thanks, Whit. I feel like I have a long way to redeem myself with Eli, and I think that will happen more quickly here."

"I haven't known her as long as you, but I'd say Eli has forgiven you. Her happiness here has helped leave all the baggage behind." Whit saw the change in Carol's expression. "I'm not saying you are baggage, but what happened between you and Sara is history best left forgotten."

Carol nodded. "I couldn't agree more. I was such a fool." She sighed. "Okay, I'm going to call Julia. What time are you thinking for dinner?"

"Between five and six?" Whit asked. "I think she closes shop at four."

"Sounds great. I'll be right back."

†

Whit could hear the shower running upstairs, and the thought of Eli's wet, naked body made her grin. She knew Eli had forgiven Carol and seemed happy to have her a part of her life. Whit didn't think she would ever sell her grandparent's place, but it was too good to leave vacant.

Carol moving in would change that and fill the home with love again.

When Carol returned, she wore a broad smile and knew that Julia had said yes.

"She's ready to go now," Carol announced.

Whit grinned. "We can make it closer to four if we're back in time from our tour."

†

Brad and Mitch hadn't made it onto the trail before Laura called.

"I just wanted to tell you two to have fun, and I love you," she told Mitch.

"We love you most." Mitch chuckled. "We'll call when we get home tomorrow night."

"Okay, son. Have fun."

"We will. Bye, Mom."

"That was pretty quick," Brad replied.

"Now we should be on our own," Mitch said. "We've got a beautiful day so far. Let's make the best of it."

As they reached the trailhead, they took a left to head south. "What a view." Brad pointed across the top of a dense forest. "The national park?" he asked.

"Yes, about five thousand acres surround Eli's place," Mitch explained.

"We could explore for weeks," Brad said.

"Yes, we could," Mitch said. "I think we've still got areas we haven't fully explored on our part of the mountain."

They walked on for another twenty minutes, until they reached their first Appalachian Trail marker. "Let's get some pictures to send to Dad," Mitch said. "You go first, then you can take one of me."

Brad posed next to the AT sign, and Mitch snapped a picture. Then they swapped places, and Brad took a picture of Mitch.

"How far do you think we are from Springer Mountain?" Brad asked.

"Less than a hundred miles, I'm sure."

"The total is over 2200 miles, correct?"

"That's correct. That's a lot of miles. I can't believe how many hikers repeat it," Mitch said. "Some of them into their seventies."

"I can't imagine doing it in my teens, much less at seventy," Brad replied.

"I think it would be a grand adventure. I could be wrong. After we do two weeks with Whit, we may both get our fill. I kind of doubt it, though. I think she's excited to go with us," Mitch said with a grin.

"I love how she teases Aunt Eli about not going," Brad said.

"I heard them talking about Eli doing one section with us in the future. I think, if she hears how fun it is, she may change her mind," Mitch said.

"Maybe so. Hey, we've made it a quarter of a mile," Brad chuckled.

Mitch looked over at his brother. "It's been pretty much downhill so far. We'll have to go up eventually. The elevation doesn't look all that bad from the maps, though." He smiled, and his braces flashed in the sunlight. "I'm glad we're doing this together."

"Me too, bro. Except for Scout trips, Dad has always been with us, or some other adult. I think this is a test for us."

"In many ways." Mitch pointed toward a dark bank of clouds in the south. "I hope those hold off until we reach the shelter."

"Me too. At least we have rain gear if we need it."

As they entered a wooded section, Brad looked at Mitch, then pointed to a broken tree limb hanging across part of the trail. "What did Whit tell us about trail maintenance? Do you think that applies?"

"She said to remove anything that could be a danger to a hiker or wildlife. I'd say a broken, dangling limb would apply. If it fell on someone as they passed, it could do some damage." Mitch was tall enough to reach the branch. "Watch out," he called out and gave the section a good jerk. The limb moved but failed to separate from the tree. "Pull out your hatchet, and I'll lift you so you can cut it."

They both dropped their packs, and Brad took out a small hatchet. "You sharpened it, right?" Mitch teased.

"Yes, Dad, I did," Brad answered. "If you lift me on your shoulders, I should be able to reach."

"For gosh sakes, don't miss and hit either one of us," Mitch warned.

"Got it, Boss," Brad teased and handed Mitch the hatchet. "Hang on to this until I'm stable."

Brad scrambled onto Mitch's shoulders. With the length of the hatchet, they should be successful in reaching the limb. He reached down for the hatchet. "I can't guarantee I can keep it from swinging back this way, so keep an eye open."

"I can hang onto it long enough to keep it from snapping back on us," Mitch answered. He grabbed the branch. "Cut as quickly as you can. You're getting heavy," Mitch teased.

Brad took aim on the branch and took a swing and then another before the limb broke free. "Good job." Mitch pushed the section away from them, and it fell to the ground with a thud. Mitch took the hatchet from Brad and lowered him to the ground.

"That was easy," Brad said.

"For you, maybe. Next time you can lift me." Mitch groaned.

"No way I'm strong enough for that," Brad said. "We'd have to figure something else out."

"I'd send you to shimmy up the tree then." Mitch laughed.

"I could do that," Brad declared.

"I know you could. I swear you're part monkey."

They started down the trail. Several minutes later, Brad stopped at an opening. "Whoa, dude, look at that."

Mitch looked across to the large rocky bald Brad was pointing out. "I think that's Clingman's Dome, but I'm not one hundred percent sure. We can check the maps later."

"That's a massive bald if we can see it from this height," Brad said. "I know we've been there, but it's been a long time, and I barely remember."

"It is huge," Mitch replied. "Cold as heck too, the last time we went. I do remember that. It started sprinkling and turned to sleet this fast." Mitch snapped his fingers. "Mom bitched the entire time it took us to get back to the car."

Mitch pointed to a pair of red-tailed hawks soaring on the thermals. "Aren't they beautiful?"

"Yeah, they are neat. Look, one of the hawks is diving after something."

"Do you have the binoculars, Brad?"

"Yeah, grab them out of my pack, and let's see what he got."

Mitch located the equipment and began scanning the area where the hawk went down. "Oh, no. Poor bunny foo foo just became lunch for those two hawks. Holy cow, you should see how that beak tears him apart." He handed the glasses to Brad and pointed out the spot to survey.

"Damn, I'd hate to be that bird's prey. The hawks must be pretty strong to rip the animal apart like that."

Mitch laughed. "I sure as heck don't want to find out firsthand." He gave Brad a few more minutes to survey the area. "You ready to roll?"

†

Thirty minutes further down the trail, they began hearing water, and Brad pointed out a quick flowing stream. We can't be too far from the trail shelter. "Check your GPS."

Mitch checked his device. "A couple of hundred yards at most. Let's go on down and see how close this stream is to it. If we need to make some repairs, we can do that, set up for tonight, and then fish."

"Let's go," Brad said. "I'm starting to get hungry."

"Me too," Mitch agreed. "We can pull out the biscuits when we arrive."

As they walked closer, Mitch heard voices coming from the shelter. They hadn't seen any other traffic on the trail, so he was excited to see hikers when they walked to the covering.

"Hello," a young man in his twenties called out when he spotted them.

"Hey," Mitch answered. "Do you mind some company?"

"Not at all. The more, the merrier. I'm Scott, and my little brother, Dennis, is in the bushes taking a leak."

Mitch stepped forward and offered his hand. "I'm Mitch, and my little bro is Brad. We're spending the summer with our aunt, and she sent us out to do some trail maintenance."

"Nice to meet you. We just arrived a few minutes ago and thought we'd layover here for tonight."

Dennis walked around from the rear of the shelter. "Hey." He smiled with a blush to his cheeks.

"Mitch and Brad," Scott shared with Dennis. "Where are you guys from?"

"Alabama," Brad said. "What about y'all?"

"Buckhead, Georgia, it's a burb of Atlanta. Dennis and I thought we'd do a few weeks of hiking before we call Dad for a ride home."

"Sounds cool," Brad said. "Are y'all hungry?"

"We've been munching on some trail mix," Dennis said.

"How about some homemade biscuits?" Mitch offered.

"Oh, heck yeah," Dennis said.

"I noticed you've got some fly rods too. Plan to do some fishing?"

"That was the plan. Biscuits for a late lunch, some work on the shelter, and catch up a mess of fish for supper." Mitch grinned. "You guys game?"

"We can help with the shelter repairs if you can catch a few extra fish," Scott said. "A hot meal would be great."

"Good deal," Mitch said. "Let's break out some grub."

The boys used the lower loft of the shelter as a table. Mitch and Brad spread out the haul of biscuits, meats, and the jar of jelly.

"That's pretty jelly. What is it?" Scott asked.

"Apple cinnamon. Made with apple juice and red hots." Brad replied.

"That sounds great. We've never had that before." Scott wiped his hands and took the biscuit and sausage patty. He added a small amount of jelly and took a bite. "Oh, my gosh. That is good."

"I made it from our Grandma's recipe," Brad said.

"You made this?" Dennis asked.

"With a little help, but yes."

"We have to exchange emails. I'd love to have this recipe for Mom," Scott said.

"No problem. Grandma always made it around Christmas time because of the bright red color," Mitch said. "How much longer you two planning to hike?"

Scott shrugged. "As long as little man can hang," he teased his brother. "Maybe two weeks."

"We're heading back tomorrow, and it's only three miles. There's a camp shelter close to our aunt's property where you could stay. You can get a hot shower, wash some clothes, and have a home-cooked meal if you want to join us."

"You sure your aunt won't mind?" Scott said.

"She may give you some work to do, but no, she won't mind," Mitch replied.

Brad piped in, "We will be headed to another shelter soon for repairs, so maybe we could hike with you when you leave."

"That sounds good. Dang, these are tasty," Scott replied.

"Much better than the trail mix. I think I've started pooping birdseed," Dennis said.

They all shared a good laugh over his comment.

"Eat up, boys, and let's get to work," Mitch said. "We have a few boards that need some work."

Mitch used the tip of his boot to open the campfire container. "We need to dump this out too." He looked at Brad. "Can you and Dennis clear this out and find some firewood for tonight?"

Brad looked at Dennis, who nodded. "I don't see why not. Do you want me to set up the camp stove, or do you want to use the grill over the firepit?"

"Let's rough it and use the pit." Mitch winked. "We can pull out the stove if we need it." Mitch surveyed the sleeping lofts. "Plenty of room for all four of us in here tonight. Hopefully, we can get done before the rains move in."

After eating a second biscuit each, the boys went to work. Mitch and Scott started adding nails to reinforce the siding on the shelter, while Brad and Dennis cleaned out the firepit and started gathering wood. They found several small branches. Brad used his hatchet to cut them into usable lengths, while Dennis snapped and piled up some kindling.

"We've only got a few boards left if you want to go check out the stream," Mitch told them.

"Now, we're talking. Stand back and watch a master perform," Brad announced.

"Dear Lord, those two are like peas in a pod." Scott nodded toward their younger brothers.

"Brad loves to fish." Mitch grinned. "I do too. We regularly have competitions with some friends and do fish fries afterward. Right now, Team Brad has bragging rights, but that will soon change."

"It sounds like you're having a lot of fun up here," Scott told Mitch.

"It's been terrific helping Aunt Eli set up her farm. I'm going to hate going back to Bama in the fall, but I only have one more year of high school. Then I'm right back up here."

"I've got one more year at Georgia Tech, then I'll join my dad's architectural firm."

"That sounds exciting," Mitch said.

"I'm looking forward to it, but I want to spend one last summer having some fun. Maybe finish the AT next year, before I dig into working full time."

"Awesome plan. I hope to do at least a few more sections next summer too. Maybe we can hook up and hike together."

"That would be fun, man." Scott hammered in the last nail. "There, that should keep us relatively dry tonight."

Mitch stored the tools, while Scott stretched out his sleeping bag on one of the top bunks. "Little dudes on the bottom?" he asked Mitch.

"Yep, that's the plan." Mitch turned when he heard a cry of excitement coming from the stream. "The great white fisherman has hooked a fish. Let's go join them," Mitch said, as he assembled his rod.

"You catch, and we'll clean," Scott volunteered.

"It doesn't get better than that." Mitch grinned.

After catching eight fish, the boys thought they would have enough for dinner. Mitch started the fire, while Scott and the others finished cleaning the fish. He took out his phone and grinned when he saw he had service.

Can we add two for burgers tomorrow night? he texted to Eli.

He watched the bubble as Eli was typing a reply. *Absolutely. Having fun?*

A blast. Tell you about it tomorrow. Told the boys you may make them work for supper. LOL

We'll pick a bunch of corn and peas for them to shuck and shell.

Way too easy. LOL Love you.

Most.

Brad had saved a Ziplock from the biscuits, and they used that for the filets after rinsing them. Dennis brought them to the shelter, while Brad and Scott cleaned their hands in the stream."

"Those look nice. You're not going to believe what Aunt Eli snuck in my pack."

"What?" Brad asked.

Mitch pulled out a container of hushpuppy mix.

Brad smiled. "Oh, hell yeah. Hushpuppies to go with the fish. You gotta love that woman."

✝

After a driving tour around the immediate area, Eli turned back toward town. Whit was sure to point out the locations of the schools for Carol. They arrived at Julia's shop, ten minutes after four, and headed to the diner.

They had just ordered, when Eli's phone pinged with a text. She grinned. Mitch had sent pictures of each of them at a trail sign. Both looked like they were having a great time. Then he sent a text asking if they could add two more to supper tomorrow night. "It appears the boys have made some trail friends," she told the group. "Mitch wants to know if we can add two more for bacon cheeseburgers tomorrow night?"

"Of course, tell him yes." Whit looked at Julia. "I think we need to make it three, though. Are you game for supper tomorrow night?"

Julia scoffed. "A country girl never passes on bacon cheeseburgers. Especially if someone else is cooking them," she teased Whit.

"Ha! Mitch told them I would put them to work in trade for a meal, a hot shower, and laundry."

"I've got plans to pick peas and a lot of corn tomorrow," Whit replied.

"There's my trade-off. The boys can shuck corn and shell peas." Eli sent him a quick text. "Sounds like they're having fun," Eli said when she put her phone away.

"That was the point in sending them off together." Carol waved her hand in a generous gesture. "They won't be young for long. Let them live it up while they can."

Eli lifted her glass of tea. "Amen to that sisters."

†

Mitch took out a small pot and frying pan from his pack and began heating oil. He used the bag of cornmeal to coat the filets. When the oil was hot, he began cooking them over the firepit. He used a spoon to drop balls of the hushpuppy mix into the pot. "You guys need to dig out camp plates and forks. It won't take long for this first batch to cook."

†

"Man, this is some good grub. We'll have to remember to bring a fishing pole next summer," Scott told Dennis.

"I'm sure we have one we could loan you until you finish hiking this year," Mitch said.

"How long have you two hiked?" Brad was curious to hear some of their trail stories.

"We've only been out for ten days this trip. Taking it easy and not pushing hard to finish big miles every day. We knew from the start we couldn't do a thru hike, so we plan on a few sections at a time."

"Do you see many other hikers on the trail?" Mitch asked.

Scott shook his head as he chewed. "We've only seen three others until we met you today. I think a lot more people are hiking southbound these days."

Mitch looked at Brad. "That's what we are planning this summer. Start in Maine and hike for a couple of weeks. Then maybe next year, pick up where we left off."

"That's what a lot of people are doing. We just figured we were this close to Springer Mountain that we'd head north."

"It's been a lot of fun, so far," Dennis said.

Brad looked at him. "Anything scary along the way?"

"We've seen a couple of bears, but they were more scared of the noise we were making. There was one river crossing that got a little hairy. The water was deeper and moving faster than we had estimated." Scott nudged his brother. "I thought I was going to go swimming after this one when he stepped in a hole, but he regained his footing and fought his way through." He smiled at Dennis. "A year ago, he couldn't have done that."

Mitch smiled. "I think being out on our own like this is a good test for us. Aunt Eli is terrified something terrible will happen, but she trusts us to do what we've learned."

"That sounds like our mom," Dennis said. "There's no way we could tell her about the bears or falling in the river. She'd never let us out of her sight again, but Dad's cool and will keep our secrets."

When the rain began to fall, the boys stoked the fire and talked until they fell asleep.

†

Mitch woke up to an aching bladder and walked outside to pee. The morning was crisp and fresh after the last night's rain shower. The repairs to the shelter had kept them dry, except for an occasional spray carried in on the breeze. Mitch loved the way the morning mist cloaked the mountains. There was a freshness in the air that only rain could bring, and he smiled at the scent of wild blossoms that filled the air. He heard a snap. He looked down at the stream to find a doe and her fawn enjoying a refreshing drink. He watched them for several minutes, then stretched before returning to the shelter.

Scott was awake and adding some kindling to the firepit. Enough embers remained from last night's fire to ignite the dry wood. "Good morning," Scott whispered.

"Morning. It's going to be a beautiful one," Mitch replied. "Did we have any water left from last night?"

"Yes, quite a bit. What do you need? Some coffee?" Scott asked.

"Naw, I'm not much on coffee. I was going to whip up some pancakes. No butter, but we've got syrup and jelly."

"That sounds good. What can I do to help?" Scott asked.

"Go rinse out the frying pan. I think I got all the fishy smell out last night, but a good rinse never hurts."

"I'm on it, man."

As Mitch foraged through his pack, he found a bag with a few pieces of sausage left. "I think we hit the jackpot." He grinned at Scott. "We had a few sausage patties left from the biscuits. I can break them up into the batter to give us some protein."

"Sounds delicious." Scott set the frying pan on the firepit grill.

"I think we have some wild blackberries, too, we can have on the side," Scott said. "We found some bushes about a mile from here. The berries are juicy and sweet."

"Bring 'em on," Mitch replied as he stirred the batter. "I should have enough for two each. That should hold us until we get home."

"Sounds great. I'm getting tired of granola and trail mix."

Mitch chuckled. "Have you thought of packing some MREs?"

"We had a few, but we've already blown through them," Scott answered.

"Aunt Eli keeps some stock for hikers in the pantry. Vienna sausage, canned meats, and that kind of stuff. We can get you restocked."

"Good, we don't have a package drop until Asheville."

"Has that process worked out for you?" Mitch asked.

"For the most part. We need to do a better job of rationing our food supplies, though. If we can fish and forage along the way, that would be a great help."

"There should be streams, lakes, and rivers along your way. Wild berries may be plentiful too."

Brad lifted his head. "That smells delicious."

"Wake up, sleepyhead," Mitch called.

Scott gave Dennis a gentle shake. "Time to get up, bro."

Brad pulled on his boots. "Nature calls." He grinned.

"Hurry back, the pancakes will be ready soon," Mitch informed him.

†

Eli smiled as she stretched. "After breakfast, I'm going to run to the store. If the boys are bringing hikers home, I'd like to restock them a bit if needed. My hiker cupboards are a little bare."

"Will you pick up more hamburger and buns, too?" Whit asked.

"Got it." Eli smiled. "Anything else?"

"I'll put a list together while you cook some breakfast." Whit snuck in a kiss.

"How about some toast and oatmeal?"

"That sounds good. Light, but gives you good energy. That might not be a bad thing to add to your pantry, some instant oatmeal. The brown sugar one is great."

Eli nodded. "That is a good idea."

CHAPTER THREE

Eli quickly filled a cart with supplies she thought would be perfect on the trail and easy to transport. She smiled when she even remembered Margret's advice on Ziplocks and toilet paper. Eli lucked up on some buy-one-get-one-free products and selected cans of peanuts and other protein snacks among her purchases. Eli was so excited about trail gear, she nearly forgot the hamburger and buns. When she went down the condiments aisle, she noted packets of salt and pepper, and foil packets of honey, ketchup, and mustard. *Shopping like this makes me almost want to hike.* She shook the thought from her head. *Naw, a warm bed and hot showers for me.*

The cashier smiled at the various purchases Eli placed on the belt. "You've either got a house chocked full of teenagers or a big donation," she said when she totaled the bill.

"I keep supplies stocked for hikers on the AT," Eli said.

"That's very thoughtful of you. The world needs a whole lot more of your brand of kindness."

"Thanks. I try to do what I can. Have a great day," Eli said after taking the receipt. She pushed the buggy out into the bright sunny morning. Eli placed the sunglasses over her eyes. She had to admit that since she began wearing the crystal necklace, her headaches had disappeared. *I'm not complaining either.*

†

"I'm glad you decided to hook up the trailer." Carol wiped the sweat from her brow with the back of her hand. "We would have needed numerous trips with just the Gator."

Whit nodded. "This corn is producing like crazy this year. I think Eli may have some ready to be picked as well." She picked up a handful of peas. "It seems like I pick one basket of peas, and two more are ready."

"Admit it, Whit. You have the Midas touch when it comes to growing food," Carol replied. "The diner is going to love all this fresh produce."

"That was a brilliant idea Mitch had. Excess food in trade for free meals. Even more critical since Eli's plot is starting to produce. We've talked about buying a big chest freezer, but I think we have plenty to make it through the winter."

"Would you mind helping me can and freeze some?" Carol asked. "I'll buy all the supplies and pay for the veggies."

Whit shook her head. "Like heck, you will. You get the supplies, but you put in the sweat to harvest and prepare them." She grinned. "I bet Brad would even help. He's getting good in the kitchen."

"It still amazes me how well they thrive up here," Carol replied. "They're both great boys but are turning into young men with you and Eli."

"I think it's easier when you're not the parent. We allow them to try and fail without repercussions. There is no perfect, and we want them to put forth their best effort and learn from mistakes." Whit turned her head at the sounds of a vehicle coming up the drive and smiled when she recognized Eli's truck.

"Dang, I almost forgot. Julia, asked if she could have a pint of your strawberries. She's making a dessert for tonight."

"Definitely, if she's making dessert. Let's pick some, then help Eli with the groceries. I bet she went overboard." Whit laughed.

"She wouldn't be Eli if she didn't."

†

"I swear, I don't know how all these bags made it into my truck." Eli winked at Whit.

"It appears you're expecting an army of hikers," Whit teased.

"You never know. Besides, we can use most of the stuff if we don't give it away this hiking season."

Eli glanced at the trailer full of fresh-picked vegetables. "You'd better park those in the shade if the boys don't show arrive soon."

Whit glanced at her watch. "I bet they roll up any minute now."

"Probably about when we get these groceries inside and make some tomato sandwiches," Carol said. "Boys always know precisely when to show up for food."

"Especially in this family." Eli grabbed an armload. "I'll carry them in if you two will start storing them in the pantry and make a dozen tomato sandwiches."

"What are the rest of us going to eat?" Whit teased.

"Every woman for herself," Eli answered.

"Well, we can all take a load in as we go." Carol chuckled at their banter.

†

"Home sweet home," Mitch said, as they stepped onto the northern boundary of Eli's property. "The camp shelter is about a quarter of a mile beyond where we'll head down the mountain. Would you like to go there first?"

"Honestly, a hot shower sounds too good to be true about now," Scott answered.

"No problem," Mitch replied.

"I think I'll take Dennis to the shelter and show him the pool too," Brad said. "Are you up for it?"

"Heck, yes," Dennis answered.

"We'll see you in about a half hour then," Brad said, when they reached the trailhead.

"Okay, we'll try not to eat all the sandwiches I'm sure they're making." Mitch told his brother. "They grow the most amazing tomatoes up here," Mitch said to Scott.

"Count me in," Scott said. "You two have fun and stay safe."

"We will," Dennis answered.

Incoming. Mitch texted Eli.

†

Eli was about to take a bite of her first tomato sandwich when Mitch's text came through. She started laughing.

"Are the boys home?" Whit asked.

"Pretty close," Eli answered, still chuckling.

"What did I tell ya? Perfect timing." Carol shook her head.

"Should I start making more?" Whit asked.

"Let's wait and see what they want. Mitch may choose something with meat." Eli answered.

†

When they reached the cabin, Cruz rushed out to meet them. "Who is this adorable little lady?" Scott asked.

"That's Cruz. In about thirty seconds, she'll bring you a tennis ball or frisbee to throw. Take my advice. If you want to eat in the next half hour, don't start a fetch game with her."

Right on cue, Cruz brought a ball over to them.

"After lunch, little lady," Scott promised.

"Now, you've done it. Cruz won't let you forget." Mitch spotted the trailer full of vegetables. "That must be our project for this afternoon."

Scott let out a low whistle. "That's a lot of vegetables."

"Don't worry. Everyone will pitch in to get 'er done. Let's drop our packs here." Mitch propped his beside the front door.

"This place is fantastic. No wonder you love it here," Scott replied.

†

"Hey, ladies," Mitch said as they entered the cabin. "This is my new friend, Scott, from Georgia. Scott, this is my Aunt Eli and her friends, Whit and Carol."

"Pleased to meet you ladies," he replied. "Mitch has told us so much about this place we just had to see if for ourselves."

Eli noted the beard growth and judged the young man to be in his early twenties. "Nice to meet you, Scott. Speaking of we, where is Brad?"

Scott grinned. "He and Dennis, my little brother, wanted to see the camp shelter we'll be staying at tonight."

"They will be a half hour or so behind us. Looks like we timed it just right." Mitch winked to Scott.

"We've got tomato sandwiches, but there's plenty of fresh deli meat in the fridge. Just wash up first, okay?" Eli instructed.

"I'll show you where the bathroom is, and I'll use the kitchen sink," Mitch said.

Whit grinned at Mitch. "Grab whatever meats and condiments you want, and we'll make you some sandwiches."

"Yes, ma'am," Mitch answered and began scrubbing his hands.

"Did you have a good time?" Carol asked.

"No," he answered with a straight face. "We had a blast."

"Did you get wet last night?" Eli asked.

"No, ma'am. Scott helped me with the shelter repairs, while Brad and Dennis gathered some firewood. We had a delicious fish dinner. Thanks for sneaking in the hushpuppy mix."

"I knew you'd catch, and what's a fish dinner without hushpuppies?" Eli asked.

"Those were the bomb. I'd love to have that recipe and the one for the jelly, too," Scott said as he reentered the room.

"We actually shared your biscuits and jelly with them for a late lunch," Mitch said. "Aren't you proud of us?"

"I'm always proud, but yes, thanks for sharing. I would have bet you would have eaten them before you made it to the shelter," Eli teased.

"We had to do some trail maintenance along the way to remove a dangling limb that was endangering the trail, so we were a bit behind schedule."

"Thank God for that limb. Those biscuits were heavenly. I was worried about the looks Dennis was giving me. I was afraid he'd gnaw my arm if I made him eat trail mix last night."

Within minutes of arriving, Scott had them all laughing. No wonder Mitch liked him. "Turkey, ham, or roast beef. Pick your poison," Eli said.

Scott grinned at Eli. "Would you mind if I have one of those tomato sandwiches first? Then ham, please, ma'am."

Eli pointed to the pile of halved tomato sandwiches on a platter. "Help yourself. You'll find tea and cold sodas in the fridge, Mitch."

"I'd love a Coke or Mountain Dew," Scott told Mitch.

Mitch opened the fridge. "We have both."

"Dew, please," Scott answered and bit into a sandwich. "These tomatoes are so sweet."

"Told you they were good," Mitch said.

Eli looked up when she heard Cruz barking. "The others must be here." Several minutes later, they heard the clunking of boots, and Brad walked in. "You must be Dennis. I'm Eli, and this is Whit and Carol."

"Happy to meet you," he said.

"Brad, show him to the bathroom, and y'all wash up and come eat."

"Yes, ma'am." Brad and Dennis disappeared down the hall.

Mitch looked at Eli and snorted. "Two peas in a pod," he said.

"Speaking of peas…and corn and carrots," Eli said.

"Yeah, we saw the trailer load when we came home," Mitch said.

"It's a small price to pay for tomato sandwiches, cheeseburgers, and a hot shower and shave," Scott said. "Mitch said we could throw a load of clothes in the wash too."

"Absolutely," Eli answered.

"Don't forget your date," Mitch said.

Scott chuckled, and Eli looked puzzled.

"He promised Cruz a game of fetch after we eat."

"She's missed you. I think Molly has too," Whit said.

"Wait until you meet Molly," Mitch told Scott. "You will die laughing at them playing."

"I am so starved," Brad said when they returned.

"Get a drink and tell me what sandwiches you want," Carol said.

"One of everything," Brad said.

"Do you have turkey?" Dennis asked.

"Yes, sir, we do. Two for starters?" Carol asked.

Dennis smiled. "Yes, please."

"Grab some chips out of the pantry, please, Brad," Eli requested.

"Dang, someone did some major shopping," Brad said.

"Eli," Whit and Carol said in unison.

Brad brought a couple of bags of chips to the table.

"I knew we were missing something," Mitch said.

"We almost had chicken," Eli teased.

"Why chicken?" Brad asked.

"Because your Miss Henny Penny pecked the crap out of me this morning for stealing her eggs."

"Which one?" Mitch asked.

"Hell, if I know. They all look the same to me," Eli answered.

"Probably Geraldine, she can be a bit grumpy in the morning," Brad said.

"Wait, don't tell me you have them all named?" Mitch asked.

Brad cocked his head and looked at him. "Of course, I do."

"Are you going to tell me you can tell the difference in twenty-four white chickens?" Carol asked.

"Yes, ma'am. That's why they call me Chicken Man," he teased.

"Did he hit his head while he was gone?" Whit asked.

Mitch shook his head. "No, but I think he's become a bit delusional."

"Eat up, Chicken Man, we've all got work to do," Eli told him and dropped her plate in the compost pile.

†

When everyone had finished eating, they walked outside to attend to the vegetables. Mitch called to Cruz, "Go get Molly." Cruz raced into the barn and returned minutes later, followed by the small goat. "I swear that never gets old." Mitch laughed. Molly rushed up to them, slid to a stop, then butted Scott's leg until he reached down to pet her.

"Oh, my goodness, what a cutie." Scott knelt to show her some attention.

"Don't worry, Cruz hasn't let you off the hook that easy, but Molly will wear her down some."

They began working on the vegetables as they watched the two play. Their antics resulted in several laughs from the group.

"You can toss the hulls into the chicken runs," Eli told Brad and Dennis. "Mitch can dump the corn husks in the compost bin, and Scott can go first in the shower."

"I can help finish up here," Scott said.

"We've got this," Mitch said. "The shower and laundry room are over there." He pointed out the building.

"There are clean towels, hygiene products, and anything you should need in the cabinets. Sorry, I only have disposable razors."

"Not a problem. I've got my own," Scott said.

"Drop your laundry in the washer while you shower, and they can dry while Dennis showers."

"Yes, ma'am." He grinned.

Eli turned to Carol and Whit. "Let's take these veggies in to rinse and package for travel. The boys can drop them off at the diner while I start cooking."

"Let's get cracking boys," Mitch said.

†

When the boys returned from town, Julia had arrived and was slicing strawberries for the cake she'd made. "Save a couple of handfuls of those berries. We made a batch of ice cream too," Carol told her.

"Not a problem. I've got all I need for the cake."

"How's the laundry coming?" Eli asked.

"Almost done," Scott said. "Do you want me to put a load of towels in?"

"Sure, if you don't mind." Eli smiled.

"Not at all," Scott answered. "That was a great shower." He looked at Eli. "I couldn't help but notice those battery banks and the solar panels. Do you generate all of your power?"

"Every single watt," Eli said. "Whit and Mitch installed the system."

Scott looked at Mitch. "That's pretty awesome, dude."

"There's not much Whit can't teach me." Mitch grinned.

"Do you want to eat at the picnic tables?" Whit asked.

"It looks like a great night out, so why not?" Eli asked.

Carol looked at Julia. "Will you help me put some tablecloths on and set the table?"

"Sure. Fine china, or the real stuff?"

"Fine china," Whit said.

Scott looked at Mitch. "Paper plates," Mitch told him.

"Gotcha," Scott answered with a grin.

†

During the meal, the boys talked about their journeys on the trail. Scott and Dennis were a welcome addition to their trail family. Mitch and Brad would accompany them the next day on their continued hike, and they would perform trail maintenance on the other shelter.

"I know it's only a few miles from here, but I think we'll lay over another night with y'all," Scott said. "It's been fun getting to know all of you."

Mitch smiled. "Good deal."

"You both are welcome to visit anytime," Eli told them as they cleaned up after the meal. "When you come down for breakfast in the morning, we'll restock some of your supplies."

"Thanks," Dennis said. "I am so sick of trail mix."

Julia's strawberry cake and ice cream were a hit for dessert. With the added company, there was little left.

Darkness was falling quickly. "Why don't you and Brad give the guys a ride up to the trailhead?"

Brad took off at a run to get a Gator.

"When you get back, you need to restock your packs, too," Eli told Mitch. "Is a big country breakfast good to send you all off tomorrow?"

"That would be fantastic, especially if there are more of those biscuits." Scott grinned. "I thought I'd died and gone to heaven when Mitch pulled those out of his pack."

Whit grinned. "Thanks, that was my contribution. I'm glad you enjoyed them. I'll cook extras in the morning."

Brad rolled up with the Gator, and after collecting their packs, Scott and Dennis thanked them for their hospitality.

"You're very welcome," Eli replied. "See you in the morning for breakfast."

She looked at Whit. "Are you ready for a shower and the bed?"

"Yes, I am," Whit replied. "I wanted to stay and help the boy's stock their bags, though."

"You go ahead. I'll take care of that when Julia heads home."

"Which should be right about now." Julia walked up to them. "Thanks for everything."

Eli returned her smile. "Thanks for the fabulous cake. That was yummy. See you this weekend?"

Julia looked at Carol. "That's a very high possibility."

"Great. Goodnight, you two." Eli took Whit's hand and they walked inside.

"I'll be up in just a few once the boys and I are done restocking their packs." Whit watched Eli climb the stairs.

Eli was sitting on the edge of the bed, preparing to set her alarm, when Mark texted.

Boys make it home?

Yes, they had a blast. Met two young men around their ages. Brought them home, and all four of them are heading back out tomorrow.

Great, remind Mitch to call me in the morning.

Will do. Love you.

Most.

CHAPTER FOUR

When the boys left Saturday morning, Eli looked at Whit. "You know what?"

"No, what?"

"I think it's time we go float in an inner tube at the swimming hole."

Whit lifted her hand to Eli's forehead. "As in, take a day off?"

"Yes, that's it exactly. It's a Saturday, and I do believe Julia closes her shop at noon, so why not?"

"We could ask her to pick up some chicken and meet us there." Carol smiled. "We can pack a cooler of drinks and some towels and head out."

"Give her a call and see if she's game. I'll grab the inner tubes if you pack a cooler," she told Whit. "I'll grab fresh towels from the laundry room too."

Eli picked up the last biscuit on the plate and took a bite. Cruz looked up at her with sad eyes. Eli broke off a piece and handed it to her. "You want to go swimming, baby girl?"

"She would have a blast out there." Whit laughed.

"Let's do it," Eli said and walked outside.

†

Eli was surprised the swimming hole was vacant when they arrived. She took the inner tubes out and set out a bowl of cold water for Cruz. Eli stripped down to her swimsuit and picked up Cruz's ball. She tossed the ball into the water and watched Cruz rush to the edge, then stop to look at Eli. Eli took off running. "Come on, scaredy-cat," she called out as she ran toward the lake. Once Eli hit the water and dove, Cruz followed her.

Eli waded over to retrieve the ball, as Cruz swam out to her. She took it from Eli and swam back to shore. Eli watched with a growing grin, as Cruz left the lake heading toward Whit. Carol stepped slowly away from Whit, suspecting what Cruz was about to do. Whit faced the truck while removing her shorts and T-shirt. She had no idea what was coming. Cruz, with the ball between her jaws, shook her body and showered Whit with cold water.

"Holy shit," Whit cried out as she spun around. Cruz dropped the ball and sat at Whit's feet.

Carol and Eli burst out laughing.

"That's not funny," Whit said, but she couldn't hold back her laughter. She picked up the ball and threw it toward Eli. "I'll get you back for that," she warned Eli.

Eli tossed up her hands. "What? I didn't do anything," she declared.

"Maybe not, but you knew what your daughter was about to do. A warning would have been nice."

"Then you would have just turned around and gotten the shower from the front side." Eli laughed.

"Hmph," Whit replied. "You want a tube and your sunglasses?"

"Yes, please," Eli answered.

"Fine, so come get them," Whit growled.

Carol nearly doubled over with laughing so hard.

Whit glared at her. "You're no better than those two."

"Sorry Whit, but it was hilarious," Carol replied.

"I know," Whit spoke softly and winked. "I can't start letting her off so easy, or she'll be relentless."

"Girl, you got that right. Eli, you'd better stay in the lake. I'd say until she cools off, but I think she's already done that," Carol said and broke out laughing.

"Don't push it," Whit said with a raised brow.

"I, ah, think I'll join you," Carol said. She picked up two tubes and Eli's sunglasses. "Holy shit, this is cold."

"It's not bad once you go under," Eli replied, as Cruz swam back to her. "Good girl." She tossed the ball toward the shore.

Carol pushed a tube toward her and handed her the sunglasses.

"Is she really pissed?" Eli asked.

"No, just startled." Carol smiled.

"Good." Eli climbed onto the inner tube. "Hey, would you hand Cruz up to me? I'll see if I can get her to lay across me."

"Sure. If that doesn't work, we can get her one with a platform across the top she can lay on."

"They make those?" Eli asked.

"Yes, they do." Carol nodded and handed Cruz up to Eli.

"I know what you'll be getting soon." Eli stroked Cruz's wet head.

Eli's attention drew back to the shore, as Whit stepped into the water. "Dang."

"Toss your tube out here and dive in. Get that initial shock over," Carol suggested.

Whit slung the tube toward them, and Carol caught up to it before it could float into deeper water. When she finally reached them and crawled up on the tube, Whit stretched out. "You couldn't have picked a better day, Eli."

"I think we were all due for a break. Besides, it's too quiet without Mitch and Brad around."

Carol frowned. "What are you going to do when they go home? Worse yet, while they hike with Whit for two weeks?"

"Honestly Carol, I don't want to think about it." She grinned. "Maybe soon you'll hear about a teaching job and I can aggravate you."

"Or you could just come with us," Whit replied.

"I just don't think I would enjoy it," Eli said.

They floated in silence for a while. Cruz fell asleep on Eli's lap, and she was on the verge of nodding off herself, when they heard a vehicle approach. Cruz heard it also and snapped to attention.

"I do believe, lunch has arrived." Carol smiled as she recognized Julia's vehicle.

"Yay! I'm starving." Eli began paddling toward shore.

When Cruz recognized Julia, she launched from Eli's lap, overturning her tube. Eli came up, sputtering from the sudden bath.

"Ain't karma a bitch?" Whit stated.

Eli wiped the hair back from her face and smiled. "Yeah, I reckon it is."

†

Eli opened the box Julia handed her and smiled when she saw the freshly fried livers. Julia gave her several packs of ranch dressing. "I hope I guessed right," Julia said.

"Perfect." Eli tore open a packet.

"I bet the boys are eating sandwiches by now," Whit said.

Eli swallowed. "They seemed to do good overnight, but what do you need to prepare them to survive a two-week hike?"

"Endurance for one thing. Mitch and Brad need to make it farther than three miles a day. The altitude will be an adjustment for them, which may be difficult for us for several days."

"High enough for altitude sickness?" Carol asked.

"No, but I don't think we'll have any problem sleeping," Whit said. "Food will also be an adjustment. Dennis's complaints about the trail mix were right on target. Chock full of protein and easy to pack, but nothing like a bite of hot fried chicken."

Eli looked at Whit. "Do I need to stock up on some jerky for ya'll?"

"Jerky is good and a couple of jars of peanut butter." She grinned at Eli. "I think you've got the nuts covered pretty well."

Eli nodded. "Can you handle some small bags of cornmeal? Especially if they plan on taking their fishing rods."

"We can go light on clothing since we won't be gone that long. That will allow for more food and supplies."

"I was thinking of something earlier when they left. Would it be okay to get you a satellite phone and each of you a solar battery charger?" Eli asked.

"That may give us a better source of communication. The solar chargers aren't a bad idea, either." Whit placed a hand on Eli's arm. "You've been giving this some thought."

Eli shrugged. "You are three of the most valued people in my world. I want to make sure you have a good time and stay safe."

"We will," Whit promised.

†

"This shelter doesn't look too bad. It's a bit smaller." Mitch looked at Brad. "Do you want to set up our hammock tents?"

"The firepit isn't as nice either," Scott said. "Shouldn't be a problem for cooking, though. "Why don't we have a sandwich and get to work on setting up camp. Did anyone notice a stream?"

"According to the map, there should be one just ahead," Dennis informed them.

Scott smiled at his brother. "Good job. Are you up to fishing with me?"

"Sure thing," Dennis grinned.

Mitch nodded. "I can round up some firewood and get ready for a fire."

Brad opened his pack. "Do you want to save the biscuits for breakfast in the morning?"

"Unless we don't catch fish." Scott grinned.

Dennis collected the plastic bags and stored them in his pack. "We may need those later."

†

Mitch left Brad to set up the hammocks as he went in search of firewood. He found plenty of broken limbs and had an armful when he returned to camp. "Looking good, bro," he said, as Brad secured the last tie. "You want to go with me?"

"Sure." Brad picked up his hatchet.

They traveled the path Mitch had taken and explored a bit farther. "Would you look at that?" Mitch pointed out a large tree.

"What is it?" Brad asked.

"A black walnut." He kicked a nut on the ground. "Too bad these are from last year. I hear they're tasty. We can't eat them, but we can these." He pointed to some blackberry brambles. "Can you take a few logs back and bring some of those plastic grocery bags in my pack?"

"I'll be back," Brad said.

Mitch ventured farther into the trees collecting wood. He had a nice stack when Brad returned. They both took a bag and started harvesting the large, juicy berries. "Damn, these are good," Mitch said as he popped a few in his mouth. "Let's get some to send with Scott and Dennis," Mitch said.

They picked for a half hour before deciding they had enough. Brad took the berries and a few sticks, while Mitch carried the remainder of the wood. Mitch stacked the limbs near the pit, while Brad hung the bags from a hook on the shelter wall.

"Let's check to see if they've caught any fish," Brad said.

†

Cruz curled up in the shade by the truck and took a nap after lunch. The ladies floated in the lake until the afternoon clouds came in. "We may get a shower today," Whit said.

"I hope the boys stay dry." Eli grinned.

"Why don't we pack up and head home?" Carol suggested. "Can we raid your creamed corn and peas for a veggie dinner tonight?"

"That does sound good, with some cornbread. I'll check to see if I've got some okra ready to fry, too," Eli said.

"If you and Julia set up a picnic table and lay us a fire in the pit for later, Carol and I can handle cooking supper," Whit said.

"You won't get any complaints from me," Eli told Whit. "Do I need to check for eggs?"

Carol laughed. "You can, but Chicken Man collected them this morning before they left."

"If you handle the picnic table, I'll cut the okra and set a fire in the pit," Eli said to Julia as they packed up. "Thanks again for the chicken livers. They are always a welcomed treat.

Julia smiled at Eli. "I'm glad you enjoyed them. You know what else I think would be good with them?"

"What?"

"Some Alabama white sauce." Julia grinned. "I bet that stuff is good on just about anything."

"I may have to try that next time," Eli said, as she closed her tailgate.

†

The boys got settled for supper just as a gentle rain began to fall. "I'm glad you thought to toss tarps over our hammocks," Brad told Mitch. "I'm pretty sure we waterproofed them well, but no need to chance getting wet."

"You will have ample opportunity for getting wet when you go on your section hike," Scott said. "There's no way you're going to be on the trail two weeks without getting soaked a few times."

"I promise you won't melt, though," Dennis said.

"How much longer until you two head back to Georgia?" Mitch asked.

Scott looked at Dennis. "We've got another food drop coming up, so maybe a week to ten days before we run through that."

Dennis nodded in agreement. "When are y'all planning to head north?"

"In three more weeks," Brad said. "I can't wait."

"You're going to have a blast. Especially with Whit. Why doesn't Eli want to go?" Dennis asked, truly curious.

"She doesn't think hiking all day is her idea of fun," Mitch said. "I think she'd enjoy it, but she has to make that decision."

Scott grinned at Mitch. "Maybe once she hears about all the fun ya'll have had on your trip, she'll want to go next time."

"Maybe so," Mitch replied and turned the fish in the pan.

†

Cruz raced toward the cabin, followed closely by her human companions. "So much for a fire in the pit tonight," Eli said as they safely reached the porch.

"At least we got to finish supper and bring most of the leftovers inside before the skies opened up." Whit smiled.

"That's true, and it seems like a gentle rain. Should we brew some coffee and enjoy it from the porch?" Carol asked.

Eli nodded. "It doesn't appear to be blowing in, so we should be safe."

Julia looked at Carol. "Let's make some coffee. We'll be out in a few minutes."

Eli offered Whit her arm. "Would you care for a swing seat or a rocking chair?"

"Let's take the rocking chairs. Let the two lovebirds see how close they can get on the swing."

"I do love that devious mind of yours." Eli smirked. She leaned down to place a tender kiss on Whit's lips.

"I love how the air smells when it rains." Whit sighed as Eli sat next to her. "Everything so fresh and clean."

"It will make for a more pronounced smoke in the valleys tomorrow morning, especially if the temps stay down. My kind of morning," Eli replied. Her phone pinged with a message from Mark.

Messaging so you can tell me how brilliant I am. LOL

What have you done now?

Wasn't me. It was Laura's fault.

What's going on?

Brad and Mitch have been begging us for months to build a forge to experiment in making custom blades.

I think I remember them mentioning that.

My early Christmas gift from Laura arrived today.

A forge?

Even better. A power hammer machine. With my right wrist bones fused, Laura knew I couldn't hammer for hours at a time. That's been my major resistance to giving it a try.

That sounds pretty cool.

It's fantastic. I can build a forge relatively quickly. The coolest idea Laura had, though, was the name.

Do tell.

Since we already have Cast Iron Farms, we can call it Cast Iron Forge.

I love it.

A handcrafted Bowie knife, with a simple design, can sell for a thousand to fifteen hundred dollars. I've got sources for the carbon steel, so little overhead, and I have two apprentices to train.

That sounds like hard work, but fun.

The power hammer takes the bulk of the heavy pounding, but there is still a lot of physical labor and skill needed to forge blades.

So, when are you starting?

I'd like to start this week. It'll take a few days to get everything set up, but I hope to have a blade done in a couple of weeks. Don't tell the boys. I want them to be completely surprised. They will do monkey flips.

Okay, I'll admit, that is brilliant. I promise not to breathe a word to the boys.

Thanks, sis. I just wanted to share my excitement with you.

I'm glad you did. Love y'all.

Most.

"I swear he's like a kid in a candy shop." Eli chuckled as she told her friends about Mark's newest adventure.

"That's a good plan for generating some income doing something he loves," Carol stated.

"Yeah, he said a basic handcrafted blade could go for a thousand or more," Eli said.

"I'd say that was a low estimate," Julia said. "Hand-forged knives are all the rage."

"Did you ever dream all of this would be happening?" Carol asked.

Eli smiled. "Not in a million years, but it makes me so happy to see how excited Mark is becoming."

†

"Since this is our last night together, I thought we might have a little celebration of our own." Scott pulled out a velvet bag.

Mitch arched an eyebrow. "You brought Crown Royal on your hike?"

"It's great for snakebites and what ails ya," Scott winked. "You in?"

"Sure," Mitch said with little hesitation. He took the bottle from Scott. He swallowed the fiery liquid and tried his best not to cough. Drinking a cold beer was one thing, but the liquor was different. "Whoa." He handed the bottle back to Scott.

Scott took a sip and offered it to Brad, who looked at Mitch with some apprehension.

"It's up to you, baby bro," Mitch replied. His eyes were watering from the robust alcohol.

Brad accepted the bottle and tried a small sip. Immediately after swallowing, he started to cough. "Man, that tastes like monkey piss." He groaned.

"It's not that bad." Mitch took a long drink, then offered the bottle to Dennis.

"Thanks, but I'm with Brad on this one. I'll pass," Dennis answered.

Brad drank from his canteen, hoping to wash the taste from his mouth. He swished the water in his mouth and spit. "Even the aftertaste is bad."

"One more for the road?" Scott offered.

Mitch swallowed another long drink. The buzz in his head should have been a clue. Enough was enough. "That's got a kick to it." He grinned when he handed the bottle back to Scott. "Thanks."

As the campfire began to burn down, Brad got up to put another log on the pile. "I'm calling it a night. See y'all in the morning."

"Right behind you, bro," Mitch called out.

Brad turned to see the goofy grin on Mitch's face. He shook his head and climbed into his hammock.

Mitch's legs felt weak. It took a few attempts to get settled inside the hammock. The sturdy fabric finally steadied under his weight, but the world started to spin.

†

In the morning, Mitch felt like he had grazed an entire field of cotton. His mouth was so dry he worried he'd never get it to open. When he stepped out of the hammock, the world began to swim again and he raced behind the shelter. Mitch dropped to his knees and proceeded to lose the remnants of the fish from last night's supper. It had been delicious going down, but the return trip was worse than he ever imagined.

His body retched until the contents of his stomach splashed on the ground in front of him. His nostrils burned with the smell of Crown Royal. Just the liquor's memory sent his body into dry heaves, and Mitch thought he was going to die.

†

Brad woke to the sound of Mitch tossing his cookies. He climbed out of his hammock and picked up Mitch's canteen. Mitch's face had a greenish tint when he turned at the sound of Brad's approach. "Man, you look awful." Brad offered him the canteen.

"Thanks. I feel horrible." Mitch groaned. He took a sip to rinse his mouth and, after spitting, took a drink. "My head is pounding. Even my throat feels like it has razor blades in it."

"I think we can scratch Crown Royal off your list of favorite drinks," Brad teased.

"Very funny," Mitch growled.

Brad walked back to the shelter. "Is he okay, Brad?" Dennis asked.

"Sicker than a dog, but I think he'll live." Brad grinned. "Hand me one of those biscuits, will ya, Dennis?"

When Mitch finally thought he had his stomach settled, he walked around the shelter to find the others eating. Brad offered him a biscuit, and Mitch's eyes grew wide as he started to gag. "No way. I'm going to the stream."

"More for me then." Brad chuckled.

Mitch shucked his clothes off and walked into the stream in his underwear. The cold water was shocking to his system, but it managed to put the fire out in his body.

When Mitch hadn't returned in a half hour, Brad finished packing his hammock and pulled a towel from his pack. He walked down to the stream to find Mitch sitting on a boulder, his feet still underwater. "You okay, Mitch?"

Mitch looked up at the genuine concern Brad had to his voice. He saw Brad was offering him a towel. "Thanks. If I ever even look at Crown Royal again, please shoot me, bro." Mitch managed a weak smile as he reached for the towel.

"With pleasure. That stuff tastes horrible," Brad replied.

"Even worse the second time around." Mitch gagged just thinking about it.

"I'm all packed. I'll get you ready to go too," Brad offered.

"Thanks man, I'll be up in a bit."

Dennis was building a small stack of firewood next to the shelter for the next hiker to use. He and Scott had both finished loading their packs.

"Is he going to make it?" Scott asked.

"Yeah. I'm not too sure Mitch will be eating fish anytime soon, and I doubt he'll ever try Crown again."

"Sorry, I thought he could handle it, or I wouldn't have offered," Scott said.

"Not everybody drinks like you, Scott." Dennis frowned at his big brother. "You didn't drink before you went to college."

"Things change, little bro, but I won't drink around you if it bothers you," Scott answered.

"I worry about you," Dennis said. "I enjoy our time together like now, and drinking seems always to ruin it."

Scott walked over to his pack and poured the rest of the liquor to the ground. "That solves that." He grinned at Dennis.

†

When Mitch made it back to the shelter, Brad and Dennis had exchanged addresses and phone numbers. "We'll drop the rod off on our way back home," Dennis promised.

"If it's too far out of the way, don't worry about it," Mitch said. "Keep it for your next trip."

"We'll see. Sorry about the liquor, man. I didn't know it was going to kick you like that."

Mitch smiled at Scott. "No worries. It was a hard lesson learned. Y'all be careful and have fun the rest of your trip."

"Will do. Hope to see you soon," Dennis said.

"Bye." Brad waved to his new friend. He turned back to Mitch, who was sitting on the shelter bench. "You want me to dig out some Tylenol?"

"Thanks. That would be great."

CHAPTER FIVE

It was nearing lunchtime, when Brad and Mitch appeared from the trail. Eli took one look at Mitch and knew something was wrong. He was pale and soaked in sweat. She placed her hand on his forehead. "You feel okay?"

"No, ma'am. I'll be honest. I feel like shit, but it's of my own doing."

Eli arched a brow. "What happened?"

"Crown Royal happened," Brad teased.

"Will you shut the fuck up, Brad?" Mitch growled.

"Whoa, here. Brad, go find somewhere else to be right now." She scowled at Mitch. "You come with me." Eli stormed toward a picnic table.

†

Brad dropped his pack on the porch and walked inside. Whit and Carol were tossing a salad for lunch.

"Where's Mitch?" Whit asked.

"Getting his butt chewed by Eli." He grinned.

Whit's frown deepened. "That is not funny. Go, hit the shower if you want some lunch. You're pretty smelly."

"Yes, ma'am," he answered and skulked out of the kitchen.

"I wonder what that was all about?" Carol asked.

"No telling, but I bet we'll get the story later from Eli." Whit looked out the kitchen window and saw Eli leaning toward Mitch. She looked none too happy with her eldest nephew.

†

"So, what's this attitude about, Mitch? I don't expect to hear that kind of language toward your brother again. You got it?" Eli was furious. She expected better from Mitch and had to remind herself he was still a teenager.

"Last night, Scott pulled a bottle of Crown Royal from his pack and offered to share it on our last night. I thought I'd be cool and have a couple of swigs with him. That was a big mistake."

"I'd say so." Eli scowled.

"The liquor hit me pretty hard, and when I got up this morning, I thought I'd have to get better to die. The mixture of the fish we had from dinner and the reek of alcohol is not an excellent blend to lose the first thing in the morning." He looked at her and saw the disappointment. "I felt like I'd eaten a whole field of cotton, and my head and body were on fire. I stripped down and hit the stream."

"Did that help?"

"Some, but my head was banging. Thank goodness Brad had some Tylenol. That, at least, brought it down to a mild roar."

"Brad is a goober this morning, too, but he was there for you when you needed him. You need to find time today to apologize."

"I know. I'm sorry I snapped. I'll talk to Brad later."

"I take it Brad didn't drink?"

"He took a small sip and said it tasted like monkey piss. I should have listened. That monkey done kicked my butt."

Eli looked at him square in the eye. "You know I can't have you drinking beer anymore now, right?"

"I don't want anything with alcohol in it right now, but yes, ma'am. I understand you're disappointed in my decision making. Honestly, so am I."

Eli nodded. "Why don't you take a cool shower and lie down for a bit? Grab a Gatorade and more Tylenol on your way to the bathroom." She sighed. "You can call your dad and tell him later."

"Aww, Aunt Eli. Do I have to tell Dad?"

"Yes, we have no secrets. You were honest with me, so you need to be honest with your dad. I was thinking about some fried fish for dinner, but I guess that's out."

Eli thought Mitch turned a bit paler at the mention of fish. She couldn't help but chuckle. "Grab a couple of slices of bread. It'll help to soak up the acid in your stomach."

"Yes, ma'am."

"Go. I'm tired of seeing how pitiful you look."

"Thanks, Aunt Eli." Mitch picked up his pack and walked to the cabin. He sat his backpack down by Brad's and disappeared inside.

†

Brad was seated at the table, eating salad, when Mitch entered the kitchen. "Sorry about snapping at you, bro." He pulled out two slices of bread.

"I'm sorry too. I was out of line," Brad replied.

Mitch grabbed a bottle of Gatorade from the fridge. "I'll see y'all later."

†

Eli walked to the garden to clear her thoughts before going back inside. Yes, she was disappointed in Mitch, but she also knew that his behavior was part of growing up. She could be proud of him for his honesty. She pulled out her phone and dialed Mark.

"Hey, I just want to give you a head's up. Mitch will be calling with a confession later today." She could hear Mark chuckle in the background.

"What did he do to piss you off?" Mark asked.

"He and Scott, the older of the two boys they met on the trail, had a bit of Crown Royal last night. It didn't sit too well with Mitch, and he looks like death warmed over this afternoon. He's showering and will take a nap. He was sweating like a dog and a bit green around the gills when they came home."

"Dear Lord. Crown. At least Scott has good taste. I was wondering when he would have his first go at hard liquor. We were about his age, too, remember?"

"I grounded him from having the occasional beer with me for a while. I do think he sincerely regrets his decision. Poor thing had eaten fried fish last night."

"Oh my word, that had to be nasty coming up with last night's Crown."

"It may be a bit before he eats fish again," Eli replied. "I won't keep you, but I wanted to forewarn you about his call."

"Thanks, sis. He should be glad it was you instead of me. I probably would have made him chop wood or something to burn it out of his system."

"I didn't have any to chop." Eli laughed. "I'm sure we don't have to worry about him trying hard liquor again for a while."

"Okay, thanks. Love ya!"

"Most!"

†

Whit served Eli a salad while she washed her hands at the sink. Eli turned around and gave Brad a stern look. "When you get done eating, you can go tend to the chickens. You can relocate the coops too."

"Yes, ma'am." Brad hurried through his last bites of salad. "I'll get your dishes," she said. "Take Cruz with you, please."

Whit and Carol looked at one another. "What was that all about?" Whit asked.

"Mitch decided it was time for him to try hard liquor. It didn't go very well, and he's hungover to beat the band."

Carol nodded. "He did look kind of rough when he breezed through here on the way to the shower." She grinned. "I figured when he grabbed plain bread, he was sick to his stomach. Now we know why."

Whit smiled at Eli. "That explains Mitch, so what did Brad do to deserve your wrath?"

"Just being a smartass teenager when Mitch was trying to ease into a confession. He needs to learn hard lessons too."

Whit chuckled. "I think he got your point."

"They both did. Mitch has to call his dad later to tell him what he did."

Carol sucked in a gasp. "Oh boy, I wouldn't want to be on that call."

Eli reached for more salad dressing. "I gave Mark a quick, heads-up."

"That's a good thing," Carol agreed. "I hope he doesn't tell Laura."

"Why?" Eli asked.

"She would probably send him to the closest Catholic church, which is thirty miles away, to say two thousand Hail Mary's."

"Yeah, you're right about that," Eli said, then took a bite of salad. "So, what are we doing for supper now that fried fish is off the menu?"

"How about I make some chicken and dumplings and some fresh veggies?" Whit suggested.

"That sounds terrific," Eli replied. "I think I'll go snag Chicken Man and put some new blocks out for the deer. Do you need me for anything?"

"Nope, we've got this. Take whatever time you need." Whit stood to clear the table.

†

Eli pulled on her cap and sunglasses and headed to the barn. She placed a new salt lick, a bag of dried corn, and a mineral block in the back, then drove over to the chicken coops. "Do you want to take a ride up with me to feed the deer?"

"Sure," he answered. "Let me finish moving this last coop."

Eli surveyed the field. "We're going to need to cut this grass again soon," she told Brad as he climbed into the Gator. Cruz hopped into the back seat. Eli turned to look at her. "I don't blame ya. It's too humid to be running today."

"I think we're supposed to get a thunderstorm this afternoon," Brad said. "That should cool things off a bit."

"Whit and Carol are cooking chicken and dumplings and fresh veggies for supper. When we get back, we can check to see if they need anything picked."

"Do you want me to text Whit and ask?" Brad asked.

Eli nodded her head. "I keep forgetting about texting. Yes, go ahead, please."

After several minutes, Brad turned to her. "Whit wants to know if you'll make street corn?"

"Tell her yes, and we'll pick some when we return," Eli instructed him.

"You got it." Brad quickly sent a text. "I'm sorry about earlier."

"Apology accepted. One of the things I hope the three of us always have is honest communications. I know we will all screw up from time to time, but it wasn't up to you to jump in this morning. However, I was happy to hear that you made a much better decision earlier. You were there for Mitch when he needed you. That's what is important to me."

"Thanks."

"You and your dad are in favorable positions by being the younger siblings. Mitch and I are the ones to screw up, and y'all can reap the benefit of our mistakes by not making the same ones."

"That does give us an advantage," Brad agreed.

"Yes, but it also means I can set the standards higher for you." Eli laughed.

Brad's grin faded quickly.

"Nothing that you can't handle with some motivation and common sense. Like you used last night," Eli said. "I was proud of you for not giving in to the peer pressure."

"Thanks. It wasn't as hard as I thought. I'm glad Scott wasn't a bully. I know some of the older guys at school can be merciless."

"It's complicated when you're searching for acceptance and your place in this world. Please know that if you ever have questions, your parents, Whit, Carol, and I will always be in your corner. Even when you do stupid shit."

†

After their talk, Brad and Eli put out the deer supplies. "You know, I haven't driven across the bridge yet. Let's see how it feels and drive down to the road. I've never been down that drive."

"Fine by me," Brad said, as he climbed into the Gator.

"Wanna drive?" Eli asked.

"Sure," he answered with a smile.

"Just don't run us off the bridge." Eli walked around to the passenger side, as Brad hurried over behind the wheel.

"Got it, no submergible trip." He grinned.

After crossing the bridge, Brad drove down the mountain. Eli pointed out a few trees that needed trimming back from the drive.

"Maybe we can work on that tomorrow," Brad suggested. "Anything large enough for firewood, we can store in the cave root cellar."

"That's not a bad idea. I've got all my racks and Whit's chocked full. We do need more little stuff for the firepit."

When they reached the bottom, Eli asked Brad to check the mail then drive over to check Whit's. They would stop off at her garden for corn and complete the circuit back home.

†

Mitch stretched out on the bed and turned the fan on full blast. The bread, Gatorade, and Tylenol had helped, but he still felt wrung out. *Nothing a long nap won't cure, I hope.* He got up to close the blinds and shut out the sunlight. *It looks like a storm is brewing.* Dark clouds were gathering in the distance.

Once more stretched out on his bed, Mitch thought back to earlier in the day. *Man, that was a colossal screwup. I'm going to have to work hard to make it up to Eli. She's put her trust in me, and now I've let her down.* Mitch fell asleep thinking of ways to get back into Eli's good graces as the first droplets of rain began to fall.

"Whoa, that was close." Eli and Whit stepped back onto the porch, each carrying a corn basket. Brad had barely parked the Gator in the barn, when the rain began to fall and a clap of thunder rolled across the meadow. "Let's get this stuff shucked and ready for cooking."

†

Whit and Carol were on the couch, watching the weather channel. "What's happening?" Eli asked, as they set the corn by the sink.

"That tropical storm is coming further inland than they had initially expected. It looks like we'll have rain for most of the night," Carol said.

Eli nodded. "Any tornadic activity associated with it?"

Carol nodded with a frown. "Unfortunately, yes. It's done a good bit of damage so far with straight-line winds and a couple of twisters touching down. Nothing close, yet."

A flash of lightning illuminated the room, and Eli waited for the lights to flicker after the loud boom. Nothing. She grinned at Whit. "Not even a flicker."

Whit turned to look at Eli. "Even if this sets in for a couple of days and drains the battery banks totally, we still have the backup generator and a week's worth of natural gas."

"You should be able to survive most anything Mother Nature throws your way," Carol stated. "Is there any chance of the streams flooding?"

Whit placed her hand on Carol's shoulder. "Some, but we're on a high enough foundation that we don't need to worry."

"Good to know," Carol spoke louder over the sounds of the rain pelting the cabin.

†

"Let's get to shucking," Eli said to Brad.

Eli dropped the last ear of corn into the pot to boil. "Man, those dumplings smell great. Will you make some biscuits?" she asked Whit. "I think I'd rather have those than cornbread."

"Yeah, that's no problem." She walked into the kitchen to begin making her dough.

The door to Mitch's room opened, and he walked out, looking significantly better. "You look and smell much better," Eli teased.

"I feel much better. Who opened up the heavens? I just looked out, and it's raining so hard I can't see Whit's cabin."

Carol joined them in the kitchen. "It's a tropical storm moving through the area. We may have it for a day or two."

"I guess I won't be mowing grass in the morning as I had planned," Mitch said.

"No, but once it dries out enough, you will have plenty to mow," Whit told him.

"Why don't you guys make a list and inventory what you'll need for your hike?" Eli suggested. "Don't you also have to apply for permits to hike Mount Katahdin?"

"Not to hike, but you will need one if you're planning to park there. It's free, but you typically need a reservation. It stays busy during the summer months." Whit looked at Eli. "It will take us eight to twelve hours to hike Mount Katahdin, round trip. We could camp there the night before, and you could wait for us to return the next day."

"That sounds like a good plan," Eli said. "You won't need to take your full packs, will you?"

Whit started to roll out her dough. "No, we can rent day packs from the ranger's station that will hold food and supplies for the roundtrip. We'll have plenty of miles to carry our full backpacks after that."

"Do I need to plan on dropping care packages for you along the trail, so we don't have to worry about shipping?"

"That does make sense, if you're going to be driving us up and waiting for us to call when we return."

"We have to climb and then come back down?" Mitch asked, scratching his head.

"To do it the traditional way, yes. We can start from the top or as close as we can get and then go down," Whit said.

"What do you recommend?" Eli asked.

"If we want the full experience, we do the roundtrip. It's not an easy climb, though, and will be our first big challenge," Whit told the boys.

Mitch nodded. "I reckon there's no sense in cutting corners, if we're doing it, let's do it the right way."

"We need to start getting some climbing in," Whit told them. "Several trips a day up and back to the trailhead with fully loaded packs. We need to increase our stamina as much as possible."

"Sounds great." Brad cleaned up from shucking corn. "I know it's not going to be easy, but I know we'll have fun."

"Since this is our first great adventure together, we need to prepare and pace ourselves. There's no requirement on how many miles we have to accomplish on this first trip. We can plan a stopping point, but even if we don't make it that far, we've started. After this trip, we'll all have lessons to use on the next leg of our journey."

"It sounds like a couple of rain days will allow you guys to do a lot of planning," Carol said. "I can help with sorting out items for packing in smaller containers or packing in general. Just tell me where I can be of help."

"You can start by handing me the large cookie sheet."

"Simple enough." Carol handed her the pan.

†

Later that evening, Eli and Whit made love while listening to the pouring rain. Flashes of lightning illuminated the room, and the sound of the rain muted the moans emitted by the two lovers. When Eli moved from under the covers to lay beside Whit, she smiled and took Whit in her arms. "I think I love you more every day."

"I know I do you," Whit replied. "The way you handled the boys this morning was just the way it should be done. They both realized the importance of making good decisions without feeling ashamed for their actions." Whit kissed Eli's cheek. "You are going to make a good mom one day."

"I'm not sure I can survive teenage years," Eli laughed. "I wanted to strangle both of them today. I knew that was not the way to handle things, but damn, I sure wanted to do just that."

Whit ran her fingertips down Eli's cheek. "I think that's a very normal response. We really have been blessed having both of them here. They could be getting into so much more trouble."

"Yes, I guess that's true. Here, they work their butts off and have our supervision most of the time. At home, with Mark and Laura working, they'd have too much time on their hands."

"The next few weeks they will be so busy and tired, they won't have time to think about getting into trouble. Me either, for that matter. I've got to get my body back in shape."

"I love the shape of your body." Eli smirked.

"I will focus on that while we're hiking. That will give me incentive to keep the boys moving, even on our tired days."

"Is Mount Katahdin going to be as hard as it seems?"

"Some hikers turn around and never hike after giving up on the mountain. For the boys and I, it will be a test to see if we are ready to commit to a two-week hike."

"I have all the confidence in the world in you and the boys," Eli purred, as she snuggled into Whit's body.

Chapter Six

The rainy days were spent mostly inside the cabin. Eli would gear up and go out to the barn to feed the animals, and Brad would tend to the chickens. Whit kept the boys busy making lists of who would pack what gear and supplies. Eli watched as the excitement grew on all three faces.

Whit looked up from the list. "I know our new boots are still in excellent shape, but it wouldn't hurt us to carry a second pair as a backup. Let's plan on taking our old boots with us."

"We'd better fumigate them well first," Brad teased.

Mitch laughed. "Amen to that."

It felt good to see them working together after the small speed bump of emotions that had exploded once they came back off the trail. "If there are items that we still need to purchase, make me a list," Eli said. She planned to go to town later to pick up the satellite phone and solar chargers. "I've got to make a run to town in a bit. How about some fried chicken for lunch?"

Mitch's head flew up. "Can we have some livers?"

"That depends. Will you make some white sauce? Julia thought it might go well with livers."

Mitch nodded. "That's not a bad idea." He smiled at Eli. "With all this rain, I could tend a butt smoking on the grill if you wanted to get one."

Whit smiled at Eli. "That sounds good. We can make everything else inside, and Brad can help me make a cake and ice cream for dessert."

"I guess I'd better get rolling then, or it will be midnight before we eat."

"Don't get a huge one like the ones Dad cooks. We aren't cooking for an army," Mitch recommended.

"Any other requests?" Eli asked.

"More street corn," Brad chimed in. "It takes me an hour to pick it out of my braces, but it's worth the effort." He grinned at Eli. "I'll volunteer to go pick some if you cook."

"Deal." Eli pulled on a rain slicker.

"Would you like some company?" Carol asked.

"Sure." Eli held a second slicker out for her. She leaned over and kissed Whit. "Call me if you think about what you need. Hey, will you do something for me?"

"Anything, what do you want?" Whit smiled up at her.

"Do you have the ingredients for an apple pie? I've been craving one for days."

"Pick up a small bag of brown sugar. I've got everything else," Whit replied. "Do you have cheese?"

"Always," Eli said with a grin. "We shall return."

Eli and Carol raced out to the truck. As they were buckling in, Eli looked at Carol. "Were you starting to get some cabin fever too?"

"Yeah, I'll admit I was. I've got everything packed in the first drop box so far, so I'm just waiting for my next set of instructions." When Eli pulled out on the highway, Carol asked, "Are we going to the outdoor shop?"

"Yes. The satellite radio and solar chargers I ordered for the crew have arrived. Did you need something?"

"Would you mind if I got something for the hikers? They'll need to pack socks, and I've noticed the boys doing their laundry. I want to buy them all a dozen pairs of DRI-FIT socks. They're light, moisture wicking, and comfortable. They need to change socks at least once a day, from everything Whit has told them."

Eli turned to her friend. "I think that's a great idea. We can browse the hiking section to see if there are any other surprises, we can get them."

Eli looked at the clock on her dash. "Can you call the chicken shack and order a bucket of chicken and three large orders of livers for pick up at ten?"

"Not a problem. Anything else?" Carol asked.

"Remind me to call Mitch, so he can go ahead and start the grill."

"When we stop for the chicken?" Carol asked.

Eli nodded. "That should be fine."

They left the outdoor shop with all their purchases, including some new super-light blankets that had just hit the market. Eli looked at the clock. "Damn, time is flying by. Would you mind going in with me at the store and finding brown sugar while I get the meat?"

Carol placed her hand on Eli's arm. "No problem. Relax, we've got this. If we eat all that chicken you ordered, we won't need to eat again for a while," she teased.

Eli made her way to the meat aisle and found the perfect sized butt for them. She also picked up some excellent steaks they could have the following evening. She met Carol at checkout. "Just had to add steaks, didn't ya? Let me run back and grab some lettuce. We can't have steak without salad. We used the last of it yesterday."

†

Eli's mouth was watering by the time they made it home with the chicken. The rain had let up temporarily, so Brad and Mitch rushed out to help carry stuff inside. "Thanks, guys." Eli handed the butt to Mitch. "Work your magic," she said.

Mitch went to work, wrapping the butt in foil and adding seasonings as he had seen his dad do so often. "I wish we would have had time to marinate this a bit, but maybe it will be edible."

"I'm almost positive nothing will go to waste," Carol said, as she began putting the groceries away.

"Brad come help me set the table," Whit called from the kitchen. "Eli, will you set the chicken out?"

"Consider it done." Eli danced around the crowded kitchen.

Mitch caught a glimpse of the steaks Carol placed in the refrigerator. "Those are some beautiful steaks," he remarked.

"Beef, it's what's for dinner tomorrow night." Eli tittered at her own joke.

"I can handle that. My inner carnivore is craving protein." Mitch smiled.

Eli opened the lid on the chicken, and the smell filled the air. "Between chicken, pork, and beef, you should fill that craving."

"Don't forget to grab the white sauce and ranch dressing from the fridge," he told her. "I'm going to put the meat on, and I'll be back. Brad, can you grab the door and open the lid for me?"

"You got it, bro." Brad raced to the door.

†

"Holy cow, this is good." The chicken liver Mitch popped in his mouth was covered in white sauce. "Please tell Julia that she's a genius."

Carol laughed at his comment. "I'll be sure to tell her you agreed with her suggestion."

"I have to admit, it is tasty," Eli agreed.

"You ready to try one, Brad?" Mitch asked. He held up a liver he had dredged through the sauce.

"Why not?" He smiled and placed the liver in his mouth. "That's a funky texture, but they are good."

"A great source of iron for energy too," Mitch said.

"That's very true," Carol said. "I hope you don't mind that we picked up a few extra items," she said to Whit.

"Not at all, I'm pretty curious to see what's in those bags."

Eli nodded. "So you shall, after lunch," she teased.

†

After lunch, they cleaned the kitchen and retired to the living room. Carol gave them each a package of specially made socks. "I heard Whit talking about your changing out socks regularly, and I've seen what you two call socks. They've got more holes than Swiss cheese." She chuckled.

Whit nodded. "These are nice and lightweight too. They'll be perfect for the trail."

Eli opened a bag and handed each of them a blanket. "We found these too, literally as the department manager was just stocking the shelves. He reports that they're supposed to be warm but lightweight, the newest to hit the market."

Whit had taken hers out of the bag and was rolling it. "Look at how small it rolls up." She smiled. "More space for food," she reminded the boys. She used a small strap to secure the roll. "Good job. Thank you, ladies. The gifts make it feel like Christmas in July."

"You are very welcome." Eli handed each of them a solar-powered battery bank. "Keep these on your packs. Each will store enough charge to recharge your phone up to three times." Eli handed each of them a carabiner to clip the charger to their bags. "Last but not least," she said as she pulled out a state-of-the-art satellite phone. "This bad boy will be our best bet for staying in touch, or God forbid you need it in an emergency, so keep those chargers filled." She handed each of them a small slip of paper. "It comes with a new number, so program it into your phone." She looked at Mitch. "You need to send it to your Mom and Dad too."

"I'm on it." Mitch picked up his phone and sent a group text to his parents. "Done." He grinned.

"When the rain stops, I'd like you and Brad to hike over to the next camp shelter and try it out."

"Return to the scene of the crime?" He laughed.

"I'm glad you can laugh about it now. Two days ago, you swore you were on the precipice of death," Whit teased him.

"It sure felt like it too. Can we work on the western drive tomorrow and give the grass a day to dry out?" Mitch asked. "I'd like to cut it, but it's too wet."

"I think that's a good plan. We can hook up the trailer and toss our gear in the Gator. Brad suggested we store some firewood in the root cellar cave."

"Not a bad idea. The small stuff we can use at the firepit," Whit said. "If y'all can handle that assignment, Carol and I can check the gardens."

Carol nodded. "Sounds like a perfect way to spend the morning after being cooped inside for days."

"Alright then. I'm going to leave y'all to planning and packing. I'm going to spend some time in the barn with the animals."

†

Eli walked into the barn, with Cruz behind her. She left the door open to add some ventilation inside. She opened the gate and watched Molly run to the door and skid to a halt when she saw the rain. "Uh-huh, I thought you might change your mind." Eli filled the cat feeders and sat on a bale of hay next to Molly's stall to watch the gang feast.

Cajun slid down from the loft and jumped beside her. "Hey there, stranger." She scratched under his chin. His purring filled the area. Eli ran her hand down his body. "I swear you are still growing." He blinked his emerald-green eyes, then stretched and reached up with a paw to stroke her face. "That is so sweet." She picked him up and cradled him in her arms. She loved on the cats as they jumped up to visit then snuggled down for a nap. "I know, nothing better to do than a nap on a day like today."

Eli stood and walked around the barn. She wasn't used to the idle time. Her eyes landed on a bucket of limbs she had cut for walking sticks. "I had forgotten about you," she said, as she picked up a beautiful length of poplar. She carried the wood to her hay bale and pulled out her knife. Eli eased the knife down the limb's spine and smiled at the memory of how relaxed this crafting made her. Eli skinned down three sections, then found her sandpaper in the toolbox. After sanding them, Eli moved away from the hay. She took the longest limb and ignited the handheld blowtorch she had bought and scorched the bare wood. Eli placed them back in the bucket to allow them to dry before she performed a final sanding and decided on whether to stain or not. She would drill a hole and tie on a wrist strap, then make a padded grip using paracord. The cord would be a handy piece of rope in case they needed one on the trail. Eli was thinking about her final plans for the sticks, when Whit entered the barn.

"Is everything okay out here?" she asked. "You've been gone so long we were starting to worry."

Eli glanced at her watch. "I didn't realize how long I'd been here. Yes, everything is fine. Just spending some time with the animals and piddling."

"You can take only so much of being cooped inside." Whit walked over and wrapped an arm around Eli's waist.

"Yeah, this has been one of the few times I've had idle time on my hands. I don't have any major projects with pressing needs, and the weather is too horrible to do much outside." She smiled up at the cats in the loft. "Even these bums have decided on a nap. I guess it is the best thing for today. Those two also." She pointed to Cruz and Molly lying side by side.

"A nap does sound pretty good," Whit replied. "Let's go stretch out for a couple of hours, then we can get cooking on supper."

"You don't even have to twist my arm." Eli reached for Whit's hand.

†

Carol was teaching the boys how to play poker when they walked back inside. "We, uh, raided your coin jar, but I promise we'll put it all back afterward," Carol said.

"That would be highly recommended. It's our Christmas gift fund, so if you expect something this year, ante up. Ha! I crack myself up sometimes." Eli cackled.

Mitch cocked his head as he looked at them. "Did she like hit her head or anything, Whit?"

"Nope, just being her usual goofy self. We're going to lie down for an hour or two, then we can all start supper."

"Have you checked the butt lately?" Eli asked.

Mitch lifted his hip off the chair. "Yup, it's doing fine." He couldn't help but grin back at Eli. "Seriously, the meat is looking and smelling awesome."

"That's good to hear. Watch Carol for dealing from the bottom of the deck," Eli warned, as she nodded toward Carol. "She thinks she's pretty slick."

Carol looked at Brad. "Hmph, she's just mad because I used to beat her all the time."

"In your dreams," Eli said, as she walked into the kitchen.

"Well, if you weren't going to 'take a nap' like a little old lady in the middle of the day, you could show us how to play," Carol challenged.

"Good Lord, go take a seat, and I'll bring you some tea. Put up or shut up Fortner," Whit teased. "So much for my nap."

Eli looked guilty. "You can still take a nap."

"What and miss a major beatdown? No way I'm missing this." Whit opened the pantry. "Who else wants snacks?"

"I'll take some chips, please," Mitch replied.

"That's going to be my line in about five minutes." Eli smirked and took a seat across from Brad. "Why are you grinning?" Eli asked. "I plan on taking all your chips, too." She winked. "Deal me in," she told Carol, as she reached into the coin jar. "How much are we starting with?"

"Five dollars, each," Brad said.

"Got it." Eli nodded.

†

Whit decided to go ahead and do her baking while the others played cards. Once the cake was in the oven, she began making her pie crust. It didn't take long for the kitchen to smell fantastic.

"I could get so used to smelling fresh baked goods," Eli said, as she raised the bet a nickel. She picked up a chip and dunked it in some salsa. "Looking a bit slim over your way Mitch," she teased, eyeing his dwindling pile of coins.

"I'm just waiting for the big hand to go all in." Mitch smiled back at her. "I fold." He tossed his cards on the table. "I'm going to go check the meat while y'all fight this one out."

Cruz trotted out with him, as Carol studied her cards. "I could die of old age," Eli teased. "You gonna raise the bet, fold, call? For goodness' sake do something."

Whit rolled out the dough, smiling as she watched and listened to their banter. Eli rarely got this animated, and it was a side of her lover that always made her smile.

"I fold, dammit," Carol growled.

Brad couldn't hide the smile on his face, as Carol tossed her cards into the pile. *He does a terrible job of bluffing.* Just you and me, little man. What's it going to be?"

"I'll see your bet and raise you a quarter," Brad said.

Eli cocked her head at him. "A quarter? That's more than you've bet yet. You must have something good to raise a quarter."

"You've got to pay up to see," Brad challenged her.

"How about two dimes and a nickel?" Eli teased. She looked over his shoulder at the smile on Whit's face. "I reckon it's worth a quarter to see what you're holding." Eli tossed in a quarter and looked at him. "Call."

Brad held his breath as he lowered his cards to the table. "I've got three of a kind." He showed three Jacks on the table.

"Well, I'll be danged, Brad. Good job."

"I won?" he cried out.

"Yes, you won." She started picking up the cards for her deal. "Congratulations."

Eli never revealed the cards she was holding, but Whit strongly suspected her hand would have beat Brad's.

Eli began shuffling the cards. "How's the meat coming?" she asked, when Mitch returned.

"It's looking good and should be up to temps within the hour," he reported.

"One more hand, then we start on dinner?" Eli asked.

"Brad and I can feed the animals and stay out of your hair. I think the rain has finally moved through."

"Don't forget to check the eggs," Whit said. "I think we should make some omelets in the morning."

"Especially if there is some butt left," Brad said.

Mitch laughed. "I wouldn't count on that."

After the last hand, which Eli won, they put their change back in the jar and put the cards away. "I'll pick up some poker chips on my next run to town," Eli said. "That was fun."

†

As they were settling into bed later, Whit looked up at Eli. "You let Brad win that hand, didn't you?"

"Who me? Let someone else win at poker? Not me." Eli smiled.

Whit crawled under the covers. "I don't believe you for a second."

"It's all good. I still came out on top." Eli smiled. "Got all my change back, too." She wore a cat-got-the-canary grin, almost devious.

Whit pulled the covers over her body. "Dinner turned out very well. Mitch did a great job on that butt."

"Yeah, he did, and your apple pie was delicious. Don't be surprised if you wake up and I'm not in bed around midnight. I already hear another slice calling my name."

Whit cracked a grin. "No honey, I think that was Carol."

"What?" Eli, bolted out of bed, ran to the bedroom door, and looked down at the foot of the stairs. Carol was standing there, holding her phone. "Is there something wrong?" she asked.

"No, I got it. I got the job. I just checked my emails," Carol said.

"That's fantastic, Carol. Congratulations." Eli turned around to Whit. "We might as well celebrate with some pie since we're up."

"I'll start the coffee," Carol said.

CHAPTER SEVEN

Carol shared her good news with the boys over breakfast. "I'm going to need to close down my apartment and bring my belongings up here."

"Do you need some help?" Mitch asked.

Carol smiled at him. "I always need help, sweetie. You, however, are in training for the AT."

"We could take a break long enough to help," Brad added.

"They do have a point," Eli replied. "You could go down to make arrangements and pack what you plan to bring here. Then we could come down, finish packing anything, load your stuff, and head back to the mountains."

"If you promise to work them hard, they will still be in training," Whit suggested.

Carol looked at Eli. "I have a few pieces of furniture, antiques that are family pieces. Could I store them at your house? At least for a while?"

Eli swallowed. "You should know you can."

"I could leave today and start working on plans," Carol said.

"How long would it take you to be ready?" Eli asked.

"I could be ready to move by Saturday at the latest," Carol answered.

Eli smiled. "So, why don't the boys and I drive down Friday? We can stay at my place, get up early Saturday and move the furniture you want to store, load your boxes, and start back if it isn't late."

"We could layover at Mom and Dad's on the way back," Mitch said.

Eli chuckled. "Mom and Dad's? Isn't that still your home?"

Mitch grinned back at her. "This place is home," he said, spreading his arms.

Eli looked at Whit. "You okay with that plan? I bet we could get Evan to stay out here and look after the animals, if you wanted to join us."

"No offense, but I'd rather my first trip to the beach be leisurely and not rushed. We can go back together later."

"Yes, I can see your point. We'll have plenty of time to visit once y'all return from the hike." Eli smiled. "That will be a much-needed break, I'm sure."

Whit smiled at Carol. "I can spend some time on my cabin, getting it ready for Carol. I'll use the bedroom in the back for storing some stuff."

"Thank you all so much," Carol said. "I'm excited to call this place home too."

†

Mitch carried out a small overnight bag for Carol and placed it in her car.

"Be sure to call to let us know you've made it," Eli said, as she walked her to the car.

"Yes, Mom," Carol teased. "I've got good underwear on too." She giggled.

"Well, I wasn't going there, but that's good to know." Eli smiled. "Be safe."

"I will. See you Friday. Maybe we can get some sushi?"

"Heck yes!" Mitch said. "That's the one thing this place is missing. A good sushi spot."

"I bet if we drove into Asheville, we could find plenty," Carol told him. "We'll check it out when I get settled."

"Yes, ma'am. See you soon." He looked at Eli. "Do you want me to hook the trailer up and load the equipment?"

"That would be fantastic. Let's get to work." Eli waved when Carol pulled down the drive, then returned inside.

Whit was placing the last plates in the dishwasher. Eli wrapped her arms around her. "Are you good with everything happening?"

"Yes, I am. It feels like another of our family puzzle pieces will be slid into place. I'll be over at my cabin getting started. Ping me when you're ready for some lunch."

"Will do." Eli kissed her softly. She hollered down the hall to Brad. "Quit primping princess; we've got work to do."

Whit chuckled. "You shouldn't tease him so."

"That boy spends more time in the bathroom than any girl I know," Eli exclaimed.

"I do not," Brad said in his own defense.

"Yeah, ya do," Eli and Whit said in unison.

"Do you want Brad to bring the other Gator around for you?"

"That would be great. Thanks. Y'all be safe."

"You too."

†

With the three of them working together, they made significant progress in clearing the western drive. When Eli decided to break for lunch, they had a full trailer. After dropping firewood at the root cellar, they sent Whit a text and started down the mountain. They dropped brush at the chipper and drove to the firepit to deposit sections of smaller branches. "What do you guys want for lunch?" Eli asked as they waited for Whit.

"May I make a suggestion?" Mitch asked.

"Fire away." Eli nodded.

"How about pizza? Brad and Whit can go to town to pick it up, while you and I knock out the chipping before it piles up and gets overwhelming."

Eli looked at Brad. "How's that sound to you?"

"Delish." Brad grinned, as Whit pulled into the yard.

Eli loved the way she moved as she walked over to join them. "How about some pizza?"

"I can always eat pizza."

"Mitch had a brilliant idea. You and Brad go to town to get it, while he and I tackle that load of brush we just dumped at the chipper."

"Perfect. Let me grab my keys." She looked at the boys. "The usual pizzas?"

"Yes, ma'am. Full of meat and extra crispy," Brad answered.

"Good, you can call it in while I drive," Whit instructed.

"All right, let's get to chipping. Text us when you get back," Eli said.

†

"That is a big pile of brush," Eli said, when they arrived at the chipper.

"Yeah, and we've still got two thirds of the drive to go."

"I think we got the thickest part already," Eli said. "Maybe we can knock the rest out this afternoon."

"How far up the drive have you been?"

"Only about four hundred yards off the highway. I've never been above where we put in the bridge. Why?"

Mitch shrugged. "I was just curious about how far up the mountain it goes."

"We can check it out later, after we've dropped the trailer if you'd like. Now you have me curious."

Mitch grinned. "Crank us up and let's shred."

"Aye, aye, Captain." Eli saluted. She handed him a pair of safety glasses and ear protection. Eli looked at Cruz, lazing under a tree. "It's going to get loud," she warned.

†

Eli was relieved when the text came through. She was starting to get hungry. She handed the last branch to Mitch and signaled for him to cut the motor. "Lunch has arrived."

"That was perfect timing," he said, as he walked to the Gator.

"Yeah, it was. My stomach agrees. It's been growling for the last fifteen minutes."

When they reached the yard, Eli saw Whit waving them over to a picnic table. Brad walked up, carrying a six-pack of sodas and a bottle of water.

Whit tore off paper towels and handed them each a plate. "Dig in."

"Man, that looks and smells good," Mitch said when Brad tossed a lid back. "Hey, there's a piece missing."

"My navigator was about to pass out from hunger, so I allowed him one piece." Whit held up her index finger. "How did y'all do with the chipping?"

Eli grabbed a slice and sat next to Whit. "We put the last limb in right after you sent the text."

"Great timing then."

"How are you progressing in the cabin?" Eli asked.

"I'm getting there, slowly but surely."

†

They devoured the pizza, and Cruz licked her lips, begging Eli for the last bite. "You are so rotten." She handed the pizza to Cruz.

"I wonder how that happened?" Whit laughed. "She's got you wrapped just a bit."

"Like someone else I know." Eli leaned in to kiss Whit.

"That is so sweet, but if you two will stop gushing, we can get back to work." Mitch broke out laughing.

"Okay, smartass, let's go."

Brad tossed the pizza boxes in the compost bin and hopped back on the Gator.

"Thanks for getting lunch," Eli said to Whit.

"No problem. Hey, do you want me to flip the steaks in the fridge as I go by the cabin?"

"That would be awesome, Whit. Thanks for remembering."

†

Whit walked back into her cabin. Oscar and Walter were still curled up on the couch and barely cracked their eyes when she stepped inside. "You two look comfortable," she said as she moved through the room, picking up framed photographs. Whit carried them to the back bedroom and sat on the bed. She wiped down the picture of her grandparents smiling back at her after her college graduation. She couldn't remember which one it was. "I wish you two were here to meet, Eli and her family. I think you would love her as much as I do." Whit set the frame on the bedside table and picked up a smaller frame. She felt her heart catch at the sight of her mother in a cheerleader uniform from high school. Whit had her mother's hair color and facial structure, but she didn't have her mom's blue eyes. Tragic was the only word she could think of to describe her. She had never recognized her as a mother growing up.

Love and nurturing came from her grandparents. As hard as she tried, Whit couldn't recall a memory of her mother that wasn't drama filled. "Nothing at all like the love I feel from Eli and our family." Whit sighed, placed the photo beside her grandparents', and walked back into the living room. It wouldn't take much more to prepare her home for Carol's arrival. She would finish sorting and clean after Eli and the boys left Friday.

Whit felt drained by the trip down memory lane the photographs had brought on. She needed sunlight and fresh air, so she picked up a basket and walked to her garden.

†

As Eli recollected, the trees along the drive thinned out the closer they got to the highway. By late afternoon, they had stored more firewood and dropped another trailer full of brush at the chipper. "Let's drop the trailer. We can pick it up on our way back through."

"From where?" Brad asked.

Eli climbed inside. "I thought we'd see how far the drive goes up the mountain. I've never been any farther than the bridge."

"Exploring, yes!" Brad pumped his fist.

†

Mitch drove and stopped at a clearing about three hundred yards up the drive. *This spot would be perfect for a tiny house. I wonder if I could get one after I graduate.* The clearing, lined with a variety of massive, old-growth hardwoods, was also home to an abundance of wildflowers that filled the air with their scent. He could tell from the darker green grass that the spot had a natural spring. *Maybe one day, he dreamed.*

†

Eli saw the peaceful expression on Mitch's face as he surveyed the clearing. She felt certain Mitch had just found his future home. "This is a very peaceful spot, isn't it?" she asked the boys.

"Yeah, it is." Mitch smiled.

"Look, it even has a spring," Brad pointed out.

"Perfect," Mitch replied. "I love those hardwoods too."

Eli nodded and looked at the trees. "It would appear they have been here a long time. I'm not sure I could reach around those trunks."

"Me either," Mitch replied. "Should we venture on?"

"Sure." Eli smiled at him.

The next clearing, they reached was no less enchanting but for different reasons. "Holy cow, would you look at that?" Brad excitedly pointed out wild blueberry and blackberry brambles. "Look at all these berries."

Eli checked the back of the Gator and found two small buckets. "Get busy." She handed them each a bucket. Cruz trotted alongside Mitch, as he headed toward the blueberries.

Smart boy. Let Brad get eaten up by the thorns in the blackberry brambles. Eli took a sip of water and stepped out of the Gator. She walked the perimeter of the clearing. They almost look intentionally planted. *I wonder if Whit knows about this.* Eli concentrated on Whit and softly asked. *Did you know there is a motherload of blueberries and blackberries farther up the mountain?*

No, but I hope you plan to bring some home.

The boys are picking some now.

Love you.

Most.

"Do you two have enough to get us started?" Eli asked. "Or you need a bit more time?"

"Can we have fifteen more minutes?" Brad asked with a mouthful of berries.

"Are you getting any in the buckets?" She shook her head. "I'm going to drive as far as I can, but I'll be back to get you. C'mon Cruz."

†

Eli returned to the Gator and drove farther up the mountain. She passed several more clearings along the way that would make beautiful home sites. When the path ended, she looked to her right to see her boundary marker. "So, we go all the way to the top. That's cool," she told Cruz. Her view on the left was spectacular. She could still see farmland in the valley miles away, but the canopy of trees from the national forest was like a green river blowing softly in the wind. "I'd bet my last dollar that, in the fall, the view here would be breathtaking once the leaves start to change." She looked over at Cruz. "This would be a perfect spot for a bench. Beautiful sunsets and the colors in the fall. Just perfect." Eli looked down and saw a footpath several hundred yards below. "I bet that's part of the AT." She strained her eyes, searching for signs of hikers. "It's probably late enough in the day that they're laying over at a shelter."

Eli started back down for the boys and stopped in a clearing she had missed from the other direction. The whispering of wind through the trees carried another sound to her ears. Buzzing, Eli was sure she heard buzzing. She parked the Gator and stepped out to investigate. "Stay," Eli told Cruz, who whined but laid down in the seat. Eli listened carefully until she picked up the direction of the sound. As she approached, the buzzing grew louder. She spotted an old hickory tree just ahead, about twenty feet beyond the edge of the clearing. A few feet above the base of the trunk, a mass of bees were busy maintaining a comb that dripped with golden honey. "Oh, my goodness." Eli took out her phone and snapped a few pictures. She wasn't sure about the boys, but Mark was deathly allergic to bee stings. She would have to check with him about the boys before they attempted to harvest some wild honey. Eli turned and hurried back to the Gator.

†

Mitch and Brad climbed in and took a seat. Each had over a half bucket of berries. "Y'all did good, but you won't believe what we found." She pulled out her phone and showed them the beehive.

"That's one big sucker. We have to keep Dad away from there," Mitch said.

Eli nodded. "I know he's extremely allergic, but what about y'all?"

"Not that we're aware of," Mitch said. "I know Dad carries an EpiPen, but neither of us has reacted. We've both been stung."

"We may need to research how to get some wild honey without dying for it," Eli teased.

"I'll ask Evan what he knows about it," Mitch said.

Eli smiled at Mitch. "We need to invite him and the girls out next week before y'all take off for the hike. Your Boston butt turned out so good; we could do a bigger one to feed everyone. I don't think you're ready for fish, are you?"

"I think I could handle fish now. Just don't ever let me get a whiff of Crown Royal again," he groaned.

"Okay, y'all decide when and what we're eating and let me know."

Brad smiled at Mitch. "Time for a fish off?"

"The others may have to work next week. Why don't we stick with the butt for now and fish when we get back?"

"I think that sounds like a great plan," Eli said, as she drove across the bridge.

"Do you want to knock out that last pile of limbs tonight?" Mitch asked.

"No, Brad and I can finish them tomorrow, while you mow."

†

"I think we need to give your dad a call to let him know we want to drop in on him and your mom Saturday night," Eli said.

"Probably so. You want to do it now?"

"Sure, give him a call."

When Mark answered, Eli gave him a quick update on Carol's new job and moving into Whit's cabin. When she told them the plan to help Carol, Mark came up with a grand idea.

"Why don't you let the boys drive down to help her?"

"What?" Mitch said.

"I said, why don't you and Brad drive down to help Carol move and let Eli and Whit have some time together. They've had very little time when one or more of us haven't been there. Plain enough, son?"

"Gotcha, Dad," Mitch replied.

"Can I at least take your truck?" he asked Eli. "I'm sure it's much more reliable than mine."

"I don't have a problem with that," Eli said.

"Are you sure, Eli? He ain't the greatest driver in the world, ya know," Mark cautioned with humor in his voice.

"You taught me to drive Dad," Mitch reminded him.

"Ha! That's why I have insurance. It would be a safer bet, and I've been riding with him, and he's done great up here."

"Just be sure to be gone in time to be through Atlanta before or after rush hour," Mark told him.

"I'll make sure they're up at the crack of dawn," Eli said.

"Alright, I'm trusting you to take care of things, Mitch. And Brad, you do everything your brother asks you too. No bickering."

"Yes, sir," they both answered.

"I'll see you Saturday night, if not before. If you roll through Opelika at lunchtime, I'll let you take me to lunch."

Mitch chuckled. "It'll probably be brunch, but you're on. Love ya!"

"Be careful, and I'll see y'all soon."

Mitch looked at Eli when they ended the call. "I certainly wasn't expecting that."

Eli looked at him. "It's a test to see if he can trust you to be a man, so don't fail him. You've come a long way, and I'm proud of you. Both of you knuckleheads." She grinned.

Whit looked at the clock. "We've got a busy day tomorrow, so we'd better clean up and hit the sack."

"Goodnight, you two," Eli said and headed up to the shower.

†

"That was very sweet of Mark to make that suggestion," Whit said. "It wasn't necessary, but I won't pass on an opportunity for time with you."

"I guess I never really thought of how little time we do get to spend together. I'm sorry for that oversight, and I promise we will have more 'us' time in the future."

Whit punched Eli in the shoulder. "I love spending time with our family. I don't feel like I'm left out at all, so don't worry about that. If I need time with you, I'll let you know. Like right now." She waggled her eyes and started to undress Eli.

Eli laughed and kissed Whit. "I love you so much. I didn't realize how lonely I was before I met you, and I never want to feel that way again."

"You'll never have to, I promise. Now, come wash my back," Whit teased and pulled her toward the shower.

CHAPTER EIGHT

After a quick breakfast, everyone started on their assignments. Whit returned to her cabin to finish preparing it for Carol, while Mitch began mowing. Eli and Brad returned to the cave and completed chipping the remainder of the limbs. Brad had taken care of the hens and brought in two dozen eggs.

Eli and Brad were taking a water break, when Eli turned to him. "Your hens have started producing nicely."

"Almost every one of them lays an egg a day." He smiled proudly. "Maybe when we move, we can add a few more coops and start selling them at the farmers' market. The free meals are excellent, but I bet we could make six dollars a dozen on them."

"That will be something to consider. It's not a difficult project to maintain," Eli agreed. "What are your plans after high school?"

Brad shrugged. "I'm not sure. I thought I wanted to be in the military, but I'm also enjoying the time here. I could go to college near here and still keep some projects going."

Eli smiled at him. "That's very true."

†

Whit finished packing up some personal knickknacks and stored them in the back bedroom. As she walked through the cabin, she smiled at the memories she had made there. The back bedroom still had pencil marks on the doorframe where Grandma had recorded her growth every year. The cabin had been home to so much love. She was sure Carol, and one day Julia, would enjoy it as much.

Oscar and Walter had followed her through the cabin. They jumped on the back of the couch for some scratches and loving, loud purrs filling the air. She smiled. "Are you boys ready to go home?"

Oscar and Walter raced her to the door and headed for the bridge. As she stepped onto the front porch, she saw Mitch coming up her drive on the riding mower. He looked up and smiled when he saw her. Whit motioned for a drink, and he nodded.

She returned inside and came out with two bottles of Gatorade. Mitch had stopped the tractor and was walking toward the porch. "Thanks," he replied when Whit handed him the drink.

They sat down on the steps. "Do you want me to cut beyond the lab?"

"No, I try to leave that wild," Whit answered. "I hope more wild berries will start to grow back there."

Mitch lifted his hat and ran his hand through his thick hair. "That makes sense." He took a long drink. "Are you two going to know what to do without a house filled with people for a couple of days?"

Whit leaned over and bumped shoulders with him. "I think we can figure something out. It will seem odd, though."

"I think we've got most of the big chores done, so why don't y'all chill? We can get back to training and other projects when we return."

"We will kick back some. We've accomplished so much in such a short time, and I think we all deserve a break. Are you nervous about driving to Florida?"

"I'd be lying if I told you I wasn't. I feel pretty confident things will be okay, but the traffic in Atlanta is no joke. I'll do my best to hit it when it's not full-on, rush hour traffic."

"That's way too many lanes all rushing at you at once for my tastes," Whit said. "Eli plans for y'all to load the truck tonight, and she's getting you up at the crack of dawn just like she promised your dad."

"I'd like to make it in time to have brunch or lunch with him. I miss the old fart."

"I'm sure he misses you too. Don't rush. The summer will be gone, and you'll be back in school before we can blink."

"Yeah, don't I know it. Brad got a text from the football coach last night. He'll have to head home after we get off the trail to start pre-season practice if he's planning on playing this year."

"Is there any doubt he won't?" Whit asked.

"Naw," Mitch said. "He enjoys playing sports. He'll bitch and moan about having to go home before the end of the summer and dying in the heat, but he loves playing."

"What about you? When will you need to head home?"

Mitch frowned. "Not long after Brad. The first of August at the latest. You can bet I'll be back up as soon as I can."

"I'm going to miss you. I've gotten used to having you around."

"I won't be gone long. Maybe I can escalate my classes online to finish early."

"You need to enjoy your senior year. You only graduate from high school once."

"Yes, ma'am, but not fast enough to suit my taste." Mitch grinned. "I reckon I should get back to mowing."

"Okay, thanks for cutting over here," Whit said. "It was starting to need it."

"I'll see ya when I get done," Mitch said.

Whit started toward the Gator. She didn't hear the chipper running, so she decided to drive up to see what was going on.

†

Eli and Brad had finished the chipping and were raking the chips in a pile. "Y'all made quite a mountain," Whit said when she pulled to a stop.

"I reckon we're going to have to start coming up with some uses for this stuff," Eli called out.

"We can start by spreading some at the firepit. The fragrance, especially the cedar, will help keep insects down."

"Perfect," Eli said. "We can do that when you boys get back," she told Brad.

"Do you have plans for what to do next?" Whit asked.

"Whatever you have in mind."

"Good answer." She propped her foot on the bumper. "I thought you might show me the honey tree at the top of the mountain."

"I'd love to. Brad, will you take our Gator back down? We can gather for some lunch when we get back. I think we need to clear out some leftovers."

"Sounds good, Aunt Eli. I'll go ahead and pack a bag for Florida."

"That's a wise decision. I know Mitch will wait until the last minute and toss something in a bag." Eli shook her head.

"I guess you would be surprised to hear that he's already got a bag packed and is ready to roll," Whit told them.

Eli's brows shot upward. "My nephew, Mitch?"

"My brother, Mitch? You've got to be kidding," Brad said.

"Yep, it's true. Mitch's bag is packed and sitting at the end of his bed."

"Wow. I guess you've got some catching up to do then," Eli told Brad.

"Yes, ma'am. I'm on my way." He walked over to the Gator and climbed inside.

Eli smiled at Whit. "Are you ready?"

"Yes, ma'am. You drive, since you know where we're going."

"Not a problem. Hop inside."

Eli drove across the bridge and turned north on the drive. "There's a great view from this side. I thought we could build some benches to go in a couple of spots." Eli slowed and pulled into a clearing. "Mitch looked like he was dreaming when he saw this place. His face was so peaceful. I think he's found his spot on the mountain."

"You have to admit it's beautiful, a small clearing, spring, good trees. Perfect place for a small home for one or two," Whit said.

"I'd bet he was thinking of one of the mini log homes, a tiny house. I saw him looking at them on the computer the other day. I went back later, and he's bookmarked several he likes."

Whit smiled. "I've looked at them too. I have to admit they are an excellent home choice. Compact, efficient, and the prices aren't bad, either." Whit smiled. "When they first became popular, a few years ago, I gave some thought into putting a couple down in my valley for vacation rental income."

"What made you change your mind?"

"I didn't change my mind, just never could pull the trigger on it. I guess there is something to be said for peaceful solitude. I didn't need the money but seeing another human's face from time to time would have been nice. Sometimes I went for months if there were no missions to get me off the mountain."

Eli pulled Whit into her arms and kissed her. "You might get sick of seeing my face one day."

"No way, man, I love this face and every square inch of you." Whit deepened the next kiss.

"I love you too, Whit." Eli reached for her hand and walked across the clearing to the spot where the spring bubbled. "What do you think about putting a tiny house here when Mitch graduates?" She pointed to the far eastern edge of the clearing. "Back close to the tree line but still a gorgeous view of the sunsets."

Whit slid an arm around Eli's waist. "I think that's a great idea. We talked for a while today. I think Mitch wants to move up here and go to mechanics school after he graduates. I think his own tiny home would be perfect. Give him some privacy, but close enough to his parents and us, if he needs anything."

Eli leaned over to kiss her forehead. "When do you find time to talk with him that I don't?"

"You had gone up the mountain with Brad. We talked during a drink break when he was mowing my grass."

"Thank you."

"For what?" Whit cocked her head in the adorable way Eli loved.

"For loving my family and me the way that you do," Eli answered.

"Excuse me?" Whit said. "It's my family too."

"You are so right. I love having you in our family."

Eli held Whit in her arms for a few minutes of comfortable silence as they gazed across the clearing toward the National Park. A sea of green treetops filled the sky for miles. "That's such a beautiful view."

"Yes, it is," Whit replied.

Eli's stomach broke the silence with a loud growl. Whit laughed softly. "It sounds like someone is getting hungry. Let's go take a look at the honey tree and head home." She reached for Eli's hand as they walked back to the Gator.

†

When Eli turned into the next clearing, she drove to where she thought she had found the tree. She turned off the motor and listened for the familiar hum. It took several minutes to locate the buzzing coming from a spot further into the meadow. She stepped out and reached for Whit's hand. "Let's go find some honey, Pooh," she called happily.

Whit slipped her hand in Eli's. "Let's go, Eeyore."

"Wow, that comb is dripping with honey," Whit said. They approached slowly.

"Yeah, it is. I don't have any experience with bees, other than getting stung. Have you?" Eli asked.

Whit shook her head. "Not really. I could do some research on harvesting honey."

"Mitch said he would ask Evan too. He seems to be our local go-to resource."

"Evan knows a lot of people who know a lot of people." Whit nodded. "If anyone had a resource, it would be him."

"I bet that honey would taste awesome."

Whit pulled out her phone and dialed Evan. "Hey, Evan, it's Whit and Eli."

"I bet you're calling about wild honey." Evan laughed. "Mitch has already called me. I'm bringing a man out Tuesday, to show y'all how to harvest."

"We should have known Mitch would be on the ball. Thanks, Evan."

"No problem. I'll see you Tuesday."

"Thanks. Bye for now."

Whit looked at Eli. "We get honey Tuesday, Eeyore." She broke out laughing.

"Let's go then, Pooh," Eli said and reached for her hand.

†

When they arrived back at the cabin, Mitch had just finished rinsing off the mower attachment. The fields looked manicured, and the smell of fresh-cut grass filled the air. Eli smiled and pointed out Molly and the hens munching on the cut grass and foraging for insects.

"The girls are doing their jobs," Whit replied.

"I think Brad was going to work on heating some leftovers. I've got the hose handy if he tries to burn anything down." Mitch snickered.

"Are you just about done here?" Eli asked.

"Yes, ma'am."

Eli let Whit off at the front door, then drove back to the barn. "Finish up, then come inside and we'll round up some lunch. It's going to be a leftover kinda day."

"That sounds good. I'll be right there," Mitch responded.

Eli looked into the cab of the tractor and saw Cruz asleep in the seat. "I was wondering where you had gotten off to. Now I know."

"She's been riding with me most of the morning," Mitch said. "She likes being in the tractor."

"Yeah, she does. Come on, sleepyhead," Eli called out to her.

†

After lunch, Eli looked at the boys. "Since you will be having brunch with your dad tomorrow, do you two want to fish and take him some filets?"

Whit looked at Mitch and grinned. "We could also have some for dinner if your stomach is up for it."

Mitch rolled his eyes at Whit. "I think I'm up for it. You'll be the first to know if I'm not."

"I bought several Styrofoam coolers the last time I shopped. You can use one of those for the fish." Eli smiled at them. "I think we've done enough work for today and need some time to play."

"Are you two going to fish with us?" Brad asked.

"I haven't fished in a long time," Whit answered. "I'll give it a try."

Brad smiled at her. "I'll take you on Team Brad. You can be my lucky charm today."

Eli looked at Mitch. "I guess that means you're stuck with me."

"I'll take you on my team any day of the week. Prepare for a butt kicking," he told Brad. "You are so going down."

Eli looked at Brad. "Are you packed yet?"

"Not completely," he answered.

"We'll clean the kitchen while you finish packing. Mitch, go ahead and set up the fish cooker, then we can start fishing."

"On my way." Mitch left the cabin with Cruz on his heels.

"Don't rush, and be sure to pack what you need," Eli told Brad. "We won't start fishing until you get done."

"Ready to tackle this kitchen?" Eli asked Whit.

"Am I ever. You rinse, and I'll load the dishwasher."

Eli could hear Brad clunking around, as he pulled out a bag and started packing. She looked out the window. Cruz hovered nearby Mitch as he set up the fish fryer. Eli smiled at Whit, who was waiting for the next dish. "You gotta love these boys."

"I do. Almost as much as I love you."

†

"For someone who hasn't fished in a long time, you sure are a natural," Brad said.

"Beginners luck." Whit winked as she reeled in her third fish. "This bench sure makes it more comfortable than sitting on buckets."

"Another great idea we had, huh?"

"Eli wants to build a few more to place along the drive on the western edge of the property. Maybe we can work on those when you get back."

"That should be a piece of cake, now that we have the design down pat."

"I'll take that as a yes." Whit smiled.

Brad grinned back at her. "Yes, ma'am, we can build those."

†

Eli cast her line perfectly into a pool and waited for a large trout to bite. She watched with anticipation, as he cautiously approached, then pounced on her fly. As soon as he struck, she set the hook and began reeling.

Mitch watched the smile grow on her face as she landed the fish. "That's an awesome catch. You should fish with us more often."

"I enjoy watching you guys just as much, and I love the competitions y'all have with the others.

"We work well together as a team. It doesn't matter who wins or loses; we all pitch in to help," Mitch said.

"I'm going to miss not having a bunch of kids around when you return to Alabama," Eli told him.

"I don't even want to think about it. The only thing that brightens my spirit is that after this school year, I'll be up here for good."

Eli started another cast. "That makes me very happy to hear. Will you keep up with Jessie when you go home?"

"I'm sure we'll talk and text, but we've agreed that if there is someone else, we want to date. It's okay. I like Jessie a lot, and I hope nobody steals her from me, but she's too sweet to think someone new won't notice her this year."

"What about you? What if you meet someone?"

"I'm not looking. I know what I want, and it's up here. No sense in starting something in Bama that will only be temporary."

Eli bumped into him. "I think that's a sweet and mature thing for you to say. I'm so proud of you, Mitch. I hope you'll never forget that."

"Even when I make stupid, bonehead decisions?" he asked.

"Even more so when you do, because you learn hard lessons quickly. We all make mistakes. The important thing is not to repeat them over and over."

Mitch nodded. "I guess that's true."

"No guessing about it at all. It's the truth, so believe what I'm saying."

"Yes, ma'am." He moved quickly to set a hook in a fish.

"Well, I'm glad we had that talk," Eli teased, as she caught another fish right after Mitch.

Mitch looked over at Eli. "I love you, Aunt Eli."

"Most," she answered and started to laugh.

†

Whit heard Eli's laughter and smiled. "They sound like they're having fun. Not as much as we are, though." She landed another fish.

"That one will fill our second bucket. Do you think we should take these down and see how Mitch and Aunt Eli are doing?"

Whit dropped her fish in the bucket. "I think that's a good idea. Let's go."

†

"Drop those filets in the freezer and wash up. Dinner is almost ready," Eli told Mitch and Brad. "Thanks for cleaning the fish while we started supper."

"It was a win-win. The fish got done, and we eat sooner than later," Mitch teased.

Brad laughed. "And only two of us smell fishy."

Eli waved her hand in front of her face. "That's for sure. Did you bathe in fish, Brad?"

"Maybe? You wanna hug me now?" Brad reached for her.

Eli held up a slotted spoon. "Not one more step closer," she warned.

"Do we have time to run through the shower?" Mitch asked.

"Yes. You, inside," Eli said to Mitch. "You," she pointed at Brad. "You get the laundry room. But no streaking across the yard. You have clean clothes on the laundry table. Put those nasty clothes in the washer. After your shower, you put the clean clothes away."

"Yes, ma'am." Brad grinned and jogged over to the laundry room.

"Go, go, go." She shooed Mitch away. "I don't want supper to get cold."

†

"The way I see it, you've got a couple of options," Eli said. "You can get up at five and beat the rush hour traffic in Atlanta. Or you can sleep until seven and wait until it dies down."

Mitch looked at Brad. "He's going to sleep the whole way anyhow. Let's get up at five. Even if I don't beat the traffic, I can pull over and wait a bit."

"That's a wise decision. Pack up what you can tonight, so all you need to do is add the cooler, Brad, and hit the road. That means you need to hit the sack early tonight."

"I'm ready," Mitch said. "I'll take my bag out and crash."

"Me too," Brad added. "It was a fun day, but man, I'm tired."

"I'll set my alarm. Do you want breakfast before you go?"

"That will only slow us down. We can hit a drive-thru down the road," Mitch said.

"How are you set for cash?"

"I'm okay, Aunt Eli."

Eli opened her wallet and handed Mitch a credit card. "Use this for gas and food."

Mitch started to argue. "Don't bother trying to argue," Eli said. "Take it, so I can sleep while you're gone."

"Yes, ma'am," Mitch relented and placed the card in his wallet.

"Are you going to sleep at all tonight?" Whit asked Eli.

"Like a rock." Eli chuckled. "After the boys leave, we can go back to bed, too." She grinned.

"I like the sound of that," Whit replied.

CHAPTER NINE

The boys were up and on the road before the sun rose. Eli kissed Whit on the top of her head. "Why don't you sleep for a little longer? I'll tend to the animals and wake you later for some breakfast."

"You sure you won't come back to bed with me?"

"I won't sleep a wink until I know they're safe."

"Who said anything about sleeping?" Whit smiled coyly.

"On second thought, let's go."

They made love until they were breathless and content. "That was very nice," Eli murmured, as Whit snuggled into her.

"I could be as loud as I wanted without worrying about who else would hear."

"Who knew you were such a vocal lover?"

"What can I say? You bring the best out in me," Whit practically purred.

"What would you like to do, since we have a couple of days to ourselves?"

"I'd like to spend some time with you in the hammock and try to relax. We've been going full speed for a while."

"It has been kind of hectic, but we've managed to get the major projects done. We've earned a break."

Whit drummed her fingers on Eli's stomach. "Why don't we play tourist? We've got such a beautiful area to explore and waterfalls to photograph. We can take Cruz with us and stop for a picnic lunch."

"We'll have to take Mitch's truck. I don't cherish the thought of spending hours penned up with Cruz in your small car." She smiled at Whit. "Maybe we can hit some roadside stands and pick up some boiled peanuts and peaches from Georgia. Those are the only two things we don't grow here that I miss."

"We could plant a few peach trees. We have plenty of room. Maybe up where the bees are," Whit suggested.

Eli tucked her hand under her head. "That's not a bad idea. Do you want to do that or wait until the boys get back?"

"Let's wait on their young muscle. We can pick out some trees, though, and bring them home."

"Will you need to work in the lab, some?" Eli asked. "I know you haven't had much time up there since you got home."

"I may go up for an hour or so to check in on things, but I won't be all night. Do you want to join me?"

"I need a few hours to finish a project for your hike."

"A surprise?" Whit asked.

"Just a little one, nothing major," Eli answered.

"Let's hit the shower then, so we can get started on our adventure."

"You shower while I go tend to the animals. If we shower together, we may not leave the house today," Eli teased.

Whit stuck out her lower lip in a pout. "Hurry back. I'll try to save you some hot water."

†

Eli plugged the camera battery in to charge, before walking out to the barn. She fed Molly and the cats, then picked up a scratch bucket for the hens and a collection basket for the eggs. Eli scattered the scratch on the ground in the first coop, and the hens left their nests, allowing Eli to collect their eggs. She repeated the process in the second coop and emerged with twenty fresh eggs. "Thank you, ladies." Eli closed the latch on the gate. Tomorrow she would leave the gate open, so they could search through the freshly mowed grass for insects and seeds. With nobody at home, Eli didn't want to take a chance leaving the hens unattended.

After depositing the eggs on the kitchen counter, Eli climbed the stairs and entered the bedroom. Whit was drying in the bathroom. "I think you'll have enough hot water left."

Eli dropped her clothes in the hamper. "You look all fresh and shiny." Eli kissed Whit on her way to the shower. "I collected twenty eggs this morning. Would you like to take some egg salad with us? We could stop for some fresh bread."

Whit was drying her hair with a towel. "Sounds delicious to me. I'll get dressed and get eggs on to boil while you shower."

Eli turned on the water. "Where are we going today?"

Whit wrapped a towel around her waist. "I thought we could drive to Whitewater Falls and work our way back here. There are numerous falls in between."

"I haven't been there in ages. I want to take you to our old homestead sometime. It's pretty much turned into a subdivision now, but the house is still standing."

"Would you rather do that today?"

"No, I want the boys to go with us. I know Brad has never been there, and I'm not sure Mitch would remember anything about it other than our stories." Eli kissed her forehead. "We had some great times there as kids."

"I can tell by the way your eyes sparkle when you talk of the place," Whit replied. "Mark's too."

"It just wasn't meant to be for us to own that property, but I'm pleased with this one. We can make our new memories here."

"Yes, we can," Whit smiled. She kissed Eli and walked into the bedroom to dress.

†

Eli grabbed Cruz's leash and the small cooler they'd filled with drinks and egg salad. "Will you grab Cruz's bowls and the bag of food I packed for her?"

"Absolutely. Do you want me to grab a bag of chips too?" Whit asked.

"Yes, please." Eli carried the cooler to Mitch's truck. Cruz jumped into the back seat, and Eli clipped a tether to her collar. "Are you ready to ride, baby girl?"

Cruz licked her cheek, and Eli hugged her neck. "Good girl."

When Whit climbed into the truck, Eli reached for her hand. "You'll have to tell me how to get there."

"I programmed Mitch's GPS while you were getting dressed," Whit said. "I can't remember all those twists and turns. Once we get on Highway 64, we'll be in good shape."

Eli started the truck and rolled the windows down for fresh air. She chuckled when she looked at the dash. "That's just like Mitch. He's got less than a quarter of a tank of gas. You can grab a loaf of bread while I fill the truck."

Whit nodded and handed Eli the sunglasses she had left on the counter.

"What would I do without you?"

"Let's not find out," Whit replied with a smile.

†

Eli enjoyed the feel of the cool morning breeze blowing through the windows and the fresh scent of mountain flowers. "Something smells sweet this morning."

"It could be so many things," Whit answered. "We picked a beautiful day for a road trip."

Eli smiled, as she watched Whit's hand cut through the air that rushed by the truck. Eli and Mark had called it window surfing when they were kids. Whit programmed the GPS for the back roads, preferring small country towns to the interstate's fast pace. Black cattle dotted the hillsides and grazed on the sweet grasses. Farmers were harvesting vegetables in the garden plots they had planted. Valley fields planted with corn would be turned into feed for cattle and hogs at the end of the season. The richness of the freshly turned earth reached Eli's nostrils, and she breathed the scent deeply. She felt Whit's hand squeeze hers, and she turned to see her lover pointing out a red-tailed hawk soaring above the turned field.

"Someone is looking for breakfast."

Eli slowed, as the bird made a dive toward the ground and captured a small rodent in its talons. "Breakfast served," Eli said with a grin. She pointed out a small roadside stand just ahead. "Mind if we stop?"

"Heck no, silly," Whit replied.

Eli eased the truck off the road and pulled to a stop in front of the stand. Whit reached for Cruz's leash. "You browse, and I'll take Cruz for a walk."

Eli smiled. "I'm sure she's ready to relieve her bladder."

"Deal."

†

"Good morning," an older woman said from behind the tables filled with fresh fruits and vegetables. "Is there anything, in particular, you're interested in?" She continued shelling the peas she had in her lap.

"Some peaches, for sure," Eli answered.

"You're in luck. We have a full table of peaches, plums too."

"They're huge. Did you grow these yourself?" Eli asked.

The woman nodded. "We've been farming for almost thirty years now. We had a great weather year for peaches."

Eli was selecting a basketful, when a young woman walked out carrying a tray. "The pies are done, Mom."

"Those smell delicious. Peach?" Eli asked.

"Yes, ma'am, and some apple leftover from last year's crop."

Whit and Cruz returned from their walk. "Something smells heavenly. Good morning." She nodded to mother and daughter.

"Good morning to you as well. What a beautiful pup."

"This is Cruz. I'm Eli, and my friend is Whit."

"Pleased to meet you. I'm Mary, and this is my daughter Sue Ellen."

Sue Ellen placed the tray of small fruit pies on the table. "May I tempt you with a sample?"

Eli looked at Whit, who nodded. "Please cut one of the peach pies in half," Eli requested.

Sue Ellen picked up two small plates, placed a section of the pie on each, and handed them a plastic fork.

Eli was the first to take a bite. "Oh, dear Lord. These are fantastic." Eli watched the woman's face light up with her praise.

"You're not kidding." Whit speared another bite.

"Do they freeze well?" Eli asked.

"You seriously think they will last long enough to go into the freezer?" Whit teased.

"The boys won't be back until Sunday," Eli reminded her.

Sue Ellen nodded. "They will be fine in the refrigerator for several days. And yes, they freeze well. Pop them in the microwave and they will taste fresh baked."

Eli swallowed. "How late do you stay open?"

"Until sundown," Mary replied. "We live in the white house there." She pointed to a small house.

"We're on our way to Whitewater Falls. Can we buy now and pick them up on the way back through?"

"Sure, that's not a problem. Just let us know what you want," Sue Ellen replied.

"Are you baking more?" Eli asked. "I don't want to wipe you out if you expect other customers."

Sue Ellen smiled. "If you're coming back, I'll bake whatever you want."

Eli looked at Whit. "A dozen of each?"

"Yes, and two more of each for us to snack on today." Whit smiled.

"A bushel of the peaches too," Eli said. "Do you like plums?" she asked Whit.

"Yeah, I do," she answered. "I can't think of a fruit I don't like."

"Please add two baskets to our order." Eli smiled.

Sue Ellen pointed to a basket next to her mom. "I picked some fresh blueberries today, as well."

"Will you add a half dozen pies to our order if you have enough blueberries?"

"That's not a problem." Sue Ellen replied. Cruz wiggled, as she watched them talking. "Can she have a treat?"

"Sure, there's not much she won't eat either." Eli chuckled.

"I make sweet potato dog biscuits for my girl." Sue Ellen reached into the pocket of her apron and pulled one out.

Cruz sat and licked her lips in anticipation. She gently took the treat from Sue Ellen's fingers. "Good girl."

Mary bagged up the four pies for them to take and grinned at them. "Are you two wine drinkers by chance?"

"On occasion," Whit replied.

"I've got some homemade strawberry and watermelon wine if you'd like to try a bottle."

"Add that to our order," Eli requested.

Eli paid the bill and got Sue Ellen's number to call if they would be late returning. "We'll see you later," they said and returned to the truck.

"That was a great stop," Whit said.

"Yes, it was. The pies were great. I haven't had watermelon wine in ages."

Whit smiled up at Eli. "I don't think I've ever had it."

"I think you'll enjoy it," Eli said, as they continued down the road.

†

When they reached the park, Eli pulled up close to a picnic table. "Do you want to eat lunch first or hike to the fall?"

"Let's hike. We can eat when we get back."

"Work up an appetite." Eli smiled. "If I remember clearly, there are some steps to climb."

"Yes, to get close up shots. I'm sure your lenses will get you up close if you don't want to climb." Whit took out the camera bag.

"I don't mind a bit of a climb," Eli answered.

They walked a quarter of a mile to the first viewing platform. Eli had forgotten how beautiful the falls were. She could hear the roar of the water before she caught a glimpse. The recent rains had filled the feeder streams, and the water cascaded down to a large pool. The sunlight cast a rainbow across the water, and Eli could see several folks enjoying the pool. "I bet that was a hike to get to." She pointed out the people to Whit. "They look like insects from this distance."

Whit traded the camera bag for Cruz's leash and watched Eli set up the equipment.

Whit was surprised that there were only a handful of people around. She remembered the park filled with tourists during previous visits. She knew that would be the case in the fall as the leaves began to change colors. The month of October, and sometimes well into November, the mountain came alive with a brilliant palette of colors marking the season's passage. During the summer months, whitewater rafting, tubing, and kayaking the plethora of streams and rivers kept the tourists visiting.

She watched Eli snap off a dozen shots. "Will you and Cruz pose for some pictures?"

Whit nodded and patted the top of a stone wall. "Up, Cruz." She smiled as Cruz jumped onto the top of the wall and licked her face. "We've got to pose for Mama." Cruz sat, and Whit placed an arm behind her.

Eli looked through the viewfinder. "That's perfect." She clicked off several photos, then set the timer. She stood on the opposite side of Cruz and listened for the click of the camera. "Do you two want to stay up here while I climb down for some close-ups?"

"Yeah, the steps are pretty steep. I think we'll stroll up the trail and meet you back here. Thirty minutes?"

"That should give me plenty of time. I don't intend to go all the way to the bottom." Eli shouldered the camera bag and picked up the camera and tripod.

"You want me to take the camera bag? You've got what you need, right?" Whit asked.

"Sure." Eli handed her the bag. "Thanks."

†

Whit watched Eli disappear down the steps, then turned and started up the trail with Cruz. Chipmunks scattered ahead of them, and Cruz pulled against the leash, waiting to give chase. "Oh no, you don't," Whit said. "This is their home." She laughed, as Cruz lowered her muzzle to the ground and examined the scents. Squirrels jumped from tree to tree above them, barking at the intrusion to their space. "We've certainly gotten everyone stirred up this morning." Whit could hear the rushing sound of water running in one of the numerous feeder creeks, and she guided Cruz in the direction of the sound. When they reached the flow, Cruz lapped up the cold water. Whit eyed a tree that had fallen across the creek. The setting was peaceful, no other sound than the rushing water, and no evidence of other humans. She sat on the trunk of the tree and enjoyed the beautiful morning. Cruz sat at her feet, and Whit felt her trembling against her leg as they watched a raccoon waddle down to take a drink higher up on the creek bank. "I see it," she said and reached down to stroke Cruz's neck. Whit breathed deeply of air filled with freshness from an early morning shower and the scent of blooms in the forest. The sun shining through the canopy of leaves made the treetops glow with color. "We have to bring Eli here. Let's go see if she's returned yet."

†

Eli made her way carefully down the steep, wooden steps. They were still damp from an earlier rain, so she took her time descending. The roaring of the falling water increased with every step she took. Eli found a rock outcrop with a beautiful view of the falls and room for the tripod at the bottom of the first landing. She set up the tripod and camera and began snapping pictures. Eli was pleased with the quality of the photographs and decided against climbing down any farther. Instead, she began the ascent to meet Whit and Cruz. A chipmunk skittered across the path in front of her and sat up to watch her. Eli snapped off several quick photos before the animal continued on its journey foraging for food. As she reached the top step, Eli could see Whit and Cruz approaching from the path that led up the mountain.

"You've got to see something we found," Whit said.

"Lead the way." Eli smiled at the excitement in Whit's voice and reached for Whit's hand. They walked up the trail until they reached the fallen tree.

"Look up," Whit said.

Eli quickly saw what Whit was so excited to show her. The sunlight breaching the canopy of trees made the leaves glow, creating a beautiful image. She switched out lenses and took several shots. "That is gorgeous."

Cruz started whining, and Whit pointed out the raccoon that had returned to the water's edge. "I see him," she said to Cruz and pointed out the raccoon to Eli. "He came back for another drink and to see what we're doing."

Eli still had her camera in hand and took photographs of the curious animal. "He is cute." Eli then turned her focus on Whit and Cruz, as they sat on the end of the fallen log. Then she snapped the lens cap on the camera. "I don't know about you two, but I'm getting hungry."

"I'm sure we could eat. Let's go set out our lunch," Whit suggested.

Whit's hand slipped comfortably into Eli's, as they made their way back to the picnic area. "I'll prepare our sandwiches, if you get Cruz fed," Whit offered.

"Deal," Eli told her.

†

After consuming the egg salad and remaining pies, Whit and Eli packed to resume their journey. They planned to visit Dry Falls and Bridal Veil Falls, before stopping back at the fruit stand for their purchases. The day was perfect for driving, and Whit picked up Eli's camera to snap photos of Cruz napping in the back seat. Bridal Veil had a light flow and was not impressive, so Eli drove on to Dry Falls. Ironically named, Dry Falls was anything but dry. Thousands of gallons of water flowed down to the waiting pool. The cascade did little to conceal the mouth of a large cave hiding behind the fall. Moviemakers had chosen the falls for many scenes, and Eli wasted no time taking photos of her own. The scenery was gorgeous, and the air temperature dropped quickly the closer you came to the falls. It took a bit of coaxing from Whit, but Cruz finally walked with her behind the curtain of water. Eli laughed, as Cruz shook her body to shed the droplets from the mist that had settled on her coat once they emerged. "One heck of a shower, huh, baby girl?" They climbed back up to the parking lot. "There's one other vantage point I'd like to get before we leave."

Whit nodded. "Lead the way."

Just below the parking area, a deck overlooked the entire falls from a distance. Eli took a few shots to get a sense of the lighting. She posed Whit and Cruz with the falls behind them and snapped several more, then used the timer to get a photo of all of them. "I think that's good for today." She lowered Cruz back onto the ground from the stone column where she'd sat for the photos. "Let's stop to pick up our goodies and drive home."

"Sounds good to me," Whit said. "It's been a beautiful day."

"Yes, it has, with such great company. We need to do this more often."

"I agree. We have such a lovely environment to explore in any season." Whit opened the door for Cruz to jump inside the truck.

Eli stowed her camera on the floorboard, next to Whit's feet, for access if they ran across anything they'd like to photograph. When Eli pulled back onto the road, Whit asked, "Would you mind if I take a look at your photographs?"

"Be my guest," Eli said.

Whit picked up the camera and scrolled through the photos Eli had taken, pausing on some shots she liked. "I would like to have some of these printed for the lab."

"We can do that. Pick out what you like, and we can send those out for processing."

"You've got an excellent eye for photography."

"Thanks. I enjoy seeing how different things look through the lens of a camera."

Whit looked into the back seat. Cruz had her head hanging out of the window, enjoying the breeze. "Would you mind if I take a few shots?"

"Not at all," Eli replied.

†

Whit took shots of Cruz, then turned her focus to Eli. She looked so relaxed as she drove through the winding curves in the road. Whit took several photographs, and when Eli looked at her briefly, snapped several more. "You're extremely photogenic," Whit said.

"You got my best side." Eli grinned.

Whit placed the camera back inside the bag and put her hand on top of Eli's. "Thanks for a great day."

"It has been fun, hasn't it? I promise we will do this more often."

Whit nodded and turned her attention to the passing scenery. She was lost in deep thought when Eli slowed down. "Grab the camera," she said. Eli pointed to a small black bear ahead beside the road. "Take a shot as I roll past, if you can."

Cruz saw the bear, and Eli tried to keep her calm to prevent her from barking at the animal. "It's okay, Cruz. We're all safe."

Whit leaned out the window and took several photographs. "Got him," she said with excitement.

Cruz could no longer restrain herself and let out a bark. The bear startled and rushed back into the forest. Eli eased over onto the side of the road and looked at the photos Whit had taken. "Good job. You got some great shots."

"Thanks." Whit took the camera back and looked at the photos.

†

The day was quickly fading, as they arrived at the fruit stand and loaded their goods. "I hope you will stop in again," Sue Ellen said, as Eli closed the tailgate.

"You can bet on seeing us again. Thanks for all the goodies," Eli replied.

"We appreciate the business. Have a safe drive home. Watch out for critters on the road."

Eli nodded. "Will do. We saw a small black bear earlier."

"They're out eating everything they can to pack on some fat for winter," Sue Ellen said.

"It's very evident how quickly the seasons are beginning to change," Whit said.

"Yeah, the mornings are getting much crisper. The foliage is going to be spectacular this year. That's always good for business."

Eli climbed in behind the wheel. "Give our thanks to your mom too. We enjoyed your pies. I'm not too sure there will be any left after my nephews return."

Sue Ellen smiled. "You have our number. Call whenever you'd like more. We'll have fruits for several months yet, enabling me to bake on demand."

"I'll put you on speed dial." Eli laughed and started the truck. "Bye for now."

Sue Ellen had given Cruz several dog biscuits. After eating her treats, Cruz settled in the seat for a nap. Whit glanced back at her. "Cruz is out like a light. I don't think any of us will have trouble sleeping tonight."

"Probably not," Eli agreed.

Eli's phone rang, and she automatically tapped the console until she remembered she was in Mitch's truck. "Damn, will you answer that?"

Whit took the phone and put Mitch on speaker. "Did you make it to Pensacola?" Eli asked.

"Yes, ma'am, we did. About an hour ago. Carol's already got a load heading to your house," Mitch said.

"Good deal. Carol has to make you earn the sushi she'll be buying tonight."

"She doesn't have near as much as what I thought. Moving Carol will be a piece of cake."

"Speaking of cake, Whit and I found a roadside fruit stand that makes the most delicious peach and apple pies today. If you're lucky, there may be one or two left for you and Brad when you get back."

"That sounds great. So, what have y'all done today?"

"We played tourist and visited some waterfalls. We needed a day to relax and enjoy a nice picnic."

"So, you haven't missed us at all?" Mitch asked.

"Of course, we miss you. It's so quiet," Eli answered.

"Are you taking care of my chickens?" Brad hollered.

"Yes, Chicken Master, we are. I collected twenty eggs this morning before we left. What are the plans for tonight?"

"Maybe one more load of Carol's belongings to your house, then a shower before we go to dinner. Dad says hello, by the way. We had a great brunch with him."

"Give him and your mom a hug and kiss from us when you get there tomorrow night."

"We will. Love you two," Mitch said.

"We love you also," Whit told them. "Be safe."

"Yes, ma'am. I'll call when we get home tomorrow. Hey, is it okay to hit your pool tonight?"

"Absolutely," Eli answered. "Enjoy and drive safe tomorrow."

"We will. Good night."

"Good night."

Eli turned to Whit. "Thanks for taking my mind off of worrying about them. I had almost forgotten they were traveling today."

"See, no need to worry. The boys made it safely without you calling every two hours." Whit chuckled.

"Yes, they did."

†

They passed meadows filled with fireflies, as the night fell around them. The tiny flashes of green and yellow lights danced across the air. Eli pointed out one field as they neared home. "I never tire of watching them dance."

"Me either. It's so relaxing. I bet we have some dancing at home too. Would you like to have a fire and watch them for a bit?" Whit asked.

"That sounds like an excellent way to cap off a perfect day. Should we try out a hammock?"

"That works for me. I'll unload the truck if you want to tend to the animals," Whit offered.

"Perfect." Eli turned into the drive. "Will you check for mail?" She stopped close to the mailbox, and Whit climbed out.

When Whit returned to the truck, she handed Eli the mail and a note from Mr. Henry. Eli read the message first. "Mr. Henry wants us to join them for dinner tomorrow night."

"Fine with me," Whit replied.

"Call and confirm. See if there is anything we can bring." Eli pulled into the yard, then exited and walked to the barn.

Cruz ran ahead to Molly and let her out of her stall, while Eli fed the cats. Several pairs of green eyes blinked at her from the loft as she filled the feeders. Tomboy weaved between her legs. "Yes, I missed you too."

Cajun slid down the slide and rushed over to her. He didn't often seek out her attention, but he was adamant about getting his fair share of chin scratches right then. She petted them both for several minutes, then filled Molly's food and checked for fresh water. When Molly heard the food poured into her trough, she rushed into her stall and began eating. Eli closed the door behind her and walked back to the cabin. Oscar and Walter were stretched out in chairs and barely cracked an eyelid when she stepped onto the porch. "Hey sleepyheads, you want some food?" Both cats followed Eli and Tomboy into the house.

"Mr. Henry said to bring hearty appetites. He seemed disappointed the boys weren't here, but I explained they would be back later this weekend."

"I think he likes them just a bit." Eli topped off the water bowls. "Do you want me to start a fire?"

"Baby, you started a fire from the moment you woke up." Whit laughed. "If you're talking about the firepit, then yes ma'am, that will do."

Eli laughed, too, and left the cabin. She lit the wood already laid in the pit and watched it burn. A glance across the creek confirmed the fireflies were dancing. She smiled, and when Whit arrived, they climbed into the hammock together.

Eli wrapped an arm around Whit and held her close, as they watched the fireflies dance and listened to the sounds of the night. The crackling of the fire and the sweet aroma of the burning wood filled the air. They rocked gently from side to side. "Nothing like living the life," Eli spoke softly. "I can't imagine anything better."

"I would never have dreamed, three months ago, that I would be in this place in my life," Whit said. "Snuggled next to a beautiful woman, who I adore, on a picture-perfect night."

"Exactly," Eli agreed. "Living here with you sets my soul on fire."

Whit lifted her head to look into Eli's eyes. "That's a beautiful thing to hear. You deserve everything life has to offer."

"I want for nothing with you in my arms. Even if I were to become penniless, as long as I have you in my life, that's all that truly matters."

Whit snuggled in closer to Eli. "You made me realize that I have so much more to offer than just my intelligence. You provided your love right when I needed it most."

"You have taught me many things, but mostly that there is such a thing as unconditional love. You don't care what I have or what I can give you. That's refreshing to not feel like what I've done is never enough."

Whit's hand softly stroked Eli's arm. "I'm sorry anyone ever made you feel that way. You are the kindest, most generous person I've ever met."

They fell silent until Eli's phone began to buzz. "Damn, I knew I should have left it in the house," she growled. Eli pulled the phone out and saw that Mitch was sending her a facetime request. "Do you mind?"

"Not at all."

"What's up, buttercup?" Eli spoke when she connected the call.

"I was just calling to tell you how nice it is in your pool," Mitch replied. "Where are you?"

Eli held the phone out the length of her arm, so Mitch could see them stretched out in the hammock.

"Oh hey, Love Muffin. It looks like you two are having a relaxing evening."

Whit laughed. "Hey, Mitch. Yes, we are. There's a fire in the firepit, the fireflies are dancing, and it's a beautiful night."

"Well, it's muggy as hell here, and I'm stuck with my little brother, but the pool is nice."

"Hey, Aunt Eli and Whit," Brad called from the side of the pool.

"Hey, Brad. Did you guys enjoy some sushi?"

"It was fantastic as usual," Mitch said. "I ate so much I thought I would explode."

"He ate two rolls by himself," Brad called out.

"You must have been hungry," Eli replied.

"I was. Dad took us for Mexican, and that stuff runs right through me. After a stop at the rest area, my tank was empty."

"That's a bit TMI, Mitch." Eli groaned. "I hope they didn't get my tag number."

"I don't think that bathroom will ever be the same." Brad laughed.

"I'll probably get a notice in the mail banning me from ever stopping in there again," Eli teased. "You know they have cameras, right?"

"What? In the bathrooms?" Mitch was surprised.

"Yes, and facial recognition software so they can track wanted felons and people who stink up the bathrooms." Eli couldn't hold back her laughter when she saw the look of terror on Mitch's face. "They do have cameras, but I'm not positive about the facial recognition software."

"That's a relief." He ran his hand through his mop of hair.

"What time are y'all supposed to be back at Carol's?"

"She said between eight and eight-thirty. I think she's anxious to get on the road. We have one final small load to bring here, then we'll load the trailer and be on our way. Do you mind me pulling the trailer with your truck?"

"It would be much safer than hooked to her small SUV. Just remember you're pulling a trailer and slow down. I know you get a lead foot like me at times, so set the cruise control."

"Yes, Mama," Mitch teased.

"I'd hate for anything to happen, and Carol's panties get strewn all over the interstate."

Mitch broke out laughing. "I'll have to remember to tell her that one."

"You two need to shower and hit the sack. You've got a busy day tomorrow. Call me when you hit the road and when you get to Montgomery."

"I will. Love y'all."

"Most," Eli and Whit answered in unison. "Good night."

After Eli ended the call, she pulled Whit closer. "I think our fire is dying down. Do you want to head upstairs for a shower?"

"I need one." Whit smiled. "How do we get out of this thing without landing on the ground?"

"Very carefully. Place your right foot on the ground, and I'll roll out and steady the hammock for you."

†

Eli's hands and mouth caressed every sensual spot on Whit's body. They moved from the shower into the bedroom, where their lovemaking continued. Whit took her leisure, exploring Eli, and soon had her on the edge of orgasm. "I'm going to die if I don't release soon." Eli groaned. Whit nibbled on Eli's left nipple and slid her fingers deep inside. "Oh, hell yes," Eli cried out. Eli reached between Whit's legs and entered her wetness. She matched Whit's pace as she thrust inside her. Whit covered Eli's mouth with a passionate kiss. They came together and Whit collapsed, breathless, onto Eli.

"Holy shit," Whit said between gasps for air. "That felt amazing." She looked into Eli's passion-filled eyes, then down to her chest. The crystal necklace glowed softly on Eli's skin. "Would you look at that?"

Eli's eyes followed Whit's. The crystal pulsed slowly against her skin. As her heart rate returned to normal, the crystal stopped pulsating and the glow faded.

Eli looked up at Whit. "What do you make of that?"

"I have no clue." Whit touched the crystal and found it warm to the touch. "I've meant to ask if this has helped with your headaches?"

Eli nodded. "I can't remember having one since I started wearing it."

"It must have some healing properties, and it certainly appears to react to our bodies." Whit rolled onto her side next to Eli. "I love you, Eli."

"I love you too. I've never been so happy in my life. You've helped to make all my dreams come true."

"Mine too. It's so nice to have a family to share again."

They lay silently together for a few moments, until Cruz's soft snoring from her bed broke the silence. "I guess she's telling us it's time for sleep," Eli whispered. Seconds later, Tomboy joined them on the bed and snuggled at Eli's feet. "Yes, we can call it a night. All present and accounted for." Eli kissed Whit. "Good night, my love."

"Good night." Whit snuggled in, happily held close in Eli's arm.

CHAPTER TEN

Eli crept from the bed and pulled on a robe before walking downstairs. She opened the refrigerator and began preparing French toast for breakfast. She used fresh strawberries and blueberries to garnish the sweet delight and placed two mugs of coffee on the tray before climbing the stairs. Whit still slept peacefully, so Eli set the tray on a table and leaned down to kiss her awake.

Whit's eyes fluttered open at the soft brush of Eli's lips on hers. "What is that wonderful smell?"

"It's called breakfast in bed." Eli smiled. She brought the tray over, as Whit propped up on pillows.

"That looks too beautiful to eat." Whit smiled and took the fork Eli offered.

Eli picked up a coffee and took a sip.

"You're going to help me eat all this, right?" Whit asked.

"Yes, ma'am, I was just giving you a head start." Eli cut a bite for herself. "Not bad."

"You can cook this for me anytime." Whit took a bite of toast and strawberry.

"It would be my pleasure, ma'am." Eli smiled and took another bite. "What time do we need to be at Mr. Henry's for dinner?"

"Five tonight. Is there something you want to do today?"

"Relax and maybe finish up a project. Will you be able to complete what you want to do in the lab in daylight?"

"Yes. Mostly check emails and review some charts on the black hole development. I shouldn't take long."

"Take whatever time you need. We don't need to rush around this morning."

†

Once they finished breakfast, Whit and Eli showered and dressed for the day. "I'm going to feed the animals. Do you want me to bring a Gator around?"

"No, I think I'll walk. I need the exercise," Whit answered. "How about a nice salad for lunch?"

"That sounds great. What do I need to prepare?"

"Nothing. I'll fry a few slices of bacon and boil some eggs. Go ahead and feed the animals and start your projects."

"Okay, I'll see you when you return." Eli kissed Whit and started toward the barn. She grabbed a bucket of chicken scratch and let Molly out of her stall. She and Cruz took off at a full run toward the garden. After feeding the cats, Eli picked up the scratch and collection baskets and walked to the coops. She opened the gate and scattered the feed in the chicken runs, before harvesting the eggs. The hens scattered, some eating scratch. Others began to sift through the cut grass for insects and seeds. She looked up to see Whit leaving the cabin and waved. Whit waved back and blew her a kiss. Eli made an extravagant gesture of catching the kiss and blew one back to her. She watched Whit until she disappeared, then began collecting eggs. After raiding the second coop, Eli exited with a haul of twenty-two eggs that she took to the kitchen counter and returned to the barn.

She examined Mitch's walking stick first. The wood torch burned a beautiful black surface, and Eli decided to add a polyurethane coat and fluorescent green paracord for the handgrip. While she waited for the sealant to dry, Eli picked up the decidedly shorter piece she had chosen for Whit. Eli inspected the wood grains and decided to apply sealant only to the staff. Whit appreciated the beauty of natural wood. Brad's walking stick received a coat of pecan stain, then Eli drilled the holes for all the wrist cords. She chose the paracord colors, selecting deep blue for Whit, then orange and blue for Brad. She tied a length of the cord long enough to wrap around Mitch's wrist, then began winding the handgrip. The polyurethane made the black shine and set off the green she had chosen for his grip. Eli hung the finished product on a nail to finish curing the sealant and worked on Whit's next. After melting the paracord's end to seal it, Eli stood and stretched. She hung Whit's walking stick next to Mitch's. Her phone rang, and she looked down to see that Mitch was calling. She hit the speaker on the phone. "Hey, buddy."

"Hey, Aunt Eli. I wanted to let you know that we've just left Pensacola."

"Any problems getting her stuff loaded?"

"No ma'am, everything went pretty smoothly. Carol had a bag full of sausage biscuits waiting for us. I took her bed over to your house, locked up, and set the security system while she and Brad started loading the trailer."

"Do you have the GPS set?"

"Yes, ma'am. It says our time of arrival at home should be two thirty. I'm sure we'll stop for some lunch along the way, which will put that ETA back some."

"No need to rush. You'll be in Montgomery before dark."

"Yes, ma'am. What are y'all doing?"

"Whit is up in the lab for a bit, and I'm piddling in the barn."

"Dad called earlier and said he had a surprise for me. Do you know what it is by chance?"

"Nope. Even if I did, I wouldn't ruin a surprise."

"Well, you're no help." Mitch chuckled.

"Where's your brother?"

"Brad's riding with Carol."

"Poor Carol," Eli said. "He'll probably talk her ears off."

"Yup. I just checked the rearview, and they are either singing or talking up a storm."

"That will make the drive pass quicker. I'm proud of y'all for doing this on your own. Whit and I are going to Mr. Henry's for dinner tonight. He was disappointed that y'all weren't here."

"We can do another cookout before we have to go back to Bama, right?"

"For sure. At least one," Eli promised.

Eli could hear a beep on Mitch's phone. "Someone calling you?"

"Gotta go. Jessie is calling. Love ya!"

"Love you too." Eli was too late. Mitch had already clicked over to pick up Jessie's call.

†

Cruz and Molly walked in and stretched out on the barn floor. "Did you two finally wear out?"

Eli checked the sealant on Brad's stick and found it dry enough to wrap his handgrip. She wondered what surprise Mark had in place for Mitch. She thought back to their conversation about the forge and wondered if Mark had made a knife for Mitch. She would find out later, when they arrived in Montgomery. Eli finished the final loops on Brad's walking stick and hung it up as well.

She returned to the cabin, and there was no sign of Whit. "Cruz, I think I hear the hammock calling my name. Let's go."

Eli climbed into the hammock and promptly fell asleep beneath a cool breeze.

†

Whit climbed the stairs to the lab and powered up her computer system. It had been days since she last checked her email. She'd been having too much fun with Eli to worry about work. Whit sorted through her emails, until she found one from the friend she had sent the crystal sample to. She hoped her friend could identify them. One of the most highly recognized geologists could not classify the piece as anything from earth. Unable to penetrate the core of the crystal, he was curious where she'd found the sample and if there were more. If she were reading correctly between the lines, he wanted to investigate possible alien origins.

Whit did not wish to have government agencies crawling all over her mountain or digging deeply into her past. She replied that she had run across the crystal on a hiking trip in Virginia and had only found the two. Whit was uncertain if he would accept the explanation, but her safety and happiness were a higher priority. Whit finished perusing her emails, finding very little of interest. She pulled up the black hole data. The dimensions appeared to have grown, but it was still young. She scanned other areas that she had been monitoring but didn't find anything new. Her thoughts came back to the crystal. Could it be something her father had left behind for her? If so, why? What purpose did they serve? Why did the crystals seem to react to her and now, Eli? Did they have healing powers as it appeared? Too many questions without answers baffled Whit. How was she going to solve this riddle? Whit opened her middle desk drawer and removed a crystal. "I wish you could answer some of those questions."

Whit replaced the crystal and walked outside. "I wonder what Eli is doing?" There was no sign of Eli moving around the farm, so Whit decided to shut down her system and go home to find her lover. She locked the lab door behind her and made a quick stop at her garden. Weeds were creeping in, and Whit made a mental note to do some hoeing soon. She picked some fragrant strawberries to share with Mr. Henry and Flora. Whit couldn't stop herself from popping a sweet gem into her mouth. "Damn, these get better every year."

Whit started across the bridge and stopped to peek over the edge. Several large fish were visible where they rested in a deep pool. Whit immediately thought of Brad. He would be disappointed to miss out on a chance at those big boys. She smiled as she thought about the instant family she'd gained by having a relationship with Eli. She couldn't ask for a better group of people.

As she approached the barn, there was still no sign of Eli. Green eyes peered back at her, but no Eli. No Cruz either, which was odd. She glanced toward the garden, but she wasn't there. Whit placed the strawberries on the porch and walked toward the firepit. As it came into view, Whit realized why Cruz hadn't met her as she crossed over. She was sleeping soundly underneath the hammock. Eli was also sleeping, tucked into the hammock. A twig snapped under Whit's boot, and Cruz jumped to attention. "Hey, pretty girl," Whit whispered. Before she could reach Eli and wake her with a kiss, Eli's phone rang and she bolted awake.

Eli looked around, startled by the phone, then relaxed when she realized what the noise was. "Hey, Baby," she said when she saw Whit approaching.

"Hey, yourself, Sleeping Beauty. You'd better get that. It's probably Mitch."

"Hello," Eli said.

"Aunt Eli, are you okay? You sound funny."

"I was napping in the hammock when you called. Did you make it home?"

"We're about to pull up now. Sorry, I woke you."

"No problem. The hammock was too enticing. I should have known I'd fall asleep."

"Where's Whit?"

"She did some work in the lab but is coming back just now."

"Tell her, I said hello."

"I will. No problems on the ride north?"

"None at all. I didn't know what time you were heading to Mr. Henry's, so I thought I'd call before I forgot."

"Dinner is at five. Do you want me to call when we get home? I know you'll be busy catching up with your parents."

"That's fine. I miss you," Mitch said.

"I miss you too. You'll be back tomorrow, so maybe we can survive one more night without you."

"Very funny. I was serious."

"I am too. We do miss you, but I'm sure your parents do too."

"Probably so."

"What did Jessie have to say?"

"She wanted to know if I would come to dinner when I get back."

"I hope you told her, yes."

"Well yeah, I did."

"Maybe we can do another cookout before y'all head out for your hike."

"That would be cool. Hayden and Brad have been texting like crazy."

"That's sweet."

"Yeah, I guess."

"Are you okay? You seem a bit down."

"I don't like how fast this summer is going."

"You still have a month and a half before you have to get ready for school. Cheer up. You'll be back up here for good in less than a year."

"I'll be counting down the days. Okay, I'm in the subdivision. Love you, and I'll be waiting for your call."

"Enjoy your surprise. I'll talk to you soon. Love you too. Bye." Eli ended the call wearing a frown.

Whit saw the look and asked, "What's wrong?"

"Mitch sounded down in the dumps. I don't like to hear him unhappy."

Whit reached for her hand. "Would you mind a suggestion?"

"Not at all. What are you thinking?"

"I think you and Mitch need to take a ride up the mountain and discuss the plan you have for setting him up in a tiny home. That would give him something to be excited about, and you can spend some time together selecting a floorplan."

"That may be some incentive for him to get through his final year of high school, too. Great idea."

"I come up with one every once in a while. Brad and I can work on building some benches, and we can install one near Mitch's spot."

"That would be perfect. Mitch could spend some time up there to dream."

"Dreams are essential, especially at his age. He'll soon be entering the adult world full time, and he needs a plan."

Eli stood and pulled Whit into a hug. "Thank you for all your love."

Whit kissed Eli. "Don't worry too much about Mitch. He'll make some mistakes, but he's grown so much from the boy I first met."

"Yes, he has. I'm very proud of him, and I try to remind him of that often."

"He knows how much you love him. That's what's important."

"Do you want to shower and get ready to go to dinner? I'll feed the animals and secure the chickens if you want to get started."

"I'll help. That way things get done sooner. Besides, I like working with you."

"We make a great team." Eli smiled.

"Yes, we do."

Eli reached for Whit's hand. "Let's go, Love Muffin."

†

Mr. Henry and Flora stuffed Eli and Whit with fried chicken and a whole mess of fresh vegetables. Flora topped off the meal with a delicious apple pie. Eli felt like she would explode if she ate another bite, but she did accept a refill on coffee.

"I hear you and the boys are going to hike part of the AT," Mr. Henry said to Whit. "That sounds like a grand adventure."

"I'm hoping it will be. We head out in two weeks."

"You couldn't convince Eli in joining you?"

"No sir, she prefers a soft bed and hot showers." Whit chuckled. "I'm hoping, one day, we can convince her to join us for a section."

"I'm giving it some serious thought." Eli smiled at Whit. "Maybe by next year, I'll be ready to leave the mountain for a hike."

"I hope those boys will be able to keep up with you." Mr. Henry shot Whit a wink.

"We have no goal other than to survive a two-week hike. It doesn't matter if we make five or ten miles a day. We are starting at Katahdin in Maine and trekking south. If we can survive that first day, we can handle the rest. The climb up can be brutal."

"I think I'm with Eli on this one," Flora said. "A hot meal and shower at day's end, and a comfortable bed to fall into is more to my liking."

Mr. Henry patted Flora's hand. "If I were twenty years younger, I'd go."

"Maybe next year you can join us for a section with Eli," Whit suggested.

"I'll give it some thought. I'd have to get Mama's permission, of course."

Flora smiled. "Silly man. You know you can do anything you want. I know you would love an adventure like that."

"Yes, I would. I just don't know if these old legs will hold up. I would need to get one of those fancy new prosthetics."

"I think it's past time you got an upgrade anyhow. You've had this one for over ten years." Flora reached over and placed a hand on her husband's arm. "You've talked about the AT all your life. I don't know why you've never hiked it."

Mr. Henry looked at Flora with complete adoration, as he lifted her hand to his lips and kissed her fingers. "I couldn't bear to be away from you for the six or more months it would have taken to hike it."

Eli looked at Whit and smiled. "Even two weeks will be a challenge." She looked back at Mr. Henry. "Would you two be up for another cookout before our hikers start their journey?"

"Will there be Boston butt?" Mr. Henry asked.

"Yes, Mitch is getting quite adept at roasting them. How about next Saturday?"

Flora nodded. "Count us in. How about more baked beans and some deviled eggs?"

"Wonderful," Whit said. "Come out in the afternoon if you want to fish with the kids. I saw some huge ones this morning that Brad would have flipped over."

Mr. Henry perked up at the mention of fishing. "I think I just might join the youngins. It's been a long time since I've fished."

"The kids would love it if you joined them." Eli gave him a big smile. "Especially, Brad. He loves to listen to your stories."

Whit chuckled. "We all do."

Eli placed her coffee on the table. "Do you have to work Saturday?"

"Yes, but it will be a short day. Probably until noon."

"Well, load Ms. Flora up and head out as soon as you can. Do you need some fresh vegetables to bring home?" Eli asked.

"We always enjoy homegrown vegetables," Flora replied.

Whit nodded. "We have two gardens producing now, so come prepared to bring home what you want. Or you can drop by this week, and we can pick when you're ready."

"I'll plan on coming out midweek, if that's okay. Maybe I can prepare something else to bring to the cookout."

"Any time. Just give us a call to let us know you're on your way." Whit winked at Mr. Henry. "You know I've got an excellent crop of strawberries this year. Stop by the cabin on Monday, and I'll pick some for you. I'm sure Flora would like them for shortcake or some other kind of dessert."

"Lordy. I can't be hungry after that delicious meal, but I swear my stomach growled at the thought of strawberry shortcake." Mr. Henry placed his hand on Flora's arm. "You do make a wonderful shortcake. If you make them, I'll gladly drive up to the cabin for strawberries, my love."

"That's an easy request to fill. Thank you, ladies."

"I'll have them ready for you on Monday then, and we'll see you both on Saturday." Whit stood and gave them both a hug.

Eli also hugged the older couple. "Bring a healthy appetite and a cooler, and we'll fill it up."

"That will be wonderful," Flora answered. "Just let me know if there is anything else, I can bring."

"Will do." Eli started toward the door. "See you soon."

"Drive safe." Mr. Henry walked them out to the porch.

Eli waved, and they started for home.

"That was a fantastic meal. I don't think I could ever fry chicken that good." Eli reached for Whit's hand.

"The secret is lard. Grandma used it instead of today's cooking oils. I suspect Flora does too. It makes a world of difference in the taste."

Eli looked at Whit. "I would have never guessed that. It makes sense, though. I guess I'll be buying a can of lard soon."

"In moderation, please, or we'll all have clogged arteries," Whit teased.

"Gotcha," Eli answered with a grin. "Will you dial Mitch for me?"

"Sure thing." Whit took Eli's phone and pressed the speed dial button for Mitch, and the speaker button.

"Hey, Aunt Eli. You ain't gonna believe what my surprise was," Mitch answered her call.

"So, tell me all about it." Eli was glad to hear the excitement in his voice.

"Dad bought a forge, and he made me a Bowie knife. I can't wait for you to see it."

"Well, send me a picture."

"I will, but it's nothing like holding it in your hand. It's beautiful and fits me perfectly."

"I can't wait to see it. Maybe I can get on the list for something a little smaller to use around the farm."

"If Dad doesn't make it for you, I will."

"That sounds like a great plan. Mr. Henry and Flora send their love. They will be coming out Saturday for a cookout. Mr. Henry is planning to fish with you guys, so I think he and Brad can team up. Have you called the crew to invite them out?"

"Not yet, but I can work on that tomorrow."

"Good deal. What time do you plan on heading out in the morning?"

"Early, so we can get there and have Carol unloaded by the afternoon."

"That sounds like a great plan. Let me know when you're on the road in the morning."

"Yes, ma'am. I'll text you when we leave, so I don't wake you if it's early."

"That works. Hugs and kisses all around. Be careful tomorrow. Love ya!"

"Most," Mitch said with a chuckle. "Goodnight."

Eli looked over at Whit. "Would you care to join me by the firepit for a glass of watermelon wine?"

"I'd love to. I'll pour the wine if you start the fire."

"You, my dear, have a deal." Eli entwined her fingers with Whit's as she drove.

"Look!" Whit pointed ahead of them in the sky. "A falling star. Make a wish."

"Done," Eli answered.

"What did you wish for?"

"Can't say, or it won't come true." Eli grinned.

"Well, I wished for…"

"Oh no you don't. Stop." Eli teased. She pulled through the gate and started up the hill to the cabin. "Look, another one."

Whit grabbed her phone and checked a site. "Ah, meteor showers tonight. That explains it."

"Should we change plans and have our wine in the bed of Mitch's truck to watch them for a while?"

"We could do that. Park away from the cabin, so there's minimal light pollution. I'll grab the bottle of wine and glasses."

"I'll grab us a couple of lawn chairs. That will be more comfortable."

"You know what would be even better?" Whit asked.

Eli looked at her. "What?"

"We take a Gator up to Mitch's spot. Completely away from light sources and a more open view."

"Perfect. I'll toss some chairs in the back of a Gator and pick you up." Eli parked the truck and kissed Whit before exiting. "Love you."

"Most," Whit answered with a twinkle in her eyes.

†

Cruz raced out of the house and followed Eli into the barn. "No, it's not time for Molly to come play, but you can ride with us."

Cruz jumped into the front seat, as Eli placed two lawn chairs in the back. "Okay, for now, but when we pick Whit up, you've got to sit in the back."

Cruz yawned and curled up in the seat. Eli drove out of the barn to collect Whit. "Alright, back seat," she told Cruz, when they stopped in front of the cabin.

"It's okay. We can share, but you do have to scoot over." Whit slipped into the seat, as Cruz moved a few inches. "Seat hog," Whit told her and laughed.

"Hold on," Eli said and started up the mountain.

When they crossed over the bridge, the noise startled a small buck, and Cruz sat up in the seat. "Sit tight, baby girl," Eli told her as she turned right to go higher. When they reached the spot, she turned the Gator toward the open skyline and set the brake. "This is beautiful. Great idea."

Whit poured them a glass of wine and handed one to Eli. "Thanks for a great night." She touched her drink to Eli's.

"To a great life with you," Eli answered. She took a sip. "This is good, not too sweet or too strong."

"I could see this sneaking up on me." Whit smiled up at Eli. "It tastes so good I might forget it's alcoholic."

"I think we can both have a glass or two and be safe. I still have to drive us home, remember?" Eli grinned.

Cruz stretched out and laid her head across Eli's thigh. "I'm glad you decided to join us. Not that I could have said otherwise once you jumped in."

"She loves her mama. So do I," Whit replied.

"I love you both." Eli stretched an arm around Whit's shoulder, and they peered into the sky, watching for the next meteor.

An hour later and two glasses of wine each had them feeling mellow. "I think we've passed the peak of the shower for tonight. Are you ready to head home?"

Eli opened her mouth to speak when she saw Whit's facial expression change. "What's wrong?"

"You're glowing." Whit pointed to Eli's crystal necklace.

Eli looked down at the blue light against her skin. "What do you think of that?"

"I've no clue." Whit's head turned toward the top of the mountain. "Do you think we should visit the cave?"

Eli reached over to unlock the glovebox. She pulled out a flashlight and a pistol. "If you're game."

"Let's see if anything is going on up there."

Eli nodded and drove the Gator to the end of the trail. She turned on the flashlight. "I think we should be able to find the cave going this way." Eli directed the beam of light ahead of them.

Cruz walked a few steps ahead of them, as they reached the outcropping of boulders in front of the cave. Eli noticed the cave's mouth was not a deep black as she would have expected, and she wondered if the crystals had come back to life. "You ready?" She reached for Whit's hand.

Whit slipped her hand inside Eli's and nodded.

When they entered, Eli could see the blue light pulsing from the back of the cave. It grew stronger as they walked closer. As they approached the entrance, Whit stopped. "Can you feel the energy?"

"Like static electricity in the air?" Eli nodded. "Yes, I can."

Eli entered first, followed by Whit and Cruz. The crystals remaining in the walls and on the floor of the cave glowed softly. Not the bright light as before, but soft with a sense of warmth. Eli looked cautiously at Whit. "You okay?"

"Yes, it's peaceful, don't you think?"

"Do you think the meteor showers have re-energized them or something? They didn't glow like that the last time I was here."

Whit looked at Eli. "I guess that could be a possibility. Your guess is as good as mine." She bent to pick up a crystal and felt its warmth on her palm. "My friend said this is nothing known to earth. His email implied it was alien, and he wanted information of where I found the crystals."

"What did you tell him?"

Whit smirked. "That I found the two of them on a hiking trip in Virginia. I don't know if he'll buy that answer, but I don't cherish anyone invading our mountain to dig for alien resources."

"That was smart," Eli agreed. "Do you want to pick up a few more?"

Whit nodded. "I told Julia that I would share one with her when she made the necklace for you. Would you mind?"

"Not at all. I do think the crystal emits positive healing energy. I'd caution her about anyone asking about the location, though."

"I know. There's no telling what lengths the government would take to find and cover up signs of an alien presence. Call me paranoid, but that's how I feel."

"Trust me. It's not paranoia at all. I see what kind of measures our government agencies are capable of taking."

Eli handed her four small crystals. "This will remain our secret."

"Do you think I should have a conversation with Mitch as a precaution?"

Eli nodded. "That might not be a bad idea. He would never do anything to affect any of us negatively, but he's naive and could easily be tricked by a smooth talker into saying something he didn't intend."

"I'll talk to him when they get back." Whit soaked in the energy of the room and turned to Eli. "Let's go home."

Eli pulled Whit close. She brushed the hair back from her face and leaned in to kiss her. The sweetness of the wine lingered on her lips, as their tongues danced slowly. Eli sensed a change in the air. When she opened her eyes, the crystals had brightened. "Look."

Whit opened her eyes and noticed the change.

"I had to know something. I think the crystals react to emotions, especially love. They always seem to brighten. Like one of the old mood rings that changed colors, but they get brighter with positive energy."

"I agree with you there. I still have so many unanswered questions, but maybe one day they will be revealed."

Eli reached for her hand. A short time later, they pulled in front of the cabin. "I'll park the Gator and be inside in just a few minutes."

Eli locked the gun inside the glove box and was surprised to find that it was already past midnight. *I had no idea we were out that long.* She closed the barn door and walked to the cabin. She turned when she heard the owl hooting in the distance. "Goodnight to you too."

She closed the door behind her and climbed the stairs to their bedroom. Whit was brushing her teeth when she entered. "Can you believe it's after midnight already?"

"I know. I didn't think we were out that long," Whit replied from the bathroom.

Eli slipped in beside Whit and brushed her teeth. When she returned to the bedroom, Whit had crawled between the covers. Eli undressed and climbed in beside her lover. She rolled onto her side and saw the peaceful look in Whit's eyes. Eli leaned down and kissed her softly.

Whit rolled Eli onto her back and snuggled into her body, her hand resting on Eli's stomach as they drifted into slumber.

CHAPTER ELEVEN

Eli and Whit were tending to Whit's garden when they heard vehicles approaching. Eli looked up to see Mitch pulling her truck up Whit's driveway. "They made good time."

Whit dropped a handful of weeds into a bucket. "Yes, they did. Mitch must have had them up at the crack of dawn."

Eli reached for her hand. "Probably. He was ready to come home."

"I love that he thinks of here as home."

Eli grinned. "Me too. I think he loves this place as much as we do."

Mitch pulled the trailer close to the front porch and got out of the truck. "We're home," he said, as he grabbed Eli in a bear hug. "I missed you."

"I missed you too. Glad you're back safe."

Carol and Brad walked up.

"Welcome home. Let's get you unloaded, and you can start settling in," Eli suggested.

"First things first. I got to pee. Mitch wouldn't stop for the last hour." Carol disappeared into the cabin.

Eli shot Mitch a grin. "You have to remember, women our age can't wait forever."

"It was only a half hour. If we would have stopped, then we'd have had to wait on Brad. You know how it is when he gets in front of a mirror."

"Hey now, I'm not that bad," Brad replied.

"Yes, Brad, you are," Eli said. "Let's open this baby up and see what we have to unload."

Mitch reached to open the door. "Mostly boxes. It shouldn't take us long. What's for lunch?"

"No clue," Eli answered. "What would you like?"

"Brad and I will unload if you go get some chicken livers."

Eli looked at Whit. "That sounds like a good deal. You want to ride along?"

"Sure thing." She walked toward the cabin. "Just let me wash my hands."

"Were you weeding or harvesting?" Mitch asked.

"Pulling a few weeds. The way Whit talked, I thought the weeds had taken over, but it wasn't bad."

"Oh hey, look at this." Mitch pulled out the knife his dad made for him and handed it to Eli.

Eli turned the knife over in her hands, admiring the craftsmanship. "This is beautiful." She saw his initials engraved in the blade's base, and *CIF* on the handle butt cap. "Your dad did a great job."

"It cuts well too. I'm excited to learn how to forge with Dad."

"I think Cast Iron Forge will be a great success. You know, I just had a thought. We could use the front portion of the cave for a forge. It's large enough for ventilation, already has some wood stacked and would be close to home for Mark."

Mitch's face beamed with a smile. "That's brilliant, Aunt Eli. We could set up a solar system to run the forge, separate from the cabin."

Whit returned from inside the cabin. "All set. You want me to drive?"

"Sure. Your car probably needs to be driven. We'll meet you back at our place," she told Mitch and Brad. "Bring Carol. She can start unpacking later."

"Will do," Mitch answered. "I'll whip us up some white sauce too. Let's get moving," he told Brad, as Eli and Whit walked to her car.

"Should we call in an order?" Whit asked.

"Naw, there's no rush. It will give them time to unload."

†

It didn't take long to settle Carol into her new home, with Whit's help. Eli and the boys worked on chores around the farm. Evan brought the Bee Man out on Tuesday, who taught them how to harvest the wild honey. It turned out that Brad was a natural, picking up the skills quickly. Eli decided honey harvesting could be one of his assignments. As the weekend approached, Whit and Eli shopped for the cookout. Mitch mowed the grass and got the grill set up for the butts he was marinating. Brad tended the chickens and helped Eli and Whit harvest vegetables when Flora came to visit. He and Mitch loaded her car with a bounty of fresh vegetables and a dozen eggs.

†

The crew began arriving early on Saturday morning. Evan assisted Mitch in getting the butts on the grill, setting up the firepit, and getting chairs arranged in the yard. Mr. Henry and Flora arrived, and Mr. Henry gladly joined the youngsters fishing.

Doc Loren and Macy arrived with a massive bowl of banana pudding, and when Julia pulled into the yard, another vehicle was right behind her. Brad was the first to recognize the SUV and hollered from the bridge. "Hey, it's Mom and Dad."

Eli spun around and smiled when she saw Mark and Laura climb out of her SUV. "We heard there was a cookout." Mark grinned. "I hope you have enough for two more."

Eli hugged him. "There's always extra. I'm so glad to see y'all."

"We thought we'd drive up and visit before Whit and the boys take off Thursday for the AT," Mark replied.

"We also heard that our oldest is getting proficient on the grill," Laura said. "Mark had to check that out for himself."

"You will always be the grill master," Mitch said. "Would you care to take over the butts?"

"Nope, I do believe I hear a fish calling my name." Mark grinned.

"You can join Mr. Henry, Jessie, and I on the bridge, Dad," Brad chimed in.

"You going to fish, Mom?" Mitch teased.

Laura shook her head. "Heaven's no. I'm going to kick back with a cold beverage and watch."

"I am so glad y'all came. It's a pleasant surprise," Eli told Mark, as they walked over to collect a fly rod.

"I wasn't sure we would make it, so I didn't say anything. But it worked out good, and here we are."

Eli hugged him again. "Hey, let's take a ride up the mountain before you start fishing. I want to talk to you about a few things."

"I'll carry our bag in while you grab a Gator," Mark said.

"Go ahead, and I'll take the bag in for you," Mitch offered.

"Thanks, son." Mark turned back to Eli. "I guess I'm ready to ride."

"Let's do it. We'll be back in a bit," Eli told Whit.

"Okay, we're going to start getting some of the vegetables ready to cook."

†

Eli and Mark walked into the barn, followed by Cruz and Molly. "You two want to follow along?"

Mark stopped long enough to pet Cajun and Tomboy. "Can I steal one of these guys when we move up?"

"Nope. I'm sure we can get plenty from Doc Loren, especially if you want black ones."

"I'd love to have black, but any that need a home would be fine," Mark answered. "The more, the merrier."

"That won't be a problem." Eli climbed into the Gator, while Mark opened the back door.

Eli drove them to the small cave near Mark's build site. "When Mitch came home and showed me his knife, I had an idea. What do you think about using the front part of the cave for your forge?"

Mark surveyed the space. "I think it's doable. We'd have to run electricity for the power hammer."

"Mitch has already planned on solar power."

Mark rubbed his head. "That makes good sense. Would the heat affect your root cellar?"

"If it does, we can move it. Will the heat make it too intense to work in here?"

"The forge is very portable. On hot days, I can roll it just outside the entrance. It will feel nice during the cooler weather."

"Should we plan on this being the home of Cast Iron Forge, then?"

Mark grinned at her use of the name. "Yes, I think we can. This spot will be great."

"There's something else I'd like to show you. Let's go."

Eli drove to the clearing that had grabbed Mitch's heart. "Mitch has fallen in love with this spot."

"I can see why. It's beautiful and has a great view."

"Whit and I have been talking. We'd like to have a tiny home set up for him as a graduation gift. It would give him a chance to be more independent, yet close to all of us."

"That's a great idea."

"I've seen where he's been researching tiny homes on my laptop. I think it may give him the incentive to buckle down and finish his last year of high school if he has something to work toward."

"It would be perfect for a single person. I like the idea. That frees up my idea for a new truck as a graduation gift, if you're going to do this."

"Ha! I might come out cheaper than you," Eli teased.

"That's true. Mitch has matured so much under your watch. I'm very proud of him."

"Me too. Mitch has had a few bumps, but he's overcome them. You should see the look on his face when he comes here. He's found his little piece of heaven, and there's plenty of room for a full-size home when it's time."

"I'd love to keep the boys close. Like Mom and Dad would have liked to have had us all on the homeplace."

"Me too. I think this is our chance to make it happen for them and us." She shrugged. "I'm not sure if Brad would be on board with that. He seems to have a bit of wanderlust in him."

"I think he'll eventually settle here. He may have to sew some wild oats first. Only time will tell," Mark added. "He's enjoying this summer and is already asking to spend Spring Break here next year."

"That would be fine with us. We love having all of you here. You ready to fish?"

"Yeah, I'm looking forward to it. Any tips?"

"You won't get skunked here. The trout bite well in this section."

"Are you okay with us staying until early Monday morning?"

"If I had my way, you'd never leave." Eli hugged him. "One day soon."

"Let's roll," Mark said.

"I'll drop you off at the bridge. Brad was getting you set up to fish with his group."

"Sounds good. Thanks, sis."

†

"Good luck," Eli told Mark when she dropped her brother off and drove on to the cabin. The aroma of cooking meat filled the air, as she stepped onto the porch. She walked toward the grill and found Mitch and Evan checking the meat. "It sure is smelling good around here," Eli told Mitch.

"I hope it turns out well. Did you know Mom and Dad were coming?"

Eli shook her head. "No clue, but I'm glad they're here."

"Me too," Mitch agreed. "Do you need me to make the white sauce?"

"No, I'll make it while you fish. Is everyone catching?"

"Mr. Henry landed a whopper. Not as big as mine, but still a big fish."

Eli smiled. "Did you get a picture?"

Mitch pulled out his phone. "I didn't, but Brad sent one to me."

"Send it to me, please, so I can show Flora."

"Done." Mitch grinned and stuffed his phone back in his pocket. "The butts have another hour or so before we can pull them off to rest."

"I'll let Whit know, so we can time things together. You guys need anything?"

"Toss us a couple of waters from the deck if you would please."

"Where are the girls?"

"They're probably chatting up a storm over on the west creek," Evan said. "Hayden is fishing with Brad."

"I'll ride over and check on them in a bit. Meet me at the deck, and I'll get you waters."

Eli walked inside to the refrigerator and took out two bottles of water. "I'll be right back," she told Whit and the ladies. When she returned, she pulled out her phone to show Flora the fish Mr. Henry had caught.

"Oh, my goodness, he'll be talking about that one for weeks," Flora exclaimed.

"Would you look at that smile on his face?" Whit said.

"He's been looking forward to today all week. He went to the garage and checked his gear after you all left Saturday night."

"I'm glad he could fish today." Eli looked at Whit. "I'm going to make the rounds with water."

Doc Loren asked, "Do you want some company?"

"Sure, let's grab six bottles. We'll be back shortly."

Doc Loren followed her to the Gator. "You couldn't have asked for a prettier day," she said, as she climbed in beside Eli.

"That's for sure. The weather has been great. How have things been with you and Macy?"

"Life is good. It's been a great summer for us. I went to the barn and checked out the crew. Everyone looks healthy and happy."

"Spoiled rotten is more like it. Mark is already planning to adopt a few when they move up."

"We'll always have cats and kittens that need a good home."

"We can probably talk Carol into a few, now that she's moved here," Eli said.

Doc Loren smiled. "We've got several ready for adoption."

"I'll drop by with her soon. Once she sees them, she won't be able to resist."

"I love the way you think."

Eli pulled up to the western creek, where the girls were fishing. "Hey, you two need something to drink?"

"We were just contemplating going to the cabin. You must have been reading our minds," Jessie said.

Erin walked over. "Hey, Doc."

"Hey, yourself. How's the fishing?"

"Great. We've almost filled our bucket," Erin answered.

"When you do, text me, and I'll bring you an empty one," Eli said.

"Thanks." Erin took a bottle of water. "The smell wafting over is killing me. How much longer until we eat?"

"Probably an hour and a half. Do you need something to snack on to hold you over? I can get Mitch to throw some kielbasa on the grill."

"That would be awesome," Jessie answered.

"I'll get him started on it now," Eli said. "We'll see you soon."

As Eli and Doc Loren walked back to the Gator, she pulled out her phone to call Whit. "Will you call out to Mitch and get him to put several packs of kielbasa on the grill?

He's killing the girls with the smell of the butt cooking." Eli listened to Whit's comment. "Thanks. We'll see you soon."

They drove onto the bridge to check on the others fishing. "Wow, you guys have been raking them in over here." Eli looked at their buckets.

"The fish are biting great today," Mr. Henry said with a smile.

"I saw that whopper you caught. He was huge."

"Biggest of the day so far," Brad said.

"We've got about an hour left before the meat comes off the grill. Why don't you fish a bit longer, then wrap it up for today so we can get these cleaned and packaged?"

"We can do that," Mark said.

"Mitch is going to put some sausage on the grill for everyone to snack on until dinner. We also brought water if anyone is thirsty."

Doc Loren passed out water and took a look in the buckets. "How do you keep the cats away from that smell?"

"We give them some fishy scraps when we clean them," Brad said. "Cajun and the crew scarf them down."

"I bet they do. No wonder the cats are growing so well."

Mark hooked a fish while they were chatting. "Reel him in Mark," Eli called out.

His smile grew as he pulled a large fish onto the bridge. "If you put the full bucket in the back, I'll ride with you and get started cleaning."

Mr. Henry stood up from his seat. "I'll help you," he told Mark.

"You two finish filling that bucket," Eli said and shot a wink to Brad. "Let's roll, boys," Eli called to Mark and Mr. Henry.

Eli dropped them off at the compost bin and helped them set up a cleaning table, while Doc Loren walked to the cabin for Ziplock bags and filet knives.

"You guys all set?" Eli asked.

"I'll grab my cooler from my truck," Mr. Henry said.

"Yep, that might help," Mark said. "I'll be right back."

The cats could smell the fish and began positioning themselves for a savory snack. Even Walter and Oscar came off the porch to watch the show. Cruz and Molly chased one another around the yard, and Eli smiled at the buzz of human and animal activity. "Let's go check on the sausage and the ladies in the house," Eli said to Doc Loren.

As they rounded the corner on the porch, Eli saw that Mitch was cutting the sausage into rounds as he took them off the grill. He was using his sodbuster instead of the knife Mark made him. "I'm surprised you aren't using your Bowie knife," she teased.

"It's a bit too much knife for mere sausage," he joked back.

"Did you guys get much fishing time in?" Eli asked.

"Enough. We managed to fill a bucket between the two of us."

"Your dad and Mr. Henry have started cleaning fish. Do you want to check on them while I take your delicious sausage inside?"

Doc Loren piped in. "I'll take them, if you want to go collect the girls. I bet they're ready to call it a day."

"I'm on my way," Eli said and walked back to the Gator. Cruz jumped in beside her. "Let's ride, baby girl." She scratched the top of Cruz's head.

Erin and Jessie had just started to walk toward the cabin when Eli arrived. "Did someone call for a taxi?" Eli grinned.

Erin laughed. "No, ma'am, but we sure won't turn down a ride."

The girls climbed in after storing their buckets and rods in the back.

"The sausage should be cool enough to eat by the time we drop these fish off, and y'all wash your hands. Mitch was pulling it off as I drove over."

Jessie cheered. "I can't wait. My stomach has been growling for at least twenty minutes."

Eli smiled back at her. "Do you think you can survive another five minutes?"

"I'm going to try my best," Jessie said.

"Hang on." A few minutes later, Eli pulled up to where the guys were cleaning fish. They dropped off their bucket and walked to the laundry room to wash their hands.

"Do you want the girls to bring out some sausage to munch on?" Eli asked Mark.

Mark nodded. "That would be great."

"Anyone want mustard?"

"Most definitely, unless you have white sauce." Mr. Henry had fallen in love with the white sauce.

"I made a big batch earlier," Eli replied. She parked the Gator and walked into a flurry of activity in the kitchen.

"I bet you want these." Whit held up a bowl of sausage slices.

"Yes'm, and a container of white sauce and some mustard." Eli grabbed a handful of plastic forks. "How are things coming in here?"

"Right on schedule. Carol and Julia will arrange the picnic tables once Mitch pulls the meat off the grill."

"Do you want me to cook the street corn on the grill?" Eli asked.

"That would be one less cook in the kitchen."

"Doc Loren can be my gopher, so that will be two less in this madhouse. Do you mind, Macy?"

"No, not at all. Loren's a bit of a nightmare in a busy kitchen," she teased.

"Hey, now. I'm right here. Don't hurt my feelings," Loren said with a smile. "More like a bull in a china shop," she told Eli.

"Come on then, let's make our exit." Eli and Loren took the bowl of sausage and sauces out to the group cleaning fish. "Who's hungry?"

Eli received a chorus of answers from the group and waited for Mark to rinse off a corner of the make-shift table to set the bowls down.

Brad and Hayden walked up, carrying a full bucket and their fishing gear. "I thought I smelled sausage," Brad called with a big grin on his face.

"Go wash up in the laundry room. You better hurry if you plan on getting sausage," Eli informed him. She turned back to look at the pile of dressed fish. "It seems like you and Mr. Henry will have a nice batch of fish to take home."

Mark nodded. "They never seem to last long around our place. There must be a black hole in the freezer they disappear into." Mark shot a wink at Mitch. "I would normally say that was Mitch, but he's been up here with you, so I can't blame it on him."

"We'll do our best to keep the fish coming," Mitch told his dad.

Eli smiled at her brother. "I guess that's one way of keeping you coming back to visit."

"You can bet we'll be here whenever possible," Mark answered. He looked at Mitch. "How much longer before the meat is ready to come off the grill?"

Mitch checked his watch. "It shouldn't be long now. I'll check the temperature and see if it's ready."

"Let me know if you need a hand."

"Evan's my gopher," Mitch said. "He does a great job too."

"Thanks for putting up with these two, Evan," Eli said.

"Eating that Boston butt makes it well worth it."

"That's the last of them," Mark said. "Do you have room in your freezer that I can store these?

"After we take out the bag of ice for Mr. Henry's cooler, we will," Eli answered.

Mr. Henry scratched his head. "Dang, I knew I forgot something."

Eli rested a hand on his shoulder. "No worries. We've got you covered. Hey, Mitch, will you and Evan carry Mr. Henry's cooler to his truck?"

"I'll grab the bag of ice to dump on these fish," Evan said.

"Thanks. I'll help you carry the cooler onto the porch," Eli told Mark.

"Thanks, sis. Brad can help me put them in the freezer."

†

Doc Loren and Macy were the last to leave. "Are you sure we can't help with anything else?" Macy asked.

"Nope, we've only got a few dishes to load into the dishwasher, but thank you," Whit answered. "Did you get your bowl and leftovers?"

"Are you kidding? Loren's already loaded her leftovers." Macy gestured toward her partner.

"Did she remember a container of white sauce?" Eli asked.

"Dangit, no, I forgot."

Eli reached into the refrigerator and pulled out a container. "Here you go."

"Thanks. See you next week?" Loren asked.

"If not, the following week for sure," Eli replied.

"Does someone have an appointment?" Whit asked.

Eli grinned. "No, I'm going to take Carol by to see some kittens."

Carol's head snapped up. "Kittens! Really Eli?"

"Yes, you need a crew, now that you are here permanently," Eli told her.

"Let's go this week then. I miss having cats," Carol replied.

"Monday it is then, Doc."

"Fantastic news. I'll cut you a great deal on altering fees if you get several," Loren said.

"I'd love to have three or four." Carol clasped her hands over her heart.

They walked Loren and Macy to their truck. Eli opened the door for Doc Loren. "Be safe, and we'll see you Monday."

Mark, Laura, and the boys were relaxing around the firepit. Eli and Whit sat beside Mark as Julia made room for Carol. "Thank you for a great job on those butts," she told Mitch.

"You did an excellent job, son," Mark added. "I don't think anyone left without leftovers."

Mitch smiled. "They did turn out well. Not as good as yours, but close."

"They were every bit as good as mine, son. Don't sell yourself short."

"Are you all set for the big adventure?" Laura asked.

"Our packs have been ready for days." Whit grinned. "We've got our drop boxes ready, and Eli has made all of our reservations."

"I wish I could go with you. You'll have to take a lot of photographs," Mark said.

Whit nodded. "I don't think that will be a problem for the three of us."

"I can't wait to see them. If the satellite phone works well, give us a call when you can. You have solar chargers, right?"

"Eli's got us stacked with chargers," Brad answered.

"Is there anything you guys need before you go?" Laura asked.

The boys looked to Whit to answer. She shook her head. "I can't think of anything that Eli hasn't already done. Eli has us well supplied for someone who's never done a long hike."

"I listened well to what you and the boys have talked about and added a few ideas of my own," Eli said.

Mark looked at Carol. "You're going to have your hands full."

Carol cocked her head. "Why is that?"

With a smirk, Mark said, "You have to keep her busy for almost two weeks."

"There is that." Whit scratched her head.

"I don't envy you that assignment." Laura laughed and gave Eli a hug.

"I can't deny I'll be anxious until I see them again," Eli said.

"At least you've given them the best means to communicate with you. It's not like you won't hear from them for two weeks," Mark reminded her.

"I know." Eli shrugged. "I can't help but worry. It's who I am."

Whit covered Eli's hand with her own. "We love who you are."

"Oh Lordy, it's getting mushy out here," Mitch teased. "I think I'll call it a night so you old folks can enjoy the rest of the night. Will you cook SOS in the morning, Dad?"

"That's easy enough," Mark answered.

"Good night then, love y'all."

"We love you too," Mark said.

"I think we'll head out too," Carol said. She reached for Julia's hand.

"Feel free to come for breakfast," Eli offered.

"Are you kidding? After today, I won't need to eat for days," Carol said. "I think it's time to sleep in for a change."

"Come over whenever. I don't think we have plans to go anywhere," Eli replied.

Whit offered a flashlight to Carol. "The bridge is well lit, but I'd hate for you to twist an ankle along the way."

"Amen to that." Carol took the flashlight. "See y'all tomorrow."

Mark waited until they were out of hearing range and chuckled. "I noticed neither of you two reminded them that Julia's car is parked in the yard."

"Nope. I think, either way, Julia was spending the night, so I let it be." Eli smirked. "I didn't want to point out the obvious and ruin a romantic adventure."

"You just wait until I get Carol off to herself tomorrow." Mark grinned.

Laura reached over and smacked him. "You leave them be," she warned.

"Ow, such a brute," Mark cried out.

"Come on, big baby, it's time for us to hit the sack. We got up early, remember?"

"Well, one of us did. The other just dragged herself to the car and went back to sleep."

Eli raised an eyebrow. "Careful, you might end up on the couch."

"You're absolutely right, my honeybunch. Let's go to bed so that these ladies can crash too."

Eli closed the lid on the firepit to choke out the fire. "It's been a long but fantastic day. I am ready for our bed, though." She reached for Whit's hand. "Lead the way, Love Muffin."

†

As it usually did, the last day of the visit passed all too quickly. When Monday morning arrived, Mark snuck back into the house after loading the bag. "The boys are still sleeping, so let them know we love them," Mark whispered.

"No, we're not. We're awake to see you off. Be safe and let us know you make it home okay. Thanks for coming this weekend."

Mark hugged his boys. "Y'all have a grand adventure. I look forward to hearing all about it. Mind what Whit tells you and have fun."

"Yes, sir," they both replied.

"Love you, boys," Laura said and kissed her sons.

"We'll be calling you," Brad said.

"Drive safe." Eli hugged Mark. "Love you most."

"No, way, man." Mark grinned. "Off to the races."

†

"Breakfast or a few more hours of sleep?" Eli asked the group.

Mitch smiled at Eli. "Breakfast, then we can go get Carol some kittens after we finish our chores."

"That sounds like a good plan." She looked at Whit. "You need more sleep?"

"Yes, but my guilty conscience won't allow it if I know y'all are up and working." She started for the kitchen. "I'll start the coffee."

Eli looked at the boys. "Why don't we scramble up a pile of eggs to go with the last of the butt?"

"Sounds good to me," Mitch replied.

"Chicken Master, go get us some fresh eggs, please."

"Yes, ma'am." Brad slipped on a pair of old boots and started toward the coops.

"You might want this," Whit called out and tossed him a collection basket.

"That would help." He smirked and tromped off the porch.

"Mitch, if you grate some of those leftover potatoes, we can have hash browns too," Eli suggested.

"Awesome. I'm on it." Mitch walked to the fridge.

"What can I help with?" Whit asked.

"You're making coffee. You could set the table, but other than that, just continue to look adorable." Eli leaned down to kiss her.

"That's so sweet. I hope you don't expect Brad and I to butter you up like that while we're gone," Mitch teased.

"It might serve you well to take notes," Eli warned him. "Two weeks can be a long time."

"Yes, ma'am. I know."

"Hey, chop some onion, too, for the hash browns, please."

"Got it, Aunt Eli. Just like the Awful Waffle." He smirked.

"The what?" Whit asked.

"Mitch's name for the Waffle House restaurants," Eli explained.

Whit grinned. "Oh, okay then."

Brad came rushing through the door. "Hey, everyone laid an egg today. That's a first."

"You must be doing something right, Chicken Master." Eli took the basket of eggs and placed them on the counter.

"Are we doing toast or bagels or something I can help with?" Brad washed his hands at the sink.

"How about some bagels?" Eli asked.

"Sounds great to me." Whit handed Eli a cup of coffee.

Whit prepared the table, then sat on a stool. She sipped her coffee and watched the three Fortners at work in the kitchen.

Mitch finished chopping some onion and handed Eli a bowl of shredded potatoes and onions. Eli spread some oil on the grill and dumped the vegetables, then gave Mitch the bowl. "Will you rinse this and crack a dozen eggs for me?" She scattered the potatoes and seasoned them.

"I'm all over it," Mitch said.

Brad steadily toasted bagels and slathered them with butter as they popped up. Eli looked at him. "Reach up and turn the microwave on for ten minutes to heat the meat, please."

"Mmm, mmm, this is gonna be a fantastic breakfast," Eli said, as she poured the eggs onto the grill.

Whit piped in from her seat. "My mouth is already watering."

"Hand me a couple of the large serving bowls." Eli pointed out the cabinet to Mitch.

"White sauce is a given, but does anyone want ketchup or any other condiment?" Whit asked, as she walked to the fridge.

"I'll take some and jelly, too, for the bagels," Brad said.

"Grape or apple cinnamon?"

"Silly question, Whit. I've given up all other jellies since we made the apple cinnamon."

"I think we'd better smuggle a jar into a pack." Whit winked at him.

"That's a marvelous idea. Will we have any bread to spread it on?"

Whit nodded. "When we arrive at our drop site, we can hit a grocery store and pick something up. We could toast some over the fire, and they might last a few days in Ziplocs."

"Maybe do some biscuits too and stuff them with sausage?" Mitch asked.

"Canned biscuits in a frying pan should be easy." Whit smiled. "We can also eat a big meal while we're off the trail, some burgers or pizza. Something loaded with tons of carbs for energy."

Mitch grinned. "We'll probably need some by then."

"Most definitely. I think we'll all lose a few pounds on this trip," Whit replied.

"I'll fatten y'all back up when you come off the trail," Eli promised.

"I still have about fifteen more pounds I'd like to lose." Mitch patted his stomach.

"I think you will lose the quickest, simply because you are bigger and will burn more calories," Whit warned him. She saw a concerned look on Eli's face. "Don't worry, Mama Bear, we'll be eating good, just not our usual home-cooked meals."

"I don't cherish the thought of any of y'all being hungry when I'm pigging out at the diner." Eli chuckled.

"If we are hungry, it will be because we chose not to eat. I don't see that happening with these two."

"Ha! Not a chance," Mitch said. "Three meals and snacks along the trail."

"See. No worries. We'll catch some fish along the way and forage to supplement what we carry."

Eli flipped the hash browns to get them crispy, then placed the eggs in a serving bowl. "Almost done," she said.

The timer on the microwave dinged. "We need another serving bowl, please, Mitch." Brad removed the steaming container of meat. "Man, this smells awesome."

"Who wants juice?" Whit asked.

A chorus of "apple" came from the kitchen.

When they placed the final bowls of food on the table, they took their seats. "Dig in," Eli said, as she took a bagel and passed the plate.

CHAPTER TWELVE

As they drove north, Eli was amazed at the beautiful colors of the passing landscapes. "I bet the colors in the fall up here are brilliant," she remarked.

Whit nodded. "They're stunning in October and sometimes early November, depending on the weather. Maybe we can make a drive up this year. You can witness them for yourself."

"I'd like that." Eli entwined her fingers with Whit's.

Mitch piped in from the back seat, "It is pretty spectacular up here. My ears sure have been popping. Will we continue to be increasing elevation?"

"Only for a little while, and the landscape will flatten back out. Do you need some chewing gum?" Eli asked.

"Naw, I'm good. It takes too long to pick it out of my braces." Mitch grinned.

Eli smiled at him in the rearview mirror. "I keep forgetting about that. We'll stop for lunch soon. Anything particular you want to eat?"

"Food and lots of it," Brad chimed in.

"Hey, I didn't realize you'd rejoined the land of the living, sleeping beauty. Will you guys jump on your phones and see what options we have coming up?"

"We'd love to, Aunt Eli."

"Is it going to take us two days of driving to get there?" Brad asked.

Whit turned around in her seat. "Two long days. It's a twenty-three-hour drive. That's if we don't hit construction or any major hang-ups."

Brad's eyebrow shot upward. "I guess I didn't realize how far it was to drive."

"We can cut it down to eight hours of driving if that's better for y'all," Eli suggested.

"That's entirely up to you, Aunt Eli. You're doing the driving," Mitch replied.

Eli let Whit decide. "Our permits for Mt. Katahdin aren't until Sunday," Whit mused. "We could scale back the driving. Stop and play tourist if you see something you want to explore a bit."

"That sounds good to me," Eli said. "We'll need to modify our hotel reservations for tonight and tomorrow."

Whit grinned at her. "I can do that while you're driving. I'll find a good stopping point for today and make arrangements, then we can decide on tomorrow's stop later."

"Works for me," Eli replied.

†

Two days later, they crossed over into Maine. Midafternoon, Eli turned on her blinker as she approached a turn. "Where are we going?" Mitch asked from the back seat.

Eli made the turn heading toward Millinocket, Maine. "The Appalachian Trail Lodge is our last stop before we reach our final destination. It's also where your resupply package will be waiting for y'all."

"That's where we're staying tonight?" Mitch asked.

"Yes, we've got a family suite reserved. I thought we could check in and scope out the town. That way, you'll know what resources are in town when you arrive to resupply."

"You know, I was just thinking of something we have forgotten about," Whit said.

"What?" Brad asked.

"We have to come up with our trail names."

Mitch looked at her, confused. "What trail names?"

"Every hiker creates a name, or someone gives them one while they're on the trail. It's been a tradition for generations. You introduce yourself and write log entries as your trail name."

"That's freaking cool," Mitch said. "Since you're our leader, will you give us names?"

Eli looked at Whit, who was smiling broadly.

"Let me think about it for a bit," Whit said.

"I've also prepaid a night for y'all to spend here, to get a hot shower, meal, some clean laundry, and a good night's sleep. You'll be halfway through the Hundred Mile Wilderness when you reach this point, and I'm sure you'll be ready for all three by the time you get here."

Whit looked at Eli. "We don't have any idea when we'll be here."

Eli shook her head. "It doesn't matter. Your room will be prepaid no matter when you arrive."

"That was very thoughtful of you," Whit replied.

"The town caters to hikers, since it's a popular stop for both north and southbound hikers. It's the first bit of civilization you'll see once you enter the Hundred Mile Wilderness, and it's the last resupply stop for a northbound hiker before they enter Baxter Park on the way to Mt. Katahdin."

"Someone's been doing some research," Mitch said.

"Yes, yes I have." Eli chuckled.

As they rolled into town, Mitch and Brad sat up when they saw how many hikers were wandering around. "I wouldn't have thought so many hikers would be in one spot like this," Brad said.

"Some are probably just coming in from the trail and some heading back out," Whit suggested. "There's no hard and fast rules about stops on the trail. You could spend a short time here to resupply or spend several days, depending on your finances and schedule."

"I would think one night would be enough," Mitch said.

"Probably so, but we all might change our minds once we've spent a week or more on the trail," Whit told them. "This is our trip, traveling at a pace that is comfortable for us. There's no race, no deadline. Our only mission is to have fun and enjoy the great outdoors."

"Now you're beginning to sound like a commercial," Brad teased.

Eli broke out laughing. "That was a good one, Brad." She pulled the truck to a stop in front of the lodge. "Here we are. Let's go inside and get checked in. Brad, can you help Mitch with your supply boxes? Whit and I will get the overnight bags."

Within minutes, Eli had them checked in and had the supply boxes stored for their arrival. "Whit Brewer," the woman behind the counter read. "No trail names yet?" She smiled.

"Not yet, but I'm thinking about them," Whit said.

"If you come up with them before you leave, I'll add them to the boxes. If not, that's no problem either."

"Thanks," Whit said. "I'll keep that in mind."

"They've also got a family suite prepaid for their supply stop," Eli mentioned. "Is there any better day of the week for them to shoot for to ensure they have a room?"

The woman waved a hand toward Eli. "Naw, most hikers stay in the bunk room. It's more of a hostel environment that the younger hikers love, and it's cheaper on their budgets. The suites are hardly ever full." She smiled at Eli. "I take it you're not joining the adventure?"

"Not this time around, but maybe one day," Eli answered.

"My name is Shirley, and I'll be around all night. Give me a call if you need anything. You all planning to scout out the town this afternoon?"

"Yes, ma'am," Mitch said.

"Aw, I do love those southern accents and good manners. Where are you from?"

"Alabama and soon to be North Carolina, when I move up with Aunt Eli after I graduate," Mitch answered proudly.

"That sounds like a grand adventure in itself." Shirley gave him a warm smile. "Have fun today. I won't be here when you check out tomorrow. Have a safe and fun trip, and I'll see you when you come in to resupply."

"Yes, ma'am." Mitch took the bag from Whit, and they climbed the stairs to the suite.

†

When they entered the room, Eli was impressed with the size and amenities. She looked at Mitch and Brad. "Are you ready to stretch your legs a bit?"

"Let's do it," Brad said. "I can't wait to get outside."

"Go ahead. I need to use the restroom, but I'll join y'all in a minute."

Whit kissed Eli. "See you soon."

They walked around town to stretch their legs, and when Mitch saw a group of young people making a beeline for a small diner, he looked at Eli. "That's where we need to eat."

"Sounds good to me. I hope there's food left," Eli said.

As the group approached, they could smell the enticing aromas. Whit sniffed the air. "That's what is calling to everyone. The smell alone is delicious."

Eli nodded. "I'd have to agree with you. Let's find out what it is."

They were lucky enough to get a table next to the group that had led them inside. "What's good here?" Mitch asked.

"Anything and everything," a young man answered. "This is one of the best spots in town and not hard on your wallet, either. I think I'm having at least one of the Philly cheese steak sandwiches. They are off the chain."

"Is that what smells so good?" Eli asked.

"That and their fried chicken, but they call it broasted up here. Still fried to me." The young man shrugged.

Whit was studying the menu. "They've got a good selection of high protein foods, great for hikers."

The waitress came and took their orders. Mitch started a conversation with the young man at the next table.

"Are y'all hiking together?"

"Yes, we've been on the trail for about two months. We did the first part of the AT northbound over the last two summers, and we've come together to finish this year. I'm Count Chocula, by the way." He grinned.

"Nice to meet you. I'm Mitch, my brother Brad, and Aunts Whit and Eli. Three of us are starting the southbound journey tomorrow."

"Getting the worst part over first, huh? I'm Samurai," a dark-haired young woman said. She reached over and shook Mitch's hand.

"We thought we'd try to tough out the first two weeks up here," Whit replied.

"That's cool. We're all from the south, so we started from Springer two summers ago," Samurai replied.

"Did you all know each other before?" Mitch asked.

"Heck no, we met each other on the trail, usually in pairs or three of us, until we grew to this group of eight. Some of us are from Georgia, Alabama, Tennessee, but we all committed to finishing together."

"Brad and I are from Alabama," Mitch offered.

"I'm from Mobile, and I go to Auburn," she replied.

"We haven't learned our trail names yet," Mitch said. "How did you come up with Samurai and Count Chocula?"

"I have an obsession with the cereal, and every time we resupply, I get a box or two."

"That makes sense." Mitch turned to Samurai. "And you?"

"On our second day of hiking, I used my walking stick to fight off a skunk. My brother, Wolfie"—she pointed at a smiling young man—"said I looked like a Samurai, wielding my stick like a sword." She looked at Mitch. "Don't sweat a trail name. It'll come along the path. Heck, it may even change a few times."

When the food arrived, the groups began to eat. Samurai looked up at Mitch. "Hey, are y'all staying at the lodge?"

"Yeah, we are."

"We're sleeping down in the bunkhouse. Why don't you two join us tonight, and we can share some of our trail stories?"

Mitch's face lit with a smile. "That would be awesome. What time?"

Samurai looked at her watch. "Seven would give us all time to shower before we head out in the morning."

"We'll be there," Mitch replied.

Eli leaned over to Whit. "I guess you're stuck with the old lady."

"That is perfect for me," Whit whispered back. She grinned and took a bite of her Philly cheese steak. "Damn, you weren't kidding about the food."

Chocula smiled. "It's the last great hot meal until we reach Mt. Katahdin and come off the trail. We'll probably have seconds and dessert to recharge."

Mitch looked at Eli. "You heard the man. Eat your fill." She grinned.

The boys took her at her word and had seconds, then a brownie and ice cream dessert. "I'm going to be dreaming of that brownie for days," Brad said.

"We will definitely eat here on our way south," Whit added. "That was an awesome meal."

"I'm glad we're walking back." Eli groaned as they left the table.

When they entered the room, Eli asked, "Mitch, do you guys want to shower before going down to the bunkhouse?"

Mitch nodded. "That's probably not a bad idea. What time are we heading out in the morning?"

"Early, like five," Whit answered. "I'd like to be on the trail by the time the sun comes up. Even going up Saddle Trail will take us ten to twelve hours for the round trip."

"I reckon we shouldn't stay out long tonight then," Brad said.

Whit nodded. "No, you need a good night's rest. What Samurai said was true. We are starting our journey with a challenging climb. Some hikers abort their trip after climbing Katahdin."

"I'd hate to have to cancel after coming all this way," Mitch said.

"Me too, but it happens all the time. Some people take for granted how strenuous hiking can be. It's not for the weak of heart," Whit warned.

Eli noted the solemn look on Mitch's face. "I wouldn't be disappointed in any of you if you choose to cancel the trip. If it isn't fun for you, I don't want you to feel pressured to go."

"I don't want to fail," Mitch replied.

Eli reached over and ruffled his hair. "There is no pass or fail here. The trip is an opportunity for adventure, but if you're not ready, you don't have to go."

"I want to go, but I'd be lying if I said I wasn't a little scared," he admitted.

Whit stepped in to hug him. "We are stepping outside of our comfort zones. It is a bit scary, but the three of us have each other to lean on. If you get tired or hungry and need to stop, I expect both of you to speak up. Lord knows I'm going to." She looked at Brad. "Are we in agreement then?"

Brad nodded. "Yes, ma'am," they said together.

"Good, now get your butt in the shower so you can go have some fun, and us old ladies can rest," Whit instructed them. "We've got our day packs in the truck, so we can wake up, dress, and be gone. If y'all want to sleep on the way, that's fine too."

Mitch grinned. "I don't want to miss a minute of this." He looked at Brad. "You go first since you take the longest."

"On my way," Brad replied.

Eli called to him. "Hey, no singing in the shower either. It's too late to find another room."

"I'm not that bad," Brad said.

"Right." Mitch tossed a towel at Brad. "Hurry, we have stories to hear."

Mitch sat on the edge of his bed, while Whit stretched out and Eli took a chair. "You know," Eli said. "I'm probably more scared of being at home alone than anything."

Mitch chuckled. "You won't be alone. You've got Cruz, Molly, the herd of cats, and chickens to keep you company. Carol's just a shout away, too."

"It's not the same as having the three of you in the house. I'll hear every little creak in the floor. It'll be so quiet."

Whit propped up on an elbow. "It's not too late for you to join us."

"Ha! I know my limits. I'm in no shape to take on Katahdin. I'll be with y'all in spirit on every step you take."

Mitch tapped his chest. "You'll be right here with us."

Eli cocked her head. "Dammit, Mitch, stop it. You're going to make my eyes leak."

Whit and Mitch broke out laughing. "Don't you join in too, Whit," she warned.

Whit did her best to put on a serious face. "So," she changed subjects. "Are you going to be okay setting up camp for us while we climb Katahdin?"

"Yep, I think I can handle that. I'll get the tents set up and pick up some wood for the firepit. I'll find something hearty for y'all to eat when you return. Twelve hours huh?"

"Worst case scenario. I'm hoping we can do a little better than that, but if not, that's fine too. We've got headlamps in our daypacks."

"Will you try to stop before dark each day on the trail?" Eli asked.

Whit nodded. "Most definitely. I'd like to have camp set and dinner underway by the time night comes."

"Good." Eli stretched her legs out in front of her.

†

When Mitch and Brad had showered, Eli had decided to join Whit on the bed. They were watching television, when

Mitch announced they were heading out. "Have fun, and don't be too late," Eli said.

"Yes, ma'am. We'll see you in a while."

"Are you really interested in television?" Eli asked.

Whit shook her head. "No, I just had it on for the weather news. Is there something on your mind?"

"I was just curious about the trail names. Have you come up with anything yet?"

"I think I have. Mine is easy. Either Star Child or Stargazer."

"Stargazer is self-explanatory and wouldn't require as much clarification," Eli said.

"Good point. I was thinking of Jester for Brad, since he's such a clown."

"Ain't that the truth. Jester is good. What about Mitch?"

"I'm struggling with Mitch. I thought of Bama Hobo, but that just doesn't sound right."

"Hmm, he loves to fish, hunt, basically anything outdoors," Eli said. "One of his favorite movies is *Top Gun*, so why not Maverick?"

"Yeah, I like that."

†

When Mitch and Brad entered the bunkhouse, they were surprised to find so many hikers. Samurai looked up to see them enter. "Over here, guys," she called to them.

Mitch and Brad joined the group. "Care for a soda?" Chocula asked. "You won't have any more once you hit the trail."

"You have two Mountain Dews?" Brad asked.

"But of course." Samurai handed them each a bottle of soda.

"So, what's your first bit of advice for two newbies?" Mitch asked.

Samurai was the first to answer. "Have fun, and don't take life on the trail so seriously. If you find a spot you like, don't be in a rush to leave."

"Monitor your food intake, so you have plenty until your next drop," Wolfie added. "I thought Samurai and I would starve our first week on the trail."

"That's right. We ate so much those first few days, because we were starving," Samurai smiled at her brother.

Chocula added. "Change clothes regularly, especially your socks, every day. Keeping your feet healthy is critical to a happy hike." He nodded and continued. "There will be creeks and lakes, but the water is cold as ice, even in midsummer. Take advantage of them to keep your feet clean and whatever you can tolerate washing."

Mitch asked. "We've got some light fly rods. Any chance of catching some fish along the trail?"

"Most definitely," Wolfie answered. "The rods are a good idea, but I think I'd only take one. That's less weight to pack. Better to pack another food or clothing item instead."

Samurai nodded her agreement. "Last year, we built a fish trap. We didn't catch anything, but it was fun trying. A couple of the guys did spear a few, so we ended up with some fish."

"Have you run across anything dangerous or that scared you?" Brad asked.

"You will see a bunch of wildlife if you travel quietly. For the most part, the animals aren't aggressive unless provoked. Especially if they have babies." Wolfie smiled. "I've been blessed to see a few wild wolves and had them answer my calls. That alone was worth the journey."

"What about other hikers? Anyone spooky out there?" Mitch asked.

"With the size of our pack, I don't think anyone would cause us any problems. You will probably run across a solo hiker or two that may seem a bit out there, but we've never run into anyone to be afraid of if that's what you're asking."

"Yeah, Samurai, it was," Mitch answered.

"You guys plan to hike for two weeks, right?" Wolfie asked.

"That's the plan," Brad replied.

"We'll cross paths again as y'all are coming south, and we're heading north. Probably somewhere toward the end of the Hundred Mile Wilderness for us," Wolfie said. "We can plan to spend a night together if the timing is right."

"Even if it's not," Samurai said. "I'm in no hurry for this adventure to end."

"That sounds great," Mitch said. "Will there be other treks for your group?"

"Most of us are still in college, so maybe we can do one more trail before reality sets in, and we have to do the adulting thing," Chocula said with a laugh.

"I bet you've had a lot of great memories to share. Do you stay in contact after your hikes?" Brad asked.

"Absolutely. We try to get together at least once a year during school breaks, and we talk on social media all the time," Samurai said. "Just look us up by our trail names. Be sure to sign in the logbooks at the camp shelters when you can. It's your way of leaving a mark on the history of the trail."

"That sounds pretty cool," Brad said.

Wolfie nudged Brad. "Don't be surprised if your name changes along the way. You may have something happen that brings out a new name. I read about a guy that got called Banana Split because he wore yellow shorts, and on his second day on the trail, he split his shorts."

Mitch broke out laughing. "Are you serious?"

"Cross my heart." Wolfie made a cross over his chest.

"That is too funny." Mitch took a drink of the soda. After another hour of listening to trail stories, he and Brad decided to call it a night. "We'll see you on the trail soon," he said as they left the bunkhouse."

"Happy trails." Samurai shot him a wink.

"You too," Mitch said, with a blush creeping up his neck.

†

"Last chance for a hot shower," Eli said, as she woke them the next morning.

Whit was packing their sleep clothes in a bag. "It's time to rise and shine hikers." She shook Brad awake.

Brad groaned, then seemed to remember it was the big day. "I'm ready, just let me pee and brush my teeth."

"Okay, we'll take our bag down and meet you at the truck," Eli said.

"Four thirty." Mitch looked at his watch. "What happened to five?"

"We wanted to give you an opportunity for one last shower." Eli smiled. "We can grab a bag of biscuits on the road."

Mitch returned her smile. "That will always get me moving."

†

When they reached the ranger station, Whit walked inside to pick up their permits and pay for the campsite Eli had reserved. When she returned, she climbed in the truck and waved the papers. "We are official." She turned to Eli. "The campsite is number fifteen, one half mile ahead on the left. You can drop us off at the trailhead, and we can start our journey."

Eli felt her heart racing, as she followed Whit's directions and pulled into a parking spot at the trailhead. Mitch and Brad climbed out of the truck and grabbed their day packs. Mitch stuffed the leftover biscuits in his, and they all filled their canteens. "I need to get a picture," Eli said. "Over there, by the trail sign," she said.

The sun was just beginning to crest the horizon as she snapped off several pictures. "Y'all have fun and be safe. I'll see you at the campsite tonight." She hugged each of them and gave Whit a soft kiss. "Take care of each other."

"Yes, Mama Bear," Brad teased.

Eli waved them away. "Go git, before I change my mind and take you back home."

Brad and Mitch started up the trail. Whit smiled and waved to Eli and followed the boys into the early morning light.

Eli watched until they disappeared, then climbed into the truck. She had a lot to do before they returned. She drove back to the campground and began setting up camp.

CHAPTER THIRTEEN

An hour into the climb, Mitch stopped and looked back at Whit and Brad. "I don't know about you guys, but I need a break."

"I was about to suggest one," Whit said, as she caught up to Mitch. They sat together on a couple of boulders.

"I'm kind of surprised we haven't seen any other hikers," Mitch said.

"I catch a glimpse of a pair every now and then, a couple hundred yards ahead of us," Brad said.

"We got a good start this morning," Whit said. "We'll probably pass a lot more on the way back down."

"We've got to get there first," Mitch said. "There's still a long way. I can't even see the top yet."

"You will as the morning mist burns off," Whit said. "I'm glad we packed some light jackets. It's getting cooler the higher we climb."

"I'm still sweating up a storm," Mitch said. "Should I put a hoodie on, so I don't get a chill?"

"That's not a bad idea," Whit agreed. "Once the sun starts warming us, we can remove them."

Brad pulled his hoodie out of the bag and pulled it over his head. "Ah, this feels better already."

"Everyone good? Or do you need more time?" Whit asked.

Mitch took another drink. "I'm good."

"Let's continue then. I think we're making decent time."

Mitch rose and continued to lead the way. When they crested a rise, he stopped and stared out across the beautiful skyline. "Is that beautiful or what?" he asked.

The sky had turned a robin's egg blue, and billowing clouds coasted on the thermals. Whit thought they could see for miles. "It is breathtaking." She looked at her watch. "We should probably have a snack before moving on. I've got bananas if anyone wants one."

"That should help my leg cramps," Brad said.

"More water, too," Mitch added. "I didn't expect this to be so tough."

Whit nodded. "We're almost halfway to the top. I won't promise you it will get any easier, but we can do this."

Each of them ate two bananas, and Whit placed the peels in a plastic bag. "Ready to roll on?" she asked.

†

Far below the mountain, Eli scurried around to set up camp. She purchased two firewood bundles from the ranger's station, got a number for a food delivery service, and placed an order for delivery at five. They would deliver the cheeseburgers in a thermal bag that she could drop off at the ranger's station on her way out the next day. Content with the arrangements, Eli placed four camp chairs around the firepit and returned to the truck for her next project. Eli pulled out a blanket-wrapped bundle from behind the back seat and an extension cord. She plugged in a wood-burning tool and opened up the blanket. Eli pulled Whit's walking stick out first and burned *Stargazer* into the wood. Then she sprayed the entire shaft with a clear polyurethane coat and hung it from a nearby branch to dry. Eli took Mitch's black stick out next and settled into her seat. She repeated the process and was delighted with the way *Maverick* shined against the blackened surface. Her activity drew the attention of a woman who was camping next to them. Eli looked up to see her walking over.

"Hello," the woman said. "I've been watching you for an hour, and I just had to come and investigate what you were doing over here. My name is Grace."

"Nice to meet you, Grace. I'm Eli. My girlfriend and my two nephews are starting their southbound journey today. I thought I'd make them a walking stick to send them on their way."

Grace looked at the two sticks hanging from the tree branch. "These are gorgeous. I see you have one more. Would you mind if I watched?"

Eli pointed to a chair. "Have a seat."

"Thanks. Did you do all the work on these?"

"Yeah, I did. It's a surprise that I've been working on for a while. Whit just decided on their trail names last night, so I thought I'd burn them into the sticks today while they tackle the mountain."

Grace smiled. "That's a great idea."

Eli picked up Brad's stick and began burning. "Are you hiking?"

"I will be. I'm waiting on my partner to drive in from Boston. We're only doing Mt. Katahdin. We wanted to start here while we had a long weekend. We're both educators, and we have a two-week trip scheduled at the end of the month."

"That's the hardest climb from what I've heard," Eli said.

"You aren't going to hike with them?"

"No, not this go 'round. I'm the support convoy," Eli laughed.

"I can understand that. Suzy, my partner, is not overly excited. I think she's secretly hoping Mt. Katahdin will scare me away from wanting to do more of the AT."

Eli smiled. "I don't think that will happen with my crew. They have been talking about this hike for a couple of months. The boys especially."

"I think it's a fabulous experience for young people. I wish I had gotten the bug earlier. It will be a good lesson for them on independence, and if they are like most teens, a nice break from video games."

Eli continued to work as they chatted. "Mitch and Brad have been with me in North Carolina most of the summer. By the time we finish our chores for the day, video games are the furthest thing from their mind." She smiled at Grace. "My partner, Whit, is a genius and has taught them so much.

They've installed solar panels and have my farm entirely off the grid. They've learned to use a chainsaw mill to make lumber, build things from a bridge across the creek to benches and picnic tables." She paused a moment and looked up. "Brad, the youngest, is our chicken master. We built portable chicken coops, and he's raising two dozen laying hens."

"I can tell you are proud of all three of them."

"Most definitely. Mitch and Brad have both grown into young men this summer. Oh, and they love to fly fish, which is perfect. We have a creek bordering both sides of the property, so they keep several families well stocked with trout."

"Sounds like a little piece of heaven," Grace said.

"If you and Suzy continue to hike, you can stop in and see us. There is a trail shelter just above our property line. We're outside Ashville a bit, but it's a beautiful section of the country. Our leaves will begin changing soon, and they make the mountains glow with brilliance." Eli finished burning Brad's trail name into the wood, sprayed it, and hung it with the others.

Grace smiled at Eli. "Those came out very nice. Maybe we can work on making our own if we choose to do more hiking."

"They have been a fun project. Nothing was too strenuous, and it's a perfect rainy-day project."

Grace's cell phone rang, and she gave Suzy directions to the campsite. When she arrived, Grace and Eli stood and welcomed her. "Eli's partner and her two nephews are tackling the mountain today. You've got to see what she's made them for their journey on the trail." Grace led Suzy over to look at the walking sticks.

Suzy turned and looked back at Eli. "These are beautiful. I love how you've seared the wood on the black one. Was it hard?"

Eli shook her head. "Not at all. A small propane torch and some patience were all it took."

"Look." Grace pointed out the names. "She even burned their trail names into the shafts."

"I reckon that's something we need to consider if we're going to climb this monster." Suzy turned her eyes toward the mountain.

"Have you checked on their progress? I've got binoculars if you want to take a look." Suzy smiled.

"Thanks, I've got a pair in the truck. I've resisted the temptation to call and check on them. I don't want to interrupt their experience." She looked at her watch. "They should be high enough to see by now. I'll be right back."

Eli walked to the truck and returned with her binoculars. She moved away from trees and began to focus on the mountain.

"What trail did they choose?" Suzy asked, as they joined Eli.

"Saddle Trail," Eli answered.

Suzy smiled. "Good choice. How long have they been gone?"

"A little over three hours."

"They're probably close to Chimney Pond." Suzy pointed in the direction Eli should be looking. "They will only have about an hour left once they reach the split."

Eli used the binoculars to scan the mountain but did not locate any hikers she recognized. She tried again for several minutes, then bounced on her feet. "Found 'em," she said. "They've moved past the pond."

Suzy let out of soft whistle. "Wow, they're making good time."

†

When they reached Chimney Pond, Whit called them to a halt. "We need to eat something before we take on this last section. Mitch, pull out the biscuits. I've got some honey packs we can use to give us a boost of energy."

Mitch placed his pack on a rock and began to pull out the food. Whit pulled out a Ziploc bag of honey packets. "How are you guys feeling?"

Brad gladly took a seat on one of the rocks. "My legs feel like Jell-O, but I'm having a blast."

"Good. Take some pictures while Mitch and I get lunch ready."

"Yes, ma'am," he answered. "I've tried to snap a few, but I was more worried about where my feet were going. That loose rock was slippery."

"Yeah, it was. I bet we hit more scree before we get to the top." Mitch pointed up the trail above them. "It's nice to see the summit, finally."

"Objects in the mirror are closer than they appear," Whit said.

"What?" Mitch asked.

"I don't know where that came from, but I was thinking of the decals they put on sideview mirrors, warning drivers that objects are closer than they seem. I know the sign says half a mile, but it's going to be a rugged half mile."

Mitch grinned at her. "For a moment, I thought you were getting delusional on us."

"Heck, I might be. Pass me one of those biscuits." Whit smiled back at Mitch.

"You can see for miles from up here." Brad snapped a few pictures.

"I think we need to send some to Dad," Mitch said.

"I'm all over it." Brad sent Mark several pictures in a text. "Still sending." He groaned after twenty seconds. He accepted the biscuit Mitch offered him and took a bite. "They aren't as good as yours, but right now, they taste fantastic."

"I wonder what Aunt Eli has planned for supper tonight?" Mitch said.

"I've got no idea, but I hope there's a lot of it," Whit replied. "We've burned a bunch of calories today, and we're not down yet."

"Do we have more biscuits?" Brad asked, having wolfed the first one down.

Whit nodded. "Yes, enough for one more each. I've got apples, too, if anyone wants one."

"Any peanut butter in that bag of yours?" Brad asked.

"Is the Pope Catholic?" Whit handed him a container of peanut butter.

"Thanks." Brad ripped the top off the container. He pulled out his sodbuster and sliced the apple. "Anyone else want an apple sliced?"

"You can do mine, please," Whit answered. She handed another apple to him, then pulled out two more containers of peanut butter. She squeezed the last of her honey into an open container. "Good to the last drop," she told them. "Everyone good on water?"

"Yes, I've got a full canteen left."

Brad nodded. "Me too."

"I've got a couple of extra bottles if we need them." Whit smiled and tossed her garbage in a plastic bag.

"You've hauled all the extras up for us today. Why didn't you share the load?" Mitch asked.

"I wanted the extra weight in my day pack. I didn't have a couple of days on the trail with a full pack like you two did."

"That makes sense, I guess, but I don't mind taking on extra," Mitch told her.

"Me either," Brad chimed into the conversation.

"I'm certain you will both have ample opportunity to carry more than your share of the load." Whit smiled at them. "Are we ready for the push to the top?"

"Yeah, I need to get moving. I'm starting to get cool from this breeze," Brad replied.

"It has dropped as we've gone higher, and the velocity has picked up too," Mitch said. "You don't think it will snow, do you?"

"I don't think so, but you never know. Anything is possible at this elevation. Only one way to find out."

†

"They look like they're moving pretty well," Eli said.

"I hope they take time to enjoy the view from the summit. It's supposed to be spectacular and it is an accomplishment to do the climb. More than a hike, it's a climb over boulders and across slippery scree fields."

"Have you been there?" Eli asked Grace.

"Only in my dreams, but I've read everything I can get my hands on and watched several videos on the climb."

Suzy placed an arm around her shoulder. "Tomorrow, that dream comes true."

Grace smiled at her. "I know. I'm scared, but I can hardly wait."

Suzy pulled her close. "We will be just fine. If we finish, we finish. If not, we regroup and try again."

Eli shrugged. "I'm sure not everyone succeeds on the first attempt at Mt. Katahdin, but as Suzy said, you can always try again. No shame in that game."

Suzy kissed Grace's cheek. "I drove straight through, so I'm starving. Would you ladies like to go grab a bite?"

Grace looked at Eli with a raised brow. "Will you join us?"

"Can you give me a minute? I want to try out the phone service."

"Do you think she'll have cell service?" Suzy asked.

Eli shook her head. "Maybe not, but she has a satellite phone that we hope will have a better chance of reception."

"That's a good idea. We can wait. Take what time you want. We can get Suzy unloaded."

Eli nodded and pulled out her phone. She pressed the button to dial the satellite phone number and lifted the binoculars to her face. It took several seconds for the phone to ring. Eli's eyes scanned the mountain for her crew. She smiled when she saw Whit stop and turn her back for Mitch to dig out the phone.

"Joe's Pizza, how can I help you?" Mitch said.

"I'd like an extra-large pizza with all the toppings you can put on it," Eli answered.

"Dang, that sounds good. Hiya, Aunt Eli."

"Hey, Mitch. I wanted to see if you had any phone reception up there."

"Excellent service. I can hear you loud and clear."

"How's the hike going? Everyone doing okay?"

"It's been more climbing than hiking, but we're close enough we can see the summit."

"Tell Brad to wave."

"Hey bro, Aunt Eli says to wave."

Eli smiled, when she saw Brad jumping up and down, waving his arms."

"You can tell him he doesn't have to jump up and down. I see him."

"You're watching us? I feel stalked," Mitch teased.

"I'm checking on your progress. Are you having fun?"

"Yes, ma'am. We're going to be sore tomorrow, but it'll be worth it. You want to talk to Love Muffin?"

"Yes, please hand her the phone." Eli waited. "Hey sweetie, how is everything going?"

"Good. We've got another half an hour or so to the top."

"Y'all have made excellent progress. I'm impressed. I just wanted to test out the phone and check on y'all. Glad you're having fun. I'll see y'all when you get back."

"Okay, we'll take some pictures and send them when we reach the summit. We'll rest for a bit there, eat a snack, and start back down."

"You've got plenty of daylight left, so enjoy the trip. Love you."

"Love you too. The boys are making googly eyes at me, but they love you too. See you soon. Oh, have lots of food. We're going to be starving."

"I've got you covered. Stay safe."

"Bye."

Eli smiled at the excitement in their voices. It was apparent they were having a great day. She tucked her phone back into the holster and walked over to meet her new friends. "It worked well." She grinned.

"That's excellent news. We may need to consider purchasing one as well if we continue to hike," Grace said.

"I'll drive," Suzy said and started walking to her SUV.

"Somebody must be hungry," Grace said.

Suzy nodded. "My stomach has been growling for an hour."

†

"Oh, my word." Whit stood at the summit and turned a full 360 degrees. "Would you look at these views?"

"It's gorgeous up here," Mitch said. "Look, there's still some snow on those mountains."

"I'm surprised there's none here," Brad said. "That wind cuts me to the bone."

"There is a massive difference at this elevation versus the campground. I'm glad we don't have to sleep up here tonight," Whit said.

"That makes two of us," Brad said.

"Do you want my jacket, bro?" Mitch asked.

"If you're not going to put it on, yeah, please."

"I've got more insulation than you." Mitch pulled his jacket from his pack.

"Let's get busy and take some pictures, sign the logbook, and we can head back down," Whit said. The three of them took several photographs, and a young couple took pictures of the three of them together. Whit returned the favor, and they walked over to the camp shelter. Brad located the logbook and looked at Whit. "We can't do this."

"Why not?" Whit asked as she pulled out an ink pen.

"We don't have trail names yet," Brad said.

"Yes, we do. Yours is Jester since you're such a clown," she said and handed Brad the pen.

"What's mine?" Mitch asked.

"Maverick from *Top Gun*." Whit grinned.

"Heck yeah, that's one of my favorite movies," Mitch exclaimed. "Maverick, I can get used to that."

"What's yours?" Brad asked.

"Eli picked mine. Stargazer."

"That fits you well," Mitch said.

"So, what do we put?" Brad asked.

Whit smiled at him. "Your name, where you're from, and today's date for starters. Then anything else you want to say."

Brad scribbled in the book, then handed Mitch the pen. Mitch wrote for a minute before returning the pen to Whit. She looked at their entries. Brad had written *This is a cool place*. Mitch had written *Starting an awesome adventure with Jester and Stargazer*. Whit thought for a second. *Life gets better with every step on the trail. Good company, great memories, and much fun to come*. She tucked the pen into her pack. "Are we ready to head back down?"

"Yeah, I'm starting to get chilled," Mitch said.

"Text Eli that we're starting back down, please. I'm not sure if she'll get it, but it's worth a shot."

"Done," Mitch said.

†

"I almost feel guilty eating this." Eli took a bite of pizza.

"We could take a couple of pies back with us," Suzy said.

"I've already made arrangements to have bacon cheeseburgers delivered at five," Eli said. "I know two boys who will be ravenous when they arrive. Even Whit said she would be starving. They must be burning some major calories."

"I bet they're pushing ten thousand calories with all the climbing," Grace said.

Eli's phone pinged with a text message. She opened it to see a picture of the three of them and a note from Mitch. *On our way back down. See you soon.* She smiled. "They're on their way back down." She typed *Be safe. Love you!*

"They look cold." Eli turned her phone to show Grace and Suzy the photo.

"It's much colder at the higher elevation," Grace said. "It could be twenty degrees cooler with the wind chill. They look like they're having fun."

"Yes, they do. I can imagine Brad talking most of the way back down." Eli looked at her watch. "The food should arrive at near the same time they return. That was a good guess."

"I've got a coffee pot that we can put on the firepit to heat some water for hot chocolate," Suzy said. "We can stop at the store for the mix and some Styrofoam cups."

Eli nodded. "That is a great idea, especially if they get chilled on the way down. I would think the temp drops with the sunset."

"Yeah, it does. A nice fire in the pit will help to warm the hikers too," Grace said. "You picked up some firewood, right?"

Eli nodded. "Two large bundles. I'll probably need to start a fire about four thirty to get it burning hot."

Suzy nodded. "We can put the water on to heat, too. That way, it will be ready when they arrive."

"Would you mind if we join you? I'd love to hear the story of their adventure," Grace said.

"The more, the merrier," Eli told them. "Just drag a chair over and join us."

Suzy boxed up the leftovers and took them back to camp. They stopped for supplies, and Eli added ingredients for s'mores to have something sweet after dinner.

†

Descending the mountain wasn't as easy as Mitch had assumed. "Even going down is tough," he told Whit on their first break. "It's a little faster but still wears on your muscles. You may need to pry me out of bed tomorrow."

"Hey, Jester," Whit called to Brad. "You're the medic on this trip. Dig out the ibuprofen and give us all a dose. We also need to drink as much water as possible tonight and finish off the bananas."

Within the first hour, they had passed several hikers on their way to the summit. "I sure hope they have headlamps," Mitch said, as they moved out of hearing range. "The sun seems to be sinking fast."

"Yes, it does," Whit agreed. "We'll need to put on our headlamps during our next stop."

For the next thirty minutes, they scrambled across the scree field, slipping and sliding. At one point, Mitch had to grab Whit's arm to keep her balanced. "Oh, good catch. Thanks."

"You okay?" he asked.

Whit nodded. "Yes, but I think I need a break."

"Hey, Jester. Pull up. Stargazer needs a break," Mitch called out to Brad.

Mitch rummaged through his bag, put on his headlamp, then took Whit's out and handed it to her. "Why is your pack still so heavy?" He saw four large bottles of water. "That explains it." He pulled them out. "Let's fill our canteens, and I'll carry anything left." After topping off their canteens, there were still two full bottles. "I've got these, so you take the empties." He handed Brad the empty bottles. "I can't believe you have been carrying this extra weight all day." He frowned. "I think it's time for our first pact."

"What?" Whit asked.

"That if there's an extra load to bear, we all share it equally," Mitch said. "Even if it means taking turns to carry an item. Agreed?" He looked at Brad, who nodded, then at Whit. She started to open her mouth, but Mitch repeated, "Agreed?"

"Okay, I'll agree," Whit promised. Whit smiled when Mitch held out his pinky finger.

"Pinky promise." He grinned.

"Pinky promise," Whit answered with a laugh and hooked fingers with Mitch. She had taken on the extra load of water to make sure they all stayed hydrated, but her pack felt much lighter with the four bottles gone. *I know he's right. I've got to have help bearing the load.*

Brad looked at his watch. "We should have another ninety minutes of sunlight according to my calculations. I think we'll be well over halfway home after that."

"That sounds about right," Whit agreed. "I'm ready for a campfire and some food."

"I heard that," Mitch said. He peeled a banana and took a bite. "These aren't all that filling."

"No, but they will help ward off cramps and soreness. I wish we had thought about some salt tablets too," Whit replied.

"I've got that covered." Brad dug through his pack, then handed each of them a tablet. Brad saw Whit's look of surprise. "I use them for summer football practices," he shrugged.

"You should be in great condition this year," Mitch said.

"This definitely beats a summer of playing Xbox," Brad said enthusiastically.

"It has been a great summer so far," Mitch agreed. "Getting better every day."

Whit felt a chill creeping in and shivered. "Time to move and get warm again," she announced and hopped to her feet.

†

Eli couldn't keep from glancing up at the mountain, as she waited for Whit and the boys to return. She tried to remain busy, laying the fire, checking the sticks to ensure they were drying, and calling Mark.

"Hey, did you get some pics from the boys?" Eli asked when he answered.

"Yes, I did. I tried calling Mitch's phone, but the call never went through."

"I tried the satellite, and it worked wonderfully, so try that number."

"Damn, I forgot all about that. The photos are gorgeous, but it looked pretty chilly up top."

"I imagine a good twenty degrees cooler with the wind chill. Even at the campsite, it's cooler than I thought."

"Are they on the way back down?"

"Yes, I'd guess a couple more hours until they return. I'll have a roaring fire, hearty food, and hot chocolate waiting for them."

"I bet they'll be ready to eat the minute they reach camp."

Eli chuckled. "All three of them. Before I forget, Whit is giving them their trail names today."

"Do tell," Mark said.

"Mitch is Maverick, and Brad is Jester since he's such a clown."

"You realize both names are in *Top Gun*, right?"

"Oh crap, I forgot about Jester. Oh well, it still suits him."

"What about Whit's?"

"I picked hers. Stargazer," Eli answered.

"That fits her well."

"I've made them all walking sticks with their names on them that I will give them tonight. I spent the morning burning the names to keep me busy."

"Shoot me a pic of them when you get a chance and ask the boys to call me after they eat."

"Will do. Love you."

"Most," Mark answered with a laugh. "Good night."

†

Whit heard the satellite phone ring and looked at the number. "It's your dad," she told the boys.

"Riley's Firewood, how may I help you?" Mitch answered.

"I'd like twelve cords delivered by tomorrow," Mark replied.

"That's a hefty order. How do you plan to pay?"

"I'm selling my son's truck to pay for it," Mark joked.

"You'd better give her a tune-up and paint job, or you'll never make enough," Mitch responded.

"Are you guys having fun? I tried to call your cell but couldn't get through. Eli reminded me of the sat phone. I hear you very well."

"Yeah, it works like a charm. It's gorgeous up here. A bit colder than we thought, but the view from the summit is fantastic. I felt like I could see halfway back to North Carolina."

"Send me some of the pics later tonight, after you eat. Eli has made a ton of tofu dishes for you."

"Dear Lord, let there be some real meat waiting for us. I feel like I could eat a whole cow."

"You know your Aunt Eli will make sure you have plenty to eat," Mark told him.

"I know. Aunt Eli's done a great job of planning on this trip. Hey, we got trail names today."

"Really? What are they?"

"Mine is Maverick, Brad's is Jester, and Whit is Stargazer. We signed our first logbook at the summit of Katahdin."

"That sounds exciting. Tell your brother we love him, and y'all be safe coming back down. Call me after you eat."

"Will do, Dad. Love you."

"Most." Mark chuckled and ended the call.

"Dad says he loves you, and we have tofu waiting for us," Mitch reported.

Whit scrunched up her nose. "She wouldn't dare. Would she?"

"Heck no, Aunt Eli only eats it when she has to." Mitch laughed.

"Phew, that's a relief."

"I'd bet that Aunt Eli is going to overload us with protein," Mitch replied.

"Phew, that sounds much better. I'm with you. I feel like I could eat a whole cow."

"Are we going to feel like this every day?" Brad asked.

Whit looked at him. "I don't think so. I would imagine our bodies will adjust to our intake a few days into the trail. In the first few days, we may feel ravenous, though, as we're burning up body fat."

"Do you even have body fat?" Mitch asked.

"I can pinch an inch here and there," Whit answered. "I'll be a lean, mean hiking machine before long, though."

"Yep, me too." Mitch nodded. "Would you look at that." He pointed to the west. "That is going to be one spectacular sunset."

"Snap some pictures along the route," Whit said. "It may disappear more quickly than at home."

Both boys raised their phones and snapped photographs. "Let's roll." Whit led them down the path. When she pulled to a stop five minutes later, they all stood in awe of the brilliant oranges and reds that were gracing the horizon. "Wow." Was the only word Whit could think of to speak. Everyone pulled their phones out and took pictures.

"I think we need to turn on our headlamps," Whit said, as they started down the trail. She turned on her lamp and was surprised at how brightly it lit the path in front of her. "These little lamps have a good shine." She turned back to Mitch, nearly blinding him in the process.

"Whoa." Mitch threw his hand up to block the blinding light.

"Sorry." Whit turned her head to the side. "Maybe we should space out just a little more."

"I'll agree to that," Mitch said. "I'm too young to go blind."

"Okay, I get it," Whit said and walked ahead.

†

Eli focused the binoculars on the site where she had spotted Whit and the boys earlier in the day. Night had fully encompassed the area, and she could see hiker's headlamps moving through the darkness. "They look like human fireflies," she said aloud.

"What was that?" Grace asked.

"I said they look like human fireflies, their headlamps cutting through the darkness with every step."

"That is a good analogy. There seems to be many more than we saw on the mountain earlier," Grace pointed out.

"I reckon I'd better go ahead and light the firepit," Eli said.

"I'll fill the kettle with water, and we can get that heating too," Grace added. "I can already feel a chill growing in the air."

"I bet they're feeling it even worse up there." Eli turned back toward camp.

"Do they plan to hit the trail in the morning?" Grace asked.

"That was the original plan. After today, Whit and the boys may decide on a day of rest. I won't know for sure until they return."

Eli picked up the lighter and got the kindling started beneath the wood. The flames grew, licking up the sides of the dried firewood, and Eli could feel the warmth growing. The wood's dried sap crackled and popped as the wood ignited, and Eli returned to her chair.

Grace and Suzy joined her around the fire. "Would you care to join us in an adult beverage?" Suzy asked, holding out a cold beer.

"That sounds good. Thanks." Eli accepted the bottle, twisted off the cap, and took a drink. "Damn, that hits the spot."

"Yes, it does," Grace agreed.

Eli was lost in thought, when Suzy broke the silence. "I think your dinner order has arrived."

Eli stood and met the driver to take a sizeable thermal bag from him and a grocery bag with chips and bananas. She pulled out her wallet and tipped the driver, thanking him for his service.

"I'm surprised you could get anything delivered out here," Suzy said, as Eli placed the bags on the table.

"One of the park rangers gave me information on several services that offer deliveries here. They leave the thermal bags to help keep food warm, and you drop them by the ranger's station when done."

Grace nodded. "That's a great idea, and I bet it supports the local economy."

Eli nodded. "It's terrific, especially for people not from the area who don't know about all the resources."

"That's true. Hey look." Suzy pointed toward the mountain. "Could that be your crew?"

Eli's head whipped around, and she saw three sets of headlamps coming in their direction. "I sure hope so." She stood and walked toward the edge of the campground. Her smile grew when she saw Whit's smiling face.

"Did you miss us?" Whit's voice had a purring quality to it.

"I didn't think the day would end." Eli pulled Whit into her arms. She looked at the boys and motioned for them to join a group hug. "So, how was it?"

Mitch was the first to answer. "Much harder than I thought it would be, but the views were amazing."

"We've got some great photos to share. The sunset alone was worth the climb," Brad added.

Eli looked at Whit. "Do you agree?"

Whit nodded. "And then some." She smiled at the boys. "It was a great first day on the trail with these two. I couldn't have asked for better partners."

"I sure hope you have some food," Mitch said.

"Plenty," Eli said. "Drop your bags, and I'll introduce you to our neighbors and get you fed."

"I've got to hit the bathhouse first," Brad said. "I seriously need to pee."

Eli grinned. "Couldn't go on the trail?"

"It's going to take some getting used to with Whit around." Brad's blush rushed to his face.

"I won't hesitate to turn around," Whit told him. "It's going to be a miserable trip if you can't go in the woods." Whit laughed. "Trust me, I'm not looking forward to that either, but I'm not carrying a bucket for hundreds of miles."

"Go quickly," Eli said and reached for his pack. She watched Brad rush toward the bathhouse. "Doesn't bother you?" she asked Mitch.

"Heck no, I've been peeing in the woods for years. Pooping is an adventure all on its own."

"Okay, enough pooh talk right before supper." Eli led them to the firepit. "This is Suzy and Grace. They will be doing the climb tomorrow." She turned back to Whit. "This is Whit, and my oldest nephew Mitch. Brad will return after a pit stop."

"Nice to meet you," Whit said, as she placed her pack on the ground. "You have a great adventure ahead of you."

Grace smiled. "We're excited to hear about your day, if you don't mind some company."

"The more, the merrier." Whit motioned them to the table.

"Grace has water ready for hot chocolate to warm you up," Eli said.

"That would be awesome," Mitch said.

"We're going to tackle the rest of the pizza." Suzy turned to get the leftovers.

Whit and Grace started making hot chocolate, and Mitch helped Eli unpack the food. She pulled out the bananas and placed them on the table. "Man, those were lifesavers today," Mitch said. "They helped to ease the muscle cramps from all that climbing."

Brad grabbed a banana, when he returned, and stood near the fire pit. "Man, this feels good."

Grace and Whit placed cups of hot chocolate on the table. "Hi, I'm Brad," he introduced himself.

"I'm Grace, and this is Suzy," Grace said, returning his smile.

"Now, this is what I'm talking about," Mitch declared, as Eli started pulling out double cheeseburgers. "They're still hot too. I love you, Aunt Eli."

"I figured you guys would be ravenous by the time you got back. There are chips, fruit, and ingredients for s'mores too."

Mitch took a bite and chewed slowly. "To die for." He looked up at her and pointed at the tree. "What are those?"

"Aww, crap, I forgot about them." Eli stood and walked over to the tree to retrieve the three walking sticks. She handed Mitch his first.

"This is freaking awesome," he said and jumped up from the table to hug Eli, nearly knocking Whit over in the process.

"You even burned our names in them," Whit pointed out. "That's why you wanted to know our trail names. Very sneaky."

"This is so cool," Brad added.

"There is plenty of room left if you pick up other names on the trail. I can add them when you get home."

Whit leaned over and kissed Eli. "These are perfect. Thank you."

"I don't have to worry about remembering how to spell Maverick now either," Mitch teased.

Eli gasped. "No, I guess you don't. Lord, I hope I spelled it right."

"You did," Whit assured her.

†

After dinner, the group sat around the fire and made s'mores, while they shared the day's adventure. Eli caught Brad nodding off and nudged Whit, who whispered, "It was a long day." She leaned over and gently shook him awake. "Why don't you turn in for the night?"

Brad groaned. "I drifted off, didn't I?"

Eli nodded. "Yes, but it's okay. Y'all had a long, physically active day." She looked at Mitch and Whit. "I don't think any of us will be far behind you."

"We need to be going, too, if we're going to hit the trail at sunrise," Suzy said. "It was great to meet you all."

Eli smiled at them. "Have a great climb tomorrow. I'll leave our address and phone numbers on your table. If you do make it our way, you can visit and not be far off the trail."

"Thanks. That sounds like fun. Have a grand adventure," Grace told Mitch. "You be careful driving home." She winked to Eli.

"Good night," Eli replied as they left the fire. She looked at Whit and Mitch. "Will you continue tomorrow or rest for a day?"

"We discussed it earlier and decided it would be better to keep moving to work the soreness off," Mitch answered. "I don't think we need to be up at the butt crack of dawn, but maybe after a hot breakfast, we can get moving."

Whit nodded. "That sounds doable. Remind your brother to use his charger on his phone. You, too, so we can stay fully charged."

"Crap, I forgot to call Dad. I'd better go do it now," Mitch said. "Good night. Love y'all, and thanks for a great day!"

"Good night, Mitch. We love you too." Eli stood and closed the lid on the firepit. She looked at Whit. "Are you too tired for a short walk?"

"No, ma'am. I'd follow you anywhere." Whit smiled.

Eli reached for her hand and walked a short distance from the camp. "It is so beautiful up here," she told Whit.

Whit nodded toward the mountain. "It's even more spectacular from up there. Before you start for home, drive up and see for yourself."

"You can drive up there?" Eli was shocked.

"Not all the way, but yes, you can go relatively high. High enough for you to experience some fantastic views."

"I will do that," Eli replied. "Look at that full moon. I bet you almost feel like you could reach out and touch it from up there." Eli leaned down and kissed Whit. "I missed you today. I don't know how I'm going to survive the next two weeks."

"I bet it will seem odd, most definitely quiet, but maybe some good 'me time' for you."

"It will be the longest time I've spent alone on the mountain. I don't want to rush your adventure, but I hope the time passes quickly for me. Is that selfish?"

"No, it's flattering to know that you will miss me like that. When I was on assignment, you had Mitch to keep you company."

"I promise we'll have plenty of 'us time' when the boys go home. We jumped right into all the projects and hard work and forgot to carve out time for ourselves."

"Eli Fortner, I wouldn't change a minute with you. I love you no matter if we're filthy dirty and tired or lazing in bed on a Sunday morning. I'm happiest when I'm with you."

Eli stood behind Whit and wrapped her arms around Whit's waist. She rested her head on her lover's shoulder, as they gazed at the mountain. "The moon makes the mountain glow," Eli whispered.

"Yes, it does. Hey, did you see that? Make a wish." Whit pointed to a falling star streaking across the sky.

"Done." Eli nuzzled Whit's neck with her lips and felt her shiver. "Are you cold?"

"A little, but I'm ready to be snuggled in next to you. I'm glad you set up a larger tent for us."

"It will be our last chance to cuddle for a while." Eli smiled. "Let's go check out this double sleeping bag." She took Whit's hand as they walked back into camp.

"Dad says hello," Mitch whispered and crawled into his tent.

"Thanks. Good night, Mitch. Love you." Eli answered.

"Most." Mitch grinned.

CHAPTER FOURTEEN

Even though Suzy and Grace tried to be quiet as they prepared to leave their campsite, Eli heard the movement and woke. Whit snuggled into her warmth. "Are you getting up?" she whispered.

"Not now," Eli whispered and pulled Whit in closer.

"Good," Whit's hand snaked beneath Eli's shirt. "You are so warm, it's going to make it hard to get up," Whit whispered.

"There's no rush, is there?" Eli asked.

"Nope," Whit answered. "The sun won't be up for another hour, at least."

Eli smiled and drifted back to sleep.

†

Mitch was the first to emerge, and he worked as quietly as he could to start a fire. The smell of the wood smoke filled the chilly morning air, as Mitch folded his hammock and attached it to his pack. He pulled out his fry pan and started cooking the bacon Eli had stored in the cooler. The aroma of bacon woke Eli, and she opened the flap to see Mitch bent over the fire, cooking breakfast.

"Mitch has started breakfast," Eli said, as she settled next to Whit. "You want to sleep in a bit while I help him?"

Whit smiled at her. "No, I'll get up and help too."

Eli sat up on the cot and slipped into her boots. "It's chilly. You may change your mind once I open the tent flap."

Whit reached up to stroke down Eli's face. "I can smell the fire, so I'll get warm around it if I get cold."

"Grace left the kettle if you'd like some hot chocolate," Eli offered.

Whit moaned. "That sounds good."

"Hang tight then, until I can get the water heating." Eli leaned down and kissed Whit. "Love you."

"More," Whit answered with a smile.

"No way, man." Eli opened the flap and stepped into the brisk morning. Mitch looked up as she approached.

"I tried to be quiet," he said.

"You were, but the smell of that bacon is irresistible. How are you feeling this morning?"

"I'm sore, but I think I'll live. Did you sleep okay?"

Eli smiled. "Like a rock. How about you?"

"I barely remember taking my boots off. If my bladder hadn't woke me, I'd probably still be sleeping."

"I would say you could lie back down, but I see you've already packed. Are you excited?"

He grinned at Eli. "Maybe just a bit."

"I packed some tortillas, thinking we could have some breakfast burritos this morning. Cook all the bacon, and I'll scramble a bunch of eggs and cheese." Eli filled the kettle with water and placed it on the grill. "You want hot chocolate?"

"That sounds good. It sure hit the spot last night. Those burgers did too. They were off the chain."

"I thought you'd need some major protein when you came back down."

"You sure nailed that. I'll be dreaming of those for days until we reach Millinocket again."

"If you reach it in good time, you can have a couple of meals there." Eli looked up when Whit approached. "Good morning. I was about to hit the bathhouse. Would you like to join me?"

"Yeah, that's a great idea. Good morning, Mitch."

"Morning, Love Muffin. Did you sleep well?" he teased.

"Like a rock until the heavenly aroma of bacon woke me," Whit teased back.

"I'm sorry," Mitch replied.

"Never be sorry about the smell of bacon. It means good food is on the way."

Mitch smiled. "We have burritos on the menu this morning."

"That sounds fantastic."

"We'll be right back," Eli said and reached for Whit's hand.

Mitch nodded. "I'll see if I can get Jester up and moving."

"Good luck." Eli laughed softly.

†

After breakfast, Mitch and Brad broke down camp. Mitch placed the larger tent back in Eli's truck, along with the cooler and chairs. "I think that has you all set."

"Thanks. If I didn't know better, I'd say you were trying to get rid of me." Eli bumped shoulders with Mitch.

"Naw, I didn't want you to be stuck packing after we're gone. I imagine you'll drive well into the night."

"I'd like to make it halfway home. No need to play tourist without y'all, but I'll keep my eyes open for interesting stops along the way."

Whit nodded. "So, y'all are all set?"

Mitch nodded. "Packs, check. Walking sticks, check. Canteens filled."

Eli felt the tears pooling in her eyes. "I guess this is it. You guys better leave before my eyes start leaking and I load you back in the truck."

Whit smiled and kissed Eli. "You'll be back to get us soon. We'll call every night, if we can, and send pictures along the way."

"That sounds good. I miss y'all already." She hugged the boys. "Take care of each other and have fun."

"We will," Mitch promised.

"Love you, Aunt Eli," Brad said.

"More," Eli responded.

Whit gave Eli a final kiss and turned back to the boys. "Let's do this."

"Love you," Eli said, as she let go of Whit's hand.

"Love you too."

Eli again watched until they disappeared down the trail. She sighed deeply and walked to her truck to begin the lonely journey home.

†

"I sure am glad we don't have to climb Katahdin again today," Mitch said, as they set a comfortable pace.

"Amen to that," Brad said. "Will we have much more climbing ahead of us?"

Whit smiled. "Yes, but nothing like we did yesterday. That was the toughest climb of the entire trail, and we knocked it out first. The rest will seem easy compared to that."

An hour later, they met the first two hikers heading north. Two young men with several week's beard growth approached. "Good morning," they said, when they spotted Whit and the boys.

"Good morning indeed. How are y'all today?" Mitch replied.

"Fine and dandy," the taller hiker answered. "I'm Snow White, and this is Puffy." He pointed to his companion.

"Maverick, Jester, and Stargazer," Whit replied.

"Nice to meet you. Are you coming from Katahdin?"

"Yes, we tackled it yesterday," Mitch said proudly. "It's an ass-kicker of a climb, but we made it."

Snow White grinned at Mitch. "That's our last bit of trail to finish our northbound trip. We did half last year, and we've been on the trail for the last three months."

"Congrats, man. We're starting small, a two-week hike this year," Mitch said.

"That's cool, at least you're on your way, and you got Katahdin done first," Puffy said. "How long did it take you?"

Whit smiled. "Right at eleven hours."

"I reckon we need to pitch camp this afternoon and start fresh in the morning," Puffy said. "How long have you been out today?"

"Just a little over two hours," Mitch replied.

"We can hit the bathhouse for a shave and shower," Snow White said.

"Yeah, I'm way past due, and I'm beginning to offend myself." Puffy laughed.

Whit laughed with them. "Check at the ranger station. There's a burger place that delivers, and the bacon cheeseburgers were to die for last night."

Puffy grinned. "Oh, my goodness, that sounds heavenly."

"Hey, where did y'all spend the night last night?" Mitch asked.

Puffy answered, "There's a shelter about eight miles ahead. You can make it by dark."

Mitch grinned. "Awesome. Any lakes or streams nearby?"

"Yeah, a good-sized stream was about a hundred yards away from the shelter. You going to try to fish?" Snow White asked.

"I'd like to, as much as possible," Mitch said.

"Good luck, man. Safe travels," Puffy said.

"You too," Mitch answered, and the two groups parted ways.

"I hope it was hair color that gave Snow White that name." Whit chuckled.

"It was pretty bright, wasn't it?" Brad grinned.

"I don't know if it's polite to ask," Mitch said. "From what we gathered from Samurai, people pretty much explain it themselves."

Whit grinned at him. "I'm sure we'll meet all kinds of colorful folks along this trail. How long do you think it will take for us to meet up with Samurai's group?"

"Probably tomorrow or the next day at the latest," Mitch said. "They're keeping a leisurely pace so they don't rush to end the adventure. They are such a cool group."

"Maybe, if we find a spot that has a lake or good stream, we can treat them to some fresh fish," Whit suggested.

"I took a peek at the trail map. We should be near a large lake tomorrow. Maybe we can get lucky there," Brad told them.

"I think we can handle a meal out of our packs tonight, if we don't arrive in time to fish," Whit said. "I'm eager to try out an MRE."

Brad nodded. "They're pretty tasty and easy enough to fix. High calories too."

"Let's plan on that as a backup then. We can get to bed early and be back on the trail when the sun comes up." Whit looked at the boys. "How are y'all feeling today? I'll admit I'm still a bit sore."

"Me too," Mitch said. "I was thankful for a comfortable pace this morning, but I think we have a bit of a climb before reaching the shelter." He pointed at the mountain looming ahead.

"Yeah, I don't think the trail is going to veer around it," Brad grimaced. "If that doesn't work the soreness out, I don't know what will."

"Only one way to find out." Whit shifted her pack. "Let's move on out."

†

Eli pushed back her tears as she drove south. She didn't realize how hard it would be to say good-bye to Whit and the boys. Eli reached to turn on the radio. Her phone rang, and she looked at the screen to see Mark was calling.

"Hey, sis. You on your way home?"

"Yeah, our trailblazers have been gone about an hour. Mitch helped me pack up camp, and after they disappeared into the woods I headed out."

"You okay? You sound down."

"I didn't realize it would be this hard to say good-bye to them. Whit and the boys seemed so excited, but I hated to see them disappear down the trail."

"It's probably a good thing Carol moved up there, or you'd go stir crazy for the next two weeks."

"I know. It'll be the longest I've gone without Whit or Mitch around."

"I'm sure you'll be fine. You can always come down and hang with us if you want."

"Thanks, but there's plenty of chores to be done. Vegetables to pick, animals to feed, eggs to gather."

"Try to do something fun for you too. Don't work yourself to death over the next two weeks."

"I'm sure I'll find something to get into."

"Okay, I just wanted to call and check on you. If you talk to the crew later, tell the boys to call when they can."

"I will. Love ya."

"Most, and don't ever forget that. Call me anytime."

"Thanks, Mark. I will."

Eli resisted the urge to call Whit. She would let them enjoy their time and cherish the calls when they came in. She dialed in a country station and enjoyed the fresh air, as she drove the winding mountain roads.

†

Whit and the boys passed several other groups of hikers making their way to Katahdin. Some stopped for a quick chat, but most kept going, eager to come to the end of the trail.

"Would you look at that?" Mitch pointed across a meadow and pulled his phone out.

"Man, they are huge," Brad said, as he spotted the two moose bulls. "Look at those racks. I bet they're eight feet across." He let out a low whistle.

Whit smiled and pointed at a female with a young calf. "Mama and a baby too," she whispered.

The animals did not seem disturbed by their presence. "I guess they see so many hikers that they have lost their fear of humans," Mitch said.

"I sure wouldn't want to press my luck in getting too close. I bet those bad boys could inflict some damage." Brad snapped off several photos.

"Did y'all remember to charge your phones last night?" Whit asked.

Brad nodded. "Yes, ma'am. Fully charged, and my power bank is full."

"Mine too," Mitch replied.

"Keep your eyes peeled. I bet we see quite a bit of wildlife on this trip." Whit smiled and snapped a photo. "I'm going to try to send a pic to Eli."

"I think they're going through, but it takes a minute or so to process," Brad said. "I did get a text from Mom this morning. I'm not sure she received my answer, though."

"How far have we walked, Jester?" Mitch asked.

Brad checked his GPS. "Almost four miles, so I think we have about six more to the shelter Puffy told us about."

Whit looked at the trail ahead. "Over this bad boy first. Do we want to break now or during the climb?"

"Let's get a jump on it. We can stop later if we need to," Mitch suggested.

Whit pointed her walking stick toward the trail. "Lead the way, Maverick."

†

Eli rounded a curve. The traffic had come to a complete stop. She looked around the car ahead of her and saw that a group of elk was crossing the road. Eli watched a dozen or more animals cross the asphalt, disappearing instantly in the dense growth of the forest. "You certainly don't see that every day," she said, as she put the truck in gear and continued on her journey. She pulled into a gas station to refuel, and her phone pinged with a message. She looked at the photo Brad had sent of two bull moose.

Damn, those are big. When no answer came, Eli walked into the store for a drink and a snack. She pulled out a Mountain Dew and perused the snack aisle. Eli wasn't surprised to learn that there were no pork rinds for sale, so she moved on to the candy aisle and picked out two packages of Twizzlers. "Thank goodness, these are universal goodies." Eli paid for her snacks and returned to her truck. She checked her phone, but there were no messages. As she pulled onto the highway, Eli could see a bank of dark clouds forming to the south. "I sure hope they make it to shelter before the skies open up." She sent a text to Whit. *Rain clouds moving north. I hope you make it to shelter before they arrive.*

†

Whit estimated they had climbed three quarters of the mountain's height when she called for a rest break. "I need to rest for a bit," she told the boys.

"Thank goodness." Mitch groaned. "I thought I was the only one punking out."

"Nope. I was hoping we could make it to the summit, but my legs have other plans." She placed her pack on the ground in front of her. "Bananas, anyone?" Whit tossed each of them a piece of fruit.

"I've got peanut butter if anyone wants some," Brad offered.

"I'll take a bit," Whit said. As she was reaching for the spoon, her phone pinged, as did Brad's and Mitch's. "I guess we have cell service."

Mitch checked his text. "Dad says that's some damn big moose."

"Mine too, except he said mices." Brad shook his head. "Dad and his autocorrect woes."

"Eli says storm clouds are heading our way, and she hopes we make it to shelter before they arrive."

Mitch looked off to the south. "I don't see anything yet, but that doesn't mean they can't blow up in a hurry."

Whit nodded. "It probably wouldn't hurt to put our rain gear in a handy spot. Just in case." She took a drink from her canteen. "Everybody good on water?"

"I'm going to refill while we're breaking," Mitch replied.

"Not a bad idea for all of us to top off," Whit added.

It took another half hour to reach the summit of the mountain. The views were gorgeous. Smaller mountains loomed ahead, and valleys were bordered by crystal blue water for miles.

Mitch lifted his sunglasses. "That looks like a massive lake, but I can't gauge the distance from up here. It could be three miles or thirty."

"I'd guess a lot more than three," Brad said.

"Hopefully, we will be close enough for some fishing," Mitch said. "I'm itching to see what the fish are like up here. I'd love to land some of the landlocked salmon. I bet they would be awesome on the grill."

"They also have a variety of trout too," Brad said. "We all know how good they are."

"Talking about food is making me hungry," Mitch warned.

"Let's gear up and find that shelter," Whit said. "The sooner we settle in, the faster we can rustle up some food."

On the descent, Mitch pointed out a swift-moving stream. "I sure hope that's the one near the shelter. It looks promising for fish."

"Only one way to find out." Whit smiled at him.

The sun was heading for the horizon when they reached level ground again. Mitch was delighted he could hear the running water. "How far to the shelter, Jester?"

Brad studied his GPS. "About a mile if my calculations are correct."

Whit hitched up her pack. "That shouldn't take us much longer, if this ground stays level."

†

Whit could hear the faint rumble of thunder, as they approached the shelter. The construction looked solid and would provide refuge from the rain. "Let's drop our packs and hunt for some firewood before this rain hits. Hopefully, it will move through quickly, and we can build a fire once it's gone."

"Sounds like a good plan to me. I'm going to scout to the east and see if I can locate that stream." Mitch placed his pack on a top layer of the shelter. "Hand yours up, and I'll put them by mine," he told them.

Whit handed him her pack. "Someone needs to stay close to watch our bags. I'm going to dig out that pit a little and rearrange the rocks around it."

"It doesn't look like it gets used much. We'll change that tonight." Mitch looked at Brad. "Let's get as much wood as we can. What we don't burn tonight, we can leave for others."

"I'm on it," Brad said.

"Keep your eyes open for any berries that may be ripe," Whit said before they broke camp. She busied herself, reestablishing a fire ring with the rocks and dug the pit deeper. Brad was the first to return with an armful of dried wood. "There's plenty more, and it's not far off," Brad said. "I'll be back with more."

A few minutes later, Mitch returned, carrying a load of larger log sections that would burn well. He added them to the pile beneath the lowest bench in the shelter. "I think I can get at least one more load," he reported.

"Did you find the stream?"

"Yes, ma'am, and it looks promising for fish."

Whit smiled up at him as she stacked the wood. "You can check it out soon. Hopefully, it won't rain long."

Brad accompanied Mitch, and they returned with another load of logs. The clouds were pregnant with rain and dropped closer to the mountain.

Whit looked at Mitch. "You sure you want to fish?"

"I can gear up and fish in the rain. Fish usually bite better as long as it isn't a monsoon."

"I don't want you getting soaked."

"I promise I won't melt." Mitch laughed. He reached into his pack for rain gear just as the first drops began to fall.

Whit climbed up to sit beside Brad. "If lightning starts, high tail it back here. We don't have to have fish that bad tonight."

Mitch pulled out a stringer and tucked it in his back pocket. "I promise I won't get fried."

"We'll get a fire going as soon as this passes over," Whit said.

Mitch nodded. "I'll be back."

Brad stretched out on the top rack, using a pack for a pillow. "Mind if I take a power nap?"

"No, go right ahead. I'm going to see if I can reach Eli."

†

Eli picked up on the second ring. "Hey, there. Did y'all make the shelter?"

"Yes, we did. It's starting to rain, but not hard. Brad is stretching out for a nap, and Mitch is trying his luck in a stream."

"Fish normally bite well in light rain."

Whit laughed. "That's precisely what Mitch said. He put on his rain gear and headed out a few minutes ago. How are you?"

"I'm doing good. Making a reasonable time. I want to drive a few more hours tonight so that I can reach home late tomorrow."

"Just please be careful. You need a hot meal and a good night's sleep."

"I promise to get both. How was the hike today?"

"It was great. We made our ten miles today. We had to cross a mountain, but it was nothing like Katahdin. Still very much a challenge, but not as physically draining."

"I got the pictures of the moose. Those are some giant creatures. I had to stop in traffic while a herd of elk crossed the road. I didn't think to snap a pic, though."

"I think if we keep our eyes and ears open, we will see quite a bit of wildlife."

"Have you met any other hikers yet?"

"Two guys were heading north. They told us about this shelter, and we shared the information on the cheeseburgers," Whit said. "I think it was a pretty fair trade of information."

"You sound good. How are the boys holding up?"

"We're all good so far. I don't think any of us will have trouble falling asleep tonight."

"That's good. I miss y'all. I caught myself looking over to talk to you earlier only to realize you weren't there. The quality of your voice comes across well on the sat phone."

"Yes, it does. That was a brilliant idea. If the boys can't reach Mark on their cells tonight, I'll have them use this one."

"Are the chargers working well?"

"Perfectly," Whit answered. "The sun brought us all back full today."

"I love you. Miss you like crazy."

"I love you too. I promise we will have tons of fun and adventure to share with you, so try not to worry. Do you want me to call later?"

"Yes, if you can. I hope Mitch catches well, and you can have a nice fish dinner."

"I hope so too. I'll talk to you soon."

"Bye, Whit."

Whit turned off the call and leaned back against the shelter wall. The soft tapping of the rain was about to lull her to sleep, when she heard laughter in the distance. *Can't be Mitch.* She sat forward and saw two young women racing toward the shelter, hand in hand.

"What the heck?" Brad sat up on the rack.

"It looks like we're about to have company," Whit answered.

When the women saw Whit, they released hands and slowed to a fast walk. Whit smiled. "Hello, come get out of the rain."

"Hey," one of the women answered. "Do y'all mind sharing the shelter tonight?"

"Absolutely not," Whit said with a smile. "Make yourself at home. As soon as this passes over, we'll start a fire. I'm Stargazer, and this is my nephew, Jester. Maverick is trying his skill as a fisherman at the creek, so we may have fish for supper if we're lucky."

"I'm Triscuit, and this is Biscuit," one of the women replied.

"Catchy and not too hard to remember," Brad said. "I won't promise I'll remember which is which, though."

"Think T for taller and Triscuit." She laughed.

"That makes it much easier." Brad grinned. "Where are y'all from?"

"Houston, Texas," Biscuit replied. "What about y'all?"

"I'm from North Carolina, and the boys are from Alabama. They're spending time with their aunt this summer."

"That's awesome," Triscuit said, as she stored their packs. "How long have you been on the trail?"

Brad smiled. "This is our second day. We did Katahdin yesterday, then started south this morning."

Biscuit chuckled. "You're still alive and walking after Katahdin, so that's a good thing."

Whit nodded. "Still a bit sore, but the next few days will work it out."

"We're finishing our last section. We've been hiking for nearly a month, I think. We kind of lose track of days out here."

Triscuit nodded her head. "We lost power on our phones a week ago, even though we used them sparingly."

"We have charging packs, and I'd be glad to charge them for you," Brad offered.

"That would be kind of you," Biscuit replied. They dug out their phones and gave them to Brad.

"You can use my charger too. I'm all charged," Whit instructed.

"Thanks a bunch. We probably need to check in with family," Biscuit replied.

"If your cell phones don't work, we've got a satellite phone that does," Whit informed them.

"Wow, y'all thought out the tech stuff well," Triscuit said.

"My partner, Eli. She wanted to make sure we could call if necessary."

Triscuit smiled at Whit's use of the word partner. "She's not with you?"

Whit shook her head. "She's sitting this one out, but we hope she'll join us on a section hike or two next year."

"That would be cool," Biscuit said. "Hiking gives us a great time to bond."

The rain had slowed to a stop. Whit looked at Brad. "Why don't you check on Maverick? Take a headlamp just in case you need it. I'll get a fire going."

"Yes, ma'am," Brad answered and hopped down from the rack. "Should I refill our water bottles and start treating?"

"That's not a bad idea. Let's top off the canteens to empty the bottles."

"I can help. We need some fresh water, too," Triscuit replied.

Whit removed a large Ziploc bag. "Better take one of these in case Maverick needs it. He'll need to clean anything he caught there, so we don't attract any critters."

Brad smiled and took the bag. "Yes, ma'am. I've got my fingers crossed he's caught a mess."

"Me too," Whit replied.

Brad placed his headlamp and picked up the bottles. "All set?" he asked Triscuit.

"Just waiting on you." She smiled back at him.

Whit and Biscuit got a fire started, and Whit set up her hammock tent. "That looks comfortable," Biscuit said.

"Much more than the ground or hard wood of the shelter. It comes in a double size too. Pretty light for packing."

"You planned this trip out well. We just fly by the seat of our pants. We get the urge, pack up more than we can carry, and hit the road," Biscuit said. "It's worked out well so far. We've been hiking for about three years, since we graduated from college."

"That sounds nice. I've always wanted to do the AT. When the boys came up and started talking about it, the trip was on from then. The AT runs just above our property line."

"We probably walked right past you on our first year," Biscuit said. "North Carolina is some beautiful country."

"Yes, it is. What do y'all do in Texas?"

"I'm a research chemist, and Triscuit works with her dad in the oil industry as an accountant."

"That's great that you can take time to trek. I know it's hard once you start adulting." Whit grinned.

"What about y'all?"

"Eli claims she's retired, but the farm keeps her busy. I'm an astrophysicist. I do research and write a few textbooks now and then."

"Hence the name Stargazer?" Biscuit asked.

"Yes, Eli thought it fit well."

"Have you been together long? If you don't mind me asking."

"Just a few months, but they have been fantastic," Whit replied. "I never knew how lonely I was until Eli came along."

"That's sweet. We've been together for six years. I plan to pop the question to Triscuit when we reach the summit of Katahdin."

"How romantic." Whit smiled. "I'm sure she'll say yes."

"I think so. We've discussed it for about a year, but never seriously. I hope Cindy's ready."

"I have no doubt she will be. Congratulations in advance."

"Thanks," Biscuit said. She saw Whit pull out a frying pan. "We've got some oil leftover that we won't need if you'd like to use that. One less thing to carry up Katahdin."

"That would be great. Thanks."

†

Mitch was having a blast. The fish acted like they were starving and struck his fly almost as fast as he could cast it. He already had six large trout on the stringer when Brad and a woman arrived. "Hey, Jester."

"Hey, Maverick." He motioned to the woman. "Meet Triscuit. She and her partner, Biscuit, are joining us at the shelter tonight."

"Triscuit and Biscuit. Those are cute names. I hope you eat fish."

"We do," Triscuit answered. "Do you need some help cleaning them?"

"No, ma'am. Jester and I can handle this," Mitch answered.

"Would you mind filling our water bottles, upstream a bit, while we clean fish?" Brad asked. "Stargazer sent a Ziploc and said we needed to clean them here, so we don't attract critters." He pulled the bag from his pocket.

"Sure, that's no problem." Triscuit reached for Brad's bottles. "I'll be right back."

"There's a couple of flat rocks we can use to clean the fish." Mitch handed the stringer to Brad. "Do you think we'll have enough?"

"I'll start cleaning if you want to try for a couple more. I don't know about you, but I'm starving."

"Let me get to it then. These trout love North Carolina flies," Mitch declared. He continued to fish, while Brad began filleting the trout. "These are some pretty fish," he told Mitch.

When Triscuit returned, she placed the filled bottles on the ground. "What can I help with?"

"You can hold the bag open. I've got some filets rinsed and ready to go," Brad told her.

"Holy cow, this one's a beauty," Mitch cried out, as he reeled a large fish toward the bank. "Two of these should work." He extracted the hook from the fish. "Man, you need a pic of this one to send to Dad," Brad said. Brad had messy hands from cleaning fish. He looked at Triscuit. "Would you mind snapping a picture? My phone's in my back pocket."

"Sure, you want to bring it over, and I'll get both of you in the frame?"

Mitch carried the fish to Brad, and they each held up an end while she took a photograph.

"Perfect." Triscuit slipped the phone back into Brad's pocket.

Mitch picked up his rod. "Okay, one more and we should be good to go."

"What should we do with the carcasses?" Brad asked.

Mitch cast his line. "I'd take them downstream just a bit and leave them. Maybe a coon or some other night-time critter will have a feast and leave our camp alone."

"That's a great idea," Triscuit replied. "You're going to have to start hanging your packs too. The bears aren't typically aggressive, but they have an incredible sense of smell."

Brad's eyes grew wide. "Have you seen many along the trail?"

"Just a few, but other than leaving a large pile of scat on the trail, they haven't been a nuisance."

"We saw two massive bull moose earlier today," Mitch replied.

Triscuit nodded. "You'll see all kinds of things from beavers to a fox if you travel quietly." She smiled at Brad. "We've even heard a few wolves howl at night but haven't seen them."

Mitch hooked the final fish. "That's probably a good thing. The last fish is coming up."

"That was perfect timing." Brad slid the filets from the monster fish into the bag. "Let me finish this one, and y'all can head back to camp while I take these downstream."

"You keep the headlamp. It's light enough for us to find our way back. Stargazer's got a fire going too. I can smell it," Mitch added.

"All set," Brad said. "I'll see you in just a bit."

Mitch nodded. "Be careful, bro."

"Always," Brad replied and picked up a handful of fish carcasses.

Mitch picked up three bottles of water and his rod. "You got the rest?" he asked Triscuit.

"No problem," she answered.

As they walked toward camp, Mitch looked up at the sky. "It's so beautiful out here."

"Yes, it is, and you have a lot more fantastic scenery ahead of you. Beautiful waterfalls and sunsets that will amaze you. I'm sad that our journey is coming to an end. Who knows, we may decide to hike it again or hit another of the big trails."

Mitch grinned. "The opportunities are there. I would love to hike some of the trails out west or maybe the Florida trail."

"There you are," Whit called as they approached. "One man down?"

"Jester is disposing of the carcasses downstream, so we don't invite critters into the camp," Mitch told her. "You must be Biscuit. I'm Maverick, also known as the Great White Fisherman." He motioned toward the bag brimming with trout filets.

"Well done, young man," Biscuit said. "I'll grab the oil so we can get it heating."

Mitch cocked his head until Whit explained. "They have some oil left and won't need it before they get to Katahdin. It's a win-win. We get oil, and they get a lighter pack."

"That makes good sense. Are we going to break out some hushpuppies?" Mitch asked.

"Why not? We've got plenty of the cornmeal, and I would gladly give up a mini can of corn out of my pack. No beer, RO-TEL, or onion, but I still think they will be tasty."

Triscuit smiled and nodded to Biscuit. "Go ahead."

Mitch and Whit turned to see Biscuit pull out a mini can of beer. "I can't help with RO-TEL or onion, but a beer I can."

"Perfect," Whit said. "We didn't find any fresh berries, so nothing sweet."

"You'll find a massive patch of blackberries two days on. They were so sweet and juicy, but we finished them off yesterday," Triscuit replied.

Whit grinned at Mitch. "It sounds like blackberry pancakes are in your future."

"I can handle that. I'm seriously craving some carbs. The hushpuppies will hold me over since I know I have pancakes to look forward to for breakfast."

"Pancakes for breakfast?" Brad asked as he returned.

"In two days, when we run across the blackberries ahead on the trail," Whit explained.

"Man, I hope Wolfie, and Samurai don't wipe them out first," Mitch said.

Whit explained to their new friends. "They're a group of about eight college kids we met at the lodge in Millinocket. We should cross paths with them tomorrow or the next day."

"We spent a night in the bunkhouse there and got resupplied. That was a great place, and they treat hikers well," Biscuit said.

"Even the dirty, stinky ones." Triscuit pinched her nose. "I was so ready for a hot shower and a razor blade."

"Do you want me to pull out our frying pan? We can do the fish and hushpuppies all at once," Biscuit offered.

"That sounds great." Whit poured oil into the frying pan for the fish. "Trout ala AT coming up. You did a great job of catching, and Jester, your filets are beautiful." Whit used a smaller bag to coat the filets and, when the oil had heated, began dropping them into the frying pan.

Mitch whipped up a batch of hushpuppy batter, as he waited on the second pan of oil to heat up, then began dropping spoonfuls of the batter into the pan. "Man, are we going to eat well tonight." He smiled at Whit.

"Jester, will you pull out our plates? Did you treat the freshwater yet?"

"No, ma'am, not yet, but I'll get on it." He reached into his pack for the drops. "We'll be all set by morning."

Triscuit and Biscuit pulled out their dinnerware and added a salt and pepper shaker. "Feel free to use that on the filets, and you can take anything that's left."

"We've got a few packets, but we'll never turn away seasoning," Whit replied.

†

"I have to admit, that was one of the best meals we've had on the trail in a long time," Triscuit said. "Before we tackle another trail, I need to learn how to fly fish."

"That's the beauty of many of the trails. There's frequently a stream or lake just brimming with free food. You have to work a bit for it, but it's well worth the effort."

They had just about finished, when they heard footsteps approach. "Hello," a solitary man called out.

"Hey." Mitch stood up to greet the visitor.

"I'm called Timeless. I was just hiking through when I saw your fire and smelled something extraordinary on the air."

Mitch looked at Whit, who nodded. "Come join us. I'm Maverick. These are Biscuit and Triscuit, Jester, and Stargazer."

"You sure you don't mind? I'm hiking on through, but I'd sure love a bite of whatever you cooked."

"There is more than a bite leftover. Pull out your utensils and dig in. I think we've eaten all we can," Whit offered.

"Why are you hiking at night?" Mitch asked.

"I don't sleep much, so I walk deep into the night until I feel like I can sleep. Then I curl up in my bag and catch a few hours, and I'm up again."

"Is that why you're called Timeless?" Brad asked.

"Yeah, I got that name years ago. I've got no concept of time, but it's great. I can get twenty to twenty-five miles a day in on the trail. This trip is my second time through."

"Good grief, that's a lot of miles," Triscuit said. "How long does it take you at that pace to do a thru hike?"

Timeless swallowed. "I did it in 110 days the first trip. Now that I know the trail, I'm going to trim that by almost a week."

"That's amazing," Mitch said. "You don't feel rushed?"

Timeless smiled and shook his head. "I've never been the kind to stop and smell the roses. If I see a pretty sight, I soak it in and move on to the next. That's why I always travel alone. Anyone else would like to take a more comfortable pace, but I challenge myself on these long hikes."

"To each his own man. As long as you're happy with your journey, that's all that matters," Mitch said.

Whit smiled at Mitch. "Well said."

"This is some great fish." He took another bite. "I've never had hushpuppies this good either."

"I caught the trout just before dark tonight. The fish up here love the North Carolina flies." He grinned.

"Is that where you're from?" he asked.

"Only for the summer. Our home is in Alabama. We're up visiting our aunts," Mitch explained.

"We're from Texas. How about you?" Triscuit asked.

"California. I'm a surgeon from San Francisco. Whenever the stress gets too much, I head for a trail somewhere."

Whit looked at him and chastised herself for doubting Timeless was anything other than what he said. "What type of surgery?"

"Neurosurgery. I'm one of the best Gamma knife surgeons in the country, but I don't mean to brag."

"It's not bragging if you are confident in your skills," Whit said. "I can imagine the stress level can be high."

Timeless nodded. "A sneeze or a cramp, and you can ruin a life in an instant. Then there are others that you just don't reach in time to save."

"That's a lot of pressure. I'll stick to my stars," Whit said.

"She's an astrophysicist, and she has the most amazing laboratory in a treehouse," Brad said.

"We lose time up there looking through the telescopes," Mitch said.

Timeless popped the last bit of hushpuppy in his mouth. "We all have our callings. It's perfect when you love what you do." He wiped his mouth with the back of his hand. "Thank you for such a delicious meal and good company. I must be on my way. Enjoy your adventure."

"You too, Timeless," Mitch said, but the tall man was already on his way down the trail, stuffing his plate back in his pack.

Whit looked at the group. "He was an interesting character," she said. "I'm going to take these down to the stream to wash them. You boys need to call home before it gets late. The sat phone is by my pack."

"Do you need some help?" Biscuit asked.

"Nope, but I'd enjoy the company," Whit replied. She strained the used oil back into the bottle, and Biscuit fished out a small bottle of dish soap.

She looked at Whit and shrugged. "I like for the dishes to be clean," she grinned. "Something else you can add to your pack."

"Thanks." They gathered the dishes and frying pans to head to the creek.

"It's turned out to be such a beautiful night. I was worried the rain would last longer than it did," Whit said, as they washed dishes.

"Hopefully, you won't run into any monsoons on the trail. The storms can be wicked. How long are y'all planning to hike?"

"Two weeks this trip. Maybe longer next summer," Whit answered. "We figured this would give us a good taste of the experience."

"I know it's still early, but are you enjoying it so far?" Biscuit asked.

"Every minute and every sore muscle," Whit replied.

"The boys appear to be good companions for you. Very respectful and easygoing."

"I love them just like they were my flesh and blood. The boys and their parents will be moving up from Bama once everyone finishes school. That's next year for Maverick, and he can't wait."

"That's terrific. I bet Maverick and Jester are a lot of fun to be around."

"They are. We work hard and play hard. That seems rare in the kids growing up today, so we feel blessed."

"Amen to that. We've talked about having one of our own, but we haven't made a final decision."

Whit smiled. "I'd like to have a baby with Eli one day too. Right now, I'm enjoying our time getting to know one another."

Biscuit returned her smile. "No need to rush. It's a big decision."

"That it is."

"Dad said to tell you hello and more." Mitch gave Whit a hug.

"Everyone okay at home?"

"Yeah, Dad's itching to come back up, and he's driving Mom crazy."

Whit nodded. "That sounds like Mark." She looked at Triscuit. "Do you need to use the phone?"

Triscuit shook her head. "Thanks, but I actually have service and called home already."

"I guess it's my turn then. I wonder how far Eli made it today?"

"Five bucks says she's still driving," Mitch said.

"You're on," Whit answered. She dialed Eli's number and winked at Mitch. "Hey, you just cost me five bucks," she told Eli. "Mitch bet me that you would still be driving."

"Yeah, but only for about another fifteen miles until I get to the hotel. Did you get fish?"

"Yes, we had a lovely fish dinner with two new friends from Texas and a fascinating man from California who blew through for a quick bite."

"That sounds interesting. Did you get caught in the rain?"

"Nope, our timing was excellent. We got the firewood under the shelter just as the first drops fell. I'll have to get Mitch to send you a pic of one of the fish he caught."

"Was it as big as the one he had mounted?"

"No, not the monster, but it was still impressive."

Whit could hear the ping of a text and glanced up at Mitch, who gave her a thumbs up. "I think he just sent you the pic."

"I'm glad y'all are having a great time. I miss you, though."

"We miss you too. I'll have to try harder to convince you to join us next time."

"I don't think that will be hard," Eli answered.

"Will you promise to get something to eat before you crash for the night?"

"Yes, Mom, I will," Eli answered with a chuckle.

"Be safe, and I'll call you in the morning. Love you."

"Most," Eli answered. "Tell the boys good night for me."

"I will. Good night." Whit ended the call and looked over at the boys. Mitch was smiling his goofy smile, and Brad was reading entries in the shelter log. "Don't forget to sign in," she told them. "Mitch, grab my pen, and you two get busy."

Triscuit laid another log on the fire. "Whose hammock?"

"Mine, but we've all got one," Whit replied. "Much more comfortable than that hardwood." She looked at Mitch. "You going to pitch your hammocks or sleep under the shelter?"

Mitch shrugged. "I reckon we should so Biscuit and Triscuit can stretch out."

Triscuit chuckled. "There's plenty of room for all of us, but I'm with Stargazer. I'd rather be comfortable."

"Hop to it then," Whit said. "Get set up, then we can enjoy the campfire until it's time to hit the sack."

†

Eli tossed her overnight bag onto the bed and ate the sandwich she had bought for dinner. After a hot shower, she stretched out and scrolled through the pictures Whit and the boys had sent. The images brought a smile to her face but an ache to her heart. She missed them and wondered how she was going to survive the next two weeks. Eli turned off the lamp and crawled under the covers, but sleep was difficult. After barely five hours, Eli woke, rinsed off in the shower, and hit the road.

She purchased a large coffee and several meat-filled biscuits, before starting onto the highway. She pulled over at a scenic overlook to eat the biscuits and watch the beautiful sunrise that blossomed across the horizon. She reached to her hip and used her cell phone to take a photo. She sent the photo to Whit. *I hope you have a great day. I love you.*

When there was no response, Eli climbed into her truck, destined for home.

CHAPTER FIFTEEN

Whit was boiling water for hot chocolate when the boys crawled out of their hammocks. Triscuit and Biscuit were drinking coffee, as they relaxed back on the bench. "You two sleepyheads ready for some hot chocolate? We had one pack left to share."

"That sounds great," Mitch said, as he stretched. "What are we having for breakfast this fine day?"

"We've got a pot of hot water, so how about some oatmeal?" Whit asked. "I've got some honey we can doctor it up with if needed."

"The brown sugar is fine for me," Brad said, as he wiped his face.

Whit snickered at his appearance. "I think, before we hike again, we should get you a high and tight haircut. That hair first thing in the morning is kind of frightening."

"But the ladies love my curly locks." Brad brushed the hair from his face.

Whit shook her head. "Go hit the creek and see if you can get it to calm down some. I'll get your oatmeal and drink ready when you get back. Take your brother with you. He could use some taming too."

"Not all of us can roll out of bed looking perfect as you," Mitch teased Whit.

"Go now, before I change my mind and feed you trail mix for breakfast," Whit taunted them. She watched them head for the creek, then turned to find Triscuit and Biscuit smiling at her.

"You're going to make a great mom one day," Biscuit said.

"They are good practice," Whit said. "We'd be blessed to have a child like one of them." She reached for her pack. "Would you two care to join us for some oatmeal?"

Triscuit shook her head. "Heavens, no, I'm still stuffed from last night. We aren't big eaters in the morning. As long as we have coffee to get us going, we're good."

"Thanks for the offer, though," Biscuit added.

"Just think, at the end of today you can have burgers or pizza or whatever your heart desires delivered," Whit reminded them.

"That is something to look forward to," Triscuit said. "Would it be okay if I share a business card with you? We'd love to hear how you and the boys make out on your trip."

"That would be awesome. We can email and maybe send a picture or two. I'll give you my information. If you're back in our neck of the woods, you can look us up."

Triscuit smiled. "I can easily see us hiking again. At least the southern half."

"We would welcome you at Cast Iron Farms, anytime you choose to visit. I'm sure the boys would love to teach you how to fly fish."

"They do have some mad skills," Biscuit said.

"Yes, they do. The boys keep half our community well fed."

Mitch and Brad returned to camp. "Better?" Brad asked.

"Much," Whit answered. "You ready to eat?"

"I'm always ready." Mitch chuckled. "Sit tight though, we can pour hot water. Let us serve you for a change."

Whit smiled. "I won't argue with that. Have at it."

Mitch handed her a mug of hot chocolate and nodded toward the sound of a phone's ping. "I think that's yours, Whit."

She reached behind her to locate her phone on the charger and smiled when she found Eli's text. "Someone was up early today." She turned the phone so the boys could see the sunrise.

"That's pretty," Brad said. "Too bad we missed it."

"I'm sure we will see plenty of beautiful sunrises on this journey." She turned the phone for Triscuit and Biscuit to see. "She didn't say where she was, but I bet she's been on the road for a bit."

"She wants to reach home today," Mitch said. "Too much time to think about missing Love Muffin when she's driving."

Whit smirked. "You're so funny. Maybe we should have named you Jester."

"No way, man," Brad said. "He's really not that funny."

Whit turned to Triscuit. "Did you camp by the lake?"

"Yeah, we did. There are several excellent shelters around the shore, just off the trail. It's a great rest stop and so beautiful they built more than one shelter."

"Can we make it there today?" Mitch asked.

Biscuit nodded. "If you hoof it. It's about twelve miles from here, but relatively level terrain."

"What did you have in mind, Stargazer?" Mitch asked.

"I thought we should get there as quickly as we can. Maybe you can fish, then keep whatever you catch live on the stringer. If Wolfie and company don't show tonight, we could save the fish and have MREs tonight."

"Would you be okay spending an extra day there, just to wait on them?" Mitch asked.

"Yeah, this isn't a race for us. The group sounds like a cool bunch, and I bet would enjoy a nice fish dinner," Whit replied.

"Heck, that's almost tempting to hike backward for," Triscuit said.

"You would be more than welcome," Whit told the girls.

Biscuit rummaged around in her pack and pulled out two more mini beers. "If you're cooking for a group, you might need these."

"Are you sure?" Whit asked.

"Yes, ma'am. We can get some fresh, cold ones when we arrive at the campground. Two less to carry." Biscuit grinned.

Whit accepted the cans and handed them to Mitch. "Will you stick these in my pack?"

"No ma'am, I'll carry them. Sharing the load remember?" Mitch smiled and dropped the cans in his pack and added the bottle of water.

"Eat up then; we can break camp and hit the trail. You've got fish to catch."

"I sure hope I can find some of those landlocked salmon. I'd love to catch some of those," Mitch said.

"If we end up having all day tomorrow to fish, can I do some fishing too?" Brad asked.

"Sure, bro. We've got a hungry group to cook for."

"I'll break down your hammock if you want to clean the dishes," Mitch offered.

"You have a deal," Whit replied. "Will you two be heading out soon? I'll go ahead and dowse the fire if you are."

"We don't have as far to go, so we'll take care of it," Triscuit said.

"I'll help you with the dishes, too, so you and the boys can hit the trail," Biscuit offered.

When Whit returned, Mitch and Brad had everything packed except for the dishes. "It was very nice to meet you, and we'll stay in touch once we get back home."

"Have fun on Katahdin," Mitch said. "Get a day pack from the rangers, so you only carry what you need."

"Pack your jackets," Brad added. "I nearly froze to death."

"It was drastically cooler the higher you climbed," Whit explained.

They hugged their new friends good-bye and started down the trail.

"Hi ho, hi ho, it's off to work we go," Brad started singing.

"If that doesn't scare away wildlife, I don't know what will." Mitch groaned.

"That's right. Shhh, Jester," Whit teased.

They could hear the laughter of Biscuit and Triscuit behind them. Jester turned and waved a final good-bye.

†

Eli sighed when she saw a road sign announcing one hundred miles to Asheville. It would be close to dark when she arrived, but at least she'd be home.

†

Whit and the boys decided to eat a snack on the trail to keep moving. Once they reached the lake, they could set up camp and eat something more substantial. Mitch was excited to fish, so he kept their pace at a nice clip. The trail was considerably more manageable than the mountainous passes, and it was late afternoon when they arrived to find the shelters empty.

The lake was immense, and Whit could barely see the far shore. "This lake is massive. Do you think you'll be able to catch from the shore?"

Mitch surveyed the lake. "Yeah, I'll try to start fishing in front of the camp, but I may have to move away from the shelters to catch."

"Go ahead and get geared up. Brad can help me set up our hammocks, and we'll round up some firewood."

"Are you sure you don't need my help?" Mitch asked, excited to start fishing.

"Nope, we've got this, bro," Brad said. "Leave your pack in the first shelter and hit the lake."

Mitch dropped his pack and started assembling his rod as he walked to the shore.

"Thank you," Whit told Brad.

"No problem. I know Mitch has been excited to fish this lake since we saw it yesterday."

"I just hope the fish are biting and that both of you will catch a big mess for us."

"If we don't have company tonight, we'll have all day tomorrow to fish, so we should have enough," Brad replied.

"I'll set up the hammocks, if you want to round up some firewood," Whit said. "Get a drink of water first. You haven't drunk much today."

"Yes, ma'am." Brad pulled out his canteen and took a long drink. "It's amazing how cold it stays, even after a day of hiking."

"A blessing," Whit agreed. "The cold feels so much better going down."

†

Whit set up the hammocks and surveyed the fire pit. Someone had recently cleaned it out, and all it needed was some wood. She turned to search for Brad, but he was nowhere in sight. She frowned but decided to give him a few more minutes before she went looking. Whit pulled out an MRE and was reading the package when Brad returned. He dropped the pile of wood next to the pit and turned to smile at her. She noticed a bright stain around his mouth.

"I need one of those plastic bags. I found a nice patch of blackberries."

"I can tell." Whit smirked and took a bag from her pack. "I'll go with you and bring back more wood while you pick berries."

"I'll get the wood. There are several nice logs I think I can drag here and chop with my hatchet."

Whit nodded. "I won't argue with you, but if you need help with the logs, let me know."

"I will. Come, and I'll show you the berry patch."

Whit followed Brad around the edge of the lake. "I'll just be a little farther down this trail if you need me."

"Thanks, Brad." Whit began plucking the ripe berries and popped a couple in her mouth. "These are sweet," she said and continued picking. A nice breeze started to blow off the lake, cooling down the air. *It may be a bit cooler tonight.* She pushed a loose strand of hair back behind her ear. *I wonder how cold that lake is? I could use a good rinsing off.* She was deep in thought about a chilly dip when Brad returned. "I thought you said a log, not the whole tree."

"It's just a branch, but this stuff should burn for a while. I think it's a cottonwood, but I can't be certain."

"You got it, or need help? I've got a decent bag of berries."

"Grab an end then," Brad answered, and they carried the log back to camp.

"I'll go look for some smaller stuff, if you want to begin chopping," Whit said. "I think you should go check on Mitch first. It's been quiet."

"Yes, ma'am." Brad jogged toward Mitch, and when he reached his brother, Mitch held up a string of two fish.

"That's my boys," Whit said and started back toward the forest. She had walked nearly fifty yards from the camp when movement ahead caught her eye. She stopped in her tracks and reached for her phone only to find her pocket empty. "No pictures of them," she said, as she watched two beavers dashing for the lake. One sat up briefly to look at her then rushed to the water's edge. Whit quickly gathered an armload of wood and walked back to camp. Brad was coming toward her and took the load from her.

"That should do us for tonight." He dropped the load next to the pit.

"I have a feeling it will be cool tonight," Whit said.

"We might want to pull closer to the fire before we go to bed, or at least closer together. We could let Mitch be the closest to the lake. He's hot natured and can block the wind for us." Brad chuckled.

Whit just shook her head. "I'm going to go check on him. It will be dark soon."

"You want me to get a fire going?" Brad asked.

"Sure, that can be your task for tonight. You can be the fire master."

Brad walked over to his pack to get his fire starter and started laughing.

"What?" Whit asked.

He pulled a Ziploc bag from his pack full of hot chocolate mix. "You've got to love Aunt Eli."

"I wonder if she's tucked away some other goodies for us to find," Whit said.

"I wouldn't be surprised." Whit walked back to her pack and opened a zippered compartment she hadn't opened yet. She lifted a washcloth, and underneath she found another plastic bag. Inside were graham crackers, chocolate bars, and marshmallows. "Looks like we're having s'mores tonight," Whit said. "Find us a couple of sticks to use before it gets dark."

"Yes, ma'am." With a grin, he took off for the woods.

Whit walked down to the water's edge and smiled at Mitch. "You having fun?"

Mitch grinned back at her. "What's not to love about being in a beautiful country, with good companions and a fishing rod in my hands?"

"How is the fishing coming along?"

"Not bad. I've got a few nice trout, but no salmon yet."

"Well, it looks like you'll have tomorrow to fish. I would think the gang would be here by now if they were close."

"That's cool with me. It's pretty here."

"Did you see a couple of beavers come swimming by?" Whit asked.

"No, not that I saw. Did you see some?"

"A pair crossed over the trail in front of me while I was gathering wood. I thought they might have swum this way."

"Nope, but I've seen turtles, ducks, and a few wading birds."

"How much longer are you going to fish?"

"Not much longer. I'm getting hungry. I'll tie off my stringer to that tree and head to camp."

"You need to check your pack. It appears your Aunt Eli left us all some surprises."

"Really? Like what?"

"Brad got a bunch of hot chocolate mix packets, and I got ingredients for s'mores."

"I wonder what she stowed away in mine?" Mitch asked.

"I reckon you'll have to find out."

"Have you called her yet?"

"Nope, not yet. I will before we eat."

"Okay, I'll see you in a few minutes." Mitch pulled up his stringer of fish and walked to the tree and tied them off.

Brad was steadily chopping on the log and had a fire blazing in the pit. "Good job on the fire," Whit said. "I'm going to put a pot of water on to use with our MRE's. I think I'm going to try the stroganoff."

"That does sound good. The beef stew is good too," Brad offered. "Do you want some hot chocolate?"

"I think I'll wait until the morning. I have a feeling we'll need something to warm us."

"I think you're right about that. I know our MREs will have a brownie or cookies, but could we have some s'mores?"

"Absolutely," Whit replied as she poured water into the pot. "I need you to get some fresh water treated for us, too, please."

"You got it." Brad stood and topped off their canteens to empty two of their large bottles. "I'll be right back," he said. "Hey bro," Brad said, as Mitch arrived.

Whit placed a pot of water on the fire to heat and sat beside Mitch. They gazed across the lake at the sun sinking into the horizon. "Beautiful, isn't it?" Whit asked.

"It's times like this that set my soul on fire," Mitch answered.

Whit smiled, remembering Eli had used the same phrase not long ago. "How so?" she asked.

Mitch looked at it, and she could see tears making his eyes shine. "I don't know if I can explain it, but being here with you and Brad, sharing these experiences, makes me feel wonderful. It's like I know this is precisely where I should be right now."

Whit slipped an arm around his shoulder. "I'd say that was a perfect explanation. This does feel right, doesn't it?"

"Yeah, it does." He wiped his eyes.

"Brad says the beef stew MRE is good, but I'm going for the stroganoff. What suits your fancy tonight?"

"I'll try the beef tips and rice. That way, we can all share a taste," Mitch answered.

"That's a great idea. We can have some s'mores too."

Mitch grinned. "That reminds me, I need to check my pack." He stood and walked over to his pack. He unzipped an outer pocket and laughed. Mitch pulled out three packages of king-size Payday candy bars. "I guess she doesn't think I'm sweet enough."

"Those are loaded with carbs and will give you a good energy boost between meals," Whit said.

"Give us. I'll share when we hit the trail again. Have you checked to see if Eli made it home yet?"

"Not yet. Bring the sat phone with you, please."

Mitch picked up the phone and handed it to Whit, who dialed Eli. Brad returned with the fresh water and joined Mitch around the fire.

"Hey, baby," Eli said. "How are you?"

"We're great. We all found some surprises in our packs tonight. Thank you."

"I thought you might enjoy some sweets. Where are y'all tonight?"

"Camped at a beautiful lake. Are you home yet?"

"I just drove through town, so maybe fifteen minutes from home."

"I know some four-legged children who will be glad to see you," Whit told her.

"Yeah, Cruz and Tomboy, for sure. I hope they haven't been too much trouble for Carol."

"I'm sure they all survived." Whit laughed. "We hoped to rendezvous with Samurai and her group tonight, but they haven't made it. We'll spend the day here tomorrow too, and the boys will fish. If they don't show by tomorrow, we'll probably have a ton of fish to eat."

"What are you eating tonight?"

"We're going to try out some MRE's and make s'mores afterward. What about you?"

"I've no clue. I'll rustle something up. There are probably a few dozen eggs, so maybe I'll make some breakfast for Carol and me."

"That sounds good. I picked some wild blackberries today, so we'll have pancakes in the morning."

"That sounds good, too. I wish I were there to share with you."

"You're coming with us next time. No argument," Whit teased.

"Yes, I am. I miss you guys."

"We miss you too," Whit said. "The boys seem to be having a great time."

"You too, I hope."

"Yes, I'm enjoying the time with them, but I miss you."

"I miss you too, but I know you've been excited about hiking since the topic first came up."

"Yes, I have and I'm so glad I have the boys for partners." She could hear the ticking of Eli's blinker.

"Okay baby, I'm home. Will you call me before you turn in?"

"I sure will. Welcome home. I love you, Eli."

"Most," Eli answered with a voice filled with emotion.

"I'll talk to you soon. The boys say hello."

"Give them a hug for me."

"I will." Whit ended the call and watched the boys as they prepared the MREs. She was so proud of them. Whit walked over and hugged them. "That's from your Aunt Eli."

"Did she make it home yet?" Brad asked.

"Just now," Whit replied. "Those smell pretty good."

Mitch nodded. "Yeah, they do. You can have the first choice of brownie, chocolate chip cookies, or oatmeal cookies."

"I'll take the oatmeal cookies. Y'all can fight over the brownie."

"Rock, paper, scissors?" Mitch asked Brad.

It took three turns for Brad to finally win the brownie. They shared the three entrees, and Whit was surprised at how good they tasted. "These are tasty."

Mitch smirked. "I reckon they'll do in a bind."

"I think I could live on these," Brad replied.

Whit and Mitch looked at him. "Naw," Whit said. "There's nothing that good to replace home cooking."

"You're right, but if I had to, I could."

"That's a scary thought, bro."

Eli was nearly knocked to the ground by Cruz, who rushed out to meet her. "Yeah, I missed you too." Eli knelt and got a shower of doggie kisses. "Have you been a good girl?"

"I thought I heard someone," Carol called from the porch. "You need some help?"

"Naw, there's nothing I need tonight. I'll unload in the morning."

Carol walked out to hug her. "I wasn't expecting you until tomorrow."

"I didn't want to spend another night alone on the road," Eli admitted.

"How are you?" Carol asked.

"I'm okay. I didn't realize how bad I'd miss Whit and the boys."

"Have you been talking with them?"

"Yeah, a couple of times a day. They send pictures and text, and we talk in the morning and at night. They're having a blast." Eli started walking toward the cabin. "How are things around here?"

"Everyone is fed except for you and me. You up for some breakfast?"

"That's what I was thinking. Are the eggs piling up?"

"I've collected seven dozen since you left," Carol said. "Time to take some to the diner?"

"Yes, I'll drop some off tomorrow. I need to stay busy."

"That won't be a problem. There's plenty of vegetables to be picked in both gardens," Carol said. "I've tried to keep up with them, but they grow faster than I can pick."

"Thanks for taking care of things while I was gone."

Carol smiled. "It's been fun, but man, this place is a lot of work. How does a big omelet sound?"

"Perfect." Eli nodded toward Cruz. "I think I've got some playing to do first."

"Yes, you do. I'm horrible at Frisbee. I can't throw near as far as you."

Cruz dropped the Frisbee at Eli's feet. "I'd better turn the lights on, so we can't see the Frisbee flying," she told Cruz and pressed a button.

"That is so cool," Carol said. "I'll get started on supper. Everything and the kitchen sink okay with you?"

"Yes, I haven't eaten since about eleven, and I was on the road before the sun came up."

"Couldn't sleep?"

"Nope, I had a bad case of a busy brain," Eli said.

"I hate when that happens. I'll call when supper's ready."

"Thanks, Carol." Eli sent the Frisbee flying toward the garden.

"Have fun."

†

"Is it my imagination, or is it getting chilly?" Mitch asked.

Whit nodded. "It's been dropping since the sun went down." She blew the marshmallow to put the fire out and made a s'more. "It's going to be a cold night next to the water."

Mitch looked at the hammocks. "Do we need to place them closer together with you in the middle?"

"That works for me," Whit said and bit into the tasty treat.

"Do you think it would be any warmer in the shelter?" Brad asked.

"No idea. You can try it out," Mitch said. "I'll be toasty in my hammock."

"Are you guys good for pancakes in the morning with some of the blackberries?"

"That sounds wonderful. I had an idea when you mentioned it earlier. What if we took some of the bacon jerky and chopped it up to go in the batter? That way, we'd have sweet and salty and some protein."

"That's a great idea, Mitch. Brad can chop some while you get our fire and water going, and I'll mix the batter." Whit stuffed another marshmallow onto her stick.

A lonesome howl broke the silence, as they roasted marshmallows. Whit looked at Mitch. "Across the lake?"

"That's what I'm thinking. Probably just saying hello." Mitch grinned.

"That's fine as long as he doesn't make a personal appearance," Whit replied.

Mitch looked across the lake. "I'm pretty sure we're safe. I doubt a wolf would approach the fire and three humans, mostly since we haven't cooked anything tonight. Now, if we had some fatty meat roasting on the fire, he might get tempted."

"I'll keep the T-bones tucked away," Brad teased.

Whit nodded. "Good idea."

"I wonder if we'll have any other visitors tonight?" Mitch said.

Brad chuckled. "At the rate, he was moving, I wouldn't be surprised if Timeless were already on his way back."

"He is something else," Whit said. "I can't imagine logging that many miles in a day, much less every day."

"That's a crazy pace, but I guess that's what he's used to doing. I hope I never get that tightly wound," Mitch added.

"I think odds are you're pretty safe." Whit punched his shoulder.

"Such a brute," Mitch teased. "Do you think we need another log before we hit the sack?"

"The pit is fairly deep, so I think it would be safe. I'm going to call Eli. Do y'all want to talk with her?"

"If she's not too tired," Brad said.

†

When Carol said the kitchen sink, Eli thought she'd been joking. The monster omelets were stuffed with meats, cheese, onions, peppers, and olives, then topped with sour cream. "I don't think I've ever eaten an omelet that good. Why have you been holding out on me all these years?" Eli asked Carol.

"It's all your fault. Since I've been up here, I've gotten more creative with cooking," Carol said and grinned. "They were pretty tasty, huh?"

"Yes, the boys will love these. You'll have to cook for them when they get home."

"I'm sure I can do that," Carol replied.

Eli stood and began clearing the table. "I've got this," Carol said. "You've had a long day. Why don't you shower and get ready for bed? I'll head home in the morning unless you need my help."

"I think I can handle things, but if you get bored, come over for lunch. I'm sure we can rustle up a tomato sandwich or something."

Carol smiled. "What do you plan to work on first?"

"After feeding the animals, I want to check the gardens and see what needs harvesting. I may run some vegetables and eggs into town. Do you want to ride with me?"

"Sure, I think I might need a few staples if you wouldn't mind hitting the store?"

"Not a problem. I probably need to pick up a few things too."

"I'll cook breakfast while you feed the animals. How about some bacon, eggs, and toast?"

Eli nodded. "That sounds like a deal too good to pass on. Thanks, again, for holding down the fort."

Carol smiled. "No problem. Julia came out and helped me when she could."

"That was sweet of her. I want to visit her soon about a Christmas present for Whit."

"Oh, she'll love that. You want to go tomorrow?"

"We could. Let's see how things go in the morning. Goodnight, my friend."

"If Whit calls, send my love to her and the boys."

"Will do." Eli climbed the stairs and found Tomboy stretched out on the bed. "I was wondering where you went. I should have known you'd get your belly full and come crash." She bent to scratch under his chin. Tomboy rewarded her with a loud purr. Eli rinsed off in the shower and had just begun relaxing when Whit called. "You have perfect timing."

"I thought I'd better call before you fell asleep."

"I just got done showering and I'm stretched out on the bed."

"Now, that's a lovely visual," Whit teased.

Eli chuckled. "Did you enjoy your first MRE experience?"

"It wasn't bad at all. Not home cooking, but it was tasty. Not nearly as tasty as the s'mores we cooked afterward. Thank you for stowing the goodies away in my pack."

"You're very welcome. Are you and the boys settled in for the night?"

"Yes, they wanted to talk with you, so I'll turn it over to them."

Brad's excited voice came across the phone, and he had Eli laughing in no time. Mitch was just as excited and eager to try again for a landlocked salmon.

"How do you plan to cook them when you catch them?" Eli asked.

"Hot rocks," Mitch answered. "I'm going to hunt up a dozen or so thin flat rocks to heat and cook them on. In theory, I think it will work."

"That does sound like it might. Keep me posted on how it turns out."

"You know I will. It's getting late, so I'll turn the phone back to Love Muffin. Love you."

"Most," Eli replied.

"I sure hope he gets a few salmon tomorrow. That sounds pretty interesting," Whit said. "He already has several lake trout on his stringer."

"I hope he does well, and the group shows up for dinner. If not, you'll be having fish and grits for breakfast," Eli teased.

"Do you have big plans for tomorrow?"

"Probably taking some eggs and produce to the diner. Brad's hens have us overflowing with eggs. I'm going to check the gardens first thing and make a trip to town with Carol."

"Has she seen much of Julia?"

"Yes, she came out to help a couple of days while I was gone. They seem to be doing good. Carol's going back to your place tomorrow, now that I'm home."

"That sounds promising. I know you've got to be tired. That was a beautiful sunrise you sent me this morning. I hope to send you some nice photos from here."

"I'll be looking forward to it. Call anytime you want to tomorrow, and I hope you sleep well. Is it cold?"

"It's a bit chillier here by the water, but it shouldn't be horrible. We've set Mitch's hammock up to block the wind from Brad and me."

"That was a smart move. Mitch's hot natured and will enjoy the breeze."

"That's what we're thinking. I hope you rest. You sound tired."

"I'm missing you and the boys. I can't wait to come and get you."

"The time will fly by, especially since you're home and will stay busy. I love you."

"Love you too. Stay warm tonight. I'll be hugging your pillow tight."

"You are such a tease. Good night, sweetie, I'll call tomorrow."

†

Eli plugged her phone in to charge and smiled at Cruz, snoring softly beside her bed. Tomboy had curled up next to her, warming her hip as she turned off the lamp and snuggled into his warmth. Eli could feel his body vibrating as he purred in contentment. Her eyes closed, and she was asleep in minutes.

CHAPTER SIXTEEN

Whit was chilled to the bone when she woke the next morning. The sun had risen, but the air had yet to warm from overnight. She slipped her feet into her boots and walked to her pack to retrieve a thick hoodie. Mitch was snoring loudly, and Brad was curled tightly in a ball. Whit picked up a stick and poked at the firepit. There were a few embers from last night, so she added some dry wood, got a flame going, and added some small limbs. The instant heat felt good against her gloved hands. *There will be no dip in the lake today.* Whit filled the pot with water and placed it over the heat to boil.

Mitch stumbled out of his tent and walked to the fire. "Even I got cold last night," he grumbled. "Man, this fire feels good."

"Yes, it does. When you get feeling back into your hands, will you chop some of the bacon jerky? We'll let Brad sleep in for a bit."

"I'm awake. I'm mustering the courage to crawl out of this sleeping bag," Brad called out from the tent.

"If you chop the jerky, I'll bring in some more firewood," Mitch said.

"I'll be right there."

"That okay with you?" he asked Whit.

"That might get your blood pumping. Hopefully, the water will be hot, and you can have some hot chocolate between loads."

"That sounds wonderful. I'll be back in a few." Mitch tossed another log into the pit before leaving.

Brad emerged from the tent with his hoodie pulled tight. Whit had to suppress a laugh when all she could see were his eyes, nose, and a flash of braces. "Come get warm by the fire. Do you have your knife on you?"

"Yes, ma'am," he answered.

Whit handed him a plate with several strips of jerky. "When you're fully awake, you can start dicing."

Brad nodded. "Man, it got cold last night."

"Yes, it did. We may need to consider moving the tents behind the shelter if the wind doesn't die down today," Whit suggested.

"That wouldn't break my heart," Brad scoffed. "Even my hair is cold."

Whit smiled. "As soon as that water heats, I'll pour us some hot chocolate. That should help."

Brad diced up the meat and poured it into the bowl Whit was using for the batter. "I'll go help Mitch gather some wood."

"Okay, I'll try to have something hot to eat and drink when you get back."

Whit watched Brad jog in the direction Mitch had gone. A honking noise sounded across the lake, and she turned her attention to a flock of geese landing on the water. Whit pulled out a frying pan and used a dollop of oil to coat the pan for heating. Mitch and Brad returned carrying loads of firewood. "That should get us through this morning. We can gather more later today when it warms up some." Whit looked at Mitch. "Check the water and pour us something hot, while I start on some pancakes."

"You got it," Mitch said with a grin.

Whit poured the first round of batter into the frying pan. She sipped the hot chocolate Mitch handed her. "That hits the spot."

"Yeah, it does, and one packet does all three of us. We may need to splurge on two packs this morning."

"I don't think it will hurt to splurge a bit since this was a bonus to begin with." She watched the pancakes begin to rise in the pan. "Those smell good. Do you want some honey for them?"

"Do you think we need it?" Mitch asked.

Whit shrugged. "Maybe not, but it's available if needed." Brad was seated on the shelter bench. "Can you dig out our plates?"

"Yes, ma'am. With pleasure," he answered.

†

Eli woke refreshed from a great night's sleep. She dressed in work clothes and tried to be quiet as she prepared coffee and left the cabin to feed the animals. Her first stop was the barn, and the cats swamped her as she entered the building. Cajun was exceptionally vocal as he took the slide down from the loft. "I know, I missed you all too," she spoke softly to them, as they wove between her legs while she filled the feeders. Cruz had opened the gate for Molly, and they rushed outside. Eli took a moment to enjoy her coffee and the cats' attention before mucking out the stall and filling Molly's feeder. Cajun hopped in her lap as she sat outside Molly's stall and purred as she scratched under his chin. "Your motor sure is running today," Eli told him as he rolled in her lap. Eli finished her coffee, exchanging her empty mug for the egg basket she had left on the porch. She opened the gates to the coops and scattered scratch on the ground, enticing the hens from the nests. Eli worked quickly to gather twenty eggs. "I'll probably have some fresh greens for you all later," she told the hens, who were searching for insects and tender grass shoots. Eli looked back toward the cabin and saw Carol emerging with fresh coffee. She walked over and joined her friend on the porch steps. "Thanks," Eli said as she took the coffee. "It's going to be a beautiful day."

"Yes, it is," Carol agreed. "I see the hens are still busy at work." She pointed to the basket of eggs.

Eli chuckled. "We had discussed setting up two more coops, but at the rate these girls are producing, eggs would be running out of our ears."

"You would have to consider opening a breakfast place or selling them at the farmer's market."

"I think we're good with what we have for now. I tell you, though, there's nothing like fresh farm eggs."

"I wouldn't have believed there was such a difference before I experienced that for myself," Carol agreed. "Are you ready for some breakfast? I can start cooking while you survey the garden. After we eat, I can help you pick."

"Yes, that sounds good. I want to shell some peas, so the girls can have the hulls."

"No problem, those zipper peas almost shell themselves," Carol said.

"Isn't that great?" Eli asked. "Okay, I'll go take a look. Maybe we can have some fresh vegetables for dinner, if you want to invite Julia out."

Carol smiled. "I'd like that."

†

"The pancakes were delicious," Brad said. "I'll clean the dishes since you cooked."

"I can't argue with that." Whit looked at Mitch. "When do you want to start fishing again?"

"No time like the present. What are you planning to do?" Mitch asked.

"I thought I'd explore around the lake a bit while you guys fish," Whit replied.

"Will you take my knife and the sat phone just in case?" Mitch removed the knife from his belt. "It won't help if you run into anything big, but at least you'll have some protection and a way to call us. I've got my phone on me."

Whit nodded and attached the large knife to her belt. She laughed when it hung down to her knee. "This thing is huge."

Mitch puffed out his chest. "Man sized."

"Alrighty then, I'm off," Whit said. "Good luck, fishing. I'll see you later."

Whit started down the now-familiar path around the lake. Fifteen minutes later, she arrived at a rock outcropping that reached nearly to the water's edge. She climbed onto the top of a large boulder. She could barely see Mitch back at camp, but she had a grand view of the entire lake. It appeared to go on forever, and she could see feeder streams on the opposite shore. Geese swam in front of her, and she could hear ducks farther down the lake. There was a faint sweetness to the air.

This spot might be useful for Mitch if he needs to reach farther into the lake for fish. Whit peered into the clear water and could see several large fish lazing near the protection of the outcropping. She picked up the phone and dialed Mitch.

"Is everything okay?" he answered in a panic.

"Yes, I'm fine. Look to your left," Whit instructed. She waved her hand above her head. "Can you see me?"

"Yes, are you okay?"

"There are some big fish swimming right in front of me. You might want to try this spot out," Whit told him.

"We'll be right there," Mitch said. "Grab the stringer," he told Brad.

Whit ended the call and dialed Eli. She figured she had a few minutes of peace left before the boys arrived.

"Hey," she said when Eli answered. "What you doing?"

"Picking peas and corn. What about you?"

"I was on a walk, but I ended up scouting a good fishing spot for the boys. Mitch and Brad are on their way."

"I'm glad to hear you survived the night. I was afraid it would be cold."

"It was, but we made it through. We had a hearty pancake breakfast, and the boys are fishing."

"Carol and I are doing some harvesting this morning. We thought we'd have a nice vegetable supper and drop some produce and eggs off at the diner. Tell Brad we've got eggs running out of our ears."

Whit laughed at her comment. "So, we don't need a few dozen more hens?"

"No, we've got more eggs than we can eat. I sure miss you," Eli said.

"I miss you too. I bet the animals were glad to see you."

"Cruz has been my second skin since I've been home. Cajun even came down for some loving. Walter and Oscar are getting spoiled by Carol. I think she feeds them at both cabins."

"I do not," Carol hollered at Eli.

"Sure, you say. We need to get the boys a kitty treadmill."

Whit could hear Carol's laughter in the background. "I'm glad you're staying busy."

"Less time to worry about the three of y'all if I keep occupied," Eli admitted.

"No need to worry, we're having a great time. I think the other group will arrive today. I sure hope they do, anyhow. Mitch and Brad are excited to see them again."

"If not, will you wait for another day?"

"Probably not, but we can package up some fish to take with us in case we run across them on the trail. It might be suitable for a day. Hang on a second. The boys just got here." Whit lowered the phone. "Look right there." She pointed out a spot to Mitch. "See them?"

"Holy cow, I think you've found the salmon," Mitch said.

"Go get 'em, tiger," Whit called to him. She put the phone back to her ear. "He thinks we found the salmon he's been hoping for."

"Send me some pics when he catches. I know he will," Eli said proudly.

"Okay, sweetie. I love you."

"Love you most," Eli answered. "Call me later. Bye."

Brad waited for Mitch to cast before gently lowering the fish into the water. Whit and Brad watched anxiously, as a large fish lunged at Mitch's lure.

"Got him," Mitch cried out as he set the hook. "Man, he's got some pull."

Several minutes later, Mitch pulled the large fish onto the rocks. "Yes." He gave Whit a high five.

"Good job, bro." Brad secured the fish on the stringer. "Several more of those, and we can feed a crowd."

"Let me land one more, then you can fish for a while."

"No problem. We've got all day," Brad answered.

"Hey, give me your phone, and y'all hold up that stringer. Eli wanted to see what your catching," she told Brad.

The boys posed for the picture, and Whit sent it to Eli and Mark. She added a text. *They have finally found the salmon.*

"You know, I was thinking. We might want to build up another firepit and put those flat rocks in there, now that you're catching salmon. I can fry the trout and hushpuppies, and you can grill the salmon."

Mitch nodded. "That's not a bad idea, but we need to see how many we can get."

"Have you already got your rocks picked out?"

Mitch nodded. "I've got a stack of them where I had been fishing. I'll bring them to camp when we finish fishing."

"I'm going to head back to camp and get a second firepit prepared," Whit told them.

"Great idea." Mitch set the hook in the next fish. "At this rate, it won't take long to catch all we need." He handed Brad the fish to place on the stringer. "Here bro, you catch a few."

"All right." Brad took the rod.

"Have fun, you two," Whit said and started back toward camp.

†

Eli scattered the pea hulls for the hens. "There, that should keep them busy for a while. Are you up to checking Whit's garden?"

Carol stretched. "Sure. If she's got some ripe tomatoes, I think I'll make us some sandwiches for lunch. Are you planning to head to town afterward?"

Eli nodded. "I think we already have enough produce to make it worth the trip. I'd like to see if there's anything at Whit's that needs harvesting. She probably has some corn that's overdue."

"Will you make some street corn tonight?" Carol asked.

"Sure will. I think we have a package of smoked butt frozen that we can heat up for some protein." Eli took the bowl of shelled peas into the kitchen and filled it with cold water.

Carol picked several tomatoes and looked at Eli. "Are you good here?"

"Yes, ma'am. You want to make some sandwiches while I finish picking corn?"

"I thought I'd get a head start on ya."

"Go ahead. I won't be too far behind you. I'll put the corn in the truck and be in for a bite as soon as I finish. Here, take six ears with you for tonight."

Eli watched Carol leave the garden with an armload of fresh veggies, then finished filling the basket with corn. She drove the Gator home and placed the corn in the truck's bed with the other produce. "This should go to good use," she said as she closed the tailgate.

Carol had sandwiches and tea ready for her when she entered the cabin. "Those look good."

Carol nodded. "I sure am going to miss these sandwiches after the growing season is over."

"I know. I don't think there's a better summertime sandwich." Eli took a bite. "Did you invite Julia out for dinner?"

"I certainly did. She'll come out around five."

"That's great. We can stop by Julia's shop, then hit the store afterward," Eli replied.

"That works for me," Carol said.

†

Whit had finished clearing out a second firepit and laying a fire when she heard hikers approach. She looked up to see

Samurai and the crew coming toward the shelter. "I'm glad you all made it," she told them. "The boys have a surprise in store for you."

"Oh, we love surprises." Samurai grinned. "Where are Jester and Maverick?"

Whit pointed at the two figures standing along the shore. "Catching dinner," she said.

"Oh, heck yeah," Wolfie replied. "A hot meal will be fantastic. What can we help you do?"

"Settle your packs. I could use a couple of extra hands to carry some rocks. We could also use more firewood for tonight. It was cold as the dickens last night."

"It was a bit chilly, and I bet even colder by the water," Samurai said.

Whit nodded. "It's so beautiful here, and the fishing has been good."

Wolfie smiled at Whit. "I'll take a couple of the guys and round up more firewood if you and Count Chocula will help Stargazer with the rocks. We'll probably need to help clean some fish too."

The group separated. "What are the rocks for?" Samurai asked Whit.

"Maverick has caught a bunch of landlocked salmon, and he wants to grill them on these flat rocks while I fry the trout and hushpuppies."

"That sounds interacting. Just point out the ones we need."

"He's already got them rinsed and stacked." Whit chuckled. "Before he even caught the fish."

"That's confidence." Samurai rubbed her belly. "I can't wait to taste them."

They carried a dozen rocks back to the firepit. "Samurai, if you'll go ahead and light the fire, we can get these heated. It may take a while."

"What can I do?" Chocula asked.

"Take this bag and pick more blackberries. We can have them with dinner tonight and in pancakes tomorrow morning," Whit said. "You'll find them about two hundred yards up the path and off to the left."

"I'm on it," he said.

Samurai lit the fire and helped Whit place the rocks around the edge. "So, how has the experience been so far?"

"It's been great. Katahdin was a butt-kicker, but we survived. The boys and I have had a great time, so far, and have met some friendly people."

Samurai grinned. "Did Timeless pay you a visit?"

Whit laughed. "Yes, he stopped in long enough for a bite to eat and blew out again. I wouldn't be surprised if he passed us again on his way south."

Samurai shook her head. "Naw, he was planning to clean up and fly back to California after Katahdin. He was a force to be reckoned with, that's for sure." She chuckled. "Wolfie thought he could keep pace with him, but we found him waiting for us about two miles down the trail."

"I can imagine it would be hard to keep up his pace," Whit said. "I plan on enjoying each step we take."

"Amen to that. We've pretty much slowed to a crawl. We don't want this adventure to end," Samurai said.

"Take heart that there will be others for your group," Whit encouraged. "Even after you start adulting, there will be fun."

"Holy cow," Samurai said. "Would you look at that?" She pointed to Brad and Wolfie, carrying a large stringer of fish.

"We are going to eat good tonight." Wolfie grinned. "We're going to start cleaning these babies, while Maverick brings in a few more."

Whit pulled out a few large plastic bags. "Send me some filets when you get the salmon done, and I'll test out Maverick's theory," Whit told Brad.

"You got it." He tucked the bags in his back pocket.

Whit checked the fire and saw that the wood had burned down to embers. There were no open flames. "Let's place some of these rocks on the embers to go ahead and begin heating them." She and Samurai placed six large, flat rocks in the pit. "I think this is going to work well."

"I'm going to mix hushpuppy batter, if you want to help."

"Just tell me what to do," Samurai said.

Whit pulled up the cornmeal mix, the two mini cans of beer, and a can of whole-kernel corn. "We'd normally add a can of RO-TEL and some chopped onions, but we'll work with what we have."

"They sound delicious already." Samurai poured the cornmeal into the bag with one beer and half of the corn.

Whit nodded. "Give it a good mix with your hand, and I'll start heating some oil." She spread a thin plastic bag across the bench. She pulled out some seasoning, some honey, and the used oil from Biscuit. "Now, all we need is fish."

Brad walked over a few minutes later and handed her six beautiful salmon steaks.

"Those look fantastic," Whit said. "Good job. Keep them coming, and we'll start cooking."

Whit laid the steaks on the plastic bag and seasoned them, then drizzled a bit of honey on the top.

"Have you done this before?" Samurai asked.

"Nope, this will be a first. Wish me luck." Whit grinned and took the oil, coated each of the rocks, and placed salmon steaks skin down on the rocks. "Can you time these for me? Ten minutes and we should be able to flip."

"Absolutely." Samurai set a timer on her watch.

Whit tested the oil. When the water droplets crackled across the surface. "Ready to make some hushpuppies?"

Samurai nodded.

Whit handed her a spoon. "Mound some on the spoon and drop it carefully into the oil. Once they start to float, we can turn them until brown on all sides."

"That sounds easy enough," Samurai said.

"I smell hushpuppies." Brad returned with more salmon and a few trout.

"Something is smelling great." Wolfie and Mitch returned to camp with three more large fish.

Mitch looked at the salmon steaks. "Those look good. Do you want me to fry the trout while you do the salmon?"

Whit nodded. "Sounds like a plan to me."

"Let me go wash my hands, and I'll be right back," he answered.

When the timer went off, Whit turned the steaks. "Man, those do look good. I think we can cook the other side for seven minutes."

"You got it." Samurai reset her timer.

Whit prepped the next round of steaks while she waited. When the timer alerted, she held her breath as she pulled the steaks off the rocks. Mitch had returned just in time to see the first batch. "Let them cool for a second and take a test bite," Whit said. "I need to see if I need to change anything."

Mitch pulled out his fork and took a bite of one of the steaks. His eyes grew wide as he chewed. "Other than the fact they are like molten lava right now the taste is fantastic. What did you put on them?"

"Salt and pepper and a little honey," Whit answered.

"You up for an experiment?" Mitch asked.

Whit laughed. "Always, you should know that by now. What are you thinking?"

Mitch pointed to the bag of blackberries. "Squeeze some of the juice on one of them."

"Great idea," Whit replied. She coated the rocks, placed the next round of steaks on to cook, then remembered to take a picture. She snapped a few more pictures of Mitch and Samurai cooking, and the others gathered around watching. When Mitch and Samurai began taking fried trout and hushpuppies out of the oil, Whit looked at the hungry guys. "What are you waiting on? Grab your plates and get to eating."

No one needed a second invitation. When the final steaks and hushpuppies were cooking, Whit sat beside Mitch and Samurai. "I think our supper turned out quite well."

"Amen to that," Mitch answered. "I now have something I can be proud to add to the shelter logbook, a Maverick-first recipe.

"Your Dad and Eli would be very proud," Whit told him. She looked at Brad. "You both worked hard to provide an excellent meal."

Wolfie let out a howl. "That was off the chain, bro." He smiled.

"You can cook for me anytime," Samurai said. "We will definitely be taking a fishing rod the next time we hike."

"That was good, and I don't think I can eat another bite," Mitch said.

"That should hold you until pancakes in the morning," Whit said.

"Will you adopt me?" Samurai asked.

"We already have." Whit winked.

The kids pitched in to clean the dishes, while Brad and Whit tended the fires. "Do we have enough wood for the night?" Brad asked.

"I think so. If not, we have a lot of help to gather more."

Trinket, a rather flamboyant young man, jumped up. "Come on, Jester, we'll go get some just in case."

Brad nodded, and Whit watched them head toward the woods. Her gaydar had pinged when Samurai introduced Trinket. Whit was proud of Brad for not shying away from him because he was gay. She sat on the shelter bench and tapped out a text to Eli. *Look what we had for dinner.* She added a few pictures. She saw the little bubbles indicating Eli was answering and waited.

Damn, those look great, and it appears everyone was enjoying themselves.

A good time was had by all. I'll call you later. Love you. More.

Whit tucked her phone away and was lost in the flames when Mitch returned.

"Where's Jester?"

"He and Trinket went out to grab more wood," Whit replied.

"Do you think I should go help?"

"No, I think they have it under control." Whit smiled.

Mitch stretched out beside her and groaned. "I am stuffed."

Whit nodded. "That was delicious. I bet we could try some of the trout that way at home. Where did you come up with the idea?"

"I must have seen a video on it somewhere. It just clicked in my head." He shrugged.

"Well, I'm glad it did. The fish was tasty and fun to cook."

Samurai plopped down beside Mitch. "Who are we missing?"

"Jester and Trinket are gathering more firewood," Mitch answered.

Samurai had a frown on her face. "I'm glad Trinket came along. He got a rough deal from his family."

"What happened?" Whit asked.

"The goofball came out to his parents. Needless to say, that didn't turn out well. They kicked him out of the house and won't pay his tuition."

"That blows," Mitch said. "What's he going to do?"

"His grandmother took him in for the summer. He was extremely depressed, and I was afraid he'd do something dumb, so I convinced him to go hiking with us."

"How far along is he in school?" Whit asked.

"This fall would have been the second semester of his junior year. He's taken a heavy load to get ahead, but now he's not sure what will happen. He's got a job at a fast-food place when we get back, but even with his academic scholarships, it won't be enough. The university won't allow him a work-study job, because his parents claimed him on their taxes."

"What is he studying?" Mitch asked.

"Veterinary medicine," Samurai said. "That dream may be out the window now."

"Is he living close to the university with his grandmother?" Whit asked.

"Yes, she's only a few blocks off campus, so he rides his bike all over town."

"Here they come," Mitch said.

Whit stood and picked up the sat phone. "I'm going to call Eli before it gets too late. I'll be back in a few."

Mitch nodded. "Would you mind if I play some music on my phone?"

"Nope, play away. Just remember to charge it tonight."

Whit walked toward the lake for some privacy. She found a fallen tree and sat looking out at the reflection of the setting sun.

†

Eli was putting away leftovers when Whit called. Carol and Julia had returned home for the evening. "Hey baby."

"I have something I need your advice on," Whit blurted out. "Oh, hey sweetie, I'm sorry."

Eli could sense the urgency in Whit's tone. "What's up?"

"There's a young man in Samurai's group. He's gay, and when he came out to his family, they kicked him out and refused to fund his college. He's almost three years into his studies to become a vet, and I'd like to offer to help him."

"So, what advice do you need? I'd say go for it. If you need help offering him a loan, I'll help. He can work at the farm and volunteer at Doc Loren's clinic during the summer breaks until he's finished."

"I didn't even think about the clinic. That's a great idea. Thank you, Eli. I don't have bills. I can loan him the money and work out repayment after he graduates."

"See how easy that was?" Eli teased. "What are the kids doing?"

"Sitting around the fire, talking and listening to country music ala Mitch."

"That's my boy. The supper looked fantastic. How did it taste?"

"It was incredible. I think we'll try cooking some trout like that when we come home."

"That sounds like a good deal. I took a bunch of eggs and produce to the diner today. They were excited about the fresh veggies. Do you think we'll do any more canning this fall?"

"Maybe a little bit, but I think we're pretty set. I believe Ms. Flora was interested in some canning. Why?"

"We're still producing vegetables almost faster than I can harvest them," Eli said. "If we put up many more, I'm going to have to build a storage building."

"Why don't you ask Mr. Henry what they're interested in, then we could probably offer some to the food bank in town."

"I can do that. Are you guys hitting the trail again tomorrow?"

"Yes, after some blackberry pancakes. I have to admit it's been fun having all the kids here tonight."

"Stay another night if you want."

"No, I think we need to move on. We'll never make it through the Hundred Mile Wilderness if we don't."

"Alright, go have some fun and call me in the morning. I'll be in the garden again." Eli chuckled. "Love ya."

"Most," Whit replied. "Good night."

†

Whit turned around and watched the young people, as they milled around the fire or sat in small groups and talked. She noticed that Brad and Samurai were talking with Trinket and decided to walk over in their direction. As she walked past the firepit, Mitch grabbed her in a bearhug.

"Love you," he said.

"Most," Whit replied. "Eli said to tell y'all hello. She was jealous of that supper."

Mitch grinned. "We'll try it out at home."

Whit smiled back at him. "We definitely will." She walked over to the shelter where Brad was sitting next to Trinket. "Hey guys, would you mind if I borrowed Trinket for a few minutes?"

"Not at all," Brad replied.

Trinket stood up. "What can I help with?"

"Let's walk for a bit." Whit smiled at him. They walked to the lake and took a seat on the fallen tree. "I've been thinking. Samurai shared a bit of your story, and I'd like to make you an offer."

Trinket looked at her, and Whit could see his eyes shining with tears as he listened to her.

"First, I am sorry for the way your family has reacted to your news. You are still their son, and they should love you no differently than they did before. Don't give up on them. Hopefully, they will come around."

Trinket shook his head. "I don't know. I've never seen my dad so angry before. He's a macho, ex-military guy, and my news was a blow to him."

"Believe it or not, there are some very macho gay men and plenty in the military," Whit assured him. "I don't know if the boys have talked much about their Aunt Eli."

"Brad told me you were lovers. I hope you don't mind me saying how jealous I am of the support you seem to get from your family. The boys love you deeply and talk of you so fondly."

Whit nodded. "We have been blessed. That's why I wanted to talk to you. I want to offer you a loan to finish vet school. You can work on our farm during the summer, volunteer at our local animal shelter, whose director is also a lesbian, and when you graduate, we can discuss a payment plan."

Trinket just stared at Whit in shock. He was speechless.

Whit smiled. "Are you okay?"

The first tear slid down his face when he nodded. "Are you serious?"

"Yes, Eli and I talked. We don't want you to miss an opportunity for an education. We'd like to help."

Trinket reached over and hugged Whit. "You don't know the load that lifts off my shoulders. I have been fast-tracking to finish school earlier, but if I have to work to save up a semester's tuition, it will take me forever to finish."

"I understand how motivated you are to graduate. Here's what I need you to do. Over the next few days, consider what you'll need for tuition, supplies, and incidentals. I'll give you my contact information in the morning, before we leave. Give me two weeks to get home and settled, then call me."

"My grandmother is offering for me to stay with her, so room and board won't be necessary. I'll work for spending money."

"I appreciate your willingness to work, but you need to concentrate on your studies and enjoying the college experience. Add spending money to your budget."

"This is freaking unbelievable. Thank you so much. I promise I will pay you back every penny, plus interest," Trinket said.

"We will worry about that later. Now, go enjoy yourself," Whit said as she stood.

Trinket stood beside her and hugged her tight.

Whit could feel him shaking and knew he was crying. She pulled back from him and smiled. "Everything's going to be all right. Go splash some of that cold-ass water on your face and come back to the fire."

Trinket wiped his tears back. "Yes, ma'am. Thank you again for your generous offer."

"You're welcome," Whit said, then turned to walk back to the camp.

CHAPTER SEVENTEEN

Mitch smiled at her when she returned to the shelter. "Everything okay?"

"Just wonderful," Whit said. "Will you two be ready to move on tomorrow?"

"Yes, ma'am. I figured we'd roll out after breakfast," Mitch replied. "We've got a river crossing ahead of us that Samurai said will be a bit of a challenge."

"Did she give you some tips on how best to cross?" Whit asked.

"They formed a human chain. With the size of the group, it was easier to keep everyone safe. I figure we can attempt the same and try to pick a safe route. Hopefully, it won't rain and make the water rise before we get there."

Trinket returned to the group and sat beside Samurai at the fire. Whit could see him talking with her. Samurai's head snapped around, and she smiled at Whit.

"What's that all about?" Mitch asked.

Whit bumped shoulders with him. "We can talk about it tomorrow. I think I'm going to stretch out and let you youngins' have your fun."

"Thanks for everything today," Mitch said. "It was a great day."

Whit nodded. "Yes it was, the first of many. Try to keep the fire going while y'all are up. It'll make a fire easier in the morning."

"I don't think that will be a problem," Mitch answered, as Wolfie added another log.

"Have fun." Whit stood to head to her tent. She stopped at each group and bid them good night.

"Thanks for such a fantastic meal," Wolfie said. "That was probably one of the best we've ever had on the trail."

"You're very welcome. It was a lot of fun. Eat a bacon cheeseburger for me when you get to Katahdin." Whit grinned at him.

"Maybe two." Wolfie smiled back at her. "We'll try to hold the noise down so you can get some sleep."

"No problem, I think I'll be out like a light as soon as I lie down."

†

Eli downloaded the pictures Whit and the boys had been sending her onto her laptop. She used some software to edit them, then sent some off for enlarging and printing. Eli wanted to surprise them with framed photographs when they returned home. She had also ordered a memory book for each of the boys to take home with them and would add additional pictures to the albums as she received them. Whit had encouraged her to do something fun for herself while they were gone, and Eli was having fun with this project. She had also met with Julia about a Christmas gift for Whit that she hoped would be a total surprise.

Eli had shut down the computer and was climbing the stairs when her phone pinged. Mitch had sent her several pictures of the group cooking and sharing the fish dinner, then spaced around campfires. They all looked happy, and the smile on Whit's face made her heart melt.

Great shots. Missing y'all. Love ya!

Love ya most. Good night.

†

Whit's bladder woke her shortly after sunrise, and she crept out of her tent. Samurai was already adding wood to the firepits. She looked up at Whit's approach.

"Did I wake you?"

"No, my bladder did. After I get some relief, I'll start some breakfast," Whit answered.

"You want me to go ahead and get the pans heating? We're doing pancakes, right?" Samurai asked.

"Yes, ma'am, we are," Whit replied as she walked past the shelter.

When she returned to camp, Whit looked at Samurai. "You ready to start some breakfast?"

"Yes, ma'am. These guys will wake up starving, no doubt."

"I'll start mixing some batter. Will you smash up some of those blackberries? We can add the juice and pulp to the mix and start cooking. I've got some honey we can use."

Samurai dug into her bag. "I can do one better. I have a bottle of syrup from our food drop."

"Perfect." Whit smiled.

As the pancakes were cooking, Mitch and the others began emerging from their sleeping bags. "You got the air smelling good." Mitch held his hands over the fire.

"Can we have some hot chocolate?" Brad asked when he arrived.

Whit smiled up to him. "That's up to you. It's your stash to share."

Brad looked at Mitch. "Put some water on to heat, and I'll grab enough to share with everyone."

"You got it, bro." Mitch filled the pot to boil.

Wolfie dug through his pack. "I've got some jerky strips we could roll up in the pancakes if anyone's interested."

Whit smiled as each of the hikers added food to the breakfast. They ended up with a smorgasbord. Brad passed around a notepad and got everyone's contact information to keep in touch once everyone returned home. Whit sipped her drink and watched the older kids interacting with Mitch and Brad. It didn't matter there was a five to seven years difference in their ages. Brad and Mitch had earned their respect with the hard work they put into the meals. A bond had formed that she hoped would continue for years. She was a bit sad when the meal was over, and they packed up camp to head down the trail. Whit hugged Trinket last. "We'll be talking soon," she whispered to him.

"Yes, ma'am, we will." He hugged her tightly. "Thank you."

"Enjoy Katahdin and your trips home. I hope, one day soon, our paths will cross again," Whit told the group as she shouldered her pack.

Samurai grinned. "They will. We've already decided to come back next summer and do another section or two with you guys."

Whit's face beamed. "That would be awesome. We'd love the company."

"It's been a lot of fun meeting y'all," Wolfie said.

"Yeah, it has, man." Mitch shook Wolfie's hand and got pulled in for a hug.

"Safe travels," Samurai said.

"Until we meet again," Brad said with a dramatic bow. "Parting is such sweet sorrow."

"Come on, you big goof." Whit threw an arm around his shoulders.

†

Eli finished her morning chores, then rode up the mountain. Cruz sat next to her, as she pulled into the open field where Mitch had fallen in love. She walked the area and tried to visualize the tiny home that they would purchase. The spot was perfect for Mitch. Close enough for assistance if needed but secluded enough for privacy and independence. Eli was filling her water bottle at the spring when Whit called.

"Hey, sweetie."

Whit's voice was crystal clear and full of excitement. "Good morning. I hope it's as beautiful there as it is here."

"It's gorgeous here. Are y'all back on the trail?"

"Yes, we broke camp about an hour ago."

"How does it feel to be on the move again?"

"Good, but it was hard to say good-bye to the others. They are such a good bunch."

"I bet you'll be hearing from them again."

"Yes, they informed us they were coming back next summer to do a section or two with us."

Eli could hear the excitement in her lover's voice. "That will be fun."

"I think so too, and I hope you'll be with us."

"I will be. I've decided I can't stand to have you out of my sight for such a long time."

"Aww, isn't that sweet?" Mitch said.

"Hey, I can be sweet," Eli said.

"Uh-huh, we're finding that out," Mitch teased.

"How far do you plan on hiking today?" Eli asked.

"We're shooting for ten miles, but we probably won't make it to a shelter with such a late start."

"You haven't been sleeping in a shelter, so that shouldn't be a problem," Eli said.

"We just won't build a fire, since there won't be an established pit," Whit replied. "We can use the heaters with the MRE's to prepare dinner. We had a great breakfast."

"Are you doing okay for supplies?" Eli asked.

"Yes, we don't lack for anything. I think we planned well."

"That's good to hear. Keep the photos coming. It looked like you had a blast last night."

"It was fun," Brad said. "The salmon was off the chain."

"I am so glad y'all decided to take a fishing rod with you. It's proven to be a great source of fun and protein added to your diet."

"Ours and many other hikers," Whit added. "I'm surprised more people don't think of fishing."

"Maybe you'll meet other fishermen along the trail."

"Maybe so," Whit answered. "Okay, sweetie. I just wanted to check in and tell you we love you. Time for us to get moving again."

"Thanks. Call me later when you get settled if you can."

"Will do. Love ya!"

"Most," Eli answered with a chuckle.

Whit tucked the sat phone away in her backpack.

Mitch offered a hand to pull her to her feet. "So, you going to fill us in on what happened with Trinket?"

"After hearing his story, I got to thinking," Whit said, as she dusted off her bottom. "I've got no bills to speak of, and I've got money coming in from the government plus book sales. I've decided that a young man's education is a good investment." She smiled at Mitch. "He got such a horrible reaction from his family; it broke my heart. He will work with us during summer breaks and volunteer with Doc Loren if she allows, which I'm sure she will."

"That's a great idea," Mitch said.

"I can't imagine my parents reacting like that because I love someone," Brad said.

"I know, but it happens all too often, especially if you're gay. That's partially the reason why suicide rates in gay teens are so high."

"Dad may not approve of our choices, but I can never see him disowning us," Mitch said.

"He wouldn't. All he wants from you two is for you to be happy and do your best in life. Who you love is your choice," Whit told the boys.

"One of us has got to make Mom a grandmother." Mitch snickered.

"Not for many years yet, so don't rush it," Whit warned.

"I know I'm nowhere ready to be a dad."

"I don't think you're ever totally ready, Mitch, but you need to have a career and the means to support a family. I think your parents and Eli are old fashioned enough to expect that you will be married before having children, so first things first."

"Yeah, I want to be more than a baby daddy. I want to be a dad like ours," Brad replied.

"I think he's done pretty well with the two of y'all," Whit said. "Let's get a move on. Daylight's a-wasting."

†

The following day, they reached the river crossing Samurai had shared with them. Whit called for a meal break, while they studied how best to ford the river.

"That's moving pretty quickly." Mitch scratched his head.

Whit frowned. "Yeah, it is."

"Do you think we should scout up and downstream for an easier place to cross?" Brad asked.

"It can't hurt." Whit took a bite of jerky. "After we eat, why don't you two split up and check it out? I would think, since the trail runs through here, this is probably the best site."

Brad pulled out his trail map. "There appears to be a bridge five miles downstream." He pointed to it on the map. "That seems like a long way to go just to cross."

"It would probably be the safest route for sure," Whit replied. "That's pretty much a whole day of hiking, when we could probably cross in thirty minutes here."

"You're the smart one, so it's your call," Mitch said. "I wonder how the fishing is?"

Whit chuckled. "You and your one-track mind."

Mitch nodded. "A hot meal of fresh trout would be nice, though. I don't think we've got enough meal left for hushpuppies, but we could do a few hoe cakes."

"Okay, then. We cross here, then set up camp on the other shore. You boys can fish, and we'll hit the trail again in the morning."

"Deal," Mitch said.

†

They decided Whit would lead, and Mitch would enter last, with the smaller Brad in the middle. They used the walking sticks Eli made for them and picked safe spots to plant their feet. "Remind me to tell Eli how much these came in handy today," Whit told Brad as they stepped safely ashore.

"It did make balancing much easier, didn't it?" Brad agreed.

Mitch nodded. "Yes. Twice, I caught myself slipping on the rocks and was able to steady myself."

"Let's slip these camp shoes off and let them start drying out while we scour for firewood, then you can start fishing," Whit said.

"Man, I never knew clean socks and broken-in boots could feel so good," Mitch said, as he laced his boots.

"That was some cold water," Whit replied. "I don't know about you guys, but I sure could use a shower."

"We should be at the lodge in two more days." Brad studied his map. "Hot showers, hot food, and a warm bed." He grinned. "Man, I can't wait."

"Me too." Mitch rubbed his face.

"Are you planning to shave or let it grow?" Whit asked. "It's filling in pretty nicely."

"I think I'll let it grow, just to see how it looks," Mitch replied.

"Makes you look old," Brad teased and ducked his brother's playful punch.

Whit laughed. "You guys get to work finding us some wood." She picked up their shoes and placed them in the sun to dry.

Brad came rushing back five minutes later. "Mitch and I found an excellent shelter fifty yards upstream. He sent me back to bring you and our packs."

"Let's go then. If you can grab Mitch's pack, I'll grab our shoes," Whit offered.

"Leave them, and I'll come back and grab them," Brad replied.

"Okay." Whit shouldered her pack. "Lead the way."

†

Mitch was successful in landing several trout. Brad was downstream cleaning, when they heard hikers. Whit looked up to see a young couple approach.

"Hello," the young man said. "Do you mind sharing the shelter tonight?"

"The more, the merrier," Whit replied. "We generally don't sleep in the shelter, so you're more than welcome."

"Thanks!" He smiled at Whit. "I'm Toby, my wife is Wicket, and this is our new trail friend, Goliath." Toby gently removed a tiger-striped kitten from the top of his pack.

"What a cutie," Whit said. "You found him out here?"

"Yes, about a day's hike out of Millinocket. We figure someone dropped him off in the woods. He was the only one we found," Wicket replied.

"He's adorable," Whit cooed. "I'm Stargazer, and these are my two nephews, Maverick and Jester." She pointed them out.

"Ah, a fellow fisherman." Toby smiled. "Mind if I join you?"

"Not at all. There's a good pool that the trout stop in for a rest break." Mitch pointed out the spot to Toby.

"That's awesome." Toby began assembling his rod. "We've been lucky so far with trout."

"You've got a terrific surprise two days ahead," Mitch told him. "There's a giant lake with some landlocked salmon.

We caught a mess that we shared with a group of friends heading north. We grilled them on flat stones."

"That sounds delicious," Toby said.

"They were tasty and fun to catch."

Wicket placed their packs in the shelter and set Goliath on the ground. The kitten tottered over and looked up at Whit. She bent to pick him up. "You are so little and cute." Whit scratched his head. "It breaks my heart to think someone could abandon something so young and fragile to die."

"It happens all too often," Wicket said. "He's a real charmer and loves to snuggle."

"Back home, we've rescued a dozen black cats from the shelter. They rule our barn," Whit replied.

"Where's home?"

"North Carolina, just west of Asheville," Whit replied. "Where are y'all from?"

"Gulfport, Mississippi," Wicket answered. "We're on our last section hike of the AT."

"We're on our first heading south," Brad said, as he delivered some filets.

Goliath purred when Brad stroked him. "Do you mind if I play with him?"

"Go for it. Goliath has some sharp teeth and claws, though, so be warned." Wicket shook her finger but wore a friendly smile.

"Yes, ma'am." Brad pulled out a shoelace, dangling it in front of the kitten. Goliath danced on his hind legs, reaching for the tip of the string.

Whit watched them play, until Goliath tired and curled up in Brad's lap and fell asleep. "You've made a new friend." She smiled.

"It makes me miss Cajun and the crew," Brad admitted.

Mitch walked over with a stringer of three more fish. "With what Toby brings in, I think this will be enough to feed everyone. Oh, how cute," Mitch said, when he saw the kitten on Brad's lap. "I'll clean these, since you have a visitor."

"Do you need help?" Whit asked.

"No, ma'am, I've got these. You can start cooking. It won't take me long to have these ready."

Whit pulled out the two frying pans, placing them above the fire to heat. She poured the remainder of the oil in the pans and began mixing a batter for the hoe cakes. She grinned at Wicket. "We had some great hushpuppies at the lake, but I'm out of supplies, so hoe cakes will have to do."

"I doubt anyone will go hungry." Wicket smiled. "I can cook our fish," she offered.

Whit shook her head. "No, need to dirty up another pan. You can help me, though."

"Just tell me what you need," Wicket replied.

"I think I'll use the remainder of the meal for the hoe cakes, but I've got a sleeve of Ritz crackers in my pack. You can smash those into a powder that we can use on the fish."

"That sounds tasty," Wicket said.

"We shall see. We have some blackberries we can crush to use as a topping too. There was a large patch close to the lake shelter that was big and juicy. We made some great pancakes with them."

"They sure tasted good," Brad agreed.

"How long do you plan to be on the trail?" Wicket asked.

"Two weeks this trip, but we'll be back next summer. We wanted to get a taste to see if this was what we wanted to do," Whit explained.

"How hard was it starting at Katahdin?"

Whit smiled. "Harder than we'd imagined, but we survived. There have been a few climbs since then, but nothing like Katahdin."

"I'll be honest, I'm not looking forward to it," Wicket said.

"Get a good night's rest and a hot meal. It took us eleven hours to finish," Whit told her. "Leave your full packs at the campsite and get a day pack from the ranger's station. That way, you carry only what you need to eat and drink."

"Don't forget a jacket. It gets cold on the climb to the top. A headlamp, too, for the end of the descent," Brad added.

Whit nodded. "It was cold up top and past dark when we returned. You two are in better condition, so it might not take as long, but be prepared."

Mitch and Toby joined them with the last of the filets. "We are going to eat good tonight," Mitch said.

"Yes, we are. Are you up to trying a blackberry topping on the filets?" Whit asked.

"We haven't made anything I won't eat yet," Mitch said.

"I've got a small bag left. Will you mash the berries? We can try it out on a piece in just a few minutes." Whit turned the filets in the pan.

"That doesn't look like cornmeal. What did you bread the filets with?" Mitch asked.

Whit shook a bag of cracker crumbs. "I saved the meal for hoe cakes and used some Ritz crackers instead."

"That was a clever idea," Toby said.

"I bet the berries will be good on the hoe cakes, too," Brad suggested.

"Yes, they will," Mitch agreed.

"I bet this little bit will enjoy the fish too," Brad said, as he petted the kitten.

"The protein will help him grow. We've been mashing up some soaked jerky for him," Toby replied. "Tonight, he can fill his belly with trout."

Whit pulled out a small filet and placed it on a plate. "Break this one into bits so it can start cooling." She handed it to Toby.

Wicket began pulling the browned hoe cakes from the oil, as Whit took out a batch of fish. "Dig in," she told the group.

Brad was the first to spoon some of the berries on his fish and cakes. Whit waited to see his reaction before spooning berries onto her plate.

"Oh, my word," Brad said. "Between the berries and crackers, these taste almost like candy."

"I was a bit skeptical about the berries and fish, but I admit, it does pair well together," Toby said.

"Trail ingenuity." Whit chuckled.

"It goes well with the salmon, too," Mitch said. "We tried some with honey drizzle and blackberry juice, and they were out of this world. By the way, you won't find the salmon near the shelter."

"Where did you find them?" Toby asked.

Mitch pointed at Whit. "Whit found them about a 150 yards north of the shelter. There's a rock outcropping that leads down to the shoreline. You'll find them there in deeper water."

Toby smiled. "That's good to know."

Mitch smiled. "We also left the rocks around the firepit. Pour a bit of oil on them and start skin side down for about ten minutes, then flip for another five to seven and you have a great treat meal."

"Do you have some oil?" Whit asked.

"No, we don't. We ran out days ago," Wicket said.

"You can strain the oil from the pan and take some with you. Did you keep your container?" Whit asked.

"Yes, we take everything with us," Wicket said.

"Great, you'll be all set then." Mitch took another bite. "I think, next year, we should pack some Old Bay or Cajun seasoning. I bet they would both work well with wild-caught fish."

"Look at you. We haven't finished this adventure, and you're already planning for next year," Whit teased.

"It's never too early to start planning," Brad said. He looked at Toby. "Is there anything you wish you would have brought along?"

"More bug spray down south." Toby scratched his arms, seeming to remember the experience. "The first week we left Springer Mountain was horrible. The mosquitoes and black flies were terrible. I'd save the last two sections for cooler weather."

"That's good to know. Stock up on garlic, too," Mitch said.

"Is there anything you'd do differently?" Brad asked.

Toby looked at Wicket and smiled. "Invest in quality supplies from the start. I cut corners on our sleeping bag, and we nearly froze to death several nights when the bag ripped wide open."

"He got a new sleeping bag for Christmas that year." Wicket grinned.

"I noticed your hammock tents. Have they been a good investment?" Toby asked.

"Priceless, and they come in a double size too," Whit offered.

"I think my Christmas list just grew, honey," Wicket said.

"Well worth the investment if you plan to do a lot of hiking and camping. A satellite phone too. My partner, Eli, got us all teched out with the sat phone and solar chargers. We've not missed a night of calling home, and the phone cameras are great for pictures."

"Speaking of which," Brad said. "Smile for the camera."

They took several group shots around the fire, then Brad played with Goliath until he was ready to sleep. He handed the kitten to Wicket. "I think he'll sleep well tonight. He's been purring up a storm."

"He's lucky you guys found him," Mitch said. "I'd like to get my hands on whoever dumped him."

"He will be a welcome addition to our family," Toby said. "He travels well too."

"Thanks for sharing a great meal with us," Wicket said. "The tips for the lake and Katahdin will serve us well, too."

"Is there anything ahead of us in the next few days that was tricky?" Mitch asked.

Toby nodded. "The next river crossing you'll encounter was a bit nerve-racking, with just the two of us. If you run across other hikers, a longer chain may help."

"Pray that it doesn't rain too. That water was moving at a good clip, and the current was strong," Wicket added. "I tucked Goliath inside my shirt just in case we took a tumble."

"That was a smart move," Brad said.

Wicket nodded. "Just don't rush and be sure of your footing. You made it across this river; you can survive the next."

"I think I'm going to wash up the dishes, call home, and crash," Whit said.

"I'll get the dishes," Mitch replied. "Tell Aunt Eli we said hello."

"You sure?" Whit asked.

"Yeah, you clean up all the time. Jester can help me." Mitch nudged his brother.

"Yes, ma'am, I will." Brad stood and began collecting dishes.

"Save the oil and give some to Wicket and Toby," Whit said and picked up the phone.

†

"Guess what?" Whit said when Eli answered.

"What?"

"We made our first river crossing today, and none of us went swimming."

Eli's soft laugh echoed over the phone. "Our connection isn't as great tonight."

"We may be at a lower elevation than normal," Whit replied. "I think we start climbing again tomorrow. The day after, we'll have another river to cross. Hopefully, the reception will be better."

"Are you eating well?"

"We had hoe cakes and fried trout tonight, with a lovely couple from Gulfport, Mississippi. Oh, and a kitten they rescued."

"A kitten? Way out there?"

"Yeah, a real cutie named Goliath. He enjoyed fish with us tonight, too." Whit chuckled. "Have you been eating well?"

"Fresh veggies and lots of eggs. I had some chicken livers for supper tonight."

"The boys send their love. They are having such a great time. So am I," Whit added. "We just miss you."

"I miss you too. I think I've walked every acre on the mountain since y'all have been gone."

"It won't be long until you came come retrieve us," Whit said.

"I've already got my bag packed," Eli told her.

"Not excited, are ya?" Whit chuckled again.

"I'm ready for y'all to be home," Eli replied. "I'm glad you're having fun, but I miss you."

"I miss you too. You may not recognize the boys when you see them," Whit warned. "I swear Brad has grown two inches, and Mitch's beard is coming in full. He's not going to shave until you pick us up, to see how it looks."

"They are growing up way too fast. Where did my little boys go?" Eli said.

"You'd be proud of them. The boys have done well on the trail together. They're washing dishes as we speak."

"I think it's a good experience for them, and it sounds like they are rising to the challenge."

"Very much so," Whit agreed.

"Are you staying warm?"

"Last night was better, but I'm ready to snuggle into you," Whit replied. "I miss my human heater."

"I'm glad to be missed for something," Eli teased.

"I miss you for many things," Whit said. "Most of all, I think I miss reaching out to hold your hand or touch you. It's so comforting to know you're there within reach."

"I can't count the times I've caught myself talking to you or one of the boys only to realize I'm alone." She sniggered. "Cruz is starting to look at me a bit funny."

"I wonder how she'd do on the trail?" Whit asked.

"She'd probably love it," Eli answered. "You think we should take her next year?"

"Yeah, I do." Whit was glad to hear that Eli was already planning to go on the next adventure. "I'm excited at the prospect of you coming with us next year."

"I won't be left behind again. I thought I could handle it, but it's been an ordeal being here alone."

"I'm sorry it's been so difficult for you," Whit said.

"It was my decision, so I have no one to blame but myself. Lesson learned."

"Do we need to come home sooner?"

"Absolutely not. I'll put my big girl panties on," Eli promised.

"We should be back at the lodge in three or four days. We'll pick up our food drop and spend a night there. Maybe we can do a FaceTime then."

"That would be good. I'll feel better if I can see you."

"I'll try to call again tomorrow morning, when we get on the trail."

"Okay, get some rest. I love you."

"Love you most," Whit said with a chuckle.

†

Whit walked back toward camp and found Mitch and Brad around the fire. "Eli said hello and she loves you."

"I bet she's lonesome without you," Mitch said.

"She is. I don't think she thought it would be as hard without me or us around." Whit smiled. "The best news is that she and Cruz will be joining us next time."

"Cruz will go crazy with all the scents to follow," Mitch said. "I think she'll love it, though."

Brad nodded. "It will be fun to find out."

"Okay, guys, it's bedtime for me. Is oatmeal good for in the morning?"

"Sounds fine to me," Mitch answered, and Brad nodded.

"Don't stay up too late."

"Yes, ma'am," Brad said.

"Good night, boys. Love y'all."

"Most," Mitch said.

CHAPTER EIGHTEEN

When the lodge came into sight, Mitch laughed. "Man, am I glad to see this place."

"Showers first, then we can go eat until we bust," Whit promised.

"We can hit the showers in the bunkhouse, while you use the one in the room," Brad offered. "It will be much faster that way."

"You must be hungry," Whit teased.

Brad grinned. "I've been dreaming of bacon cheeseburgers, pizza, and Philly cheesesteaks all morning."

"I knew you had some pep to your step. Now, I know why." Whit ruffled his hair. "Let's get checked in."

"I've already placed your food drop in the suite," the young man working the counter said. "I had a feeling y'all would make it in today."

"Thanks. That saves us from having to lug it upstairs. You boys hit the showers, and I'll see you in a bit." Whit handed Mitch a key.

†

Several hours later, they were clean and glutted on protein. "Are you guys ready to FaceTime with Eli?" Whit asked, as they stretched out on the king-sized bed with her.

"Yeah. Maybe we can do Mom and Dad tonight?" Brad said.

"We most certainly can," Whit assured him. "Grab my phone and hand it to Brad, since he's in the middle. He can play cameraman."

Brad placed a FaceTime request to Eli. She was sitting on the front porch steps with Cruz. "Good afternoon, gang," Eli answered. "You guys sure look comfy."

"Clean and stuffed to the gills," Whit answered. "How are you?"

"Doing good. Cruz finally wore out from playing, so I'm taking a break. Mitch, all that hair looks good on you. Do you plan on keeping it?"

Mitch ran his hand over his face. "Just until we come off the trail. It's kind of itchy."

"We're trying to convince him to keep a Fu Manchu or something," Brad said. "All I got was more peach fuzz," he laughed.

"Don't worry. You'll wish that's all you had once you have to start shaving regularly," Eli told him.

"We hit the diner already and have plans to return for supper," Whit told her. "I was amazed at the food we consumed."

"Y'all have been burning a lot of calories," Eli reminded her.

"Yes, we have. That last river crossing was a bear. If it weren't for Brad's quick reflexes and Mitch's muscle, I would have been a drowned rat."

"What? You didn't mention that last night."

"I didn't want you to worry, but we're safe, full for the moment, and clean again. Brad did a load of clothes, too, so we don't have the funky smell in our packs."

"Did you pick up your food drop?"

"It was waiting in the room for us," Whit replied. "We're going to pick up some fresh oil and more hot chocolate mix. That came in very handy."

"Is there anything else you ran out of that we need to add more for next time?" Eli asked.

Mitch answered, "More cornmeal, because we've been able to fish so much and some syrup for pancakes. We've been able to find blackberries, and we cut up some jerky too."

"That was creative," Eli said.

"We made a garnish of blackberries for fish and hoe cakes. That was very tasty. Oh, we want to add some Old Bay and Cajun seasoning too," Mitch added.

"It sounds like y'all have done some experimenting," Eli said.

"We've had fun cooking experiences. The salmon on the flat rocks was, by far, the best, especially with the honey or berries," Whit replied.

"We may have to continue to experiment," Eli said. "Those all sound delicious."

"I have to admit they all were pretty good," Whit told her.

"What are your plans for this afternoon?" Eli asked.

"Packing our bags with the fresh supplies and maybe stroll to the grocery for a few other items before hitting the diner again," Whit answered.

Eli smiled. "That sounds like a plan. Are you heading back to the trail in the morning?"

"Yes, we need to do that to make it to our extraction point on time. We've had a rather leisurely pace up to this point." She looked at Mitch and Brad. "Not that I would change a minute of our experience."

"We're only four days away, right?" Mitch asked.

"Yes, that's right," Whit answered.

"We have five days left," Brad corrected.

"Does that mean you want an extra night in town?" Eli asked.

"No, that means we have an extra night on the trail if we find another exceptional spot to camp," Mitch said.

"I wouldn't think that would be too hard to do. It seems like you've enjoyed your spots thus far."

"Yes, we have. I wish you could have seen the lake. It was gorgeous," Mitch said.

"Except for being cold at night, I could have stayed there a week," Brad said.

Whit nodded. "It was pretty cold there."

"You will be all warm and toasty tonight," Eli reminded him. "Get your grocery store run in and call me before y'all hit the sack."

"Okay, sweetie. I'll have a Philly cheesesteak in your honor tonight." Whit grinned. "Love you."

"More."

"You heard the lady; let's rock and roll." Whit climbed from the bed. "Man, that sure was comfortable."

"It won't be long until you can climb into it for the night. Do we need to make a grocery list?" Mitch asked.

"That may be a safer bet," Whit replied. "I'll write."

"More hot chocolate and Paydays," Mitch said.

"Cornmeal and syrup," Brad added.

"Do we want to try out some different seasonings on the fish? More oil too." Whit added to the list.

"You think we can get Cajun spices?" Mitch asked.

"We can certainly look. I want to order some ham biscuits, from downstairs, that we can eat on the trail." She grinned at the boys. "Unless you want to sleep in."

"Heck, no," Brad said. "We've got twelve miles to the next shelter, so we're going to need to pick up the pace a bit to make it before dark."

"Is there a lake or stream nearby?" Mitch asked.

"Looks to be a decent-sized river, and a bridge to cross it." Brad smiled.

Whit looked up at him. "That's good news. I'm not ready for a swim."

"Are we good on everything else?" Mitch asked.

"Yes, I think so, unless we find something irresistible at the store." Whit turned to Mitch. "Do y'all want to hang out in the bunkhouse for a bit tonight?"

"We could check to see if anyone is interesting to talk to," Mitch said. "You can have a bit of private time with Aunt Eli."

"That would be nice. Not that we don't love you two, but I can't get mushy with y'all around."

Mitch broke out laughing. "Is that what they call it now, getting mushy?"

"You know what I mean." Whit broke out laughing.

"Is that like sexting or phone sex?" Brad asked.

Whit smacked him on the back of the head. "No, silly. That's for you, young folks."

"Ouch, I was just teasing," Brad complained.

"I didn't smack ya that hard, cream puff." Whit chuckled.

"We'd better go before blood starts flowing." Mitch laughed.

"Let's go, then." Whit ripped off the list.

†

They returned with half an extra-large pizza and a two-liter of Mountain Dew "for later," as Mitch called it. They quickly packed the additional supplies in their packs. "Order a dozen biscuits for in the morning," Whit told Mitch, as they started for the door.

"Got it," Mitch said, and they disappeared.

Whit changed into some shorts and a T-shirt and climbed onto the bed. She clicked on the FaceTime button and called Eli. "Hello, gorgeous," she said, when Eli picked up the call.

"Hey, beautiful. How are you?"

"Stuffed with cheesesteak and comfy on this big, old bed. I wish you were here to share it with me."

"Aww, that sounds so sweet. Where are the boys?"

"I sent them off to the bunkhouse so we could have some private time."

"Oh, I bet they loved that." Eli chuckled.

"Ha! Brad accused us of having phone sex or sexting."

"Sexting? What the heck is that?"

"My point exactly. That must be a young person's thing. I do wish you were here, though. I miss snuggling into you."

"Just five more days, and you can snuggle all you want."

"I can hardly wait. I will need a long, hot shower."

"Someone to wash your back too?"

"Oh, yes. I've got several spots I can't reach."

"I will be more than happy to wash anything you want," Eli promised.

"I love the sound of that," Whit replied with a purr to her voice.

Eli fell silent for a few long seconds.

"Are you still there?" Whit asked.

Eli started to laugh. "I was thinking of how easily this could evolve into phone sex. I'd rather hold out and wait for the real thing, though."

Whit laughed. "Me too. There's nothing like that personal touch."

"Amen to that," Eli replied. "I picked a bucket full of blackberries today. I think Carol and I are going to try our hand at making jelly tomorrow."

"That sounds like a good way to keep you occupied," Whit teased.

"We've gotten our freezers full of fresh vegetables, and I've taken two loads to the diner."

"We may end up needing to make a trip to the farmer's market one weekend. Have you asked Ms. Flora if she has room for more?"

"I knew I forgot someone. I dropped corn and peas for Doc Loren and Macy."

"Once we get home, we can get Mitch to cook some butts or barbequed chicken, and we can have a harvest day instead of a fish off."

"That's a good idea. We can send our guests home with all the fresh vegetables they can handle. I like that. I'll send an invite for the weekend after you get home if that's okay."

"Sounds wonderful. That will give us time to settle back in and do some shopping. I do like the idea of butts. They can cook all day while we work."

"Let's make it happen."

Whit was silent until she said, "Welcome back, boys. Nothing going on downstairs?"

"Naw, it was pretty dead down there," Mitch replied.

"Say hey, to Eli," Whit told them.

"Hey, sugar britches," Mitch called out as he climbed onto the bed next to Whit.

"I got your sugar britches, buttercup." Eli laughed.

Brad crawled onto the bed so Eli could see him.

"Hey, there you are. So, nothing happening in the bunkhouse?" Eli asked.

"Just an older couple, no youngsters to chat with," Mitch replied. "What are you doing tonight?"

"Planning your homecoming with Whit. We want you to cook some butts, and we'll call everyone out for a harvest party."

"What's a harvest party?" Brad asked.

"We'll pick everything we can from the gardens and send our friends home with plenty of fresh vegetables. I've already taken two loads to the diner, and there will be more ready soon."

"That sounds doable," Brad replied. "How are my girls?"

Eli laughed. "We've got eggs coming out of our ears. We're getting two dozen nearly every day. Carol and I have cooked eggs every way you can imagine. She cooked a monster omelet the other day that you guys will love. It was so delicious."

"That does sound good," Brad said. "When are you starting up this way?"

"In three days. I'll layover and drive to the extraction spot the next day. I'll be waiting for y'all at the hotel."

Mitch leaned over closer to Whit. "That sounds good. I don't want this trip to end, but it will be good to see you."

"For reals," Eli said. "I've missed y'all."

"Five more days, and you can see our stinky butts again," Brad teased.

Eli laughed. "Have you mastered pooping in the woods yet?"

"I'm good as long as there's a tree near," Brad admitted. "It took a few attempts, but I'm good."

"That's good to know," Eli replied. "I'm glad you're learning some new skills this summer."

"This has been the best summer yet," Brad said. "I've learned and experienced so much. I can't wait to do it again next year."

"We can start planning early this year," Eli promised.

Whit stifled a yawn. "Okay, well, I guess we'd better get some sleep. We've got miles ahead of us tomorrow and another river crossing."

"Be safe and know that I love y'all. Call when you can and keep the pictures coming. I love seeing them."

"Will do, Aunt Eli. Love you most!"

"No way, man," Eli answered Mitch. "Good night."

"Good night," Whit replied.

†

Eli swept a pile of shavings from the floor of the porch. She had been working on a dozen new walking sticks to keep her mind occupied. Eli had listened to the boys chatting about their new friends and thought it would be a thoughtful gift to them for Christmas. Eli knew Brad was collecting trail names and contact information. She'd help them burn the words and finish the sticks when they returned. With a deep sigh, she entered the empty cabin. "Are you ready for bed?" Cruz fixed her chocolate brown eyes on her and licked Eli's hand. "I love you, too, baby girl."

CHAPTER NINETEEN

Carol came over to fix breakfast for them and was working on omelets, when she heard Eli's phone vibrating on the counter where it was charging. After the previous day of mowing, Eli had forgotten to place it on the charger overnight. She'd gone out to feed the animals and collect the eggs, while Carol started cooking. When the phone vibrated again, Carol looked at the message from Mark.

Call me ASAP.

Carol grabbed the phone and rushed out to find Eli, who was scattering scratch in the chicken coops. "Hey, Mark is blowing up your phone." Carol waved the phone in the air.

Eli rushed toward her and took the phone. She saw the message to call Mark and felt the blood drain from her face. Something terrible must have happened for him to message like that. Eli dialed Mark immediately. "What's up?"

"There was a murder on the AT last night—a woman who was traveling with two men. They aren't reporting any names or locations. I've been trying to reach Whit and the boys for hours, and I can't get any of them."

Eli sank to her knees.

Carol rushed to her. "Are you okay?"

"Put me on speaker," Mark requested.

Carol took the phone from Eli and pushed the speaker button. "What's happening? Eli is ghost white."

"There's been a murder on the AT, and I can't reach Whit or the boys."

"What the hell?" Carol cried out.

"The news isn't releasing any names or locations yet, but they say it was a woman traveling with two men."

"Oh, no. What can we do?"

"Tell Eli to get ready. I'm already on my way, and I'll be there to get her in an hour."

"Okay, I'll have her ready. She's already packed her bag."

"See if you can get some food in her. I'll keep trying to reach them. Thanks, Carol."

"You're welcome, Mark. Pray everything turns out okay," she answered.

"I'll see you soon."

"Be careful."

Carol ended the call. "Let's get you fed and ready. Mark will be here soon."

Carol reached her hand out and helped Eli to her feet. "Everything is going to be okay. Go bring your bag down, and I'll finish breakfast."

"I can't eat, Carol," Eli cried.

"Yes, you can. You and Mark will be driving all night, so he needs you strong right now. Go and get your bag and bring it downstairs. You can keep calling while I cook."

Eli nodded. She rushed into the cabin and flew up the stairs. She brought her bag down and sat it on the porch, then poured a mug of coffee.

"Why don't you pack a small cooler? You both will need some caffeine and snacks to keep you going. I can whip up some biscuits and sausage to take or some egg salad?"

"Egg salad would be easy, and Lord knows we have enough eggs."

Carol smiled at Eli. "Yes, we do. I'll put them on to boil, while you ice down some drinks. There's a fresh loaf of bread and chips in the pantry." She was relieved to see the color returning to Eli's face.

Eli rushed out to the workshop to retrieve a cooler, placed a twelve pack of Mountain Dew inside, and added ice.

Carol whipped up a large omelet and split it between the two of them with toast. She added sour cream and handed Eli a fork. "Get busy."

Eli hung up the phone. She had tried the sat phone, but it rang without being picked up. The three cell phones were out of service range. "Dammit," Eli growled. "It just can't be them."

"It's not. Somehow, I think you'd know if Whit was in danger. Try to relax and eat. You need to be strong."

"I know. Thanks, Carol. I don't know what I'd do if I lost Whit or the boys," Eli said, as tears filled her eyes.

"I don't wish that on any family, but it's not Whit. I know it's not."

Eli was picking at the omelet. "Eat now, until it's gone," Carol said gruffly.

"Yes, ma'am," Eli replied and took a bite.

†

Eli's stomach revolted against the food, but she knew Carol was right. She needed to eat and be ready to drive straight through to Maine. Her finger pushed the redial button. Still no answer. Eli's mind whirled with images. For a moment, she felt faint. Carol was right. Somehow, she would know if Whit was harmed or in danger. Her hand reflexively went to the crystal around her neck. It was warm but not glowing. She closed her eyes and imagined speaking with Whit. *Are you okay?* Nothing happened. Eli didn't think they would connect with this much distance between them, but it was worth a shot. She opened her eyes and found Carol staring at her.

"Are you okay?"

"Yes, just sending up a prayer that Whit and the boys are fine."

"Oh, alright, then." The worry on Carol's face didn't fade.

Eli finished the omelet and started the egg salad, while Carol packed chips, bread, and a variety of other snacks. "Is there anything particular I need to do while you're gone?"

"No, keep everyone fed. Hopefully, we'll be home safe and sound soon."

"I can do that." Carol bent down to pet Cruz. "Looks like you're stuck with me again for a few days."

Eli frowned. "I had hoped to take her, but not now. We need to get up there and find our family."

"That's the main priority right now." Carol pulled ingredients out of the fridge.

Eli tossed Cruz an egg white. "I'll be back soon. Try not to get too spoiled while I'm gone."

Carol laughed. "Ha! Like I could spoil her any more than you already have." Carol took the bowl of egg yolks and began adding the mixture.

Eli washed her hands and walked over to the cabinet. She pulled down her pistol and attached it to her belt.

"Do you think that's needed?" Carol asked.

"As crazy as this world has gotten, I won't travel again without protection," Eli answered.

Carol nodded. "Crazy indeed."

Eli tried calling all four phones and still got no response. "Dammit, I hate not being able to get in touch."

"Scour the internet and see if there's any news," Carol suggested.

Eli's fingers flew across the keys, as she typed in keywords. "Holy shit," she called out.

"What?"

"Still no names or locations, but a man wielding a machete attacked her. Her companions had minor injuries and the state police are in pursuit of the suspect. Damn, damn, damn. It can't be them. Why would anyone want to attack them?"

"Okay, so maybe that wasn't the best idea I had today." Carol frowned and snapped the lid on the container. "Toss this in your cooler. Add more ice if you need to cover it up."

Eli reached for the container and carried it to the cooler. She placed it inside and decided another bowl of ice would be enough. Eli dropped the last cubes into the cooler and looked up when she heard Mark's truck come roaring up the mountain. Eli could see a dust cloud following him.

Carol rushed out onto the porch, as Mark's truck slid to a stop. Cruz ran out to greet him.

Eli could see the panicked look on his face. "Have you heard anything yet?"

"Nothing. Still no answer. The boys and Whit will be fine," Eli told him, as she pulled him into a hug. Her words didn't ring with confidence in her ears. She could feel the pistol strapped to his waist. Mark was worried too.

"Let's roll," he said. "We've got a long drive ahead of us."

Eli rushed back for her bag, and Carol carried the cooler. "Keep me posted on any news," Carol said. "I'll turn the television on and see if they are reporting anything yet."

"Thanks for everything," Eli replied and climbed in beside Mark. "Let's go get our family."

†

Whit stared at the river ahead of them. The water was rushing by from the rain that had fallen the night before. She turned and looked at Mitch. "What do you think? Should we cross or wait it out and hope for better tomorrow?"

Mitch looked up at the sky. "I'm afraid we're going to get more rain, which will make it even worse."

It began sprinkling as he spoke. "Damn, just talking about it, brought it down." Brad covered his mouth.

Whit laughed. "It's okay. I was thinking the same thing." She looked back at Mitch. "Let's get our camp shoes on, so we can keep our boots dry."

He nodded, and they changed into shoes. "Let's not get in a rush. This water is more powerful than it looks. Same order as before?"

"No, you first, then Brad and I'll bring up the rear," Whit agreed. "I hope we don't go swimming."

"Me too. I can already feel how cold that water is, and we haven't stepped in yet."

"Hey, wait a minute. I've got an idea." She lifted her walking stick. "Eli wrapped these with twenty feet of paracord. We can use mine to tether us together. If one of us does slip, we'll have a bit of a safety net."

"Unless it's Mitch. I don't think you and I could hold him," Brad teased.

"You'd be surprised what adrenalin can help you do," Whit told him. "Mothers lifting cars and buses off of children. I think we can hold Mitch until he gains his feet." Whit punched Brad.

"You're right, Whit," Brad said. "I'd never doubt you for a second."

Whit nodded. "Okay, then. Are we ready?" She wound the cord around Mitch's waist, then Brad's, and finally her own. "Slow and steady. Use your sticks for balance."

Mitch stepped into the water and cringed as the cold liquid soaked up to his knees. "That's invigorating. I think my balls just shrunk to peanut size."

"That's a bit TMI." Whit laughed. "They will thaw out after we get across."

Mitch nodded and stepped forward, carefully choosing the placement of his feet. Brad followed him into the water and squealed when it filled his shoes. Whit braced herself for the rush of cold against her skin.

The first third went smoothly, and the depth shrunk as they reached the middle of the river. "That wasn't too bad," Mitch said, as he stepped back into the deeper water.

They were twenty feet from the shore when the disaster happened. Brad's left foot slipped off a rock, plunging him into deep water. He cried out in fright, and Whit's hand locked in on the cord. Mitch had already looped the line around his hand, which was probably the only thing that kept Brad's head above the water. Brad lost his grip on his walking stick. As he lunged for it, he pulled Whit off balance, causing her to tumble into the water. "Holy shit," Mitch cried out, supporting the weight of both of them without losing balance. "I need you guys to get to your feet," he said through gritted teeth.

Whit grabbed Brad's pack, rose to her feet, then pulled Brad upward as he sputtered and spat out water. "Got him. Let's move." Whit was beginning to shiver.

Mitch pulled them across the remaining distance and tossed his pack onshore, as he helped Brad and Whit emerge from the water. "You two are soaked. Get out of those clothes and dry off as best you can. I'll find wood for a fire."

Whit and Brad stumbled over to several large boulders and dropped their packs. "Grab your towel and blanket," Whit instructed, as she pulled the shirt over her head. "No time for modesty." She laughed, as she stripped off her pants and shoes. "Damn. that was cold."

Brad's teeth were chattering, and his lips were pale. "Nnnnot my idea of a bath," he stuttered.

Whit was worried for him. Brad had the least amount of body fat of the three of them. She took her towel and started rubbing his back and chest furiously to get his blood flowing again. "Drop those pants and let's get you wrapped up," Whit told him, even as the cold water ran down her face from her hair.

"I'm okay. You get dry." Brad managed to pull his shoes and socks off and rubbed his legs dry before wrapping up in his blanket.

Whit was drying off, when she looked up and saw him crying. "What's wrong? Are you hurt?"

"I lost my walking stick," he frowned.

"I promise you; Eli will be more than glad to make you another."

"I know, but it's not the same."

Whit saw his eyes grow wide. He pointed at her. "You're bleeding."

Whit looked down at the towel and saw the blood Brad was pointing out. She didn't feel anything but the cold, but when she turned around, Brad said, "You've got a big scrape on your right shoulder and down your back."

"It'll be okay," Whit said. "Let's get warm." She sat next to him and pulled her blanket around them both. They huddled together, sharing warmth.

Mitch returned a few moments later, carrying an armload of wood. He dropped it at the pit. "Let me get a fire going, and I'll gather more wood."

"You go, and I'll get the fire started. I love you, but you suck at that, bro," Brad said with a smile.

"You're right about that. Are you two alright?" Mitch asked.

Whit nodded. "Yes, thanks to your strength. You did great, but I see you need some doctoring up too." Whit pointed to the blood dripping from his right hand to the ground.

"It's not bad, but where did all that blood come from?" He pointed to her towel.

"I scraped my back when I fell. Jester can patch us both up later. I'm just happy to feel my toes again." Whit smiled up at him.

"Do you need me to pull out dry clothes and socks?" Mitch asked.

Whit shook her head. "No, we can get them. Gather another load of wood, then come and get dry yourself. None of us needs to be sick."

"I'm good. I'll change pants and socks when I get back and get my boots back on my feet. Be right back."

Brad huddled around the wood until smoke began rising and a flame burst out of the wood. "Here we go. I'll keep feeding the fire, if you want to get dressed in dry clothes. Please don't put a shirt on until I can treat that scrape."

"No problem," Whit replied. Brad turned back toward the fire, so Whit slipped into dry panties and pants. She wrapped the towel around her shoulders and bent down for clean socks. "Damn," she cried out, and Brad spun around.

"You okay?"

"Yes, that scrape hurt when I bent over. I wasn't expecting that," Whit explained.

Brad smiled at her. "Sit back on the boulder. I'll put your socks and boots on for you."

"I can do that," Whit replied.

"Please?" Brad reached for her socks.

"Okay," Whit relented and sat back on the boulder, while Brad put the warm, dry socks on her feet. She had to admit her boots were toasty once he laced them up. "Thanks, that's much better."

"You're welcome. Now go stand by the fire and get warm while I get dressed. Then I'll take a look at your back."

"Yes, sir." Whit chuckled with a salute. "Aw man, this feels good." She held her hands over the pit.

"Mitch would still be trying to light it." Brad pulled a dry shirt over his head.

"It's good that we all have our unique talents. Mitch saved our asses today with his strength. If he couldn't have held us, we might be floating down the river somewhere."

"I know. I was terrified for a second. Then I felt you pulling on my pack and I knew we were going to be alright."

Whit shivered. "I hope that's the last river we have to cross this trip."

"It is," Brad said. "I think we need some practice before next year."

"I agree," Whit said.

Brad rubbed his head with the towel and finger brushed his hair. "Let me get my first-aid kit and get you fixed up."

Mitch brought in more wood and placed a few large logs on the fire before pulling his shoes and socks off. "That looks painful." He motioned to Whit's shoulder.

"Grab her canteen and a couple of Tylenols from the kit, please," Brad requested. "That will take the edge off, at least. I'm sorry the peroxide stings, but I've got to make sure it's clean before I put a bandage on it."

Mitch handed her the pills and water. "Are you hurting anywhere else?"

"No. But I'm sure we'll be sore tomorrow. How's your hand?"

"Nothing a little Neosporin won't fix," Mitch said.

Brad looked at his hand. "Go rinse that in the cold water and rinse the blood out of Whit's towel. When you get back, I'll doctor you."

"Thanks, bro," Mitch said.

Whit felt Brad gently spread the antibiotic ointment across her damaged skin. "I don't have big Band-Aids, so I'll have to improvise." He laid a large sheet of gauze over the scrape, then taped it to her skin as best he could. "Can you get a bra and a shirt over your head?"

"Yes, I think I can manage. Thank you for fixing me."

"Thanks for not letting me drown." Brad offered her a clean shirt and sports bra.

Whit pulled the shirt over her head. "I'm going to put us some water on to boil. We could use some hot chocolate right now."

"Amen to that." Mitch returned and spread Whit's towel to dry.

Whit placed the water over the fire and watched as Brad ministered to Mitch's hand. The cord had burned deeply across his hand, and it looked painful. "Does that hurt bad?"

"No, not bad at all. That ointment sure helps," Mitch said, as Brad wound a roll of gauze around the wounded hand.

Brad grinned at him. "We need a bigger first-aid kit next trip."

"That one sure came in handy today," Whit replied.

"Yeah, it did. Thanks, bro." Mitch pressed the tape into his hand.

"Are y'all good with some pancakes and jerky tonight?" Mitch asked. He frowned. "I broke my rod when y'all fell."

"Your rod, my walking stick, some skin. That was a heck of a river crossing," Brad said.

"Man, I'm sorry about your stick," Mitch said.

"Yeah, and that was your lucky fly rod," Brad replied.

"I'll break another one in before the summer is through," Mitch smiled. "No more fish this trip, though."

"We've got enough supplies that we won't starve," Whit assured him.

"I'm going to gather more wood. I won't be long." Mitch disappeared into the woods.

†

Mitch stashed wood along the path beside the river that he would pick up on his return. A breeze had picked up, dropping the temperature, but at least it served to push the rain clouds through quickly. They had a nice fire, but they didn't need to be soaked in rain. He didn't hold out much hope of finding Brad's walking stick, but he knew he had to try. His heart raced when he saw the bright orange and blue paracord dangling from a limb. Brad's walking stick had lodged on a fallen tree about three feet offshore. Mitch carefully reached across to retrieve the walking stick, then returned down the path, picking up wood as he went. He couldn't carry it all with Brad's stick, but he would return with Brad for another load to get them through the night. Brad and Whit had their backs to him when he returned.

"Y'all ain't gonna believe this," he said, and they turned toward him.

"You found it," Brad cried out and jumped to his feet. "Thanks, Mitch."

"You got lucky, and it hung up on a fallen tree branch." He handed the walking stick to Brad. "I need you to help me carry in the rest of the wood, though."

"No problem." Brad placed his walking stick next to his pack and followed Mitch.

Whit watched them disappear down the path. She was very proud of how both of them had responded. Their strength and actions prevented a crisis from occurring. It could have been easy to become lost in the raging cold river. *Eli and Mark will be amazed by this story.* She pulled out the sat phone, tried to dial out, and realized the water had seeped into the battery pack. "Well, shit." Whit searched her backpack for a bag of rice to pull out the water. Her cell phone was dry but not in service. "I guess this story will have to wait." She tucked her phone back in her pack.

When the boys returned, Mitch saw the sat phone in the bag of rice. "Water damage?" he asked.

"Yes, and my cell doesn't have service. Check yours when you can," Whit told them.

Mitch pulled out his phone. "Nope, out of range of a tower," he replied.

"Mine too," Brad answered. "I guess we won't be calling out tonight."

"No, our grand adventure story will have to wait. Who's ready for some hot chocolate?"

"I am so ready," Mitch said, as he stacked the wood next to the pit. "I guess the shelter is farther down the trail. "Are you okay staying here tonight?"

Whit began pouring hot water. "Absolutely. We can pitch our hammocks and crash here. "I'm not sure I have the energy to walk any farther today."

"Are you okay?" Mitch asked.

"Yes, just a bit drained emotionally. That was quite a scare, but you both reacted well and didn't panic. I'm very proud of you."

"It was scary, but we worked together, and we're all okay," Brad said. "A few battle scars, but they will add to our story." He grinned.

"That they will." Whit handed them a hot drink. "To surviving," she toasted, and they took a sip of the hot chocolate.

"Man, that's good," Brad said.

Mitch nodded. "When we get done drinking, you can help me pitch the hammocks while Whit starts on pancakes."

"We can all relax around the fire after dinner," Whit replied.

†

"Still nothing," Eli growled and plugged her phone into the charger. They had crossed over two state lines and were approaching a third.

"I'm going to have to stop for fuel soon. Will you make us a sandwich? Can you drive for a bit afterward?"

"Sure, Mark. You've got to be exhausted."

"Just worried. I don't know what I'd do if we lost any one of the crew," Mark admitted.

"I know. I have faith Whit and the boys are okay, though. I feel like I would know it if something happened. Don't ask me to explain that."

"I won't. I'd feel for anyone's family in this situation, but I'm praying with all I have that it's not ours."

"I know. One or two sandwiches?"

Mark pulled into the station to fuel the truck. "Just one for now," he answered and stepped out of the truck.

Eli stepped out to open the cooler and assembled a couple of sandwiches, while Mark filled the tank. She ate her sandwich while she waited on him to return from the restroom. "I'd better make a pit stop too. Are you okay with Mountain Dew, or do you want some coffee?"

"A Dew will have me wired for hours." Mark chuckled. "We can swap over to coffee later."

Eli relieved her aching bladder and climbed into the truck. She pulled back onto the Interstate. They had been driving about an hour, when both their phones started ringing. Laura called Mark, and Carol was calling Eli. "Let's hope this is good news," Mark said as he answered.

Eli answered Carol's call.

"Hey, Eli, the news just broke in for a special announcement. The hiker killed was a woman from Tennessee, and they have apprehended her ex-boyfriend for the murder."

"Dear Lord, that's a relief," Eli said. "I think Laura is giving Mark the same news. Thank you for calling and letting us know. I'll call you back later."

Eli looked over and saw tears running down Mark's face. "That is excellent news. I feel for the woman's family, but I'm glad the boys and Whit are okay. Thanks, honey. Yes, I promise we will stop and get a room now. I'll call you later."

Mark ended the call. "You were right; it wasn't our crew. I'll feel better once we hear from them to know they are all right."

"Me too. Hopefully, the gang is in a terrible reception area, and we can call tomorrow. Are you up to driving a few more hours?"

"Yes, I don't think I can sleep right now, anyhow. I'll need to find a store, too. I have no clothes or hygiene goodies. I jumped in my truck when I heard the news and told my boss I'd call him later."

"You need to call him and let him know everyone is okay. You can head home Monday after we pick up the crew and drive home." Eli reached over and covered his hand with hers. "Find a store. I can't look at you in those same clothes for the next five days." Eli made a face.

"I'm on it, sis." Mark picked up his phone.

†

"I think we need another cup of hot chocolate," Mitch said as they sat around the fire.

"I won't argue with that," Whit replied.

"You two relax and I'll pour this round," Brad told them.

Mitch looked at Whit. "How's your shoulder feeling?"

"I won't lie. It feels a bit raw. How's your hand?"

"Burns a bit, too, but I think I'll live." Mitch gave her a sly grin. "May I make a suggestion?"

"I'm all ears," Whit said.

"Will you let Brad and I transfer stuff from your pack to take some weight off your back?"

"No, I can carry my share of the load."

Mitch nodded. "We both know that, but the strap is going to run across that scrape. We can wrap a towel around it, but taking some weight out would help tremendously."

"What he's saying is true. Just a few items would be a help," Brad added. "Especially since we have a climb ahead of us."

Whit tossed her hands up in the air. "Okay, I can't argue with logic."

"Thank you," Mitch said. "I feel better now."

"I'll change both your bandages in the morning before we leave, so you'll both have a fresh layer of ointment and pain relief. It wouldn't hurt either of you to take another dose of Tylenol either."

"Dish them out," Mitch said. Brad gave them each two tablets. "Thank you."

"Three more days on the trail?" Mitch asked.

Whit shook her head. "Probably a little over two before we head into town to meet Eli."

"It's been so much fun. I know, not long after we get home, Brad will be going back to Bama and I'll only have a few weeks left." Mitch opened his arms. "I'm going to miss all this. Even though parts of it have kicked our butts, it's been quite an adventure."

"Yes, it has, and I'm thankful that I waited for the two of y'all to come into my life to share it with me," Whit told them. She felt her eyes tearing up. "It does seem like the summer has passed so fast."

"I'll be wishing for these days when the coach is running our butts off during football practice," Brad said.

"I don't miss those days of puking your guts up from being too hot," Mitch said.

"Yeah, there are those. I feel like I'm in better shape this year than ever before." Brad flexed his arms. "I'm almost getting guns."

Whit nodded. "Hard work will do that to you. I bet you've grown at least two inches this summer."

"If you continue to eat more, you'll start to fill out. It'll be muscle, which will help with football," Mitch told him.

"No more tofu." Brad laughed.

"Tofu is healthy for you, but you need more meat. Fish and chicken are some of the best you can have to build muscle." Whit smiled. "I bet, by this time next year, you'll have added another twenty pounds of muscle."

"Do you think we can catch up a bunch of trout to put in the freezer?" Brad asked Mitch.

"I don't see a problem with that. We can catch a cooler full for you to take home, and I'll bring a couple of coolers full when I come back. That should last you for a few months. I'll even help Mom and Dad with cooking."

Brad smiled. "I'd love that. You've gotten great at cooking this summer. I hope you will continue to experiment. You've created some tasty meals."

"Maybe Dad will allow me to do more of the cooking. I know it would ease some of the weight off his shoulders," Mitch added. "I think he would appreciate getting home after a long day to a meal that was ready for him to sit and enjoy."

"I'm sure he would," Whit agreed. "You need to be sure to take some of the flat river rocks home, so you can grill some salmon for them too."

"Yeah, that was off the chain," Brad said.

"We need to change topics. All this food talk is making me hungry," Whit said. "We got any Paydays left?"

"We sure do. You want one, bro?" Mitch asked Brad.

Brad nodded. "That does sound good."

"Something sweet to eat, then we need to hit the sack. We've got miles to walk tomorrow." Whit took the candy bar that Mitch offered.

"That sounds good to me. I'm ready for some sleep." Mitch sat down next to Whit and looked up at the moon. He pointed up to the sky. "We're going to have a full moon tomorrow night or the next."

"That will be a great way to celebrate the end of our journey, under the light of a big, full moon," Whit said.

"Yes, it will," Brad agreed. "What are we doing for breakfast in the morning? We could do one of the MRE breakfast meals, for quick and filling."

"That's a good idea," Mitch said. "We haven't eaten any of those yet."

Whit dropped her wrapper into the fire. "Sounds like a plan."

"I'm going to sit up for a bit and make sure this fire gets dowsed," Brad said.

"Fine by me. Good night boys."

✝

Eli pulled into the parking lot of the hotel. "I'm glad we can rest easier tonight, but I wish we could have talked to them."

"Maybe by tomorrow we'll be able to reach them. You good with one room?" Mark asked.

"Yes, now that you've got some new clothes." Eli poked his ribs. "I'll get us checked in if you'll park and bring the bags."

"Deal," Mark replied. "Don't let me forget to call Laura when we get into the room."

"Yeah, I'll just send Carol a text. It's too late to call her. She knows Whit and the boys are safe. I'll call tomorrow to give her an update."

CHAPTER TWENTY

Whit woke early and felt the tightness in her back and shoulder. It was a minor injury, but it had made sleeping in the hammock difficult and painful. The sun was cresting over the horizon when she stepped out of the tent. The morning air was crisp, but she did not have the chill she'd experienced after falling in the river. She glanced over to find Mitch's tent empty and wondered where he had gone. Brad was still softly snoring, buried beneath his covers. Whit pulled out her cell phone only to find she still had no service. She picked up the bag of rice and looked at the sat phone. Whit pushed the power button, but nothing showed on display. She would try again once they started down the trail. Whit looked up at the sound of footsteps and saw Mitch approaching, holding his phone. "No service for you either?"

"No, ma'am. I even walked fifteen minutes down the trail and still nothing," Mitch answered. "Maybe something later today."

"We can continue to try as we hike today." Whit walked over to the shelter and saw that Mitch had already laid out MRE's for breakfast. "Do you want to break down camp or eat first?"

Mitch nodded toward the packages. "If you want to use the heaters to warm up the food, I'll get Brad up and start breaking down camp."

Whit nodded and started working on breakfast. She listened to Mitch calling for Brad to wake up.

"Time to wake up and get a move on, little bro," Mitch spoke.

"Just thirty more minutes, Mom." Brad groaned.

"I'm not your mom, so get your butt out of bed," Mitch growled loudly.

Brad's hands moved quickly to remove the covers as he sat up in the hammock. He looked at Mitch and wiped his face. "You are definitely not Mom."

"Not even close. Whit is making breakfast, so we need to break down camp and get ready to roll. We've got miles to make up today," Mitch informed him.

"All right, I'm up," Brad mumbled, as he reached for his boots. "I gotta go pee first." He stepped out of the hammock.

"All right, but get the lead out of your butt this morning." Mitch began disassembling Whit's hammock.

Whit used the heater to warm the food, after adding some water. She looked up at Mitch. "I'm not too sure how this is going to taste. It doesn't look or smell half as good as the other meals."

"If we don't like them, we can have some jerky and stop for an early lunch," Mitch said.

Whit nodded and continued preparing the meals. Brad returned and started breaking down his tent. "I smell sausage," he said.

"Yeah, I think that's what this mystery meat is," Whit replied. "These eggs have a unique color, too," she added.

"Maybe we can doctor them with some honey or syrup," Mitch offered.

Whit made a face full of doubt. "I'm not sure that's going to help. Come and get it," she called to them.

Whit opened a seasoning packet and poured the contents into the container. She stirred the food and took a tentative bite and was surprised by the flavor. "Looks like hell, but the taste isn't bad. Try it. You might like it."

"My name's not Mikey." Mitch laughed. He took a bite and nodded. "Not something I want to eat every day, but I reckon it's tolerable."

"What are you talking about? This stuff is Marine gourmet," Brad teased.

"Man, I hope I don't get drafted by the Marines," Mitch said.

"What do you mean?" Whit replied.

"I turn eighteen soon, and I have to register for the draft."

"They still have that?" Whit shrugged. "I thought that went out of fashion years ago."

"Nope, every young man who turns eighteen must register in case our country goes to war," Mitch explained.

"See, you learn something new every day, even at my old age," Whit replied.

"Yep, you're ancient," Mitch teased.

"How's your back feel this morning?" Brad asked.

Whit shrugged. "Tight and tender. It woke me several times, when I turned in my hammock last night." She smiled at Brad. "I reckon I'll live."

"Would you mind if I dressed it again before we move out this morning?"

"That's fine. Thanks, Brad," Whit said.

"I've already wrapped a towel around the strap to give it some extra padding," Mitch told them.

"Does your hand need more ointment?" Brad asked.

"Naw, I think I'm good for now. You can dress it again later."

Whit finished her meal and dropped the packaging in their refuse bag. "I'm going to empty my bladder, then I'll be ready."

"We'll finish packing and be ready to go when you return," Mitch said.

"All right." Whit took a portion of the paper and headed down the trail.

"It's so much easier for us," Brad mused.

"Thank goodness," Mitch said.

†

Eli and Mark tried the phones before they left the room, to no avail. "Either they still don't have service, or they aren't on the move yet," Mark said.

"I would bet they've been up, so they must be in a horrible spot for cell reception," Eli replied.

"Let's have some breakfast and hit the road. How much longer do we have?"

"A good nine hours from here to reach our extraction point," Eli answered.

Mark sighed. "I guess it could be worse."

"A good fifteen to Katahdin." Eli smirked.

†

Whit and the boys trekked for an hour before they reached the next shelter. They stopped for a quick break and soon met up with a pair of young men on the trail.

"Good morning," Mitch said.

"Morning indeed," one of the men replied. "I can't say how good yet. Have you heard the news?"

"I guess not. What's going on?" Mitch asked.

"Murder," the other man replied. "There was a murder on the trail in Virginia."

"What?" Whit cried out.

"A crazy ex-boyfriend attacked a woman from Tennessee, who was hiking with two men. Cut her up bad with a machete, from what we heard. She was pronounced dead on-site."

Whit gasped. "Oh, my goodness. What a horrible way to die. What about the two men?"

"Minor cuts, but they'll survive. I'm not sure if they caught the suspect yet, so be careful if you're trekking further south. You may see some forestry workers on the trail that you normally wouldn't see."

"Does that often happen on the trail?" Brad asked.

"Murder?" The taller young man shook his head. "About once every ten to fifteen years, that we know of anyway.

There are places on the trail you could hide a body no one could ever find."

Mitch nodded. "Sad but all too true."

Whit looked at Mitch whose eyes suddenly grew wide. "A woman and two men, you said?" he asked.

"Yeah, that's what we heard."

Mitch looked at Whit. "We better find a way to call Dad and Eli today. If they've heard the news, they're probably freaking out."

"Good luck. You probably won't have cell reception for another three hours south of here. Even then, it can be spotty. When you crest the ridge on the next mountain will probably be your best bet."

"Thanks for the information." Mitch shook hands with the men. "Be careful ahead. You've got a wicked river crossing in a few hours," he informed them.

"Some cold, powerful water," Brad added with a shiver.

"Noted. Thanks, man. Y'all, be careful, and watch your backs. I think they'll catch that maniac quickly, unless he's one of those survivalists that can hide for months right under your nose."

"We've only got a couple of days to go," Whit answered. "Thanks for the information."

"Stay frosty," one man said, and they moved on up the trail.

Whit looked at Mitch and Brad. "Can we pick up the pace? If your dad and Eli have heard, they're probably freaking out. Especially since we haven't had cell service for a while."

Mitch pulled out his phone. "Yeah, if Dad knows there's been a murder and he can't reach us, I'm sure he's climbing the walls." He shook his head. "Still no service."

"Let's hoof it until we reach the top of that mountain." Whit pointed at a mountain a few miles ahead.

†

Eli listened to the phone's ringing until the prompt for a voice mail kicked on for Mitch. "Dammit. I hate this. The sat phone won't even connect. I thought that would work most anyplace on the trail."

"We'll keep trying," Mark said.

"So, talk to me. Tell me how things are going at home. Anything to keep my mind off the phone," Eli pleaded.

"I'm getting pretty damn good on the forge," Mark said. "I've managed to make several more knives, working on them at night and on the weekends."

"Mitch loves the one you made for him," Eli said. "I wouldn't mind having a smaller version for Whit and me."

"I do believe I can arrange that." Mark grinned. "I've got several orders already strictly by word of mouth. It's obscene what people will pay for hand-forged steel."

"Enough to replace your work income?"

"If I were to get serious and forge, at least on a part-time basis. The power hammer saves me hours of grueling hammering. I think Brad will excel at using the forge. He has a good sense of technical things."

"What about Mitch? Will he play a part in the process?"

"He's the brute strength I no longer have. He will be invaluable in cutting the springs we need to forge the blades.

I think he'll be excellent in cutting and assembling a variety of mediums for handles."

"You seem to be enjoying the process," Eli said.

"I want to learn everything I need to teach them, so that we can produce as a team."

"I think the boys will love that. They're both quick learners and hard workers when it's a skill they're interested in," Eli replied. "Are you okay with Whit and I setting Mitch up in a tiny home once he graduates?"

"Laura and I both love the idea," Mark answered. "We've been impressed with how much he's matured with you."

"Can I be honest?"

"Please, feel free," Mark answered.

"You need to allow him to try more new things. If he fails, he fails. He's not perfect, but I think he feels shackled by a need to make you proud of him."

"I can see that. I don't often have the patience to move at his pace," Mark admitted. "I see something that needs doing, and I want to get it done right away."

"Mitch works well with deadlines. Please give him a time frame when you need something done right away. One easy thing I think he could do would be to take over more of the cooking duties. He's a creative cook and could help take some of the pressure off of you."

"That would be nice. Some days, I drag in from work and could be satisfied with a peanut butter sandwich, but two growing boys need more solid food."

Eli's phone pinged with a text, and she lunged for her phone. "From Carol. She sent a link and said to watch the video."

"Let me pull over first." Mark pulled the truck to a stop on the side of the road.

Eli pushed play, and a video regarding the capture of the murder suspect began to run. His picture popped up on her screen. "He looks crazy." Eli shook her head, as the reporter commented that the suspect had made a full confession. The killer had been smoking meth for three days as he raced to catch up with the hikers. Julie Carter, his victim, had broken up with him over his addiction to illegal drugs. He exacted his revenge in a drug-fueled rage, brutally killing her and injuring her two male companions.

"Crazy fucker," Mark growled.

"Drugs are the root of so much violence," Eli said. "I had to do some research. Given the thousands of AT hikers each year, there have been few violent encounters and only a handful of murders."

"If you're trying to make me feel better, it's not working," Mark replied.

"Mitch and Brad probably have a higher risk of gang-related or school-shooter scenarios than they have while hiking the AT. I just hope you won't prevent them from continuing this adventure."

"The thought had crossed my mind, but I know you're right. If Mitch and Brad have had as much fun as it sounds, I won't prevent them from continuing next year." He shrugged. "That doesn't mean I won't worry, but I can't protect them forever."

"Good. I plan on going next year. I know it's against the rules, but I will be packing," Eli said. "Something small, but I won't go unprotected."

Mark grinned at his sister. "You're such a rebel," he teased. "I wish I was physically fit to go. I think it would be fun."

"Maybe you couldn't hike, but there's nothing to say you couldn't meet us at a few of the shelters for some overnight stays. Some sections wouldn't require much walking to reach a shelter. You could resupply us with food."

"That's not a bad idea." Mark nodded. "Indeed, it's very doable." He pulled back onto the road. "Maybe, after we move for good, we can do some camping."

"For sure," Eli answered. "There are so many excellent places to explore in North Carolina alone."

"I am so ready to be there," Mark replied. "I dream of waking up to the beautiful mornings of the mountains."

"It has been a dream come true for me, and I can't wait for your family to join Whit and me."

"You were so fortunate to find her. It's like all your lucky stars fell into one place. I love seeing how happy she makes you after that nightmare ending with Sara."

Eli nodded. "Water under the bridge, bro. I'm not looking back, just moving forward."

"I hear that!"

†

Even with a towel wrapped around the strap for extra padding, Whit could feel the pressure on her injured back with every step. She was relieved when they reached the summit of the mountain and stopped for a break. "Check to see if a phone works from up here," she told Mitch, as she eased her pack to the ground.

Mitch saw the grimace on her face. "You're hurting, aren't you?"

"My back is stinging a bit," Whit admitted.

"Let's add some ointment and get some Tylenol in you," Brad said.

"I won't argue." Whit waited until Brad had the first-aid kit, then pulled her shirt up in the back. Even that movement was painful.

Mitch took out his phone. "Yay, we do have service, but I'll wait until Brad finishes doctoring you to call."

"Thanks." Mitch handed her a canteen of cool water, and Brad doled out Tylenol.

"How's your hand, bro? Do you need a fresh dressing?"

"Naw, I'm good."

Brad looked at the irritated skin across Whit's shoulder blade and winced as he applied new ointment. "I know it's painful. I'm trying to be gentle."

Whit forced a smile. "You're doing great, Brad. Thank you."

Mitch saw the concern on Brad's face. "Will you let me carry your pack for a while?"

"No," Whit answered. "I can manage."

"I'm taking more weight out of it then," Mitch said. "You can probably feel it. Your shoulder is raw, and the straps are irritating it with every step you take."

Whit nodded. "I'm well aware of that."

Mitch smiled. "I can double up. It'll be comfortable going down the mountain."

"I refuse to allow you to carry my pack," Whit snapped a bit too sharply. "I know you're willing, but it's not fair to you."

"Who said life was fair?" Mitch tossed back at her. He grinned and started removing items from her pack, placing them in his. "I'll lighten the load then, if you insist on being stubborn."

"I've got room in my pack too, bro," Brad said.

Mitch spotted the pack of candy bars in his bag and handed Whit and Brad one. "We could all use some sugar." He chuckled.

Brad replaced the dressing and lowered Whit's shirt. "There you go. I hope it helps to ease some of the pain."

"Thanks, Brad." She gave them a stern look. "Not a word of this to Eli. I don't want her worrying unnecessarily."

"Got it," Mitch said.

†

Mark had climbed into the truck after refueling when Eli's phone rang. "It's about damn time," she told Mark.

"Hello, how are y'all?"

"We're fine," Mitch replied. "We've been out of range of a tower for a bit. We just got service again."

"Even on the sat phone?" Eli asked.

"It's out of commission right now. I messed up, and the battery got wet," Whit replied.

"How on earth did that happen?" Eli asked.

"I forgot to secure it in a plastic bag before a river crossing. I'll replace it if it's fried."

"I'm not worried about the phone. I'm just glad y'all are okay. Do you know there was a murder on the trail?"

"Yes, we learned about it this morning, from two guys heading north. I hope you weren't worried."

"Ha! Mark and I are about four hours from the extraction spot. He heard about it first and called me from the road to tell me to be ready. We were coming to find you. So, say hello to your dad, boys."

"Hey, Dad," Mitch and Brad called out.

"Hey, boys. I'm glad you are safe and sound. The damn media didn't give out much information, and we were both worried about the similarities, so we came to find you," Mark explained.

"We only found out late yesterday that it was in a totally different state, and the woman was from Tennessee," Eli added.

"I can only imagine how scary that must of been, not knowing all the details, but I assure you we are all fine," Whit replied. "We're about a day and a half away. If we push it, we could make it there late tomorrow."

"There's no need to rush. Enjoy your time on the trail. Eli and I will check into the hotel and relax until you make it. We'll have a nice hot shower and some good food."

"Oh, now that's just cruel, Dad," Mitch said.

"Sorry, son, I shouldn't have said anything about a thick bacon cheeseburger and fries," Mark teased.

"I feel like I could eat three or four of those," Brad said.

"I'll buy as many as you can eat," Mark told him. "Please, call your mom, so she knows you are safe."

"We will," Mitch assured him. "Hey, can I go to FaceTime for a minute? You've got to see the view from up here."

"Sure," Eli replied.

Mitch panned the camera 360 degrees, so Eli and Mark could share the view from the top of the mountain.

"It is a gorgeous view," Eli said. "Thanks for sharing it with us."

"I can't wait for you to join us next year," Mitch replied. "You're going to have so much fun."

"I'm looking forward to it. How much farther do you have to the next shelter?" Eli asked.

Brad checked his GPS. "Six miles."

"Well, at least part of it is downhill," Mark said.

"Yes, it is," Whit agreed. "If we don't make it before dark, we'll set up camp, but we should have plenty of time."

Eli asked. "Are y'all doing okay for food?"

"Yes, we're still loaded down. We'll have a quick lunch and head out again shortly," Whit replied.

Eli nodded. "All right, then. Call us when you get to the shelter if you have service. If not, we'll be waiting for you at the hotel."

"Sounds great. I hate that y'all had to go through that stress, but it'll be nice to see Mark again. Love you, and we'll see you both soon."

"Most," Eli replied. "Stay safe."

"Bye for now." Whit ended the call. "I can only imagine what those two were thinking." She handed Mitch the phone. "Call your mom before we forget."

Mitch dialed Laura, while Whit sorted through her pack. She took out a bag of trail mix and some jerky. "We should eat what we can today to lighten our packs for the last few miles."

"That won't be a problem," Brad replied. "I'm crazy hungry today for some reason."

"Another growth spurt, probably," Whit told him.

Brad grinned. "I hope so." He took a bite of jerky and dug out some peanut butter. "I can't wait to sink my teeth into a cheeseburger."

"Or three," Whit replied. "I'm right there with you."

"Mom said to tell y'all hello," Mitch said. "I assured her we are all safe and sound." He picked up a strip of jerky and took a bite. "I've got a packet of chicken if anyone wants some."

"I'll take some," Brad said.

"I'm good, thanks." Whit gazed across the valley and enjoyed the jerky. "We need to take some pics from up here. I don't know what that river is to the east, but I sure hope we don't have to cross it," she said with a chuckle.

Brad shook his head. "Nope, no more water crossings for us. All solid ground from here until we reach the town."

"That's good news," Mitch said. He took the two bottles of water from Whit's pack and put them in his bag. He lifted her backpack. "There, that should be significantly better."

"Thanks, Mitch. I don't want you to be overloaded, though," Whit said.

"I'm good," Mitch replied. "Smile," he said and snapped a photo of Whit. "Let's do a group selfie." He moved next to Whit. Mitch snapped off several more pictures and sent Eli some through a text.

"Are we ready to head down?" Whit asked.

Brad nodded. "Hi ho, hi ho," he started singing.

"Good Lord." Mitch groaned and lifted Whit's lighter pack onto her back. He shouldered his own and led them down the trail.

†

Later that evening, they sorted through their packs to create a smorgasbord for their last night on the trail. They sat around the fire and watched the full moon rise through the night sky. "It's so beautiful out here," Mitch said. He popped a handful of peanuts into his mouth.

"The moon looks big from up here," Brad said.

"Yeah, it does," Whit agreed. "It's not yet a harvest moon, but I'm sure the increased elevation up here makes it appear larger."

"Do you miss your lab?" Mitch asked.

Whit smiled at him. "Yes, but in a way, this view is just as good. No electric light pollution to distort how beautiful the night sky can be."

Whit spent the next half hour pointing out the different constellations to them. When a light breeze began to blow, the temperature dropped and Brad shivered. "It amazes me how quickly the temperature can change up here." He pulled a hoodie over his head.

"Less than two months ago, this spot was likely still covered by snow," Whit told him.

"Do you think we'll have snow at Christmas?" Mitch asked.

"It's a very likely possibility," Whit replied. "It may not be a huge amount, but we often have a white Christmas."

"That would be so cool," Brad said as he sat next to Whit.

"This Christmas will be extra special with you and the family at the farm. I know Eli is already excited about y'all being there."

"I'll be halfway through my final year of high school by then," Mitch said. "I can start counting the days until I come to the mountains for good."

"We are looking forward to that, too," Whit said. "I bet Eli will have a list of a hundred projects by then," she teased.

"I'll be ready," Mitch promised. "Look." Mitch pointed out a falling star. "Make a wish."

"Done," Whit said. "Let's hope they all come true."

"Amen to that," Mitch replied. "The last of the oatmeal for breakfast?" he suggested.

"That sounds good to me," Whit agreed. "Are you ready for bed?"

"Yeah, I think I'll hit the sack." He looked at his watch. "It's incredible how quickly time gets away from you out here. Can you believe it's almost one?"

Whit stifled a yawn. "Yes, I can. Let's all call it a night," she suggested. Whit burrowed down in her sleeping bag and found a comfortable resting position. She closed her eyes and thought of Eli. *I love you*, she whispered in her mind.

†

Eli and Mark had crashed hours earlier, but the crystal glowing on her chest woke her. Her fingers touched the crystal and found it warm. Then she heard Whit's whisper. *I love you most*, she answered back. *Tomorrow night, you will be back in my arms.*

Eli closed her eyes and fell asleep, a smile playing across her lips as she dreamed of Whit.

†

The next day, the final miles passed quickly. When they were a half mile from stepping off the trail, Whit called them to a halt. "I just want to tell you both that this has been a dream come true for me, and I'm glad to have shared this time with you. Today may be the ending to our first adventure together on the AT, but I promise you it's not the last." She pulled them into a hug. "I've had so much fun with y'all, and I'm so proud of what we've accomplished."

"It's been a blast," Mitch said. "The time passed way too quickly, but I know we'll hike again next summer."

Brad nodded. With tears in his eyes, he said, "I know I'll be going home soon, but one day will come when I never have to leave."

"You both will always have a home with us," Whit promised. "Even if it's only temporary as you move through life, you can always come home to the mountain."

They both nodded with understanding. "Now, who's ready for a cheeseburger?"

"Or three," Brad added.

"Let's go." Mitch led them on the final steps of their journey.

Eli and Mark were sitting in front of the hotel, talking and enjoying the creek's sound, when the crew arrived. Eli saw them first and jumped to her feet. "Welcome back," she said, as she wrapped her arms around them in a group hug.

"Hey, sweetie." Whit kissed her softly.

The boys walked over to Mark. "I'm glad you came, Dad," Mitch said. "We have so much to tell you about our adventure."

"I can hardly wait to hear your stories." Mark grinned and hugged his sons. He looked at Brad. "I think you've grown a few inches. And you, look at that beard." He grinned at Mitch. "Mine never grew in that good. I'm jealous."

"I don't think I'm keeping it, though. It's hot and itchy," Mitch complained.

"We've been trying to convince him to keep part of it," Whit said. "A Fu Manchu or something."

"We'll see how that goes. Right now, I just want a hot shower and a lot of food."

"Let's go then," Mark said. "We've scouted out a great place to eat."

†

When Eli closed the door behind them, she spun Whit around and kissed her deeply. "I have missed you so much."

"I've missed you, too, and plan to show you just how much tonight when we return. Right now, I need a shower and a razor. Someone to wash my back too," she teased.

Whit brushed her teeth for several minutes before starting to strip out of her clothes. When Eli saw the bandage on her back, she rushed over to her lover.

"What happened?"

"Our last river crossing was a bit hairy. Brad decided to go for a swim, and I decided to join him. If it weren't for Mitch's strength, we would probably both be in much worse shape. But that's a story for them to tell. I got a nice scrape out of the deal, and Mitch got a nasty rope burn, but we survived to tell the story." She grinned at Eli. "By the way, the paracord from my walking stick helped save us, too. I'll need you to wrap it again."

"That's no problem at all. Call me when you're ready for me to wash your back, and I promise to be gentle."

"You can start by taking the bandage off for me, please." Whit turned around.

Eli slowly removed the bandage and saw the healing wound. "I bet that hurt."

"It was a challenge to sleep with, and Mitch insisted on removing half of my gear from my bag to lighten the load."

"Good boy," Eli said.

"He's a good man," Whit corrected her. "I think the young boy is all gone."

Eli nodded. "He sure looks more mature with that beard."

"Mitch has grown a lot in the last few months."

"I'm very proud of both of them. I'll be back in a minute." Eli leaned forward to kiss Whit.

"Where are you going?"

"Next door to get some first-aid supplies from Brad, so I can dress your wound, unless you prefer he does it for you."

"Oh, okay. No, I know you are more than capable. Thank you."

"I'll be right back then."

†

When they returned from dinner, Eli and Whit undressed and slipped between the covers. "It is so comforting to feel your skin against mine," Whit purred, as Eli's hand caressed her.

"I have missed you terribly. The nights are the worst. I reach over to touch you, but you're not there. Or I start talking to you and realize you're not with me. Cruz has been giving me some worried looks." Eli chuckled.

"I'm home in your arms now, so you don't need to worry." Whit's finger traced Eli's lips.

"Right where I need you to be." Eli rolled on top of Whit and kissed her deeply, as their bodies began a sensual dance, leaving them both gasping for air.

"I need you inside me, please," Whit whispered to Eli.

Eli entered her slowly and took her leisure, exploring the depths of Whit's arousal until she could hold back no more and Whit's body trembled with the release. Eli curled Whit's body into her arms and caressed her tenderly, until Whit fell asleep in her arms.

†

Whit woke with a start the next morning and found Eli watching her sleep. "I'm sorry I fell asleep on you. I wanted you to feel as satisfied as I was."

"Trust me, I was, and nothing could have felt better than having you in my arms again."

"I promise I won't fall asleep on you tonight." Whit leaned over to kiss Eli.

Eli smiled. "Let's get showered and dressed so we can meet the boys for breakfast."

†

Mitch sat in front with Mark on the drive home. For two days, the boys kept them entertained with stories from the trail. Eli wrapped her arm around Whit and held her close the entire trip home.

Mark was up early Monday morning for his drive home. He'd go straight to work, then home afterward.

"If you need a break from driving, I can bring Brad home in two weeks," Eli offered.

"Naw, I'm good. I'd hate to miss out on a chance to be up here," Mark said as he climbed into his truck. "Love ya!"

"Most. Be careful and let me know when you make it home tonight." Eli closed the door behind him. "Give our love to Laura."

"Will do," Mark said. "One day, I'll never have to leave."

"That's right," Eli replied and stepped back, as Mark started the truck.

She watched him drive away and went back inside to pour another cup of coffee. "It's good to be home," she told Cruz.

CHRISTMAS AT CAST IRON FARM

Eli was fighting to get a Christmas sweater over Cruz's head, when Whit called from the front room.

"I see headlights coming up the drive!"

"Be still, Cruz. I know you're excited to see everyone, too, but really? Sit still."

The living room was filled with the scent of the Blue Ice Christmas tree Eli had purchased. The fragrant tree had its roots wrapped in a burlap sack for protection and was soaking in a galvanized trough full of water. Eli and Whit had decided on a live tree that they would plant in the yard after the holidays.

"There." Eli released the squirming pup. "Aren't you pretty?" Eli had initially chosen a red and green sweater with bells on it, until Whit reminded her how active Cruz was. They'd probably go crazy listening to the sounds of the jingling bells. Instead, they settled on a green sweater with large red poinsettias. Whit did concede to a festive collar with flashing LED lights. It at least had an on-off switch.

Eli was excited for Mark and his family to arrive for their first Christmas celebration in North Carolina. She and Whit had entered into a relationship and they wanted to share their first Christmas with family. Whit had admitted to her that she hadn't celebrated the holidays since her grandparents passed. Eli was determined to make this an extraordinary Christmas. They had spent hours hanging lights around the cabin and selecting ornaments for the tree. Eli had spent days shopping in Asheville, and the presents were nestled around the tree. There were two unique gifts she had hidden that she would bring out when the time was right.

The kitchen brimmed with aromas of the foods they would share for Christmas dinner. A turkey and ham were baking in one of the double ovens, while casseroles bubbled in the other. Eli and Whit had stayed up Christmas Eve baking cookies and apple pies from the recent apple crop. They shared hot chocolate as they toiled and brought Christmas Day in after a round of passionate lovemaking in front of the fireplace. Eli was excited to make this the best Christmas ever. All they needed was family, and they had just arrived.

Eli reached for Whit's hand. "Let's go greet the family." They stepped out onto the porch and were met by a brisk breeze. Eli had been feverishly checking the weather, and she prayed the promised snowfall would arrive soon.

Mark pulled the SUV to a stop, and the boys came barreling out of the back seat. Mitch wrapped her in a bear hug, while Brad hugged Whit.

"Did you hear? We're supposed to have snow today." Brad reported excitedly.

Whit nodded. "We heard. I hope it comes soon."

Cruz raced to the vehicle and showered Laura and Mark with kisses. "Hey mutt, we missed you too." Mark lifted Cruz in his arms for a hug.

Mark placed her back on the ground, as he and Laura approached. "Merry Christmas," Laura said, as she hugged both women.

Eli grinned at her brother. "We are so glad y'all finally made it."

Cruz rushed to Brad and dropped a tennis ball at his feet. The group laughed at her excitement. "Some things haven't changed." Brad picked up the ball and hurled it.

The winds picked up again. "Brrr," Laura said. "It's cold up here."

"The fire's burning hot, so go inside and warm up," Eli said. "Mark, the boys, and I will get you unloaded."

"You heard the lady, let's get to it boys," Mark said.

Mitch was already at the back of the vehicle and handed out suitcases and boxes full of presents. "Yeah, we are a bit loaded down." He shot a grin at Eli.

"You're staying for a week right, not a month?" Eli teased, as she took two suitcases.

Laura hollered back to Eli as she walked up to the door. "You should know by now this tribe never travels light."

"Yes, ma'am," Eli replied and handed the bags up to Whit.

Twenty minutes later, they had unloaded and the bags were stored in the bedrooms. Laura and the boys huddled around the fireplace, as Mark and Whit arranged the presents around the tree.

"It's sure smelling good in here, Aunt Eli," Mitch said, as he rubbed his hands together.

"We will have a feast in a couple of hours. There are cookies and coffee made, if you need a snack. I can make hot chocolate if you boys want some," Whit said.

"Or milk to go with the cookies. We made them from Mom's oatmeal, chocolate chip recipe," Eli told them.

"Bust out the milk then," Mark replied.

After munching on several cookies, the boys wanted to go outside. "Take Cruz with you and tell her to go get Molly. She could probably use some exercise."

The boys rushed to the door, with Cruz on their heels. "Go get Molly," Mitch directed.

"Mark, you've got to come to see this." Eli and Whit had installed a doggie door in the barn for Cruz and Molly. Eli chuckled, as they stepped outside. "Whit taught Cruz how to use a rope, hanging from the stall, to open the gate and let Molly out to play."

They waited for a few seconds, then Cruz and Molly came flying through the doggie door, ready to play. "That's hilarious," Mark said as the pup and baby goat charged after the boys. "This place is gorgeous. I'm so happy for you, sis."

"It has turned into our little piece of heaven. I couldn't be happier."

"I'm glad that you and Whit have gotten together too. She seems like a perfect match for you." Mark saw the smile grow on his sister's face.

"She's the best thing that has ever happened to me. Keeps me on my toes and loves me, just for me."

They watched the boys and animals play for several minutes. Mark wrapped an arm around Eli's shoulder. "I hear the fireplace calling us," he teased.

"Okay, just a second. Mitch, will you make sure Molly has food when y'all get done playing?"

"Yes, ma'am," he hollered back.

"I think we'd better carry in another armful of wood," Eli said, as they passed the rack filled with cut wood. She pulled the cover back, and Mark let out a whistle.

"You've been busy," Mark said, after seeing the full rack of wood.

"I'm getting pretty good with the chainsaw. Haven't cut anything off with it yet, either. I've been trimming back trees from the path up to the trailhead and cutting some downed logs over the property."

"Do you think you'll be ready for livestock this summer?" Mark asked, as he opened the door.

"Yeah, I think so. This year has gotten away from me so fast."

"Well, you've been pretty busy." He closed the door. "Livestock can wait."

Whit was checking the meat when they arrived. "The turkey and ham will be ready in about thirty minutes," she told Eli.

"You sure have it smelling wonderful in here," Mark repeated. "Is there anything I can help with?"

"You can carve the bird when it comes out. I'll slice the ham."

"Laura and I got the table all set," Whit chimed in. "The rolls have risen, just let me know when I need to pop them into the oven."

"You can wait until we take the meats out." Eli hugged her lover close. "This is going to be a great meal."

"Yes, it is," Whit agreed.

Mark spied the apple pies sitting on the counter. "Are all the fruits and vegetables from your gardens?"

"Yes, they are," Whit replied. "Mostly from mine. We've pretty much eaten or canned what Eli was able to grow. We'll save them for the winter."

"Wait until you taste those zipper peas. These are the best I've ever grown. Which reminds me, I need to put some rice on," Eli said.

Mark joined Laura by the fire. "That tree is beautiful. Is it a Blue Ice?"

"Yes, we wanted a live tree that we can plant in the yard. That will be a chore for the boys before you head home." Eli grinned, "I've got to put them to work while they're here, to keep them busy."

"You have more firewood to cut and stack?" Mark asked.

"I've got several more logs down that can be cut and split," she answered.

Mark rubbed his hands together. "Sounds like a good chore for tomorrow, so we can work off all this food we're about to eat."

The door opened, and Brad burst into the cabin. "Whoa, slow your roll youngin'," Mark called out.

"Y'all ain't gonna believe this, it's snowing," he cried out. "Huge flakes, you gotta come and see."

Laura pulled on her coat, and the group followed Brad outside. Mitch, Cruz, and Molly were jumping in the air, trying to catch the flakes as they swirled slowly toward the ground. Laughter filled the air, as Brad joined them in the yard.

"This is so beautiful," Laura announced. "Do you think it will stick?"

"From the size of the flakes, I'd have to say yes," Whit answered. "It's certainly cold enough."

"I hope we get several inches," Mark said, as he placed an arm around Laura. "We're going to have a white Christmas." He grinned.

The timer sounded from the kitchen, and Whit returned inside. "Let them play and enjoy themselves while we finish setting up the meal," Eli said.

"Okay, I'll be in to carve the turkey in just a few minutes." Mark watched his sons enjoying the snow.

Eli snuck a kiss from Whit, as she walked past her in the kitchen. "Man, that bird looks good," she said, as Whit carried the pan to the counter.

"The ham looks just as yummy," Whit replied.

"I don't think anyone is going to go hungry," Eli said. "Will you pop the rolls in the oven?"

"With pleasure." Whit smiled and placed a soft kiss on Eli's lips.

"I am so ready for more of those," Eli teased.

"And more you shall have, but later. We've got work to do."

Mark and Laura returned inside. "The boys are putting Molly up and feeding her and the cats, then they'll be in to clean up. Ready for me to start carving?"

"Most definitely." Eli handed him a large carving knife. "No sampling," she said.

"You take all my fun." Mark laughed and surveyed the bird.

"Laura, will you pull down two large platters from up there?" Eli pointed to a nearby cabinet.

"Absolutely, what else can I do?"

"You can help me serve dishes to the table. Oh, and don't let me burn the rolls," Whit answered.

"What's a family meal without burned rolls?" Mark asked.

"Not this meal," Eli said.

†

The meal was a huge success, and even Cruz was stuffed and napping by the fireplace. "Can we open presents now?" Brad asked. He had been eyeing a particular package with his name on it ever since the meal finished.

"I reckon so," Eli answered. "Whit, do you want to play Santa?"

"Sure," she answered and pulled on a red cap with a white tassel. "Ho, ho, ho," she said, as she got up from her seat.

She began handing out presents, and they enjoyed watching the boys tear into theirs. The two large gifts for the boys were a new twenty-two rifle and scope for Brad and a top-of-the-line compound bow for Mitch. They were thrilled with the gifts and eager to try them out.

"We have targets set up in the barn, but it will have to wait until tomorrow," Eli announced.

"Aww." They both groaned.

"Is it still snowing outside?" Eli asked Whit.

Whit looked out the large window. "Coming down fast," she answered.

"I have one more gift for the family." Eli walked over to the entertainment unit and pulled out four small boxes. She handed one to each of Mark's family.

They opened the boxes to find a set of keys. Mitch looked confused. "I already have a set of keys to your house, Aunt Eli."

"I know you do, but this set belongs to your new home," she answered.

It took a few seconds for her words to sink in, and the boys erupted in screams. "You're freaking kidding me?" Mitch said.

"Nope, I'm not. Will you and Brad go to the barn and pull the Gators around front?"

"Heck yeah," they answered in unison and bolted toward the door.

Eli looked at Mark and saw a tear running down his cheek. "I didn't think we would start building the cabin until next spring," he said, as he wiped the tear away.

"Have you ever known me to be that patient?" Eli asked.

Mark stood and hugged her tightly, as his tears fell in earnest. "Thank you. I love you so much."

Laura still seemed in shock. Whit offered her a hand and pulled her to her feet. "We put the bare necessities in for furniture, so you'll have lots of decorating still to do."

"Thank you, both." Laura hugged them.

"Ready to go? I think I hear Santa's sleigh pulling up," Eli said.

Mark burst into laughter, when he saw the two Gators donned with flashing Christmas lights. He turned to look at Eli. "What can I say? It was her idea." She pointed to Whit.

"This is awesome. Move over, Brad. I'm driving."

Brad hurried over to the passenger seat, and Laura climbed in the back. Eli climbed into the rear of the Gator Mitch was driving, and Whit took the passenger seat. "Careful, the road still needs some work," she told Mitch and Mark.

"Yeehaw," Mark yelled and took off. Cruz raced ahead, confident of where they were going.

When they reached the building site, Mark pulled to a stop. Whit and Eli had decorated the front of the cabin with Christmas lights, and the interior lights shone brightly through the large picture window. In the early winter light, the cabin glowed with color.

"Merry Christmas, all," Eli called out.

They drove on to the cabin, and Laura had the privilege of opening the door to their new home. They knocked the snow off their feet, and the family scattered, as they walked through the cabin.

"Oh my gosh, Dad, you've got to come to see this," Mitch called out from the downstairs master bedroom. Everyone walked into the room where Mitch had pulled the blinds back. Out on the deck, a large hot tub laid in wait.

"You've got to be kidding me?" Mark said.

"Nope, after you start working around here putting in a garden and all your other plans, you're going to need a good soak. I think Whit and I will break it in for you," she teased.

"This is perfect timing," Laura exclaimed. Eli looked at her, a bit confused. "Go ahead and tell them," Laura told Mitch, who was about to burst at the seams.

"Dad and I were planning on moving up after I graduate this year. Mom and Brad will come up when he graduates."

"Really? That is so awesome," Eli cried out.

Mark nodded. "Mitch and I wanted to get a head start on the garden and other projects. He's also going to apply for a local mechanics school. With all the equipment around, we need someone who can keep us running."

"We will still go to Montgomery once or twice a month, especially during football season, but we're all ready to be here." Mitch smiled broadly.

"That's fantastic. You boys haven't been upstairs yet, have you?"

"No, ma'am." Brad bolted from the room, with Mitch hot on his trail.

In addition to the two large bedrooms, Eli had furnished the loft area with a billiards table, ping-pong table, and a substantial flat-screen television they could use for their games.

The adults were climbing the stairs, when the boys started screaming. "This is so awesome," Mitch cried out.

"This is perfect," Laura said. "My mind is whirling with decorating ideas."

"Oh, I almost forgot." Whit pulled out an envelope to hand to Laura.

She opened the envelope and pulled out a credit card. "Fifty thousand," she cried out.

"If that's not enough, we'll add to it," Eli said.

"No, you will not. You have been too generous as it is. I'm sure I can decorate with this and have some leftover for your projects," Laura told Mark.

The group wandered through the house for an hour, as Whit and Eli pointed out a few special touches they'd added. Laura was surprised to learn that the entire house was running off solar power, with a standby generator.

"We have a new wood rack too, for the front porch, but we ran out of time to put it together and fill it with wood. Maybe you and the boys can help with that tomorrow?"

"That is going to be so much fun," Mitch said.

"We have one more present for y'all. It's still in the SUV. That will be our first chore tomorrow, to hang it," Mark said. "I'll go down and get our suitcases and bring them up, if you're ready to spend the night here."

Laura looked at Eli. "Would you mind?"

"Heaven's no. I'd expect nothing less, but you'll have to come to our place to eat."

"We know where the grub is, Aunt Eli," Brad said, still wearing a grin.

"Let's go then. The road and bridge are in, so you can drive the SUV here. We can leave a Gator up here too, so you can take the shortcut to our place."

"I'll drive it back," Mitch volunteered.

They drove back down the mountain, leaving Laura and Brad to start a fire in the fireplace.

"This is all too much," Mark said, as he and Eli pulled into the yard. "I can't thank you enough."

"You don't have to. The tears in your eyes are good enough. I know you'll be happy here, too."

He nodded. "I surely will. Come on then, let me show you what we made for you."

Mitch opened the back of the SUV and pulled out a blanket-wrapped item. "You remember that slab of white poplar I took home last summer?"

"Yes, I do," Eli answered.

"Dad and I made this for you." He opened the blanket and revealed a beautifully stained and routed sign. "Dad did the routing, and I did the stain and attachments. We thought it would be perfect on the front gate."

"Cast Iron Farm," Eli read aloud. "I thought you had forgotten that conversation we had so many years ago."

"No way, it's been in my dreams ever since that Christmas, years ago, when we first started talking about North Carolina. The boys and I will hang it tomorrow, if you agree."

"I love it." Eli hugged them both. "Let's take it inside for now and get you two headed back up the mountain."

After they had loaded the bags, Eli looked at her watch. "Do you want to come back down around six for leftovers?"

"Sounds great, I'm already getting hungry again," Mitch said.

"Take that Gator up. You can park it in the garage for now, until we can build a barn." Eli turned to Mark. "Go back out on the road and turn right. A hundred yards or so, you'll see a new mailbox. Turn there, and the drive will lead you back to the cabin. See you at six."

Mark hugged her and climbed into the SUV. "Drive careful," she told Mitch.

"I will, Aunt Eli."

Eli and Whit watched them leave, as the snow continued to fall. "I think everyone had a good Christmas," she said.

"I do too. I'm so glad to hear Mitch and Mark will be joining us in a few months." She looked at Eli. "No offense, but I hear he's a great cook." Whit chuckled.

"As I'm sure you will find out this week. Mark has promised me some cooking lessons, so watch out waistline. C' mon lady, let's go snuggle by the fireplace."

"You won't get any argument from me," Whit replied.

†

Later that evening, after Mark and his family had left for their new home, Eli and Whit settled back onto the couch. "I don't know about you, but it's been a long day. Thank you for helping everything go so well. I couldn't have done all this without you, Whit."

"Sure you could, but it wouldn't have been near as much fun," she teased her lover.

"There is one more thing I need to do tonight," Eli said.

"What is that, my love?"

"This." Eli knelt on one knee in front of Whit. She pulled out a small box and opened it. "Will you honor me by becoming my wife?"

Whit's eyes grew wide, and her hands covered her mouth to keep from screaming. She nodded her head rapidly, then answered. "Yes, I'd love to be your wife." She pulled Eli in for a passionate kiss.

After the kiss, Eli's phone pinged. Whit saw Mitch's picture beside a message. *Well, what did she say?*

They both chuckled, and Eli typed. *She said, yes!*

Fan-freakin-tastic.
Good night Mitch, love y'all.
Love you most.

ABOUT THE AUTHOR

Ali Spooner lives in beautiful northwest Florida with her long-term partner and several fur babies. Ali's writing began as a hobby. The assistance of the Affinity Rainbow Publishing team has advanced her love of storytelling to a new level.

Ali's characters are primarily everyday people, from cowgirls to psychics. Ali also has created a few supernatural characters in her paranormal series. Several of her twenty-plus books have been Amazon-rated number one choices and always include a happily ever after. Ali's hobbies include photography, reading, travel, college sports, and spending time with family and friends.

OTHER AFFINITY BOOKS

The Boss's Daughter by Samantha Hicks

Vivian Westfall, CFO of *Bridger Holdings*, meets her boss's estranged daughter, Lauren, when a disturbance at the company spring party piques her interest. Lauren is clearly drunk and making a fool of herself. To prevent embarrassment, Vivian forces Lauren away from the party. They have angry words, and things take an unexpected turn when Lauren kisses her. Months later Lauren pitches a proposal to her father to loan her the funds to start her own health club. Her father reluctantly agrees with a caveat; Vivian must go with her to Scotland to keep an eye on the money. It doesn't take long for the sparks to fly in all emotional directions. When Gregory Bridger finds out about their relationship, he does everything in his power to break them apart. Trust is at the heart of this love story, a fragile emotion that without it, things can and do fall apart.

The Ghost of East Texas by Ali Spooner

Agent Blair Cooper and her partner, psychic Tally Rainwater (Terminal Event), are back in a gripping new murder mystery investigation. When the serial killer Casper Caruso, known as The Ghost of East Texas, was sent to death row, Agent Blair Cooper was adamant that there were more victims of his killing spree. As his execution day approaches, Casper reaches out to Blair. If she agrees to a face-to-face meeting, he will give the whereabouts of 10 additional bodies left in his wake. Blair and Tally must piece together the clues to bring closure for some of the victim's families. However, when you bargain with the devil, there is always a price to be paid.

Terminal Event by Ali Spooner

Tally Rainwater was born with the gift of second sight, something she never understood. A near-fatal accident, at age twelve, makes her visions clearer, but not the reason for them. As she matures, Lisa, a spirit, enters her visions to guide her in using her gift, but still not the reason why. Can Tally and Blair's budding romance survive the possibility? Read this intense murder mystery romance and find out.

The Star Child by Ali Spooner

Eli and Whit are enjoying their life together on the mountain when Whit is called into action for a secret mission at the Pentagon. While she is gone, the Cast Iron Farm comes to life, literally, when Eli discovers a mysterious cave that has a connection to Whit's past. Younger brother Brad joins the gang. When Whit returns, she plans an Appalachian Trail adventure with Brad and Mitch. Join Eli and family as their adventure at Cast Iron Farm continues.

My Dear Vet by JM Dragon

Ava Lawrence, a research veterinarian, is thrown in the deep end when her uncle asks her to cover his country practice while he has a vacation of a lifetime. How could she refuse? His team shouldn't be any different than the crew at her parents' practice, oh, was she so wrong. What she now has to work with is a sassy nurse, an obnoxious receptionist, and an animal whisperer, or so it seems. Ava finds herself embroiled in taking care of animals in the area and local issues outside her experience, making her question her sanity. Throw in chickens, cats, dogs, and a donkey named Theo, along with various other animals. This turns out to be Ava's unexpected adventure with far reaching romantic benefits.

One Shot at Love by Annette Mori

Blair returns to her hometown after the death of her sister. Always an activist she vows to use her voice to advocate for better gun control. She meets Maribel, an irresistible, sexy woman who proves to be an enigma to Blair. Maribel can't help approaching the weeping woman and learning the origin of Blair's grief, Maribel thinks she is the last person who should form a friendship with Blair. Ultimately, the allure is too much for Maribel, but how long can she keep her secret and continue to nurture their burgeoning feelings for one another. A committed left-wing social activist could never fall for the poster child of the

NRA. Unless taking that one shot at love matters more than anything else.

The Mountain Whispers by Ali Spooner

Arriving home and discovering the betrayal by her best friend and lover, Eli Fortner leaves to run off her anger and hurt. A chance stop at a convenience store and the purchase of lottery tickets sends Eli's life into a whirlwind of change. Able to now pursue her dreams, Eli heads off to see what else fate has in store for her.

Whit Brewer, Eli's neighbor, is everything Eli never knew she needed and wanted. But can she let go of the betrayal long enough to let Whit in? Thirteen black cats, a baby goat, and Cruz, her furry best friend, join Eli on her adventure, new life, and the possibility of real love.

Charlie by Erin O'Reilly

At fourteen, Hannah Garvin met 'the one,' Charlene Gaines, and her life was never the same. They were inseparable and spent every moment they could together. One day, Charlie left without a word and again, Hannah's life took a dramatic change. Hannah vowed to never fall in love again. When she meets Mick, a new arrival to the small Texas panhandle town near her family's farm, her heart remembers what being in love was like, and yearns for more. Will Hannah let the memory of Charlie go so she can start a new life with Mick? Or will her heart betray her and hold on to her love for Charlie?

<u>Misha's Promise</u> by Renee MacKenzie

Misha Wyatt has settled into a peaceful existence as a healer in Karst, New America. When an airplane crashes in the meadow outside of Karst, Misha hurries to help the pilot. Misha is not expecting the pilot to be alive...or so beautiful. Will her uncontrollable desire to keep the pilot safe be her downfall? Can *they* survive their journey? The last book in the Karst series brings our characters to their physical and emotional limits. Don't miss the culmination of this exciting series!

<u>Heart Strings Attached</u> by Ali Spooner & Annette Mori

Socialite Remy has her world shaken. Bartender Chancy has her orderly life turned around. A mutually beneficial business agreement between Remy and Chancy turns into undeniable attraction. Will the two ignore culture norms to explore their intense desire for each other?

<u>The Panty Thief</u> by Annette Mori

Someone is stealing panties, but who? And why? Joey Hartford is a fourth-year medical student who insists she doesn't have time for a relationship. A new tenant in her apartment building is proving too tempting to ignore. Sabrina is in her final year of her doctoral program and focused on completing her dissertation. Meeting Joey is dangerous for so many reasons. Add a suicidal ex-girlfriend who suddenly reappears in Sabrina's life and Joey's jealous friend-with-benefits, and things get complicated quickly.

Country Living by Jen Silver

Peri Sanderson achieves her dream of moving from London to a cottage in the English countryside with her wife, Karla. Peri sees their future as pastoral while chatting with the locals in a quaint village pub. Sexy urbanite, Karla, has other ideas. Secrets are everywhere. Peri quickly senses something not quite right among her rural neighbours and also with Karla. Temptation, betrayal, and intrigue combine to change the lives of both women beyond anything they could have imagined.

Before the Light by Samantha Hicks

One year after her long-time partner Meredith's abduction and their subsequent break-up, Kathleen Bowden-Scott's life is spiralling out of control. She meets Bethany Jones and despite an instant attraction Kathleen shies away. In this fast-paced, romantic suspense, lies are exposed and hearts unite as Kathleen and Beth fight for their future.

Wanted for Christmas by JM Dragon

Belle Farrow knew what she wanted for Christmas—work. She had little to offer but a minor degree in cookery and household management. Certainly not enough for a decent chef or housekeeper position. Then she saw an advert in the local newspaper. Wanted: Housekeeper/cook/nanny for the period of Christmas until the New Year. This is Christmas. Perhaps Santa reads the ad column too and pushes a little spirit of the season to that request.

Affinity
Rainbow Publications

eBooks, Print, Free eBooks

Visit our website for more publications available online.

www.affinityrainbowpublications.com

Published by Affinity Rainbow Publications
A Division of Affinity eBook Press NZ LTD
Canterbury, New Zealand

Registered Company 2517228

www.ingramcontent.com/pod-product-compliance
Lightning Source LLC
Chambersburg PA
CBHW070752280626
47162CB00016B/165